Never

He arched an eyebrow at her but said nothing as he retraced his steps back to the hitching rail. As he tied his horse to it, Glory's gaze slipped to his long-fingered hands. She watched his precise motions, and felt a hot thrill she couldn't name course through her and weaken her knees. It made her angry that it should be so.

He might have grown into a man, but he hadn't changed a bit from the irksome half-grown boy she remembered. She still couldn't shake a response out of him—not if her very life depended on it. He just stared at her and kept his thoughts to himself. Even when they'd been children, he'd behaved this same way. And back then, she'd been the prettiest child—everyone said so. Everyone else fell victim to her little-girl charms—even his two brothers sitting out on the hill right now. But not Riley. Never Riley . . .

Seasons of Glory

Cheryl Anne Porter

St. Martin's Paperbacks

ISBN: 0-312-96625-3

Printed in the United States of America

St. Martin's Paperbacks edition / July 1998

St. Martin's Paperbacks are published by St. Martin's Press, 175 Fifth Avenue, New York, NY 10010.

10 9 8 7 6 5 4 3 2 1

The *Lawless Women* trilogy is dedicated to the memory of Jimmie H. Deal, Sr., my beloved father who passed away on December 24, 1995.

Chapter 1

Please don't leave me, Jacey. Please don't. When I open my eyes, you'll be riding back on Knight and you'll say you were just teasing. Oh please, Jacey. Don't leave me here with the graves and the memories. Don't.

Glory slid her hands down her face to press her cold fingers against her mouth. Taking a deep breath for courage, she opened her eyes. Where only moments ago her older sister had reared her black gelding atop a bald hill, that gentle swell now stood barren, washed in the autumn morning's cool shadows.

She's really gone. Glory slumped, defeated, her hands now at her sides. No amount of prayer or pleading or injured silence on her part had kept Jacey here. Glory turned to her plump little elf of a nanny. "I should've stayed in my room like I said I would, Biddy. Jacey didn't deserve a farewell from me. How could she just up and leave like this? I hate her for going."

Her apple-cheeked face lining with her frown, Biddy patted Glory's arm. "Now, darlin', ye know ye don't hate yer sister. We've worries enough—with Hannah in Boston and Jacey riding off to certain trouble in the Arizona Territory—without ye addin' to it. Yer just scared."

Glory's bottom lip quivered with the truth of that. "Well, I have every right to be. I've never been alone on the ranch like this. And after everything else that's happened—all the killings and the funerals and such—it just seems that there's an emptiness here now, Biddy, as if you and I are the only ones left in the world. Are . . . are you scared, too?''

Biddy tipped her double chins up and struck what to Glory was a brave but unconvincing pose. ''Of course I'm scared. Only a fool wouldn't be.'' Having thickened the air with that observation, she turned her frowning attention back to the washboard roll of the low hills beyond the Lawless ranch yard.

A sudden and brisk gust lifted Glory's skirt hem, chilling her and chasing goose bumps over her exposed flesh. Shivering, she hugged her shawl around her shoulders and stepped back into the shelter provided by the verandah's overhanging roof. From there, she surveyed the patch of land she knew as home. The Lawless spread. A vast cattle ranch sprawling across the tallgrass plains and rolling hills of no-man's-land.

Mama and Papa had dreamed of a better life for them all. But now . . . they were buried out back, alongside Old Pete. And her older sisters? Gone from home, looking for answers, for vengeance. That left her in charge. Glory swallowed, feeling the responsibility press on her shoulders for every man, horse, cow, and blade of grass for miles around.

She couldn't do this. A prick of panic gripped her belly, urged her to run after Jacey and again beg her to stay. *No.* Glory stubbornly fisted her hands in her shawl's folds. *No. It's best to think about what I can do.* Which wasn't much, she admitted. After all, Papa'd seen to the day-to-day running of the ranch, the hiring and firing, the buying and selling of the cattle, the ordering of supplies. Jacey'd dogged his every step, so she knew all the ins-and-outs. But she was gone.

And Mama . . . *Well, she tried to teach me,* Glory grimaced, remembering how she'd dawdled so long over household tasks that Mama'd shake her elegant head, shoo her away, and put the work in Hannah's capable hands. Thus freed—the memory now pricked at Glory's conscience—she'd fritter away the hours in her room, indulging her romantic daydreams of her own home, a loving husband, and her own beautiful children. *Just how you intend to take care of them,* Mama'd fussed, *when you won't lend your hand to the simplest of tasks, I'll never know, Glory Bea Lawless.*

Oh, why hadn't she paid more attention, asked more questions? Because here she was now—nineteen and helpless. And in charge. *Well, surely I know something.* Glory bit thoughtfully at her lower lip. She'd helped Mama with the bookkeeping. And gotten in the way when Biddy was baking. And she'd also . . . Nothing else came to mind. Surprised realization stiffened her spine. *That's it? That's all I know?*

Glory blinked, and found she was staring at Biddy's wide and capable back. Solace and reassurance rested with her. In a blaze of emotion, Glory hurried to her and clutched at her beloved nanny. Biddy's squawk of startlement at being grabbed from behind blended with Glory's heartfelt and sobbing cry of "You're the only one who hasn't left me, Biddy. I love you."

Biddy turned in Glory's embrace and hugged her tightly. "There, there, child. I love ye, too. Yer sisters will be back. We must believe that. But right now 'tis ye I'm worried about. Yer breakin' me heart—all that time ye spend at yer poor parents' graves. 'Tis not good for ye. Why, look at yerself—ye haven't eaten or slept properly for the past month. Are ye still havin' those nightmares?"

Nestling her face in the warm crook of her nanny's neck and shoulder, her fragmented world momentarily warm and secure, Glory nodded her head and sniffed inconsolably. Then she pulled away and turned to stare out at the wind-stirred tallgrass. "I keep . . . seeing them, Biddy. Mama and Papa. Just lying there. All that blood."

"I know, child. But ye must let go. Ye must look to tomorrow, to what needs to be done. It's what ye do from here on out that'll cure what ails ye."

Glory pivoted to face Biddy. "I know what needs to be done—everything. With Hannah and now Jacey gone, I ought to be cured inside of a week, wouldn't you say? Because I'm now the Lawless in charge, even though I don't have the first idea what to do." Glory sighed, lifting her chin. "But I suppose I have to try. Because this ranch was Mama's and Papa's dream. And now, I must see that the dream lives. There's no one else to do it.''

Having made that brave speech, Glory stood there, fearing she was already bested by circumstances. Her shoulders slumped right along with her resolve. "Oh, what am I saying? I don't know a thing about running a cattle ranch. It'll dry up and blow away because of me.'' The enormity of it all brought her hands to her mouth. She stared teary-eyed at her grandmotherly nanny.

Biddy leapt into action. "You'll do a fine job of it. And plenty of help ye'll have. Why, Smiley's been the foreman since yer father settled the place. He'll still make the everyday ranching decisions. An' Sourdough's out in the cook shack stirrin' up the men's breakfast this minute. He knows what supplies are needed and when to get them. An' there's me, darlin'. I'll be takin' care of ye. Now see? Ye'll be naught but an overseer until yer sisters come home.''

Heartened by Biddy's cheery picture, Glory smiled—and exhaled for the first time since Jacey'd announced yesterday afternoon that she was leaving. "You're right. We'll be just fine. Hannah and Jacey will be so proud when they come home. The ranch'll be better than ever.''

"That's the spirit!'' Biddy beamed with pride. "Those are the first words ye've uttered in a month that show some gumption.'' She clasped Glory's hand with both of hers. "Proud of me baby, I am.''

"Now, Biddy, you can't go on calling me a baby,'' Glory chided, feeling stronger by the minute. "I'm a grown woman in charge of a cattle ranch. And I'm a Lawless. Papa's blood flows through my veins. And the way I see it, that more than makes up for whatever I don't know. I don't need anyone's help.''

A sudden and stark expression puckered Biddy's mouth, catching Glory off guard. "What is it, Biddy? What's wrong?''

Biddy shook her head, unsettling gray, wispy curls from her knot of a bun. She then gripped Glory's arm with a fierceness that surprised her. "Listen to me. Ye'll need other help besides that of a bunch of old folks who maybe canna protect you, should them murderers decide to ambush us again. So I'll hear no talk of Lawless pride and how ye can take care of yer own without outside help. 'Tis rubbish and will see us all dead. I want a promise from you. Should outside help come a-callin', promise me ye'll accept it, Glory Bea. Promise me.''

Truly alarmed now—she hadn't considered the possibility that the unknown men who killed Mama and Papa might return—Glory cried, "I promise, Biddy. I swear it. Do you really think they might come back?''

Biddy relaxed her grip on Glory's arm and nodded up at her. "I fear it, I do. Child, we don't know the who or the why of my beloved Catherine and yer father bein' cut down like they were . . . and in their own home. So we must keep a watch. 'Tis not much, but 'tis all we can do—be prepared and be careful. And go on living.''

With that, Biddy released Glory and turned to stare out at the prairie vista beyond the security of the Lawless fence. In a moment, she waved her pudgy, brown-spotted hand, urging Glory to join her at the low railing that ran the circumference of the wraparound verandah. "Come here, child. Look.''

Glory immediately obeyed. "What am I looking for?'' She searched the horizon, but could detect no movement. Only the autumn-browned tallgrass waved in the wind. Realizing Biddy hadn't answered her, Glory repeated, "Biddy, what are you looking for? What do you want me to see?''

"Yer sisters,'' came her answer.

Glory's stomach flopped with a creeping fear. Could the sweet old lady's mind be slipping? Did Biddy really know what was going on around her? She appeared to, and yet she'd been muttering to herself all morning—even before Jacey left. And she'd looked out the curtains, searching the outdoors from every window in the house—on both floors. Twice.

One way or the other, she had to know, Glory decided. She took a deep breath and blurted, "Biddy, how can I see my sisters? You know Hannah's in Boston, don't you? Remember—she left last month with that letter from Mama's family, thinking they may have had a hand in her and Papa's deaths?''

Biddy nodded up at Glory. "Of course I know."

But Glory wasn't so sure. She searched her nanny's faded-blue eyes, saw they were clear and focused on her. But still, she challenged, "Good. Do you also recall that Jacey just left with that broken spur? She thinks it proves someone from Papa's old gang was here the day of the . . . murders."

Biddy pursed her lips, as if exasperated. " 'Tis not addled I am, Glory. I know full well where yer sisters are and the why of it. 'Twas just an old lady's hope to see them riding over them hills, all safe and sound, that had me looking for them. But they're out of me nest now, and there's naught I can do to protect them. But I have ye here, and I'll not see anything happen to ye. Mark me words—I'd do anything to see that yer safe. Anything."

Ashamed for having doubted Biddy, Glory looked down at her feet and mumbled, "I know, Biddy. And I'm sorry. It's just that . . . I wish Mama and Papa were still here. And Old Pete. And his cats and dogs."

Biddy sighed and said, "Oh, me too, child. I miss 'em all somethin' fierce, I do." Then she became all bustling business as she tugged Glory by her hand. "Come on, then. Yer stubborn sister is gone. We should go inside before ye catch yer death from this October air."

Glory dug in her heels, resisting Biddy's pulling on her. If she was going to be in charge here, she couldn't allow her nanny to boss her around. "You go inside. I'd better go check with Smiley about the—"

Biddy's sudden flapping of her other hand in Glory's face startled her, cut off her words. "Shh, Glory. Did ye hear that?"

"Hear what?" Glory heard only the fear in her own voice. She bit down on her bottom lip. Could the murderers be coming back?

Biddy flapped her hand again for quiet. She cocked her head, listened, and then dragged Glory back to the porch railing with her. Relinquishing her hold there, Biddy shaded her eyes with one hand and pointed with the other. "Look there. Who the devil is that comin' down the path? 'Tis early of a morn yet, and our closest neighbor is a half-day's ride away.''

Glory saw them, all right. A wagon and two outriders. Only one family lived a half-day's ride away. "The Thornes," she entoned, her features set in disapproving lines. "They'll never get past the men Smiley has at the gate.''

Biddy harrumphed her opinion and followed it with, "We'll see.''

Glory shot her a look and then turned her attention to the dust-raising approach of their neighbors. Perched on the buckboard's seat were a man and a woman. A leggy gray horse, tied to its gate, trotted along behind. But just as Glory had predicted, the guards posted at the gate stepped boldly in the wagon's path, their rifles raised in a challenge. The wagon drew to a harness-jingling halt at the gated archway proclaiming this land Lawless property.

The wagon's driver—Glory's heart lurched with the certainty it was Riley, the oldest Thorne offspring—spoke with the guards and gestured to the main house. Glory cut her gaze to the two outriders and saw they'd reined in a good twenty yards up the rutted dirt path. Two more Thorne sons, no doubt. "What do you suppose *they* want?''

"An' how would I be knowin' what they want? 'Tis not as if I invited them here, now is it? When would I have done that, pray tell?''

Biddy's high-pitched protests stiffened Glory with sudden suspicion. She turned to her nanny and clutched at her ample arm. "All morning you've been looking for someone. And now they're here. Am I right?''

Looking everywhere but at Glory, Biddy snapped, "I've no idea what yer talkin' about, child. 'Tis merely an innocent visit by our neighbors. Where's the harm in that?''

Rising temper strangled Glory's words into a fierce whisper. "Where's the harm? The Thorne men have never been welcome on Lawless land, and well you know it. Papa tolerated Louise Thorne's visits with Mama, but that was the extent of it. And you know the why of that, too.''

"I know a lot of things, child. And not all of them right and good," Biddy countered. " 'Tis not Mrs. Thorne upsetting you. 'Tis her son Riley. I know it, and you know it. Now look—the men have allowed them to pass. You just remember yer manners, young lady.''

Glory pivoted to see for herself. Unbelievably, the guards waved the Thornes onto Lawless property. They'd never do that—unless they'd been told to by someone in authority. What was her nanny up to now? *Remember my manners? Bad manners, maybe.*

Invited or not, Riley Thorne would get a piece of her mind, she fumed. Did he think just because Papa was departed that the land dispute and the bad blood would be forgotten? Nursing her family's grudge, Glory silently watched the wagon draw near. Suddenly, Biddy rounded on her, drawing Glory's angry attention her way. ''Here they come. And you'll treat them with the respect yer dear mother always did. Feud or no, she counted Louise Thorne a friend.''

''I'll be nice to Mrs. Thorne. For Mama.'' Giving up only that one inch, Glory pointedly looked away from the team and wagon that drew near. Arms crossed under her shawl-covered bosom, she remained stiffly quiet, even when Biddy called out a greeting and got one in return from the folks in the wagon.

Glory heard the team drawing up to the hitching post. The Thornes could all fall into a deep hole, for all they mattered to her. But her harsh sentiment couldn't prevent her from stealing a glimpse over her shoulder. Intense curiosity compelled her to look, to see what changes the past five years had wrought in Riley. Her breath caught with what she saw. Tall and all filled out. A man. Not at all the skinny, coltish boy she remembered.

Was he also handsome? She flicked her gaze up to his face, but his stiff-brimmed Stetson shaded his features from her view. *If only he'd raise it up so I can*—Riley caught sight of her and made the sparest gesture of greeting. Glory stiffened and jerked back around. She had nothing to say to him.

But she did have something to say to Biddy. Leaning over and speaking under her breath, she fussed, ''Here I am, the only Lawless around to take care of everyone and everything.

And what's the first thing out of the chute? A wagonload of Thornes. If this is about the grazing lands—''

"Shush, child. Maybe 'tis naught to do with the land. Now, do ye want them to hear ye?"

Glory straightened up and purposely raised her voice. "I don't care if they do. This is *my* land now, and I'll do as I see fit."

Biddy pulled Glory to her plump side and spoke right into her ear. "Listen to ye. Yer poor mother must be turning—''

"Yoo-hoo, Glory? Biddy? Good morning to you," came Louise Thorne's booming voice. "I hope we're not too early of a morning for paying a call?"

Freeing herself from Biddy's grip, and purposely freezing Riley out of her welcome, Glory forced a smile to her lips and a friendly tone into her voice. "Why no, Mrs. Thorne. It's always a pleasure to see *you*."

A sudden stinging pain tweaked her arm. Glory blinked several times to keep from tearing up. That darned Biddy had pinched her.

She stole another glance at Riley and sucked in sharply when he nimbly jumped down from the buckboard. Her brows arched in appreciation for his long legs and muscular grace. Riley Thorne cut a most pleasing figure of a man. In profile to Glory as he helped his mother alight, he spoke over the creaking of the wagon's springs. "Morning, Miss Biddy, Miss Glory. Ma insisted on dropping by. Seems she's worried about you."

Glory's rising awareness withered as she turned to Louise Thorne, a squarely built, brown-haired, cheerful woman. "Worried? Why on earth—?"

"Because, pretty child, it's just not right—you having to shoulder all this man's work." Louise Thorne hitched her skirt and her bulk up the two steps to the verandah. With a pitying smile on her kind face, she reached out to smooth a work-roughened hand down Glory's cheek. "What *was* that Jacey thinking, to light out like she did? Why, your mama must be turning over in her grave at the thought of her youngest all alone here."

In the face of such sympathy, Glory's chin quivered. She hung her head. A sniffle or two escaped her. "Thank you, Mrs. Thorne, but I'm not alone. Biddy's here and Smiley and all the men—" Up popped Glory's head and her eyebrows. "How'd you know Jacey left? Why, she didn't even know herself she was heading for Tucson until we got Hannah's letter—and that was only yesterday afternoon."

Biddy and both Thornes struck such quiet poses that Glory could hear the wind blow, could hear the men's voices as they called out to one another over by the horse barn. Could hear a dog bark and a chicken cluck. Then it was true—she'd been betrayed. Glory rounded on her red-faced nanny. "Biddy Jensen, shame on you! You sent someone over to the Thorne place yesterday. You *were* looking for them all morning, weren't you? I cannot believe you—"

"Now hold on, Glory."

Glory pivoted to Riley. "Perhaps you ought to mind your own—"

He grabbed her arm and propelled her firmly toward the porch steps. Speechless with this uninvited familiarity, Glory could only stare up at his clean-shaven profile. Once on the ground, she was forced to turn with him to face the two older women still standing on the porch. "You two sit and visit. John and Zeke will keep a while out on the hill. I'd like a word with *Miss Lawless* here."

Needing no further encouragement, Biddy and his mother lifted their skirts and scurried for the front door. Jerking it open, they got stuck together in the opening, but then barged through, slamming it closed behind themselves. With those targets out of her range, Glory turned a properly authoritative expression up to Riley. "If you think you can just ride onto *my* land and handle me like this, then you are sorely mistaken."

Something sparked in the depths of his dark eyes, giving him the appearance of a hunting hawk as he stared down at her. "I'd hoped we could be civil to each other."

The deep and intimate timbre of his voice went all over Glory. Another wave of unnerving awareness had her swallowing convulsively. "We...we can," she stammered, barely able to meet his steady gaze. Her next breath allowed her to add, "Once you've taken your hand off me."

But he didn't. Nor did he answer her. Or allow her to look away. Glory's heart thumped, her mouth dried. The moment stretched taut with unspoken appetites. Then, without warning, Riley released her and stepped back, causing her to stumble. Why, she'd been leaning into the man. She jerked her gaze down, needlessly straightening her clothes all around. Yes, her heart beat too fast, her hands shook, and her stomach fluttered. But only because the oldest son of Papa's enemy stood on Lawless land.

"You've changed a lot, Glory."

Her hands stilled. What did he think of those changes? Glory finally lifted her head, met his gaze. His eyes, dark-brown, almost black, blazed under the low brim of his hat. His straight nose pointed to his wide mouth. Glory swallowed. "So have you. Five years is a long time."

"I reckon so."

When he didn't say anything else, sudden self-consciousness made Glory blurt, "I see you're a man now. And not the...boy I remember...playing with...when your mama called on mine. You quit coming around with her."

Riley's lips twitched, as if around a grin. "I got too big to pay calls with my mother." With that, he turned from her, strode to his wagon's tailgate, and began untying the big, finely muscled gray horse tethered there.

Watching Riley's every movement as if she'd never seen a man before, Glory called out, "Is that Pride—that yearling you told me about on your last visit?"

Riley's hands stilled over the knots he worked to undo. He sent her a considering look. "That was five years ago."

Glory felt suddenly ill. If she *could* move—and she realized she couldn't—she'd march right over to Biddy's wildflower plot and bury herself. Why had she let on that she'd remembered—for five years!—the name he'd given to some dumb old horse? But stuck with it, she persisted, "Well, is it?"

Riley smoothed a hand along the animal's arched and muscled neck, and drawled, "Yep. This is him—all grown up and gelded."

Glory blinked in shock. "Riley Thorne! What a bold thing to say."

He arched an eyebrow at her but said nothing as he retraced his steps back to the hitching rail. As he tied his horse to it, Glory's gaze slipped to his long-fingered hands. She watched his precise motions, and felt a hot thrill she couldn't name course through her and weaken her knees. It made her angry that it should be so.

He might have grown into a man, but he hadn't changed a bit from the irksome half-grown boy she remembered. She still couldn't shake a response out of him—not if her very life depended on it. He just stared at her and kept his thoughts to himself. Even when they'd been children, he'd behaved this same way. And back then, she'd been the prettiest child—everyone said so. Everyone else fell victim to her little-girl charms—even his two brothers sitting out on the hill right now. But not Riley. Never Riley.

Glory cocked her head as she considered him. *Was* he still immune to her charms? Or did she just think he was? After all, a man he may be, but she was now also a woman—one ready to test her powers. Before she could think twice, she blurted, "Riley, look at me."

He did. He notched up the brim of his Stetson, crossed his arms over his broad chest . . . and stared at her, waiting.

Glory suffered a moment of panic. He wouldn't take kindly to being toyed with. She could see it in the tilt of his dark eyes. She immediately abandoned any notion of a flirtation and cast about for something casual to say. "Umm, are you staying long?"

"That depends on you."

Glory's cheeks blazed. Why, his tone of voice alone made his words sound like an invitation to a kiss. Or was it just the way she was hearing things today? Feigning uncomprehension, she amended, "I meant, what's the reason for your . . . visit?"

"That's a good question. Walk with me a minute, Glory?"

Sudden irritation with the whole situation—he hadn't changed a bit—made her drop her prim pose. She forced her breath out in an impatient puff. "I shouldn't. I should just tell you to mount that gray of yours and get off my place."

Riley's eyes narrowed. "Is that your answer?"

Yes rode the tip of her tongue, but she just couldn't say it. Not with his mother inside with Biddy. That would be impolite. Telling herself that was her only reason, Glory relented. "Well, you did come all this way. I suppose I have a few minutes before I go see about . . ." *See about what? Think, Glory.* But she couldn't come up with a blasted thing. And so finished lamely with "Something important."

And he knew it, darn him. Riley dipped his Stetson to her. "Yes, ma'am. Wouldn't want to keep the boss lady from her work." With that, he turned and started walking.

Glory stayed where she was. Did he just expect her to fall in beside him? But then she did, hurrying to catch up to his long-striding figure. He didn't say anything, but he did slow his steps to match hers. As they walked side by side, Glory looked up at him from under her lashes and considered his square-jawed profile. And suddenly wanted to cry. Why did it have to be that Riley Thorne had grown into a most handsome man? A tall, big-muscled handsome man? It wasn't fair. He was a Thorne. And she wanted him.

Just then, he looked down at her. Caught staring, Glory felt yet another splash of warmth spread over her cheeks. Why, she hadn't blushed this much in her whole life. She quickly looked away, concentrating on the yard and the barn, the horses in the corrals, a dog stretching in the sun.

"Glory, I wanted to come see you before now and tell you how sorry I am for your losses."

Glory stopped, unable to look at him. He'd caught her off guard with his condolences. She looked out at the hills, blinked back her tears, and mumbled, "It's okay. Your mother came. It was enough."

"I suppose." He was quiet another moment but then added, "Ma told me . . . how it was here that day. Looking around now . . . well, it looks like things have been set to rights.''

A deep breath helped Glory get her words out. "Yes. You'd never know that only a month ago—" A hitch in her voice cut off her words. Unwilling to discuss it further, she resumed walking, Riley easily keeping pace with her.

A few steps later, it was Riley who stopped them. Glory turned her questioning eyes up to his. "I should have come. When I think about what you and your sisters and Biddy came home to that day, I want to hit something." He took a deep breath and then added, "I'm trying to say I'm real sorry, Glory. I've thought about you a lot, and felt for you. I shouldn't have stayed away."

Glory knew why he had—the hard feelings between the Lawlesses and the Thornes over their ongoing land feud. But more disconcerted by the deep concern he'd just confessed to having for her, she stumbled around her words. "I thank you for that. But there's no call to feel bad. The funerals . . . well, we were all upset. Why, I couldn't tell you to this day who was there, and who wasn't.''

Thinking only of a comforting gesture, Glory reached up and squeezed Riley's arm. And froze. She'd touched him a thousand times over their childhood years. But this time . . . well, the feel of him was different somehow. More . . . physical. Seeing him watch her, she jerked her hand back and held it self-consciously in her other one. "I just . . . well, it's not your place to see to me. I can take care of myself.''

"I reckon.'' He then looked down, drawing Glory's gaze with his to his boots. A kitten meowed plaintively at his feet. He bent over, scooped it up, and then held the little tabby against his chest to pet it gently. After a quiet moment of that, he spoke as if to the kitten. "Taking care of yourself can be a mighty lonesome business. You ever consider letting . . . someone lend a hand?''

Caught up with watching his hands hold the purring kitten so gently, and lost in wishing he'd hold her like that and keep her safe and warm, Glory smiled and nodded yes. And then realized she was. She stiffened. Great merciful heavens, she'd almost—She shot Riley a look. And wanted to die. His serious expression, his wordless consideration of her, his knowing eyes. They spoke volumes.

Mercifully, he returned his attention to the tabby. Glory came close to stomping her foot. Yes, she wanted help. She *needed* help. She was scared out of her skin. But she was a Lawless. Oh, she was such a betrayal to her family, to everything they stood for. They were all so strong. But not her. She was the weak one. They knew it, and she knew it. Here was the proof—she'd all but jumped at the first offer of help to come her way. And from a Thorne, no less. Worst of all, she still wanted it. Wanted him.

In an agony of silence, she watched Riley squat down to set the little furball free. She couldn't help but notice the way his denims stretched tight over his muscled thighs. Nor could she deny that the sight was pleasing to her. Just then, Riley looked up at her. Caught staring yet again, Glory quickly looked away from the warmth in his dark eyes.

"Glory? Look." She flicked her attention back to him, but saw him nodding in the direction of the kitten. Together they watched its hopping, zigzagging retreat. Chuckling, Riley smiled up at her. "It must be good to see some new life around here. Old Pete would be proud. He did love his animals."

Glory nodded and took a deep breath. "Yes. We found the mother up in the loft about three weeks ago. She'd birthed five kittens."

"Good. I'm glad." Still, Riley stared up at her. Glory noticed that the sun in his eyes lightened their brown to a honey-eyed gold. And knew this moment was about so much more than cats and kittens.

Close to running into his arms and crying like a baby, Glory jerked around, showing him her back. She concentrated on picking at her fingernails as she chided, "Get up, Riley. You look like you're begging . . . or proposing, or something."

He was customarily quiet a moment before answering. "One and the same, the way I see it. Won't catch me doing either."

Stung by his implied rejection, Glory stiffened and put a hand to her chest. "Well, it's a good thing. Because your name's Thorne. And mine is Lawless. There's too much bad blood between our families. But even if that weren't true, we couldn't . . . I wouldn't. . . ."

Staring at the horse barn, with Riley still behind her, Glory stood lost in her acute embarrassment. What was she doing, saying these words to him? She had to get herself out of this. "Well, darn it, Riley, I just don't fancy you . . . in *that* way. And darn you for making me have to say it."

Her words hung in the air. She swished her skirt aside as she pivoted to face him. He'd stood up. Her voice faltered as his gaze hardened. "I'm sorry. I didn't mean to say that . . . like that. I just meant—"

"No need to apologize."

Her anger fueled by his solemn composure, Glory again spoke more sharply than she intended. "Even if I did feel otherwise, *now* would not be the right time. I made a blood oath with my sisters to avenge my parents' deaths. And my part is to keep this spread going, so Hannah and Jacey have a place to call home. My sisters are counting on me—for the first time in my life—and I won't let them down."

"No one's asking you to do otherwise." Riley took a chest-expanding breath and peered off into the distance. When he again looked down at her, his frown produced lines to either side of his wide mouth. "I came here out of simple neighborliness to see if I could be of any help to you. That's all."

Such noble words. And she was such a spoiled child. Stricken, Glory hung her head. "I'm sorry, Riley. I don't know what's gotten into me today. First Hannah left. And now Jacey. Then Biddy and I got into a fuss. And now you show up. I . . . well, I just don't know what's going on anymore."

She again sought his eyes. Her heart fluttered at his unapproachable handsomeness. "I thank you for your concern, but we'll be fine. We . . . we don't need any outside help."

"From a Thorne, you mean?" The angled planes of Riley's face sharpened. "This is no time to be stubborn and prideful, Glory. There're things going on you have no idea about. Dangerous things. I just wish you weren't the one left here to face them. Hannah or Jacey'd be better fit to—"

"Is that what you think? That I can't handle myself and

this ranch?'' It was true: Everyone—even the Thornes—obviously believed she couldn't dress herself without help. Forgetting any notion of female flutterings over this man, Glory shook a finger at her childhood friend. "You listen to me, Riley Thorne. I may be the youngest, but I'm learning. And I'm learning fast. I'll just show you that I don't need any help.''

Riley's eyebrows rose. "That damned Lawless nature of yours hasn't suffered any for being so spoiled by your family, has it? Folks around here believe you to be a sweet-natured, kind girl. I must be the only one who sees past that to the prideful girl underneath.''

Beyond insulted, Glory sucked in a breath and lit into him. "Well, thank you for that. Did you come all this way just to find fault with me and my upbringing?''

Riley glared at her from under the brim of his Stetson. Then he spoke in a deadly calm manner. "No. But go ahead—make your own way. Just get the hell out of *my* head.'' With that, he pivoted and stalked away, showing her his squared shoulders and broad back.

Get the hell out of my head? Glory's mouth slacked open in surprise. Why, the big ox—he did feel something for her. Triumphant, Glory poked her tongue out at his retreating figure. Riley stopped, as if he'd seen her do it, and spun to face her. Glory instantly struck a sober pose and raised her chin a proud notch. Raking her gaze over his dad-blamed handsome face under his dusty old Stetson, she waited for him to speak.

And speak he did. "I came to tell you I can't sleep nights, knowing you're here by yourself. There're bad men roaming these hills. Maybe even the ones responsible for your folks being dead. If you'd think a minute, you'd realize that Smiley and your men can't sit around protecting you day and night and still see to the cattle.'' He paused, looked her up and down, and then added, "So, you can try, Glory . . . but you can't run me off.''

Glory narrowed her eyes. "I already did. I want you off my property.''

"No. I'm here, and I'm staying. Until Hannah or Jacey gets back. And I don't care if you don't like it, boss lady.''

Chapter 2

"Well now, Mrs. Thorne, it would appear your Riley's told my Glory that he plans to stay." Her pudgy hands folded atop her rounded belly, Biddy braced her bulk against the dry sink as she stared out the kitchen window. When Louise Thorne came to stand next to her, Biddy pointed out Riley's stiff-legged approach and Glory's bustling at his back, her mouth going as fast as her feet.

A secret smile on her lips, Biddy reflected that she'd known Riley was just the thing Glory needed to pull her out of her mourning self. He could always get a rise out of the girl just by being around.

"Lord above, Biddy, if you thought she was mad when we pulled up and I spilled the beans—me and my big mouth— well, just look at that child now. What are we going to do?"

Keeping her pleased gaze trained on the spectacle outside, Biddy countered, "Not a thing. As you said, 'tis up to the Lord above." She watched Glory and Riley a moment more before turning to Louise. "Thank you for talking Riley into coming today. I'm only sorry that Zeke and John felt they couldn't come inside."

Still peering through the pane of glass, Louise waved a hand at Biddy, as if dismissing her thanks and her concern. "Oh, stubborn boys. They're Thornes through and through—like their big brother. I dang near had to hog-tie Riley to get him to agree to stay on Lawless land. And Ben? That husband of

mine liked to have turned purple, he was so mad at the idea.
I'll tell you who you need to thank—that poor rider you sent
with your note. He came close to gettin' hisself shot before
he could give me your message.''

Louise now turned mischievous brown eyes and a wide grin
on Biddy. "But now that Riley's here? Why, you couldn't
throw him off the place. That sweet little Glory gets his goat
every time. All she has to do is bat those pretty eyes and my
boy's mush in her hands. Only he'd never admit it.''

Biddy smiled at Louise, taking in the strong profile of her
kind face, which suddenly crumpled with lines of worry as
she shot Biddy a worried look. "You do know that his heart
and mind are set on Glory, don't you?''

Biddy sighed. "Oh, aye. We've all known since Glory was
a babe and him only six years old. The only one who doesn't
seem to know is Glory herself. 'Tis probably for the best she
doesn't, bein' as your Mr. Thorne would be none too happy
with such a match.''

It was Louise's turn to sigh. "Ben would as soon be dead
as see Riley hitched to Glory. But what his pa thinks won't
stop Riley, if it's Glory he wants. I tell you, if she feels the
same about him, there'll be no end to the trouble.''

Biddy shook her head. "I know. But should it come to pass,
I'll have none to blame but meself. I did ask him here and
thus threw the children together.'' Having said that, she focused on her friend's face, now seeing a hint of doubt or a
degree of hesitation in Louise's features. Biddy pursed her
lips, ordering, "Come on, then. Out with it. Whatever it is,
ye'll feel better for havin' said it.''

Louise slumped. "You're right. There's . . . talk, Biddy,
among the cattlemen, what with J. C. bein' gone. Talk about
taking back their grazing lands. I'm afraid it could go beyond
talk . . . and real soon. They've had meetings, and folks are all
riled up.''

Biddy's hand went to her throat. "The saints preserve us.''
She turned again to gaze out the window. This time she looked
past the farmyard to the hills beyond. "All this land. A body'd

think there'd be no need to come to a blood feud over grass for cattle."

Behind her, Louise spoke quietly. "J. C. did start it, Biddy."

"I know." In the somewhat strained silence that followed, Biddy focused on Riley's and Glory's advance on the house. Through the glass pane, the young'uns' muffled shouts grew louder. "Through it all, my Catherine counted you as a friend. She hated the feuding between the men. Tell me I wasn't wrong to send word to you last evening of Jacey's leaving."

Biddy felt a gentle squeeze on her shoulder. "You weren't wrong," came Louise's earnest words. Biddy exhaled. When Louise withdrew her hand, Biddy turned from the window and watched her guest walk back to her chair, to the coffee cup that sat waiting for her. It was so easy to forget she was a Thorne. And that Riley was one, as well.

Easing down onto the cane chair, Louise Thorne then cupped her mug with both hands. Finally, she turned misting brown eyes Biddy's way. "I miss Catherine, Biddy. You know what she meant to me—how she defied J. C. to help me in my birthing bed all those times. I just hated it that there was nothing more I could do after the funerals. But Ben insisted I come right home."

" 'Tis yer place to be beside yer man." Biddy crossed the orderly kitchen and patted Louise's sturdy shoulder. *No matter how pigheaded he can be*, she added to herself before continuing. "The place hasn't so much the feel of a home without me Catherine—I raised her from a babe, came all the way from Boston with her, I did. But we're getting by. 'Tis day-to-day, but now there's naught to remind us . . . except for three graves out back. And our heavy hearts."

Louise tsk-tsked. "To think Catherine's own family might've had a hand in her death. It's just too horrible. But J. C., for all his faults, loved her . . . even unto the grave." Sniffling, dabbing her eyes with a folded hanky she pulled from a pocket, Louise waved it at Biddy and gave her a watery smile. "We'll both be blubberin' like babies if we keep on like this."

"We're near enough as it is," Biddy confirmed, using her apron's ruffle to wipe her own eyes. "Come on, let's go save yer son from Glory's Lawless wrath."

The two women exchanged a glance and then bustled out of the kitchen. They rounded the corner into the great room, stopping just as the front door slammed open. Riley burst inside. Glory was quick on his heels and shouting, "I should've known what you were about when you unhitched your horse from the wagon!"

Biddy clutched at the cross on a chain around her neck. Maybe she'd been wrong to ask Riley here. But it was too late now for second thoughts. Because the young man's arms were full of his belongings. And wasn't he the fine one, ignoring as he did Glory's tuggings on his coat and her shouted words? Biddy's eyes widened as Riley, without so much as a how-do-you-do, marched straight for the stairs and the second-floor bedrooms.

The Lawless nanny exchanged another look with Riley's mother, who looked as taken aback as she felt. Biddy knew she had to step in. This was all her fault. "Now, Glory Bea, yer forgetting yer manners. I'd like to think I've done a better job with yer upbringing than this."

Her admonition garnered for her the blazing glare of her youngest charge. "Not according to Riley, you haven't." The girl advanced on her as if she thought her old nanny a wayward hen out of the coop. She pointed at Riley as she spoke. "Tell him he can't stay. Tell him he's not wanted *or* needed here. Tell him to get off my property right this minute."

Before Biddy could open her mouth, Riley stopped his boot-scuffing progress up the wooden stairs long enough to call out, "Or you'll what, Glory?"

Glory spun on him. "Or I'll have my men *throw* you off, Riley Eugene Thorne. *That's* what. You *and* your horse *and* your wagon *and* your moth—." Glory went stock-still before slowly turning to face Riley's mother.

Recognizing Glory's gaffe for the opening it was, Biddy pursed her lips and crossed her arms over her bosom. In censuring silence, she watched her precious baby's grass-green eyes widen as she bit at her bottom lip hard enough to redden it. The child was so delicate and so beautiful. It was true—she was spoiled to the bone.

But Biddy let none of her tenderness for Glory show when she reminded, "What was it ye promised me—and not an hour ago—about outside help? There now. Look at your face. I thought ye might remember. So, what do ye have to say for yerself?"

Glory blinked and crumpled two-handed at her brown wool skirt. A guilty pinch of skin appeared between her finely arched but lowered brows. "I'm sorry, Mrs. Thorne. I meant no disrespect. It's just that . . . Riley can't stay here. Won't you make him see that?"

Biddy spared Louise by answering for her and drawing Glory's repentant gaze to her face. "She'll do nothing of the sort. I invited them here today, as ye now know, and 'tis here they'll stay—as my guests. Do ye think, Miss Lawless, ye can be tellin' *me* who I can and cannot have to visit?"

Glory gasped and covered her mouth with her hands. She then flew into Biddy's arms, blubbering out her apologies. "Oh, Biddy, I never meant—Of course, you don't need my permission. You're my family. I love you. I'm so sorry. I don't know what's gotten into me today."

Thinking she knew exactly what—and who—had gotten into Glory, Biddy patted the child's slender back and looked beyond her to Riley, still paused on the stairs. Silently she nodded for him to continue on. He nodded back and trudged upward.

Biddy then held Glory away from her and smoothed from the girl's tear-dampened face her darkly auburn hair, all but undone from the severe bun she'd taken to wearing since the . . . recent deaths. "Now, there, there, baby. I know ye meant no harm. Come, make yer manners to Mrs. Thorne. She's kept her boys waitin' long enough outside the gate."

Her hands folded in front of her, her head down, Glory stood before Biddy and sniffed as she nodded. "Yes, ma'am." She then turned to Mrs. Thorne. "Forgive me, please. I've just been so . . . so . . . since Mama and Papa—"

Louise Thorne grabbed Glory to her in a bear hug and came near to pounding the breath out of the girl, in Biddy's alarmed estimation. "You think no more on it, honey. It's already forgotten."

She then held Glory out at arm's length and smiled into her stricken face. "Biddy was right to send for us. We're neighbors, and we've got to look out for one another. Womenfolk understand these things, even if our men don't." She looked long and hard into Glory's face and then laughed in her loud, cheerful way before adding, "Now promise me that once I leave, you won't throw Riley off the place."

Glory nodded her promise, following it up with her words. "I promise."

A wrench of emotion shook Biddy as she stared at Glory's high coloring, her petite but exquisite figure, that mess of rich brown hair and those bright-green eyes. She looked so much like her mother.

Just then, Louise released Glory, turned to Biddy, and smiled as she said, "I'd best get on home. I thank you for the coffee and the hospitality. I'll get by when next I can."

"See that ye do, Mrs. Thorne. Yer visits are always a pleasure. Can I fix ye and the boys a little something to tide ye over?"

"No thank you. We got our own basket in the wagon." Louise turned again to Glory. "You don't be a stranger, either, honey. A woman gets hungry for female company, what with only a husband and five sons and a bunch of rowdy cowhands for company." Then she laughed. "Well, four sons now, what with Riley's being here. You try not to kill him now, you hear? I set an awful lot of store by my eldest."

Biddy kept her watchful gaze on Glory, noting with a nanny's pride and satisfaction the girl's obedient nod to the older woman. Louise then swept by Glory and made her brisk way toward the front door. Biddy watched her neighbor's departing back a moment and then glanced at Glory . . . in time to catch a flash of gold-flecked will in those narrowed green eyes.

* * *

Up on the second floor of the Lawless main house, Riley looked around the room that he'd claimed by its unused look. The bedroom he shared at home with his brothers was more like a bunkhouse, he supposed, crowded as it was with the five of them and the stacked bedding. In contrast, this quiet and strange room loomed huge and airy and . . . unwelcoming.

He studied the neatly made narrow bed with its polished wood headboard and footboard, the matching dresser and washstand. Off to one side sat a tall armoire that looked too fancy for the house. Starched curtains hung at the two long windows. On an impulse, Riley crossed to them and looked out. Just as he'd calculated—and hoped. The barn and its service court. And the wagon yard. A good view of the working part of the Lawless spread.

For a moment, he concentrated on the activity outside. Even though all the chores being done were no different than those performed at home, Riley couldn't shake the feeling of strangeness at being here. *Actually*, he asked himself, *just what the hell am I doing here?*

Receiving no answer, he huffed out his breath and retrieved his carpetbag from where he'd tossed it onto the floor a moment ago. *Quit trying to second-guess yourself, Thorne. You made your decision yesterday to come here. And here you are. You might as well unpack and make it official.* Flopping the bag on the bed, he opened it. And stared at its contents.

Then, with deliberate, determined motions, as if someone dared him to do otherwise, Riley began pulling out shirts and socks, extra denims, a combination suit . . . but, unexpectedly, his hands stilled. He stared again at his clothes. *I must be plumb loco. I'm liable to get a bullet in the back at any minute. And yet here I stand, playing at houseguest.*

Feeling a sudden need for outside activity, Riley abandoned his unpacking and reached for his Stetson on the bureau top. Settling it firmly on his head, he cast about for an idea on what he could do. Then his expression and his mood cleared when he remembered Pride. He'd left his horse tied to the rail out front. He needed to go see to him. Feeling better for having a purpose, he turned to exit the room. And jerked up short in surprise.

Framed in the doorway and blocking his exit stood Glory. Riley considered her presence here at the door to his bedroom and frowned. "How long you been standing there?"

She shrugged. "Since just now."

Had he been so deep in thought that he'd missed her approaching footsteps? Well, here she was, so obviously he had been. When she said nothing else, when the moment stretched beyond awkwardness, Riley prompted, "Say your piece, gal. I've got to see to my horse."

His words hung in the air for long moments. Glory again looked from him . . . to the bedroom behind him . . . then at him in the bedroom. Finally, she met his waiting gaze and said, "I want you out of this house. Right now."

Riley's eyes narrowed. "I understood you to accept my presence here."

She raised that Lawless chin of hers. "I did. But 'here' doesn't mean in the main house and only two doors from my . . . bedroom. It's not seemly. You can bed down with the other hands out in the bunkhouse."

Riley put his hands to his waist. "I'm not a hand. And I wouldn't last five minutes out in that bunkhouse."

Glory cocked her head at a considering angle and looked him up and down. A disobedient deep-brown curl straggled across her brow. "Just why *did* Biddy send for you? What *are* you supposed to be doing?"

Riley saw no need at this point to mince words—or to tell her the entire truth. "I'm here to see that no harm comes to you. Or Biddy. You need a man about the place."

Glory's eyebrows shot up. "We have plenty of men about the place."

"And two of them raised their rifles at us when we rode in. But you know what I mean."

"No, I don't."

Riley exhaled, resigning himself to having to put his fear for her well-being into terms she'd accept. "You need someone to oversee your spread."

"A Thorne overseeing Lawless concerns? Hardly. If anything needs overseeing, I'll do it."

Riley ignored her comeback and continued with his list. "You need someone to keep an eye on the hills for strangers, for folks who don't belong here."

"You're the only one who doesn't belong here."

A flash of irritation jerked a muscle in Riley's cheek. "Maybe so. But Smiley and your hands will be out riding fence and checking on strays. So who'll order supplies and pick them up? Direct the grazing of the remaining herd? Oversee equipment repairs? Settle disputes? Take on new—"

"Smiley, me, and Biddy. We can do all those things. Plus keep the books. I know how to do that."

Frustrated, and feeling somewhat useless, Riley blurted, "You need someone to be the man *inside* this house."

"No, I don't. I can be the—Well, no I can't, can I?"

There. That got her. Riley hitched his pants all around and glared out his importance. "That's what I thought. Now, clear on out. I've got to see to my horse." He headed for the door.

Glory didn't budge. "Biddy already had Pops take Pride to the barn."

It seemed to Riley that there was a heap of pride in this room, too. But he thought better of mentioning that, and so he changed the subject. "I need to say my farewell to my mother."

"She already left. She said for you to behave yourself while you're here."

Riley frowned so deeply he felt his eyebrows meet over his nose. "My mother hasn't told me how to behave since I was in knee pants."

"She did this time. She also said for you to watch your language around a lady."

Now that did it. Riley strutted over to Glory and bodily pressed her out of his way. Sweeping past her, his long-legged strides carrying him handily down the hall, he called over his shoulder, "Find me a lady, Glory Bea Lawless, and I'll watch more than my language."

Glory yelled something back. Riley didn't catch it, but figured he knew the gist of her words. His disgruntled mood swept him down the stairs, through the great room, out of the house, and across the hard-packed dirt of the wagon yard to the barn.

Muttering to himself, calling himself three kinds of a fool—a Thorne bedding down on Lawless property—Riley's better nature argued with him to remember the whys and wherefores of his being here. "I ought to do just like she said—get on Pride and head for home," he told himself. "What do I care if Glory ends up in a heap of trouble? Serve her right, the little—"

Riley stopped, looking around. He'd been talking out loud to himself. And it'd been noted. A couple of men in the yard stared his way, their hands no longer busy saddling their horses. An old dog raised up from his nap long enough to assess and then dismiss the disturbance before flopping back down on his side.

Frowning fiercely, denying the steady heat in his face, Riley strode—closemouthed—into the barn. He looked down the central aisle of the building, marveling as he always did at the sheer size of the Lawless horse barn. Apparently it took a lot of horses to run a spread this size.

A spread this size. More than one man had died trying to take back from J. C. what he'd stolen from them—the best of their grazing lands. And he'd taken, with muscle and guns, the most land from the Thornes. There'd been blood shed and hard feelings throughout the territory since those days. But now with J. C. gone, the ranchers were talking again of taking back what rightfully belonged to them.

Riley thought he could hear again the shouts for justice from the cattlemen last week when they'd held a meeting on Thorne land. True, none of them had wanted to go up against a shootist like J. C., but the old man was no longer a factor. Only his youngest daughter stood in their way. *And here I am in the middle of it. Good timing, Thorne.*

Willing away that troublesome prick of conscience, Riley searched the stalls for his horse. When the first few yielded no Pride, and with his patience for this day wearing thin, Riley whistled sharply. About halfway down the corridor, the gray gelding poked its head out of a stall and pricked its ears at him. Glad for a friendly face, human or otherwise, Riley started for his horse.

Behind him, the cheerful whistling coming from the tack room stopped short and a door opened. Alert to any threat, Riley paused to glance over his shoulder. A group of men filed out and stared his way. Reluctant to show his edginess, Riley faced forward and forced a nonchalance into his step. Best to ignore what wasn't his business.

"Riley Thorne? We'd like a word with you."

Now it was his business. Stopping, he turned around to find himself faced with a knot of Lawless hands—among them the man Biddy'd sent with her note. At their front stood their foreman, Smiley Rankin. Readying himself for anything, Riley opened up the dialogue. "You call my name, Mr. Rankin?"

"I shorely did. We wuz wonderin' why Miz Biddy had Pops here bring yer mount around to the barn. You ain't planning to stay on, are you?"

"Only as long as I have to."

The men stirred and muttered, taking a collective step toward him. But the grizzled old foreman, never looking away from Riley, flung an arm out to stop them. "It's already been long enough, son. Don't rightly know as we can stomach yer sort on Lawless property."

Narrowing his eyes at the insult, even as his guts churned with a dose of fear and a heap of bravado, Riley countered, "Well, I don't know that you have any say in the matter, Mr. Rankin."

Smiley jutted his stubbly chin out. "Be that as it may, who's ta say you ain't up to no good?"

"Me. I say I'm not." Riley looked into each man's face, gauging the effect of his words. And promptly decided that maybe he ought to backtrack a little, give them all a chance to walk away. "I'm not looking for trouble here. I accept that you've got every right to be on edge, in light of your recent tragedies, but—"

"There ain't no 'but' to it. Now, the Lawless girls figure

as how some of their family back east had somethin' ta do
with their folks bein' dead. But me and the boys . . . well,
we're not so sure that the blame don't lie closer ta home. A
lot closer, if you git my drift.''

Riley's gut tightened. "I get it. Loud and clear. And I'm
here to tell you you're wrong." Even while he paused to let
that sink in, Riley wished he could believe his own words.
Truth to tell, he had his own doubts about the Lawless murders, too. "I'm here to see after Miss Lawless, is all. Times
like these, with killers on the loose, neighbors have to stick
together, land feuds or no."

Smiley's weather-tanned and lined face hardened. "Them's
mighty peculiar words, comin' like they do from a Thorne."

"If you're accusing me or mine of something, Mr. Rankin,
have the guts to come right out with it. I've never killed a
man before, but I figure there's always a first time." Riley
distributed his weight evenly on his feet. With his heartbeat
pounding at his temples, he waited.

"One against six? Are you *loco*, boy?"

"Some would say so. Now what's it going to be? I'm all
for staying out of your way, if you'll do the same for me while
I'm here."

That caused a muttering conference between the hired hands
and their foreman. Finally, Mr. Rankin turned back to Riley
with their decision. "We don't want no trouble, neither. And
we ain't accusin' anyone of anything. Our concern is Miz
Glory. She's no more'n a girl and needs pertection, because
there's trouble coming out on the range. Now, that bein' the
way of it, we're thinking it'd be best if'n you just saddle up
that gray of yers and head on home."

Riley's forced-out breath puffed his cheeks. "Much as I'd
like to, I can't do that, Mr. Rankin. Miss Glory wants me here.
For the why of it, you'll have to ask her." His palms slick
with sweat, Riley then did a most foolish thing. He turned his
back on the men and took measured steps to the stall where
Pride silently watched him.

He didn't dare breathe until he entered the large stall and
put himself out of a bullet's path. Remaining still and listen-

ing, he heard no more than muttered curses and shuffling foot-steps out in the corridor. Finally he exhaled and caught Pride's bridle. Lowering the animal's head, he stroked his hand down the horse's velvety muzzle. "Damn, boy, that was a close one."

"Closer'n you'd care to think, son."

Riley spun around.

The Lawless foreman stood outside the stall's closed half-gate. "I'm sorry it has ta be this way. I've knowed you since you wuz a boy. And I've knowed you to be a good man—the best of the Thorne bunch. But times have changed." Smiley then paused, frowned, and took a deep breath. "We'll be keep-in' an eye on you, so watch yer step. And I ain't just a-talkin' about the horse droppin's, neither." With that, he turned and continued on his way.

Not knowing what to make of that speech—a friendly warn-ing or a threat?—Riley stared at the empty space where the man had stood. He was surrounded by enemies . . . which put him under Glory's protection, somewhat like the hen protect-ing the fox once it was inside the chicken coop. Riley chuckled at that image.

"This has been one hell of a day, and it's not even half over yet," he told his horse as he picked up the currycomb from a ledge in the stall.

Chapter 3

About an hour later, having seen to Pride's needs, Riley stepped out of the barn. Cautiously. He wasn't a man to make light of any confrontation. But a quick scan of the open yard between him and the main house showed him nothing out of the ordinary. Two men wrestled a heavy wooden wheel off a wagon axle, another one walked a horse from a corral, and the rest ambled slowly toward the dining hall attached to the cook shack. Not a one of them, so far as he could tell, paid him any mind. *Good.*

But after only a few steps, his name was again called out. This time, in a low hiss. Riley spun around, his hand gripping his Colt. Seeing who was there, he straightened up and exhaled. "Miss Biddy, you aiming to get yourself shot?"

Half hidden by the barn's heavy door and peeking around it, Biddy clucked out, "And who would be shootin' at the likes o' me?"

Riley chuckled as he strode over to her. "You tell me. You're the one hiding behind a door."

" 'Tis not hiding I am." She frowned and cocked her head as if in thought. Then, "Well, perhaps I am. Not that I'm afraid, mind ye. I just wish a word in private. Can ye spare me a moment?"

Riley gestured his consent. "Sure. I was just heading for the house, anyway. What's wrong, Biddy?"

She stepped out from the door's shadows and stood before

him, wringing her plump hands. " 'Tis Glory, I'm afraid."

Riley's gut tightened. "What's wrong with Glory?"

"She's out to the graves again. She's not herself when she's there. Why, ye'd scarce recognize her as the same girl ye spoke with earlier." Biddy put her hand to her mouth and stared past him for a long moment. Then she turned concerned, faded-blue eyes up to him. "I just don't know what to do, Riley. She'd been coming along in her grief until she fussed yesterday with Jacey. An' now 'tis no better than a month ago."

"No better? In what ways?"

Biddy gestured helplessly. "In all ways. Oh, Riley, I just came from the hill, but there's naught I can say or do to relieve her sorrow. She's fair wallowin' in it, an' 'tis that afraid I am for her. 'Tis one of the reasons I sent for you." Biddy gripped his arm. "Would ye go and see to her? Perhaps she'll listen to ye. For sure, she's not hearin' a word I say today. She's beyond angry at me."

Riley frowned in uncertainty. "I don't know, Biddy. She's just as put' out with me as she is with you. And it seems only fitting that she'd want to be alone with her departed ones. I'm not sure I should—"

Biddy's grip on his arm tightened. " 'Tis not alone she's needin' ta be, but with company. Now, go on with ye. The graves are out back of the house, up that first hill. Tell her I sent ye to fetch her in for a meal. I can barely get her to eat as it is. Take a good look at her, Riley. You'll see what I mean."

"I've seen." Riley was quiet a moment, but then exhaled. "All right, I'll go get her, Biddy. You just set up the vittles, and we'll be along directly. A growing girl like her needs to eat."

A sigh laden with relief escaped Biddy. She removed her hand from his sleeve and patted his arm. "Thank ye, Riley. Yer a good man. Just don't let on that any of this was my idea." Before Riley could protest that this whole thing was her idea, Biddy quick-stepped around him and lit out for the house.

Riley shook his head and started for the back of the big two-story main house. Walking beside it, he couldn't help but compare its size and fineness to his family's low, rough-wood dwelling. A spasm of anger shot through him. *Pa's right. Everything the Lawlesses have came as a result of J. C.'s stealing from his cattlemen neighbors more than twenty years ago.*

But all thoughts of old feuds fled his mind when he rounded the house and spied the three white-crossed graves that capped the hill. Through the wide-spaced slats of the low fence that hugged the cemetery, Riley could make out the small figure kneeling between two graves.

Feeling grim and not up to this, he looked heavenward. *What am I doing here?* he wondered. Getting no answer, he tugged his hat down low on his brow. Taking long, determined strides across the yard, he was soon trudging up the sloping land to Glory.

But the closer he got to the fenced-off graves, the slower he walked. He just couldn't shake the feeling that he was intruding. He changed his mind about disturbing her there and started to move away. Then the sounds of soft crying carried to him on the almost cold breeze. Turning back to her, staring at Glory's slender back, marking that she didn't even have her shawl to warm her, and watching her shoulders wrench with each sob, Riley mouthed a curse.

Approaching with due respect, he opened the gate, grimaced at its rusty-hinge squeal, and swung it closed behind him. Glory had to have heard him, but she said or did nothing to acknowledge his presence. So he just stood there. It suddenly occurred to him that he should remove his hat. Jerking it off, he ran a hand through his hair and held his Stetson in front of himself.

Twice he started to say something, but didn't. He then reached a hand out to Glory where she knelt between her parents' graves and worked at pulling weeds from around them. She was still crying. Riley fisted his hand and dropped his arm to his side.

The scene was almost too painful for him to look at. Biddy

was right. He barely recognized her. Everything inside him told him to grab her up and hold her as close to his heart as he could. He wanted to kiss away her tears and tell her everything would be okay. But most of all, he wanted to tell her he would never let anything or anyone hurt her ever again.

But he couldn't do that. There was too much between them. Between their families. And even if there weren't, she didn't care for him in the way he did her. She'd said it plain enough earlier. And he had to respect that.

Just as he did her mourning. Giving her more time to be alone with her thoughts, Riley turned his attention to the third grave—Old Pete's grave—and raised his eyebrows with surprise. A mongrel hound lay draped across it. The dog's head rested atop his paws. His floppy ears and sagging jowls grazed the dirt. Big, dark, sad eyes stared up at Riley. Skeeter, wasn't it?

Then he saw the bowl of water and a tin plate of dried-up scraps placed at the graveside, and considered what they meant. He looked from the food to the dog, seeing now the healed wound that grazed the hound's shoulder. A bony shoulder. Riley frowned with his dawning awareness of the dog's overall thinness and his dull coat. Apparently Glory wasn't the only one not eating.

Stepping over to the dog and squatting down on his haunches, Riley rested his Stetson atop a thigh and scratched the big-boned dog between its ears. Skeeter thumped his tail halfheartedly. Petting the hound and staring at Glory's back, Riley felt weighed down by the oppressive sadness of the place. A windswept hill. Three graves. Raw mounds of dirt. Whitewashed crosses. Glory kneeling between the first two, Skeeter draped over the third one, and himself squatting on the other side of that third grave. Completely separated.

Quite unexpectedly, Glory stilled her hands and spoke over her shoulder to him. "Skeeter was shot . . . that day. I guess he took off to nurse his wound. Anyway, we didn't see him for the longest time. We thought he was dead. Then last week, he just showed up. He won't eat. And he won't leave Old Pete's grave."

A sob tore from her and ripped at Riley's heart. He watched her swipe at her eyes with her wrists, heard her shuddering breath. And didn't know what to do, how to help her. Surely, if he touched her, she'd shatter.

No small amount of anger and anguish laced her next words. "He's going to die, Riley. Look at him. He's just letting himself waste away. And I can't do a thing to stop it. I've even picked him up, as big as he is, and carried him to the house. But he set up such a mournful howling that Biddy let him back out."

Riley suspended thought as he watched her pull a tiny weed from beside her father's grave. She then smoothed her hand lovingly over the mounded dirt itself. Without warning, she pivoted until she could look into his face. Riley noted that her eyes were red and raw, her brows drawn. She glared at him as if she held him responsible for all the bad things happening to her family. "Do you know Skeeter came right back up here, when Biddy let him out? And he hasn't left since. Just what am I supposed to do, Riley?"

As if he *were* guilty somehow, Riley looked away from her face, from her trembling chin. He stared at the ground and said, "I don't rightly know, Glory." He then looked up at her, at the wild tangle of her hair, at her cheeks wet with tears and pale with grief. She looked so frail . . . like a sick, old woman. Fear for her lanced through him.

Glory narrowed her eyes at him. "What are you doing up here? You come to pay your respects?"

Riley looked at each grave in turn and then back at Glory. "I suppose so. But mostly, I came to get you. I talked to Biddy." He looked pointedly at Skeeter and then back at her, raising an eyebrow. "She says you're not eating."

An unheeded tear rolled down her cheek as she glared at him. "I eat."

"Yeah? When was the last time?"

She stared blankly at him for a long moment before blurting, "I forget."

Riley stood up and jammed his Stetson on his head. He held his hand out to her. "Come on, you're going inside. And you're going to eat. Right now. And I'm going to see that you do.''

She shook her head, looked around wild-eyed. ''I can't. I have to . . . to . . .''

''To what, Glory? If you make me, I'll pick you up like you did Skeeter and carry you to the house. I swear I will. And *no one* will let you back out.'' To underscore his seriousness, Riley stepped over Old Pete's grave. He now stood in the space between the old cowboy's and J. C. Lawless's final resting places.

Only to realize he didn't have the heart to be rough with her. Especially when she clutched at her rumpled skirt and stared up at him with washed-out and pleading green eyes.

''Dammit, Glory,'' he muttered as he squatted where he was. ''I can't stand to see you like this.'' On an impulse, he held his hand out across the father's grave to the daughter. Glory eyed his offer of help, but nothing more. Determined, Riley didn't withdraw it. ''Honey, I'm speaking as your friend now. You're not doing anybody any good—especially yourself—by making yourself sick like this. You've got to eat and stay strong. There're too many folks around here who need you.''

Glory stared at his hand, at him. Her chin quivered.

Riley smiled, hoping the tenderness he felt for her showed on his face. ''*I* need you, Glory. These cowhands of yours aren't about to listen to me.. And Biddy . . . who's going to take care of her? She's getting on in years, you know. And what about your sisters? Are you going to let them come back to find you buried on this hill, too, and the Lawless spread dried up and blown away?''

Glory shook her head. Riley took a deep breath and found it to be painful. ''Give me your hand, Glory. I'll help you through this.''

Glory dropped her gaze to his hand. She then turned to study each of her parents' graves. Finally, she focused on him, but only to shake her head. ''No. You'll leave me, too. Everyone else has left me.''

Riley's heart wept for her injured soul. ''Biddy hasn't left you. And I won't leave you, Glory. Not ever."

She searched his face, apparently found what she sought, and then haltingly reached out a hand to his. At the last moment, just before her fingers touched his, she snatched them back. Her green eyes blazed with a dark intensity. "Promise me it'll be all right, Riley. You *promise* me."

Riley nodded, praying all the while that he wasn't lying. "I promise you, Glory. Now take my hand."

The light in her eyes faded. She stared at him as if she'd just now realized who he was. Then, almost shyly, she reached out across the empty space . . . and took Riley's hand.

Relief weakened him. He clamped his fingers around hers before she could change her mind. Her skin was cold, her fingers long and thin and heartbreakingly fragile. But this was a good start. Riley pushed to his feet. With his help, Glory rose to hers. Together they turned to look at Skeeter.

The old dog's eyes were closed. His bony chest rose and fell with each shallow breath. "We have to save him," Glory said.

His gaze resting on her, Riley nodded. "Yeah, I know."

Then, her hand still held in his, Glory turned to look out across the tallgrass prairie. A gust of wind ruffled her hair. "Can you feel it, Riley? This"—with her free hand she indicated the three graves—"This was only the beginning. There's more trouble coming, isn't there?"

Knowing what he knew about the other ranchers, what he suspected about the murders here, Riley eyed the treeless horizon with her. A cloud passed over the sun, turning the breeze colder, the day darker. "I don't think the trouble ever left, Glory."

Over the next few days, while Riley settled in, Glory found more than one reason to believe what he'd said to her out at the cemetery hill. About the trouble not leaving. She now believed it had stayed on when his mother rode off without him.

Looking up from the ranch's accounting ledger, she peered out the picture window in Papa's office. Well, her office now, she supposed on a sad sigh. Twiddling the ink pen in her hand, distracted by the day's bright sunshine, Glory caught sight of Riley approaching the house. A smile claimed her mouth. Without thinking too much about it, she ran her gaze from his Stetson-shaded face, to his broad shoulders and his flannel-shirt-covered chest, down his long, muscular, denim-clad legs to his booted feet.

A girlish sigh escaped her as she rested her chin in her palm. *He is a most pleasing man to look at. A girl'd be lucky to have him look with favor on her.* Glory jerked upright. She stared blankly at the cheerfully crackling flames in the small fireplace grate across the room. And reminded herself that both she and the Lawless spread would best be served if she kept her mind on her figures. And she meant the ones on the pages in front of her.

Clearing her throat, frowning, Glory bent again over the numbers and concentrated on reconciling them with the accounts due. In only a matter of moments, though, a knock sounded on the open door. Glory looked up. Her heart skipped a beat. "Riley. Come in."

Nodding at her invitation, and slapping a leather glove against his other gloved hand, he approached her desk and stood in front of it. Looking up at him, Glory noted he was dusty and smelled of horse, hay, and sunshine. But when he just stood there, quietly staring, she began to fidget. Finally, she blurted, "What do you want? I'm busy with the account books."

"You're looking better."

The unexpected thrill of his sharp, brown-eyed gaze roving over her person dropped Glory's gaze to her lap. "I feel better."

He was quiet a moment. No surprise there. Riley almost never spoke without first weighing every word he said, as if he only had a certain amount of words allowed him and so had to use them sparingly. "Good."

She brushed an imaginary speck off the page in front of her. "Is that what you came to say?"

Another silence, then, "Yes and no. I checked on Skeeter." Her heart jumped. "How is he?"

"About the same. I carried some hay from an open bale up there for him to bed down on. The nights are getting colder."

Glory swallowed the lump in her throat and finally looked up at this kind man in front of her. "Thank you. I haven't been out there to check on him since you . . ." She took a deep breath and tried again. "I'm afraid I'll find him . . . gone. I don't think I could stand that."

Riley nodded. "I know. No one faults you, Glory. You've had a tough time here."

She nodded her thanks for his understanding. Then not knowing if she wanted him to stay or to leave, she straightened up in her chair, shot him a shy glance, and busied herself with moving the inkstand here, the blotter there. "Is that what you wanted to tell me?"

When he didn't answer her right away, Glory looked up to see him making himself at home. He removed his Stetson, perched it on the desk's edge, then removed his other glove and stuffed them both in a back pocket of his denims. Running a hand through his unkempt, almost-black hair, he nodded toward the open page in front of her. "Does the ciphering come out right?"

Glory frowned as she scanned the page and then looked up at him. "I don't know. I'm not finished yet. Why?"

"I want you to ride out with me and look the ranch over, see some things."

So, they were back to that again. Her moment of gratitude evaporated into Lawless stubbornness. Glory leaned back in her father's worn leather chair. "There's not a thing wrong with the way this place runs, Riley. It's done well enough all these years without your direction, I'll warrant."

"That's true enough. But your pa was here then. And you're new at this, no more'n a girl who—"

"A girl who helped her mother with these same books. A girl whose own hand has done the writing in the ledgers for years."

"With your mama directing every entry."

In a sudden snit because he was right, Glory pushed the open ledger toward him. "Fine. Why don't you show me some of these cutbacks that've occurred to you—in only two days of looking around—that haven't occurred to anyone else living here for more than twenty years?''

Riley stared at her and then stepped around the desk, tugged the ledger back in front of her, and leaned over her shoulder. With his face right next to hers, he looked down at the page. ''Winter's coming on. You don't need as many men now.''

''I won't let any men go. They'd starve.''

Riley shook his head. ''No, they won't. They're grub-line riders. They don't stay in one place long because they don't want to. They know where to find work and food.''

Glory poked out her bottom lip. ''Yes, they do. Right here.''

Riley met her gaze. ''All right. Then, look at this. And this.'' He pointed to item after item on the page. Glory's darkening gaze followed his finger's trail. ''Don't order any more salt pork and coffee before next spring. You have plenty. But see that? You're low on oats for your horses. If you keep the men, you've got to have more horses. More horses mean more feed. Then you'll have to spare some men to go up to Kansas to the feed stores for that.'' He withdrew his hand and frowned at her. ''Smiley didn't tell you any of this?''

Glory turned her face up to the big prickly Thorne at her side. ''I'm sure he would, given half a chance. But mostly he's in here complaining about you interfering with him.'' Having thus accused him, Glory pressed her lips together and glared.

Riley's perfectly calm expression never changed. ''If the man was doing his job, there'd be no need for interfering.'' With that, he concentrated again on the columns of numbers, running that long finger down them and frowning.

Her teeth gritted, Glory slammed her hands down atop the pages, spreading her fingers out to block as much as she could from Riley's view.

He straightened up and stared at her. ''That's not helpful, Glory.''

Bending protectively over the pages now, Glory fought for control and spoke in her normal tone of voice—normal for when she was furious. ''I thank you for your efforts, Riley.

Truly, I do. But I *really* wish you wouldn't trouble yourself with *my* business.''

Riley settled his hands at his waist. ''Then you trouble yourself with your business. Get out of this office and ride over your land. See what it is those numbers stand for.''

Glory's muscles were beginning to ache. ''Why do I need to?''

Riley quirked his mouth. ''Do you have any idea what's going on under your nose?''

''How can I? Everywhere I turn, I keep bumping into you.''

Riley's frown deepened. ''I thought you wanted my help.''

Glory slowly, deliberately fisted her hands, crumpling the pages and her hours of work into so much rubbish. ''Whatever made you think that?''

''You did.'' He reached behind himself to pull up a slat-backed chair and turn it so that, when he sat, he straddled the seat and rested his arms atop the chair's wooden back. ''For the last two days I've been looking your place over and telling you where changes need to be made.''

Glory nodded. ''I know.''

''You're not going to make any of the changes I suggested, are you?''

Glory shook her head. ''No, I'm not.''

Riley's jaw set. A muscle jerked in his cheek. ''Because they're not good changes? Or because it was me who told you about them?''

Glory released the green and crumpled pages, made a great show of straightening them, and then closed the ledger. She turned a sincere expression to Riley. ''Both.''

Riley sat still and unblinking. His gaze bored into hers. Heavy with warring wills, the minutes ticked by. ''Fine,'' he blurted, jumping up and dismounting his chair, much as he would a horse. He placed it back where he'd found it, snatched his Stetson off the desk, jammed it on his head, turned his back on her, and strode toward the office door. The dull thud of his boots across the polished floor marked his retreat.

Shrinking back into the soft leather of her chair, her hands gripping the padded armrests, Glory watched Riley's denim-covered behind a moment longer than her surprised state warranted. Rousing herself, she jumped up and called out to him. "Wait, Riley. Where are you going?"

Without slowing down, he exited the room and called out, "Straight to hell for trying to help you." He then turned to his left and disappeared from sight.

Glory gritted her teeth in mounting anger and frustration. He'd most likely tattle to Biddy, who'd come give her yet another long and Irish lecture on manners. "Darn him to heck," Glory muttered, already on her way around the big oak desk. With her striped cotton skirt slowing her strides, she stalked across the room and turned left into the hallway.

Only to stop short to avoid running into Riley, who was leaning up against the white-painted wall, his arms crossed over his chest. Glaring at her, he shrugged away from the wall, pulled his riding gloves out of his back pocket and began pulling them on. "I see you're out of the office, boss lady. Care to take a ride over your property to see what exactly it is you own?"

Caught chasing after him, and prepared to die before she'd admit it, Glory looked everywhere but at his smug self. "I thought you were leaving."

He eyed her from under his lowered lids. "I thought you didn't care."

Glory narrowed her eyes as he stretched his fingers inside the glove he was pulling on. "I don't. I just—"

"You just what?"

"Well, let me finish." She looked all around the hall, searching for something, anything. Like an answer to a prayer, Biddy rounded the corner behind Riley. "Aha. I was looking for Biddy." Glory swept past him, ignoring his warm closeness as he turned with her. "There you are, Biddy. I've been looking all over for you."

Biddy frowned. "Ye have, child? Why, I've been in the kitchen all this time. Ye knew that—"

"Well, I guess I forgot." Glory glared at Biddy and, with a nod of her head, indicated Riley.

Biddy looked from her to Riley and then back to Glory. Her

eyes widened with dawning understanding. "Oh, that's right. I wasn't in the kitchen—"

"You were just now when I came through there," Riley reminded her. He stood now beside Glory.

Biddy nodded vigorously, putting her upswept gray hair in jeopardy of coming undone. Already, wispy strands framed her reddening face. "You're right, of course. I *was* just in there. But before that, I wasn't. Then I went back in there and left again. I had to . . . had to . . . Oh, dear."

Glory waved a hand at her. "Oh, never mind, Biddy. You're a terrible liar." She turned to Riley. "Let's take that ride. I'll just change my clothes."

Riley's expression never changed. "Whatever you say, boss lady."

The front door closed. Slammed. In the kitchen, Biddy exhaled. The children had left the house for that ride. She dusted her hands on her apron and looked around, trying to remember what she'd been doing when Glory'd stopped her. Fresh loaves of bread cooled on the sideboard, filling the sunlit room with a warm yeasty scent. The makings of a midday meal awaited her on the chopping block.

Aha, that was it! Meat scraps for Skeeter, the poor thing. Biddy grabbed her shawl off a peg, wrapped it around herself, knotting it over her bosom. She then grabbed up the tin plate of scraps she'd put together earlier and headed out the kitchen door. Outside, stark-blue skies, not a cloud to be seen, and bright-yellow sunshine greeted her. *'Tis a good day to be alive*, she grinned while breathing in deeply of the Indian-summer air.

Stepping off the small wooden landing and down the two steps to the yard, Biddy looked off to her left, spying Riley and Glory riding side-by-side toward the arched entry to the Lawless spread. She shook her head and muttered a prayer for young people today as she ambled out to the cross-topped hill. Thinking of Skeeter, she clutched the tin plate fiercely. *Like as not, I'll find that poor critter wasted away.*

But at the end of her trudging steps up the hill, Biddy had

reason to smile when Skeeter sat up and thumped his tail at her approach. "Well then, sir, is it better yer feelin'? Look what Biddy's brought ye—yer favorite."

She opened the wooden gate and stepped through, allowing it to swing closed behind her as she offered the dog the plate. Letting him smell it first, she then placed it on the ground in front of him. Skeeter lowered his head, sniffed it again, and then turned away, resettling himself atop Old Pete's grave.

Biddy frowned at this behavior, as much as she did the hay strewn about. Who'd done that? she wondered. Again addressing the old hound, she put her hands on her hips and fussed, "Is it that ungrateful ye are, then, to turn yer nose up so?" She bent over and picked up a fatty meat scrap, holding it under the disinterested dog's nose. "Here now, don't ye be insultin' me like this. There's naught wrong with me cookin'."

Skeeter dutifully sniffed the meat. He then turned mournful eyes on Biddy and licked her hand. But that was all. He lowered his big brown head to rest it atop his paws, and blinked up at her. Biddy's heart melted. She tossed the meat chunk back into the dish and looked around. Plenty of water in his bowl. Perhaps a bite or two of last night's supper gone. Some hay for his bed. Biddy picked up yesterday's plate and tossed the remaining scraps over the fence. "May as well let the other animals have it, eh, Skeeter?"

Skeeter's only response was the polite raising of an ear a fraction of an inch. Biddy tsk-tsked and shook her head. She turned to address Catherine Lawless's grave. "An' will ye look at him, Catherine? Here's food and water and warm hay for him. 'Twas good enough for the Baby Jesus, but not for Skeeter. What am I goin' to do with him? I can't let him die. 'Twould kill Glory. How I wish ye were here, me baby, to help us—"

" 'Scuse me, Miss Biddy?"

Squawking her startlement as she wrenched around, Biddy saw Smiley Rankin standing outside the gate. The man, as tall and thin as he was balding, held his sweat-banded slouch hat in front of himself and twisted it around by its brim. "Sorry, ma'am. I didn't mean ta scare you so."

Her plump and brown-spotted hand to her chest, Biddy felt the rising heat of embarrassment on her face. Had he been standing there long, listening to her talk to a dog and then to a grave? "Well, ye did. Ye came near to stoppin' me heart, Mr. Rankin."

Smiley ducked his head, showing a long string or two of dark hair combed over his tanned scalp. He then turned an apologetic brown-eyed gaze on her. "I'm right sorry. I reckon my gettin' close enough to scare you is a sign of how far gone ole Skeeter is, though. Before, he would've raised the dead—uh, sorry, ma'am. I didn't mean no disrespect."

"None taken." Biddy settled her speculative gaze on the foreman. A sudden girlish shyness overcame her at the way the man reddened whenever she looked at him. Despite her surroundings, Biddy smiled encouragingly. "An' what is it yer needin' with me, Mr. Rankin?"

Smiley choked on his first attempt to speak. Then, clearing his throat, he started over. "I'm needin' ta speak with you about Riley Thorne. I hate cuttin' into yer visitin' time up here, but I seen him ridin' out with Miz Glory just now and figgered this might be the best chance I had."

Biddy sobered as she stared at Smiley Rankin. "Riley, is it? Then, let's go where we can talk without bein' seen by the entire territory." Patting Skeeter's head in parting, she pushed through the cemetery's gate and approached the foreman. Pointing downhill to the wooden swing in the backyard, she instructed, "Walk with me down there, Mr. Rankin."

"Yes, ma'am," he entoned, stuffing his hat on his head and falling in step beside her.

Down the hill they walked. The windmill's creaking turns in the breeze, a ranch hand's distant laughter, and the bawl of a calf accompanied their silence. Despite her awareness of the man's physical closeness—and how pleasing it was, too—Biddy felt her motherly defensiveness stir to life. She could remain quiet no longer. Holding her skirt up out of the dusty dirt, she stopped and turned to Smiley. "An' what is it about Riley Thorne that yer needin' to say?"

Smiley squinted down at her. "Me an' the boys don't think

it's a good idea for him ta be on the property like this, him bein' a Thorne an' all.''

Biddy pursed her lips. ''I see. I'm not surprised. I know yer reasons why—the feud and all. But his bein' here is a family matter, nothing more.''

Smiley's features pinched in disapproval. ''Well, ma'am, it ain't just the family he's concernin' himself with. He's stickin' his nose in *all* our affairs. Askin' questions about the cattle, about the runnin' of the place, questionin' how many men we got, how many horses, things like that. Some think he's spyin' on us. Seems the boys have heard tell of some talk—''

''Talk, Mr. Rankin? Of what?'' Having asked him, Biddy wasn't sure she wanted to hear his answer, and so braced herself for bad news.

''Well, ma'am—an' this ain't easy for me to say, carin' like I do for ya . . . uh, for the Lawless girls, I mean. But there's a feeling out in the bunkhouse that the men what shot Old Pete and J. C. and the missus wasn't . . . well, wasn't only strangers, ma'am. Nor no kin from back east.''

Chapter 4

Biddy's heart beat painfully against her ribs. She wet her lips. "Whatever do you mean, Mr. Rankin?"

Frowning, shifting his weight, the foreman slid his gaze from Biddy's face. "They've heard some of the ranchers hereabouts had a hand in it. An' made it look like it was strangers actin' alone. Now, there's no proof of such, an' I'm not sayin' as I believe it, but . . . I thought you should know."

With her knees weakening and her heart fluttering, Biddy feared she would collapse where she stood. Mr. Rankin being the only support in reach, she clutched at his sleeve. He gripped her other arm. "You okay, ma'am? Here, let me help you to the swing. It's just over there."

"If you'd be so kind." Was that wavery voice hers? Biddy leaned heavily on Smiley's strength as he guided her to the wooden swing. Standing in front of her and holding her shoulders until she plopped onto the broad seat, Smiley gave her arm an awkward pat. Fanning her hot and sweating face with a hand, Biddy breathed out, "Thank ye, Mr. Rankin. I do believe I'll be fine now."

"If yer sure, Miss Biddy." But still, he backed up a few paces and frowned in apparent concern at her. "You want a drink of water? Or somethin' stronger?"

Biddy shook her head and waved away his offer. "No. 'Twas just the shock. It will pass." She folded her hands in her lap, stared at them, thought about what Mr. Rankin had just told her, and then sought his gaze. "I don't see how the boys could think such a thing. Why, we found writing paper from Boston and a broken spur of the sort only the Lawless gang wore. How could our"—she swallowed on the word—"neighbors get those things?"

"Well, that's the hell—pardon me—the heck of it, ma'am. The boys are hearin' that some of the ranchers acted in cahoots with shootists from back east. Otherwise, how come it is that no one reported any strangers hereabouts? Nor found no bodies other'n those?" He nodded his head to indicate the three graves on the hill.

After a silent moment, the foreman added, "We know J. C. didn't go down without no fight. And as good a shot as he was . . . well, it just seems there would have been . . . others. The thinkin' is, there *was* others, but they was carried off. At the very least, folks hereabouts seen somethin', and they know. But they just ain't sayin'."

"Merciful heavens." Biddy raised a hand to shade her eyes from the sun as she focused on Smiley. "Are ye sayin' that some of the folks who came to the funeral could be the ones who killed me Catherine and Mr. Lawless and Old Pete?"

Smiley looked down at his boots. "Could be." He then raised his head to look directly into her eyes. "I'm thinking, fer her own pertection, you need to tell Miz Glory . . . the truth about her folks."

Biddy's blood ran cold in her veins. "No. 'Twould kill her. She has so much pride."

"I reckon. But pride can be a hurtful thing. Just thought I'd mention it. The truth is bound to come out sooner or later. Which is another reason to want Riley Thorne off the property. He can't be trusted. Especially with Miz Glory."

Glory didn't trust Riley one whit. How could she? The man was a Thorne. Why, even though he'd been a perfect gentleman so far on their ride, he could at any time choose to assault her virtue. Riding her chestnut mare alongside his big gray gelding, she cut her gaze over to the silent man next to her.

He'd all but ignored her once they'd ridden out of the yard and onto the grazing lands.

Vexed with his inattention, Glory wondered if it wasn't her he was interested in, then what? She narrowed her eyes in thought until it came to her. Why, the land, of course. The thousands of acres of prime grazing land were what occupied his days and his conversations. Her grip tightened reflexively on her mare's reins, even as her features set in stubborn lines. Not one inch would he, or anyone else, take from her. It was Lawless land. Her land. Hannah's and Jacey's land.

Riley suddenly reined in his gelding. Reining in her thoughts and her mare, Glory watched the source of her pout-ish mood dismount. Holding the gray's reins, he bent over to pick at something in the dirt. Then he pulled a handful of tallgrass. Glory rolled her eyes. "What now? We've examined cattle droppings, frowned at the dried-up rills, shook our heads at holding pens needing repairs. Are you now going to have me graze?"

"Hardly." Riley straightened up, studied the grass fisted in his hand and walked his gloved fingers up a stalk or two. Lifting it to his nose, he smelled it, and then opened his fist to sort through the roots. Shaking his head, he cast it to the wind. He turned to her and said, "It's awfully dry."

At her limit with his endless concerns for her land—and now apparently every blade of grass on Lawless property—Glory fussed, "And I suppose that too is my fault? Maybe you think I can withhold the rain."

Riley chuckled. Finally. He'd been so deadly serious for the past two hours that she'd been ready to scream. "You would to spite me, wouldn't you?"

Glory raised her chin a prideful notch. "Most likely I would. Now tell me why you said 'It's awfully dry' like it's a judgment from heaven."

"It may be—for your stubbornness." Riley dusted his gloved hands together and grinned at her, showing startlingly white teeth against his tanned face. He then sobered, notched his Stetson up, and put his hands to his trim waist. "But I was thinking of fire."

Glory sucked in a breath and dismounted. Holding Daisy's reins, and mimicking Riley's actions, she squatted down to paw a strand of tallgrass. She noted its yellow-brownish color and how it snapped easily in two when she bent it. She then sought Riley's gaze. "It is October, Riley. Shouldn't it—? Why are you looking at me like that?"

Something in the considering way he stared at her alerted Glory's feminine sixth sense. Right now, grass didn't concern him half as much as she did. Her stomach quivering, her mouth dry, she all but whispered, "Is something wrong?"

Riley nodded, scaring her further. "About a hundred things I can think of."

Slowly, Glory rose to her feet. The prairie wind settled, seemed to hold its breath and wait, like she did. The sudden awareness of their aloneness, of him as a man and herself as a woman, and what that meant, made Glory's heart thump in slow beats. Looking at him now, she focused on the finer characteristics of Riley's face. The straightness of his nose, the wideness of his mouth, the tiny scar on his chin.

Knowing she was staring—but so was he—Glory lowered her gaze a fraction. And caught her breath. Crisply curling and blackish hairs peeked over the top of his combination suit. She wanted to touch them. It was that simple. That complicated. And touch his neck, his broad shoulders. They were so thickly muscled and . . . manly.

Gone was the skinny boy her sisters had teased her about during her growing-up years. He'd been her best friend, Glory mused, and her worst enemy over the years, depending on her age and the state of the feud between their fathers. But gone now was the boy who'd cradled her in his arms when she was a baby. Who'd held her hands to help her with her first steps. Who'd dried her tears when her black kitty got crushed under a horse's hooves.

The boy was gone. The man stood here in his place. Almost close enough to touch. All she had to do was reach out. If she did, he'd come to her. She knew it. She looked into his eyes. He knew it, too. Glory'd never been so afraid in all her nineteen years. Being aware of a man was one thing. Knowing what to do about it was a whole other thing. True enough, Mama'd always said that the love between a man and a woman was sacred and beautiful and good.

Until this moment, though, Glory'd always pictured love as paper hearts and ribbon-tied wildflowers and store-bought candy. But looking at Riley, she'd bet none of those pretty pictures danced in his head. No, she suspected she danced there instead. So, this quivering in her belly, this wanting him, this yearning for his touch, was what Mama'd really meant. This . . . physical side to love. What a married man and woman did in bed.

Glory sucked in a deep breath at her wayward thoughts. She'd never looked at any other boy and thought beyond the hearts and flowers part of love. *Riley's not a boy*, her heart reminded her. Glory bit at her bottom lip. A single tear clouded her vision, spilled over, and rolled down her cheek. Her soul was damned. He was a Thorne.

Straightening up, Riley's expression quickened. His gelding trailing behind him since he still held its reins, he took a step toward her, his other hand out. "What's wrong, Glory?"

She sniffed and hauled in a stuttering breath. "Nothing," she gurgled out before spinning away from him and nearly colliding with her mare. The normally docile creature reared its head and sidestepped in alarm. Glory held tightly to the reins and cried out over her shoulder, "Don't you touch me."

Too late. Riley's hands were on her shoulders. He turned her to face him and his big-boned gray. "I asked you what's wrong. Why are you crying?"

"I'm not." Then she burst into tears and flung herself into his embrace. Against the soft fabric of his red-and-black flannel shirt, she wailed, "You. You're what's wrong. How come you have to be so—? So—oh, I don't know . . . such a *man*, Riley Thorne?"

"Such a—? What are you talking about?"

When he tried to hold her away from him, Glory clung tightly. She just couldn't look into his brown eyes right now. "No, leave me be."

His chuckle echoed in his chest, vibrating against her cheek.

She breathed in his musky scent with each breath and listened to the sound of his husky voice. "How can I leave you be while you're holding onto me? And honey, if I could leave you be at all, I wouldn't be on your place now."

Glory blinked, stared at the indifferent wilderness beyond the security of Riley's arms, and sniffed. "Why *are* you here—really?"

Riley shifted his weight, settling her more against him. His hand rubbed up and down her back. "Because I . . ." He huffed out a breath and started over. "Because . . . it's the neighborly thing to do."

Glory frowned at the large-checked pattern of his shirt, and then pushed back until she was held loosely in his embrace. Her hands now on his chest, she looked up into his eyes, noting the fine lines at their corners. "Liar," she accused.

Riley gripped her arms, rocking her gently as he admonished, "Don't do this, Glory. Don't you look up at me like this."

"Why not?" Glory tipped her tongue out to moisten her parted lips and waited for what seemed a breathless eternity for Riley to move, or to answer her. Surely if she looked away now, the season would be a different one. Perhaps frozen winter. Or scorching summer.

Caught up in his arms, she watched the play of emotion over his handsome face. And realized he was a stranger to her in more ways than he was familiar. Whatever battle raged in his head, it seemed to deepen the sharp angles of his high cheekbones and square jaw. A subtle change in the shade of his tanned and taut skin alerted her to his decision, just as surely as did his tightening grip on her arms. His brown eyes narrowed, sighting on her lips with the singular intensity of a crouching predator.

Glory became afraid. Something wild, something untamed and unknown lurked just beneath the calm exterior of this man. And this barely controlled fierceness in him wanted her. A trembling overtook her. His kiss would sear her heart, scar it for life, she just knew it. And yet . . . she still wanted it.

Wanted him. What was wrong with her that she'd feel this way? How could she betray—

Riley's head lowered with the frightening suddenness and deliberation of a hammer on a nail. His lips claimed hers. Shocked, Glory opened her mouth to protest. But the words curled up and died like paper in fire. Wide-eyed, she stiffened until her rigid stance made her legs ache. But Riley's demanding kiss only deepened. He pulled her tight against him, his tongue dueling with hers.

To her shock, Glory realized her eyes were closing, realized she liked the firmness, the moistness, the hunger in his lips. She liked the taste of him, too. She liked the hotness between them, the melting together of their bodies. The wonderful tingling and surrender of her—

Riley broke off the kiss. He pulled back sharply, let go of her, stared at her. With eyes wild and fierce, he faced her, staring as if at a phantom. As if he'd been jarred awake while sleepwalking. Glory steadied her feet and clutched her hands together over her heart. She couldn't look away from him, not even when he wiped her kiss off his lips.

Something in her heart tore at such a gesture. He hadn't liked her kiss.

"That's why," he said, his voice no more than a hoarse growl. "That's why you can't look up at me like that. Because that kiss . . . that's only the beginning, Glory. And you don't know the first thing about what goes on between a man and a woman."

Hurt, angry, a study in insulted innocence, Glory poked out her lip. "I do too know the first thing. It's that kiss. And guess what, Riley Eugene Thorne? I don't care if you didn't like it. Because I did."

Satisfied when his brown eyes widened, Glory spun on her heel and realized she was still holding Daisy's reins. With a quick flick of her wrist, she tossed them over the horse's head and mounted the docile creature, settling herself in the saddle. From her seated height, she then looked down at Riley.

He didn't move or protest or do anything else to sweeten the moment for her. *He's going to make this hard, darn him.*

Her first kiss, and it was done out of anger. And he hadn't even liked it. Glory swallowed, called on her Lawless strength, and hissed down at him. "Did you hear me? I said I liked it. And you—a Thorne, no less."

With that, she put her heels to the chestnut. And left Riley standing there.

The front door slammed. Determined footfalls, all the louder for being booted, echoed through the main house. Seated in the sunny, formal parlor—her departed Catherine's favorite room—Biddy paused in her mending and looked up, frowning at the noise and then sighing. With Jacey gone, there was only one person who'd tear through the house this way. *Glory be, 'tis Glory Bea.*

"Biddy? Where are you? I want Riley Thorne thrown off this property!" The footfalls and the yelling stopped. Then, "Do you hear me? Biddy, where are you? I hate him, and I want him gone by nightfall."

"The saints preserve us," Biddy muttered aloud. "First Mr. Rankin and now this." Laying aside her blouse and the button she intended to sew on it, the put-upon nanny came reluctantly to her feet.

"Biddy?! Where are you?" Glory's shouts and trodding steps heralded her approach to the parlor.

" 'Tis in the parlor I am, young lady," Biddy sang out, following it with, "Not that young ladies would be bellowing and stomping around like a man in a barn, mind ye."

That brought Glory to the door. Her high color, windblown hair, and frowning mouth elicited a raised eyebrow from her nanny. In a pouting temper, one which would last for days if not checked, the child stood in the doorway, her feet apart, her hands fisted at her waist. And glared. "I want him gone, Biddy. Today. This minute. Now."

Even knowing full well who she meant, Biddy stalled the inevitable by asking, "Who is it yer wantin' gone, and why?"

Glory advanced into the room, flinging her papa's sheepskin coat off and tossing it onto an upholstered wingback chair. "Riley Thorne is who," she all but snarled as she passed by.

Swept up in the windstorm that was Glory, Biddy turned and watched her stomp to the window by the piano and stare outside. Suddenly she spun around. "He kissed me. And then didn't like it."

Biddy's hand went to her mouth. "Merciful heavens," she mumbled through her fingers. It was happening. Her and Louise Thorne's worst fear . . . and secret fondest hope.

Glory tromped back to her and crossed her arms under her bosom. Her green eyes flashed with gold specks, rivaling a spring meadow dotted with marigolds. "Who does he think he is, kissing me? I never invited him to do such a thing. Why, the man's a Thorne. You asked him here, Biddy, and so you can tell him to leave. I want no part of a conversation with him."

Understanding as she did the real reason for Glory's fit of temper, and biting the inside of her cheek against the urge to chuckle, Biddy lowered her hand from her mouth. "Are ye telling me ye want Riley gone *because* he kissed ye? Or because he didn't *like* yer kiss?"

Glory stared wide-eyed at her, screeched, and spun around. Biddy allowed herself a secretive smile. *So young Mr. Thorne took a liberty with our little miss, and she liked it more'n he had. Or so he told her, the devil.* Watching her baby's slender back, right now so rigid with temper . . . and no small amount of wounded feminine pride, Biddy admonished, "Now, Glory, yer not thinking straight."

Hands fisted at her sides, Glory pivoted like a toy spinning-top to face her. "Oh, yes, I am. I never want to see his face again. How dare he . . . *kiss* me—a Lawless? Now, are you going to tell him to get his gear and clear out?"

Biddy pursed her lips. This had gone far enough. Hands held together at her waist, she narrowed her eyes at her baby. "No, I'm not, young lady. 'Tis only yer pride that's wounded."

Looking every bit the spoiled youngest child that she was, Glory backed up a step. "The only wounds there'll be—if he's still here come suppertime—will be on Riley's Thorne-y old hide, if I have my way."

"And there it is, miss, the crux of your behavior—'yer way.' Granted, 'tis no one's fault but me own and yer dear mother's for that. But true it is, yer so used to getting *yer way* in all things that ye can't abide someone who'd dare deny ye."

Warming up to her subject, seeing but not heeding the suddenly crestfallen expression that claimed Glory's features, Biddy pointed a finger and shook it to emphasize her words. "Yer no longer a babe now. Yer a woman. And high time ye acted it. Look around ye. 'Tis ye who are responsible for keeping this ranch going. Ye made a blood oath with yer sisters to do just that. And ye can't do it alone. 'Tis help yer needin'— Riley Thorne's help, as it turns out. An' ye'll just have to swallow yer dislike for it bein' that way. From now on, ye must do what's right for all, and not what's good for just yerself."

A heavy silence followed Biddy's outburst. Staring now into Glory's wounded face, seeing her stiff posture, and hearing her own words, Biddy put a hand to her chest, felt her heart beating dully. She'd never spoken to Glory thus. The child was doing the best she could. It was all so new to her, and she'd just not found her way yet. *And what did ye do, Margaret Jensen? Ye told her she's failing everyone.*

Biddy never knew she could be so cruel. Yes, it'd felt good to unburden her troubled and fearful heart, but not at the expense of her precious Glory. She reached a hand out to her baby. "Glory, child, I didn't mean—"

"Yes, you did." Glory's quivering chin went up a notch. "I never knew until this past week just how everyone saw me. First Jacey told me to grow up. Then Riley found fault with everything I've tried to do for the ranch. And now you tell me I'm a willful, stubborn child who thinks only of herself— at the expense of my family and this ranch."

Tears spilled down her pinkening cheeks. "I'm sorry, Biddy. I never meant to cause you shame. Or bring shame to Mama's and Papa's memories."

She stopped, blinked, and pressed her lips together. Biddy wanted to die. She'd hurt Glory to the quick. Before she could move or say anything, though, Glory looked down and then raised her head. "If you'll excuse me, I think I'd like to go to my room."

Her own eyes filling with hot tears, her chest hurting, Biddy shook her head. "Oh, child, what have I done?"

Glory walked slowly, sedately past her. "You've told the truth. Nothing more." At the doorway, a hand resting on the wood casing, Glory turned and studied the parlor. "Mama loved this room. I remember that night in here, after the funerals, when Hannah told us she was leaving and how scared I was. I can still feel Jacey's knife prick my finger as we made our oath to avenge the murders." She pointed to the carpet at Biddy's feet. "Look. That little spot there is Hannah's blood from her knife-prick. We said, 'We swear it. And so be it.' "

Looking wounded and elegant, and suddenly older than her years, Glory exhaled and raised her head. "I swore it. Then . . . so be it."

With that, she turned around and walked away.

Biddy stayed in place. She couldn't move, could only helplessly listen to Glory's retreating steps down the hall. Suddenly physically ill, Biddy clutched at her chest, reached for a chair to steady herself, and mouthed again, "Margaret Jensen, what have ye done?"

Riley swung his leg over Pride's back and dismounted as if this were his last act on Earth. Remembering how mad Glory was at him because of their kiss—What had given her the idea that he hadn't liked it?—Riley figured walking inside just might *be* his last act.

Looping the gelding's reins around the hitching post, he absently rubbed his gloved hand down the horse's muscled neck as he stared at the Lawless main house. The notion that he could just open the door and walk inside was still taking some getting used to.

Not that he was wanted here. Not that he really wanted to be here. Just then Glory's face, so sweet, so angry, so stubborn and prideful, sprang to his mind's eye. Again, he could taste her hungry but innocent kiss. *Okay, she's what's keeping me here—that and my own wanting to be,* he admitted to himself.

He steeled his resolve with a deep breath and hitched at his gunbelt. Then he tugged his Stetson forward on his brow. *I'm acting like a danged bull pawing the ground right before it charges,* he thought. He turned to his gray gelding. "Well, here goes nothing. If Glory strips my hide from the bone, you know your way home, don't you?"

Pride made a chuffing noise and nodded his head. Riley chuckled . . . at his horse, at himself for talking to his horse. And for being afraid of a woman half his size. *Yeah, but one who's most likely gripping a fire iron with my name on it.* Accepting his fate, Riley trudged up the steps, crossed to the indifferent door, grasped its heavy brass knob, and turned it.

He opened the door with the studied slowness of a thief and poked his head in. Listening, he heard only the sound of his own breathing. "Glory?" he called out as he pushed the door open enough to step inside. "You in here?" He closed the door behind himself and took off his Stetson. "Wherever you are, I'm sorry."

He cut his gaze all around the homey, inviting great room. He then sighted on the stairs. No one there. Then to the left toward the kitchen. No sounds greeted his ears from that direction, either.

"Biddy?" he ventured. No answer. Frowning, knowing that with the sun starting to set, she'd normally be in there filling the house with the evening meal's aromas, Riley headed in that direction. "Where is everyone?" he muttered, increasingly edgy about the quiet.

As he strode by the long, broad hallway which opened onto the office and the parlor, something on the floor caught his attention. His gut clenching, he stopped and concentrated on what he was seeing. "What the hell?"

A limp hand poked out of the parlor and into the hallway. Palm-up, fingers spread, a bit of ruffled sleeve encased the wrist. Struck numb, Riley stared for a long second, not accepting what he was seeing. Then he recognized the pattern in the ruffle. He'd seen it this morning. "Biddy. My God."

Mindful of the recent murders, Riley drew his gun before

approaching the parlor. At the double-wide arch, he jerked into the opening, crouching and waving his pistol. No one but him and Biddy. Still wary, Riley knelt beside the older woman's prostrate form and looked her up and down. No blood. No wounds that he could see. He cut his gaze around the room. No furniture overturned, nothing disturbed. No sign of a struggle.

He reholstered his Colt, ripped off his gloves and Stetson, tossing them aside. Then he felt her cheek. Cold, clammy. Her complexion appeared ashen, almost Pride's gray color. Fearing it was her heart and that she might be . . . gone, Riley leaned over and placed his ear to her chest. Holding his own breath, he listened. And then exhaled. There it was. A strong, steady heartbeat. He raised up on a knee and shook her shoulder. "Biddy, can you hear me? What happened?"

No answer. Riley scooted his arms under her shoulders and knees and lifted her off the floor. His teeth gritting with his effort, he staggered under her bulk and made for the stuffed horsehair sofa. Depositing her there, he stood up and stared down at her. She remained unconscious.

More than a little concerned now, Riley leaned over and smoothed her hair back. He had to get help. Straightening up, stepping over his Stetson and gloves, he loped down the hallway, turned into the great room, threaded a path around the scattered pieces of leather furniture, and took the steps two at a time. "Glory?" he called out as he ran.

Chapter 5

Glory pushed her teary-eyed self up to a sitting position on her bed. Bracing herself with her hands flattened atop the quilted bedspread, she cocked her head and listened. Was someone calling her name? Shifting her weight until she was balanced, she rubbed her fingers over her hot, damp cheeks and listened. The sounds of someone bounding up the stairs greeted her ears.

"Glory? Are you up here?"

Riley. He was the last person in the whole world she wanted to see. Still, swinging her legs over the side of her bed, she stood and put her hands to her all-but-undone bun. Grimacing, she hastily pulled out the hairpins and raked her fingers through her long curls. She stepped to the closed door but then stopped to rearrange her skirt's folds.

The door flew open, startling a squawk out of her as she jumped back out of the way. Clasping her hands over her heart, she glared at Riley as, a hand still on the knob, his other clutching the door's frame, he leaned into the room. Glory frowned at his entrance. "Didn't your mother teach you to knock—?"

"Something's wrong with Biddy."

Glory stared at him. "What did you say?"

Riley let go of the jamb to grab her arm. Shock and uncertainty had her resisting his pull on her. His grip tightened. He put his face right in front of hers. "Listen to me, Glory. Something's wrong with Biddy."

With Riley's brown eyes no more than a few inches from her nose, Glory blinked and swallowed. "Biddy?" she repeated, hearing her own voice, which sounded strangely like a kitten's mewling.

"Yes." Riley tugged her out into the hall with him. "I came in just now and found her—"

"Something's wrong with Biddy," Glory repeated, suddenly understanding. She wrenched out of Riley's grip and made for the stairs. Thankful for her split riding skirt that didn't tangle around her legs, Glory loped downstairs in a worried frenzy. Right behind her, Riley's heavier steps dogged hers. On the first floor, she stopped, looking both ways.

Riley passed her by, heading for the hallway. "This way," he called over his shoulder. "In the parlor."

Glory followed his back. Her heart pounding, her palms sweaty, she became aware of a prayer repeating itself in her head. *Please, no. Not Biddy. I need her. I'm sorry. I'll do anything. Just let her be all right. Please, God.*

But still, when she burst into the parlor, Glory wrenched to a stop, stared at Biddy's lifeless form on the maroon sofa, and then rushed to her side. Going down on her knees, hugging Biddy's limp form to herself, Glory whimpered, "No."

She then turned her wide-eyed gaze to Riley, who stood across the room, an unreadable expression on his face. "What's wrong with her? What did you do?" The words were out of her mouth before she knew she was thinking them.

Riley's face closed, his features firmed. "I don't *know* what's wrong with her, but I sure as hell didn't *do* anything to her—and you know it. I found her on the floor in here and carried her to the sofa."

Glory stiffened and glared at him. "Did you hurt her when she told you I want you off my land?"

Apparent confusion knit his brow. He shook his head. "She never told me anything. I came in looking for you and found her like that—only on the floor. We can stand here arguing, or we can see to Biddy. Which is it going to be?"

Glory glared at him and then peered down at her nanny, more a grandmother to her than anything else. She took a deep, calming breath—*I can do this . . . I can do this*—and smoothed a hand over Biddy's soft but clammy cheek. She turned to Riley. "Go out to the cook shack and get Sourdough. He'll know what to do."

Tight-lipped and glaring, Riley nevertheless nodded and quickly exited the room. Glory spared his hurrying figure a glance and then began loosening Biddy's collar. "Oh, please, Biddy, be all right. I'm so sorry we fussed. I didn't mean anything I said, I swear it. If you're not okay, I'll just die. Don't leave me, Biddy. Please don't leave me. I won't know what to do."

When her whimpering threatened to become sobs, Glory jerked to her feet. All but panicked, she searched the room, the framed pictures on the walls, the delicate tables, the upholstered chairs, as if she would find a plotted-out course of action attached to them. But nothing presented itself. Glory lowered her gaze to study her cherubic, gray-haired nanny's breathing. Thankfully, her chest rose and fell in even breaths. *Do something*, she thought frantically.

Suddenly galvanized, Glory raced out of the parlor and threaded her way through the maze of rooms to the kitchen. Once there, and swiping at her eyes with the backs of her wrists, she sighted on a clean cloth covering a pan of cornbread. Snatching it up, she turned to the deep sink, worked the lever, and moistened the white, loosely woven cloth. Wringing out the rag, she ran back to the parlor.

And stopped, staring. Biddy was rousing. Making little moaning sounds, her movements weak and uncoordinated, the older woman tried to push herself upright on the sofa. Glory's thankful heart soared. "Oh, dear God, thank you," she breathed as she rushed to Biddy's side. "No, Biddy, you just stay lying down for now. Do you hurt anywhere?"

Her faded-blue eyes rounded, Biddy stared at her as if she'd never seen her before. "Hurt?" She appeared to think about that before she shook her head. "No." Then her expression cleared and she put a hand to her wrinkling brow. "What happened, child? I don't know how I . . ."

Gripping Biddy's plump shoulders, Glory gently urged her to lie back down. "You must've fainted. Riley found you on the floor." While she talked, Glory folded the wet cloth and pressed it to Biddy's broad forehead.

Biddy suddenly gripped Glory's hand. "On the floor? What on earth would I be doin' on the floor?"

Thinking of the accusations she'd just flung at Riley, Glory remarked, "I was hoping you could tell me that." She glanced at the doorway. Feeling the imminence of *his* return, Glory rushed her words. "Did you tell Riley he had to leave?"

Biddy frowned at her and shook her head. Glory slumped but then jerked upright when something caused her nanny to stiffen and widen her eyes and then narrow them. Glory all but cried out her fear. "What's wrong? Do you hurt somewhere?"

Biddy further mussed her straggling hair by vigorously shaking her head. "No, child, 'tis not a—ooooh. Ow. 'Tis a pain." She clutched at her heart . . . no, her stomach. No, her head. Her hip. She then grabbed Glory's arm with surprising strength. "Ye must have Riley stay. Ye must. I'm ailin', child, and I cannot help ye. Promise me."

Desperately scared, Glory covered Biddy's hand with her own and swore, "I promise, Biddy, I swear it. Riley can stay. Just please be okay."

Biddy exhaled deeply on a sigh and settled herself on the pink brocade sofa. "Oh, 'tis much better I'm feelin' right away." She pulled her hand out from under Glory's and patted her cheek. Then, frowning in thought, her gaze cast to the ceiling, she said, "The last I recall . . . you left the room . . . in tears. Because I—"

Her mouth agape, Biddy sat up, swinging her legs over the side of the sofa, and sending the damp cloth to her lap. Glory fell on her bottom trying to get out of the way, but Biddy bent over her, clutching at her shoulders. "Oh, child, I said such horrible things to you."

Glory shook her head and clasped one of Biddy's hands.

"It doesn't matter, Biddy. All that matters is you getting better." Her chin a-tremble, Glory lay her head on Biddy's ample lap. "I thought you . . . I thought . . . Oh, Biddy, you scared me."

"There, there, child, 'tis just . . . fine I . . . am."

Catching the note of hesitation in Biddy's voice, Glory looked up in time to see Biddy make a swooning dive for the sofa's pillows under her. Screeching, Glory reached for her nanny and realized two sets of male hands helped her settle Biddy again. Frantic, panicky, she didn't question their sudden appearance. Instead, she searched Riley's and Sourdough's faces. "Do something!"

"Ah aim ta do just that, Miz Glory. Now, you be a good girl and git on outta muh way, ya hear?" Sourdough, the old camp cook and a short, grizzled man so bowlegged he couldn't catch a hog in a ditch, as Papa'd always said, put a gnarled but strong hand under her arm to help her stand.

Riley stepped in, easily lifting Glory to her feet. Frightened out of her wits, she wrenched into his arms and allowed him to walk her out of the room.

Biddy opened her eyes and cut her gaze around the room. "Are they gone?" she whispered to the white-aproned Sourdough, who'd pulled a chair up to the sofa.

"As gone as it gits." Leaning forward on the dainty piece, looking as out of place in the ladyish parlor as a badger would in a baby's pram, Sourdough pulled a pocket knife out of his grubby denims and began patiently cleaning under his fingernails. Keeping his eyes on his handiwork, he drawled, "That Thorne boy sez yer ailin'. Ah'm supposed to be doctorin' you, like Ah do the men out on the trail. But it don't appear there's no such need." He paused, looked up to give her an assessing, eyebrow-raised look, and added, "You aim ta tell me what's goin' on, Miz Biddy?"

Biddy sat up in a rush, primly straightening her clothes and her hair. "Shh. Keep yer voice down."

Sourdough grunted as he turned back to his personal task. "Ah ain't the one yellin'. Now, Ah got more'n thirty hungry men a-grousin' fer their supper out to the bunkhouse. Ah'd appreciate it if we could hurry things along, seein' as how there ain't nothin' wrong with you.''

Biddy clucked her tongue at the man. '' 'Twas in a faint, I was, I'll have ye know.''

Sourdough shot her a sly glance and raised a bushy eyebrow. ''Maybe so, but you ain't now.''

Biddy settled herself more on the sofa and folded her hands in her lap. ''I became weak of a sudden . . . after fussin' with Glory, 'tis all. But yer right—I'm fine now. And I'm not wantin' Glory to know that.''

The old camp cook nodded as he folded his knife and repocketed it. Only then did he ask, ''How come?''

Biddy considered him a moment. The man was as testy as a bantam rooster. But she'd need his silence for her just-hatched plan to work. ''Because she'll send Riley Thorne away.''

Sourdough stared at her as he ran a bony-fingered hand over his stubbly chin. ''Seems ta me you're the only one hereabouts as wants him around.''

Biddy fluffed up on the sofa. ''That may be—an' think what ye will about me—but I'm doing what I feel's best for Glory.''

Sourdough chuckled with a gap-toothed grin. ''Cain't no one fault you there, ma'am. You always have put the girls first. So if you say the Thorne boy needs to be on the place, Ah'll abide by that . . . for now. What goes on in the main house ain't none of my business, nohow.''

Biddy exhaled in relief. ''I do thank ye, Mr. Sourdough. Now, here's what I'm wantin' ye to do. I want ye to tell Glory I can't be out of bed, that I need rest. Just say I'm old and tired, and can't take all the strain. But also tell her I'll be well in time. No sense scaring the life out of the child . . . again.''

''Ah can do that. But it's goin' ta cost you.'' With his expression the carefully blank one of a seasoned poker player, Sourdough sat back in his chair, clamped his hands onto his knees, and waited.

Why, the old rascal. Knowing from past experience exactly

what it was he'd want from her, Biddy narrowed her eyes. "How many and when?"

The cook's whiskery mouth worked. He looked up at the ceiling as he thought. Then, like a soaring eagle sighting on a mouse a hundred feet below, he swooped his gaze down to Biddy. "Ten. In three days' time."

Biddy sucked in a shocked breath. But what choice did she have? "Done. What kind?"

Sourdough shrugged his shoulders. "Ah'll leave that up ta you, ma'am. You know what you have on hand."

"Ye drive a hard bargain, Mr. Sourdough."

He rose stiffly to his feet. "Ah been told that before." Then, nodding his head, he added, "Nice doing business with you. Ah'll go tell Miz Glory yer ailin' and need some rest."

He'd taken no more than two or three bowlegged steps before Biddy called out to him. "Mr. Sourdough? I've had a sudden thought."

The conniving old cook turned back to her. "An' what's that?"

"How in the world is it that I'm going to bake ten pies in three days when I'm supposed to be in my sickbed?"

Sourdough scratched his head and worked his mouth. Then nodding at her, he drawled, "A smart woman lak you? You'll think up somethin', Miz Biddy."

Up to her elbows in flour and lard and sugar and cream, with endless pie pans scattered atop every available bit of space, with the cast-iron stove hot and ready, and surrounded by bowls of shelled pecans and opened jars of fruit preserves, an aproned Glory rubbed her wrist under her itching nose as she bent over to read Biddy's recipe.

How in the world ten pies would make her nanny feel better, she had no idea. But there it was. And she *had* promised God only yesterday in the parlor that she'd do anything if Biddy would be okay.

Sighing, denying the tired throbbing in her shoulders—she'd been baking since sunup—she floured the rolling pin and rounded out yet another crust. Handling it gingerly, daring it to tear apart as many others had, she successfully wrangled it into a tin pan and then pinched the edges up. *This one will be pecan*, she told herself, being absurdly defiant. *Only one crust required.*

Setting the crust aside, Glory turned to the stovetop where a heavy pot bubbled with the syrupy filling. Stirring it, glad for the moment's relative inactivity, she didn't realize she'd blanked her mind until a knocking on the open back door recalled her to her surroundings. Jumping at the sound, she leaned back to see her foreman standing outside on the landing. "Come in, Smiley," she sang out. "I'm just making these infernal pies."

Smiley hesitated a moment but finally stepped inside, his hat in his hand. He stayed just inside the doorway. Glory glanced at him and saw him looking in confusion all around the thoroughly messy kitchen. "Ah ain't never knowed you to bake a pie . . . nor nuthin' else, Miz Glory."

"And this is why," Glory teased, seeing through his eyes the flour-dusted shelves and counters, the fallen-over jars of preserves, and the gaping sacks of sugar floundering about. "Now, what can I do for you?"

Smiley scratched his head and quirked his mouth, his face turning reddish. " 'Scuse me, ma'am, but you got some . . . flour on yer nose."

Glory felt her own face heating up as she quickly swiped at it with her doughy fingers. Smiley's widening eyes confirmed her fear that she'd only made it worse. "Oh, the devil with it, Smiley. Tell me what you need."

"Yes, ma'am. I'm takin' some of the men and headin' out—while this here nice weather lasts—to round up some stray cattle Heck said he seen close to the . . . Thorne place."

Glory stilled, nodding silently. They'd been steadily losing cattle over that way. Smiley knew it, and she knew it. "All right. How many men and how long you figure on being gone?"

"Five. And at least overnight." He pursed his lips together, looked at his boots, and then back up at her. "I don't like leavin' you like this, Miz Glory."

Glory frowned at the man. She suddenly realized he'd never come even this far into the main house. And he'd certainly never said two words about . . . well, caring. About her or anybody. Glory's heart heated up to meet the kitchen's warmth. "I'll be fine, Smiley. Biddy's here, and so's Riley." His name hung in the air between then. Glory looked down and then up again. "And the other men. Nothing will happen."

"Yes, ma'am. I just wish I could believe that. I never . . . well, I never said much about it afore, Miz Glory, but you an' yer sisters . . . it's like yer my own girls. I ain't never had a family 'cepting you-all. An' it's right sorry I am that me and the boys was off on that cattle drive and wasn't here . . . that day. 'Cause it woulda turned out a whole lot different, ma'am. A whole lot."

Her eyes tearing up, her throat tightening, Glory raised her chin as if that could forestall emotion. There was a time—no less than a few days ago—when she would have rushed to hug Smiley and gush all over him and tease him about caring. That she didn't now was testament to her new grown-up status. That, and her being the Lawless-in-charge. You couldn't cut the fool with your hired help, if you were the boss, Papa'd always said.

Finally, when she was able, Glory all but whispered, "Thank you, Smiley. What you said means a lot to me. More than you know."

Frowning, red-faced, and obviously embarrassed, Smiley pointed with his sweat-banded slouch hat toward the hallway. "I'm wonderin', Miz Glory, if'n it'd be okay for me to have a few words with Miz Biddy—if'n she's up to visitors, that is."

Glory's eyebrows raised, almost of their own volition. She swallowed the smile that tugged at her lips. "Certainly. Please—go ahead. She's in the parlor. I believe she'll be heartened for having the company."

Smiley frowned, dipped his eyebrows, trying his best, Glory figured, to look properly male and businesslike. "Yes, ma'am. I'll just . . . go see to her for you, seein' as how yer so busy an' all in here."

Glory nodded. "I'd appreciate it, if you would."

Still, Smiley stood where he was, looking everywhere but at her.

Glory bit her lip . . . hard. "Have you grown roots, Smiley? I've got pies to see to. And the accounting books. And the wash. Now, go on with you. She doesn't bite."

Smiley stiffened the least bit. "Yes, ma'am." He pointed to the kitchen's entry and the hallway beyond. "This a-way?"

Glory nodded. "Yes. Just call out. She'll hear you and yoo-hoo back."

"Yes, ma'am." Smiley took a deep breath and crossed the kitchen, acting for all the world as if a hangman's noose awaited him around the corner.

Glory chuckled and shook her head. But then wrinkled her nose. It smelled like something was burning. *Burning?* She jerked around to the stove. The pecan pie filling bubbled up and over the sauce pot's sides. Shrieking in disgust, Glory grabbed up a portion of her apron, wrapped it around her hands, clutched the pot's handle and lifted it off the stove. In a temper now, she plopped it down harder than necessary, spilling its blackening contents all over the wood counter.

Angry beyond measure, close to tears of frustration, and surveying her mess, she kicked at a chair leg and griped, "Damn it all to hell and back three ways from Sunday."

"It certainly smells that way."

Her heart leaping, Glory spun toward the sound, only to see Riley stepping over the back door's threshhold and into the too-warm kitchen with her. "You'd best get," she mock-warned, her hands at her waist, "or risk getting put to work in here, Riley Eugene Thorne."

"Is that so?" He stepped into the room, sized up the unholy mess, then looked her up and down, and laughed. "I don't know which one you do worse—bake or swear. Come to think on it, I don't think I've ever seen or heard you do either before now."

Glory's Lawless chin came up. "Mama and Biddy taught me to bake, and Jacey taught me to swear. When the need arises, I can do both equally well, thank you."

Riley grinned and shook his head. "Well, from the looks of this place, you might want to stick to the swearing." He then frowned at her and pointed. "You've got flour . . . and something else on your nose, Glory."

Mortified, Glory put her sleeve to her face, rubbing as hard as she could. When she lowered her arm, she cried out, "Well, did I get it?"

"No. Come here, silly." But he came to her. Taking her chin in his hand, he used his other to brush and rub her nose—and then her cheeks and her chin. Glory blinked with his efforts. "Mercy, girl, you're a walking dessert. Just look at this apron. There's blackberry and . . . what's this?"

Glory tugged her chin out of his hand to look down at herself, at where he pointed. She held her apron out, commenting, "I think it's pecan-pie filling. But it could be . . . well, almost anything in the kitchen, I suspect."

Riley raised her chin again. Glory's heart sank. His warm smile lit his so-dark-brown eyes. He smelled of the outdoors, of windswept plains, of endless meadows. "You look good enough to eat, sweetheart." With that, he slanted his head down to kiss her.

Glory had time only to suck in a breath before his lips covered hers. Gone was the memory of their angry words from yesterday in the parlor. She melted against him. He held her tightly, jealously close to him. When their kiss deepened, when his tongue found hers, Glory heard a moan, knew it was hers. Aching for him, she clutched at his denim jacket, stood on tiptoes, sought instinctively to offer more of herself up to him. With urgent, answering motions, Riley's hands moved over her back, her waist, down to her hips—

"Damn you to *hell*, Riley Thorne!"

Glory shoved away from Riley at the same moment he let go of her and spun to face . . . Smiley Rankin. A picture of angry outrage, the foreman stood framed in the doorway, his hands poised inches above his twin six-shooters.

Glory stepped back, her hands pressed to her wet and swollen mouth. Even though she'd caused this standoff, the moment belonged to the two armed men. There was nothing she could do to stop them. Life on the prairie had taught her that much.

Riley straightened up to his full height and stilled dangerously. "Easy does it, Mr. Rankin," he warned the Lawless foreman. "This isn't any of your business."

Hands fisted, Smiley advanced stiff-legged into the kitchen, stopping a few feet short of Riley's ground. His neck steadily reddened and corded as he jutted his chin out. "An' I say it is. Don't forgit yer standin' on Lawless land. An' Miz Glory here ain't much more'n a girl yet. Ain't you—nor no one else—goin' to mess with her, neither."

Glory sucked in a breath laden with the kitchen's deliciously homey aromas, so at odds with the threatening words that peppered the air. As she watched, Riley's broad chest seemed to expand in a flagrant challenge. "The way I see it, Mr. Rankin, this is Miss Lawless's call."

For one dark second, the men glared like enraged bulls before turning hard yet questioning faces to her. Glory's stomach chose that moment to flop about sickeningly. Her knees weakened. She had to choose between Lawless concerns . . . and a Thorne.

A thinking part of her brain told her this wouldn't be the last time she did, either. Begging for some of Hannah's strength and Mama's soft way with words, Glory straightened up. "It's okay, Smiley. I can take care of . . . this. You go on. I'm sure the men are waiting for you."

Smiley jumped as if snakebit. "But, Miz Glory, I cain't leave him with—"

"Yes—you can, Smiley. I'm *telling* you, you can."

Smiley narrowed his eyes at her. "Yes, ma'am, Miz Lawless. Yer the boss. But I don't lak it one little bit. An' neither do the rest of the men." He then shoved past Riley and stomped out of the kitchen, slamming the heavy door behind himself.

Still weakened by the angry confrontation between the two men, Glory didn't move for long moments. Neither did Riley. But then, suddenly overcome, she bent over, her hands gripping her knees, and took several deep breaths. Absurdly, she noted that the flour-dusted puncheon floor under her feet needed to be swept.

"You'll 'take care of *this*?' Just what does that mean?"

Glory's stomach muscles clenched at the tone in Riley's voice. Straightening up, she sought his gaze. As she'd expected—wide mouth a grim line, his brown eyes staring a hole through her. She exhaled a huff of air which feathered out her bangs. Seemed like she couldn't please anybody anymore. Used to be that was all she did. Still, despite her thumping heart and slick palms, she met Riley's stare. "I don't know what it means. I was just trying to calm you both down."

"Calm us down? Neither one of us is *calm*, Glory."

Her sudden vexation with this man pinched her face into an angry mask. "I don't care one whit if you are or not. You're alive, aren't you?"

Then, sighting on something promising which could make her point, Glory scooped up two balls of raw dough and hefted them, one in each hand. "Now get the all-fired heck out of my kitchen, Riley Thorne." Without warning, she heaved back and threw a dough ball at him, hitting him square in his chest.

Time stopped. Riley stared at his chest as if he'd just realized he had one. Then he raised his head. His gaze slipped around the kitchen, hunting for something to toss right back at her, no doubt. Then, an eyebrow rising, he smirked at her.

Glory's eyes widened. "Don't you dare, Riley Thorne. And don't you ever kiss me again, either." She chunked her other crust-in-waiting, but missed because her target ducked. The dough ball flew past him to plop with a wet, sickly sound onto the hallway floor.

Hot-faced, sweating, damp of hair, tight of chest, and absolutely beyond her limit with piemaking and peacemaking, Glory searched her immediate surroundings for something . . . anything . . .

"Now, Glory, calm down. I mean it. You're just going to—"

"Calm down?" Glory jerked her gaze to Riley's fuming face. "Calm down?" she screeched. "I'll show you 'calm down.' " She yanked an innocent bowl of pecans off the old sawbuck table and heaved them at Riley's head. Again he ducked. The bowl hit the wall and broke. Pecans and crockery shards showered down, pelting the floor.

Riley stared at the mess, then at her. "That's it—the last straw, Glory Bea Lawless." His face a mask of determination, Riley came after her.

Glory shrieked and took off around the table. Riley went one way, she went the other. A strained and grunting few moments of hedging and feinting finally saw Glory grabbed up and dragged over to the nearest chair, yelling for all she was worth, and kicking like a Missouri mule. Riley sat down, threw her over his thighs, and proceeded to spank the temper right out of her.

Over the sounds of her own outraged screeching, Glory's ears picked up an approaching voice, one she knew from her earliest childhood. Sucking in air, she clawed at Riley's arm wrapped around her ribs. "Riley, stop it," she hissed frantically. "Stop it!"

But too late. The voice and its owner came nearer and nearer. "What in thunderation is all the noise? Must a body leave her sickbed to see to—?"

The voice was in the kitchen now. It gasped. Thrown across Riley's unyielding lap like she was, Glory felt Riley's jerk of surprise. Undone to be caught in such a state, she slumped, hands and feet trailing on the floor, her long hair dusting through the spilled flour and sugar.

The voice spoke again . . . in a changed, almost reverent tone. "Oh my, 'tis shocked, I am. I never thought to see the like in all me born days. Such a turn me pride and joy has come to."

Glory strained upward to see Biddy's face, but held in the manner she was, the most she could see was her nanny's ample bosom. But she didn't need to see her face to know that Riley was about to get his comeuppance. Because Biddy would abide no one laying a hand on her darling, her pride and joy. Why, as like as not, she'd throw him off the place herself now.

Glory watched as Biddy came into the kitchen, walking right past her. The beloved invalid's daygown and wrapper dragged across the food-smeared floor. "Will ye look at this mess in me kitchen—me pride and joy? Glory, get up this instant and start cleaning. Have ye taken leave of yer senses, girl?"

Chapter 6

It was cold and late that same evening. A wild wind whipped and whistled about the eaves and doors, hunting, searching for a loose or rattling way inside the Lawless main house. On the other, warm side of those same walls, Glory made her evening rounds. The kerosene lamps were out, the front and back doors were locked. Gliding through the great room, her way lit by the glowing embers in the fireplace, she made her way to Biddy's downstairs bedroom, just on the other side of the stairs.

She put an ear to the door and listened. Only quiet greeted her. She'd best be sure, she decided, in light of this afternoon's pie-making and kitchen-scrubbing excitement. Glory opened the door and peered into the darkness. Deep, even breathing from the bed brought an indulgent smile to her face. Finally, her little patient was asleep. That liberal dose of whiskey she'd asked for, in her evening toddy, had seen her nodding off in contentment.

Taking great care to close the door quietly, Glory turned and rubbed her fingers across her forehead. Bone-tired, headachy, she wondered how Mama had so effortlessly taken care of them all. Straightening her spine, Glory resisted feeling sorry for herself and strode briskly toward the stairs. She had one remaining chore before she sought her own bed.

And that chore's name was Riley Thorne. How dare he hire two new men, she intended to ask him. He had neither the right nor the authority to take on hands in her name. If a couple of drifters came hunting a station, all Riley need do was point them to her. Period. The end of his involvement. But no, she had to find out about the two new hands from Sourdough, who'd come to gripe about two more mouths to feed. Glory could only shake her head.

Worse, who was it again who'd preached cutting corners and letting men go? And here two new ones slept in the bunkhouse. It was a good thing Smiley wasn't here. More than pie dough would have flown through the air if he had been. Just who did Riley think he was—a Lawless?

Granted, she conceded as she took the stairs one weary step at a time, he acted every bit as bold and rash as any Lawless, but the man was still a Thorne—one in her side, if anyone cared to ask her. Once upstairs, Glory passed her own room to stop two doors down in front of Riley's. She fisted her hand to knock but, hearing Riley moving about inside the room, found she needed a moment to boost her courage.

She smoothed a hand over her hair, knotted back in its usual bun, and then ran it down her skirt. A clean skirt. A different skirt than the piemaking and paddling skirt of that afternoon.

Her determination thus restored, she knocked on the door and waited, listening. Riley's whistling and bustling about continued. Glory pursed her lips and knocked again . . . a little harder. Again she waited and listened. Again, in vain. Shaking her head, the least bit angry now—was he ignoring her?— Glory knocked hard enough to make her knuckles hurt. And listened.

Now the man was singing . . . after a fashion. She listened another moment and then frowned. What awful, lilting lyrics he belted out.

"*. . . Old Jake rode his mule to the valley town./It'd been a while since he'd come down, uh-huh./A rich man now from his gold-mining claim/He hunted some fun without no blame, uh-huh./He looked forward to spending* all *his money/And getting him a taste of Miss Bawdy's honey. Uh-huh, uh-huh . . .*"

Miss Bawdy's honey? Certain now that Riley had heard her knocking and meant to embarrass her with such language, Glory pressed her lips into a peevish line, grabbed the knob, twisted it, and burst into his bedroom. Her pointing finger raised, her words already tipped against her tongue, Glory didn't realize—in that first instant—exactly what it was that . . . faced her.

But then, *it* registered. Her breath—and her words—sucked right back down her throat. Every instinct implored her to turn away, to run. To cover her eyes, at least. But shocked beyond measure, Glory posed as she was—frozen, numb, blank. Staring.

A towel over his head, his . . . front facing her, and wearing only his boots, Riley was drying his hair. Perhaps sensing a draft or her presence or the thickened air—or all three—his hands stilled and he straightened up. Slowly he dragged the towel off his head. And stared openmouthed at her. "Glory."

Then, he looked down at himself and whipped the towel around his waist. Holding it secure with one hand, he dragged his Stetson off the bureau and plopped it on his head. Red-faced, frowning his eyebrows into a V, he griped, "Don't you ever knock? And close your mouth before you catch a fly."

Glory closed her mouth so abruptly her teeth clacked together. She realized she was still pointing at his . . . at him. And jerked her arm down to her side. Words came and went, all unspoken. Finally she managed, "I did knock. I'm sorry." Her hand still on the knob, she began backing up.

Riley reached out to her. "Wait. You're here now. What'd you want?"

Still backing up in a hot-faced, lead-limbed retreat, Glory assured him, "It can wait. I'm sorry. I didn't mean to—" There was no need to finish her sentence as she finally stood in the hall and pulled the door closed.

Safe now on the other side of the wood barrier, she put her shaking hands to her face. How could she ever face him again? It just wasn't possible. The door opened. Glory sucked in a breath and jerked back one clumsy step. And held her breath, since it, and certainly not her spine, was the only thing keeping her erect.

Still attired only in his towel and hat, Riley asked, "What can wait until tomorrow?"

Even though the man loomed large in her vision, Glory tried her best not to . . . see him. In sheer desperation, she cast her gaze both ways down the darkened hall, but found no help, no escape. Giving up, she finally settled her gaze on his chest—his face. *Look at his face*. "M-men," she stammered. "The men. They can wait until tomorrow."

Riley cocked his head. His Stetson's brim shaded his face, made him appear sinister. "What men?"

Glory took another step back, only to conk her head against the wall behind her. Almost grateful for the physical jarring, she flattened her hands against the wall and began sidling down the hallway as she hedged, "The ones you hired. You can't hire them. But they can wait. They're alseep now. I should be, too. And you. Asleep. Both of us. But not to-gether—I mean, in the same room. No. Umm, good night, Riley."

Having edged her way down to her room's door, Glory flung herself inside and slammed it closed. Wide-eyed and unblinking in the smoky light of the kerosene lamp on her dresser, she stared at her familiar surroundings as if she'd never seen them before. Mortified reaction set in. She clapped a hand over her mouth and doubled over, the better to trap her embarrassment inside. But it erupted. Glory stood straight up with her next gulping breath and burst out laughing.

Weak-kneed, she made her way to her bed, collapsing on it in a knees-drawn-to-her-chest heap. She groped for a pillow, found one, and stuffed it over her head. *Oh, dear heavens, I saw Riley as God made him. I cannot ever come out of my room again. How will I face him? I just can't. Never again can I look him in the eye after seeing his . . . him.*

Glory sat up in the tangled heap of her clothing and stared blindly at the opposite wall. She'd seen Riley naked. Imme-diately, she flopped back onto the feather comfort of her bed, and lay there sprawled and again seeing Riley in all his glory.

Then she rolled over onto her tummy and settled her head on her pillow, thinking *My, he is magnificent.*

Absently focusing on her lady's vanity perched against the room's opposite wall, Glory declared Riley's physique perfect. Like one of those statues in the art books Mama included in their lessons. He was muscles everywhere. Long-limbed. Solid. And that hair on his chest. It had a most interesting pattern, thinning as it did down to a line below his waist that widened out into a—

A knocking on her door, accompanied by a husky drawl of "Glory?" sat her straight up. "Go away," she called out, using the same childhood intensity she had when shooing scary monsters from the armoire on dark nights.

Only this monster was real. And apparently it didn't shoo very well. "I'm not going away," it said. "Now open this door, please."

Her wary gaze trained on the door in question, Glory shook her head. "No," she called out. "Go away. I'm sleeping."

An exhalation from out in the hallway preceded, "No you're not. You're talking to me."

Darn. He had her there. Glory swung her legs over the side of her bed and sat there, hands folded in her lap. "What do you want?"

Silence. Then, "I don't rightly know. But here I am."

Glory frowned. "Go to bed. You're already undressed for it." Her hand clamped itself over her mouth as her eyes widened and hot blooms burst upon her cheeks.

Silence. Then, "I suppose you're right. Are you okay?"

Glory considered the door a moment, tried to see Riley on the other side of it. She gained an instant image of him . . . bare-chested, Stetson on, towel-wrapped hips. And bit her lip to keep from giggling again. "I'm fine. Why wouldn't I be?"

Silence. Then, "No reason, I guess. Umm, good night, Glory."

Glory's lips twitched, but finally she blurted a respectable, "Good night, Riley."

*   *   *

"Biddy, something happened last night."

Biddy frowned at Glory's words as she watched the girl butter a flaky biscuit. Perched on the side of Biddy's bed, and sharing her breakfast tray, Glory took a big bite and turned those grass-green eyes on her as she chewed.

Frowning, Biddy absently brushed a wispy gray hair back under her mobcap. She next lowered her china teacup and saucer onto the silver tray atop her lap. "Well, child, are ye going to tell me what, or must I guess?"

Glory shrugged, handed Biddy the other half of the biscuit. "Here. Eat this. Sourdough sent in a plate of them. The ones I baked . . . or tried to . . . could bring a jackrabbit down, if you hit him just right." Satisfied only when Biddy accepted the treat and bit into it, Glory continued, "I saw Riley naked."

The biscuit would go neither up nor down, neither in nor out. Biddy could get no air. She pitched forward, jerked her knees up, and knocked the tray in a slanting slide over the edge of the bed. Gasping, Glory jumped up and caught it at the last moment, saving most of the spill for the tray. She quickly sat it aside.

Hands clawing at her throat, lungs screaming for air, Biddy couldn't even protest when Glory grabbed her arm up over her mobcapped head and shook it while she pounded on her hunched shoulders with her other.

"My word, Biddy, are you all right? Your face is absolutely purple."

Biddy wrenched her arm out of Glory's grasp and flapped her hand, wanting Glory to leave her be. Glory stepped back and stared wide-eyed, her hands clutching at her skirt. Just then, Biddy felt the biscuit dislodge. She swallowed in sheer relief, cleared her throat, and then waved at the tray. "Water," she gurgled out, barely recognizing the raspy voice as her own.

As Glory hopped to, scampered to the porcelain pitcher and cup on the nightstand, and poured out a measure of water, Biddy decided that today was the day she got out of bed . . . if she lived past this conversation, that was. And all these years, she'd thought for sure it would be Jacey who'd be the death of her. Breathing shallowly, Biddy accepted the water and drank it down as if it were a stiff tot of whiskey.

Sitting the glass back on the nightstand, she took a deep breath, testing her capabilities, and exhaled in relief. She'd live. Hand to her chest, wheezing, still coughing, she lay her head back against her pillows and stared up at the ceiling. Blessedly, her breathing slowly became normal.

When she could speak, she raised her head and patted the bed next to her. "Sit yerself right back down here, young lady. And tell me exactly how it was ye saw Riley without a stitch on."

Settling herself atop the covers, Glory chirped, "Oh, he wasn't completely naked, Biddy. Don't be silly. He had his hat on. And then a towel."

Biddy shrank against her plumped pillows and folded her hands together. "Well, in that case, the man was fully clothed." She glared at Glory to let her know she didn't mean that at all.

The child tried to smile, but it wouldn't hold. She immediately found reason to jump up and begin straightening the large, sunny room. And apparently felt she should start as far away from the bed as possible. "Now, Biddy," she chided, rearranging a silverbacked comb and brush set on the oak vanity across the room, "it's not like you're thinking."

"Ha. Tell me what I'm thinkin'."

Glory spun around, a hand over her heart. The girl at least had the decency to blush. "You're thinking that we—? I think not. Riley was toweling off after his bath, and I heard him singing this awful tune. I merely went to his door and—Why, Biddy Jensen, shame on you for thinking we'd—"

Biddy stiffened. "Shame on me, is it? Let me remind ye, young lady, yer the one talking about seeing Riley as God made him." Then, like a hen sitting on its roost, she settled into her covers and focused on Glory, shaking her head. " 'Tis better I'm feelin'. I believe I'll be up and on me feet by this afternoon." Then she muttered, "Before I'm a grandmother and right under me own nose."

"What?"

Biddy huffed out her breath. "Never ye mind. Just take the

tray, child. I can eat no more. I said I'd be up and around today.''

"I don't know, Biddy. It's only been a few days."

"And I'm much stronger for the rest. Now, go on. Be off with ye.''

Glory stayed where she was and looked consideringly at her. Biddy raised an eyebrow, daring her to challenge her word. Finally, Glory huffed out her breath and flounced over to the nightstand. Picking up the tray, she turned to Biddy and said, ''Well, I'm glad you feel like getting up. The Good Lord knows I can use the help. But I want you to be careful because I can't be inside with you, watching your every step, since I have to go out to the bunkhouse and—''

Biddy grabbed Glory's wrist, rattling the tray precariously. Glory divided her attention between balancing her load and peering wide-eyed at Biddy. ''Yer not hopin' to see the rest of the men in their altogether, are ye?''

Glory's jaw dropped. ''Biddy! What a scandalous notion! I hardly think I'd—'' She stopped, huffed out her breath and added, ''I'll be out at the bunkhouse—but having a few words with two new hands Riley hired yesterday. And that's all.''

Biddy released her wrist, sat back. ''I should hope so.'' Then she frowned. '' 'Riley hired,' is it?''

"Yes. I intend to find him and remind him he's not a Lawless. Then, because Smiley and some of the men are still out looking for strays, I also—''

"Oh? Smiley—umm, Mr. Rankin, I mean—is . . . away?'' Biddy looked down, fiddled with her quilted spread, and then sought Glory's gaze.

The shameless girl chuckled. ''When are you going to tell him you're sweet on him?''

Biddy puffed up in indignation. ''I'm no such thing. Ye mind yer tongue, young lady.''

Glory's green eyes lit with humor. ''Of course, you're not. And he didn't come to see about you yesterday.''

Biddy ignored the heat on her cheeks and managed a tone of voice as blustery as the day outside her window. '' 'Twas about business, his call was. Nothing more. Now, go on with yer list of chores. The day's gettin' no younger."

Glory grinned before wisely—to Biddy's way of thinking—changing the subject. "Yes, ma'am. After I greet the new hands, I need to go check on the repairs to the corral fence. And then I'll get an accounting from Sourdough on what he'll need to outfit the chuck wagon for the spring drive up to Kansas."

Biddy sat still, suddenly content just to listen to the doll-like, auburn-haired girl chatter on. She didn't know what was stranger—having a conversation with Glory about seeing a man naked or one about the workings of the ranch. Up until the last few days, the girl hadn't cared about either. Her baby was growing up.

She flicked her attentive nanny's gaze over Glory's person, from her neatly coiffed hair—still in that blasted bun—to her tucked white blouse and tan pocket-skirt, which met at her tiny, belted waist. Gone was the stringy hair and the pallor and indifference about her appearance of only a few days ago. Gone was the moping spirit, too. What had caused this rapid change in her? Not what, but who, Biddy realized. Riley Thorne. Her secret smile found its way to her face.

"Oh, and the good news is Skeeter came to the—Biddy, what on earth are you smiling about? I'm telling you all the troubles around here and you're smiling at me as if I've just successfully baked a cake."

Her heart full, Biddy's smile became tremulous. "Will ye listen to yerself? Yer quite the strong one, Glory Bea, taking charge like ye have. Ye remind me of Hannah. I'm right proud of you. And yer sisters will be, too."

Glory blinked at her and then her mouth worked, her eyes shone. She looked down at the spilled mess that was the breakfast tray, and then back up at Biddy. "That means a lot to me. I just want to do a good job and be the best darned Lawless that I can."

Glory grabbed Papa's big old sheepskin coat off its peg by the kitchen door. Looking back at the messy room—not at all the way Biddy usually kept it—she renewed her efforts to be nowhere around when her doting nanny dressed and found what awaited her. The sight could end her doting era.

Slinging the heavy garment across her shoulders, feeling its hem hit her behind her knees, Glory poked her hands through the armholes, already rolled up to thick cuffs from her new habit of wearing it. She nestled down into its woolly folds, pulling its comforting weight and memories around herself. She had other, better coats, certainly ones more suited to her size, but Papa's was . . . well, Papa's.

Looking down at herself as she pushed the big leather buttons through their corresponding holes, Glory marveled anew at how close she felt to Papa when engulfed in his favorite coat. Perhaps she was being superstitious, but she believed her judgment and decisions about the ranch were sharper when she had it on. For sure, the men recognized it as J. C. Lawless's. They didn't say anything, but they eyed it and then her, and called her Miss Lawless. Some of these men had known her since she was a baby, had always called her Miss Glory. But now she was Miss Lawless, boss lady.

Smiling at the thought, still flushed with Biddy's high praise of her, Glory stepped outside. And caught her breath. A cold blast of air, laden with choking dust, brought tears to her eyes and nearly blew her off the landing. Coughing, blinking, she grabbed the heavy kitchen door and held on when the wind threatened to wrench it free of its hinges and send it spiraling about the yard.

Barely able to see, her watery eyes scratchy with dust, Glory suddenly realized she was no longer alone on the narrow clapboard landing. Someone—a strong someone—helped her slam the uncooperative door closed. Wrenching around, tugging the coat's collar up around her neck, Glory found herself pressed up against a stranger's body.

His head ducked, his broad, pockmarked face turned in profile to hers as he too fought the wind, the man held her pinioned between his strong arms as he forced the door into its frame. Even though he was helping her, and his actions were the most innocent, Glory felt her heartbeat thud, as if in warning. This man had to be one of the drifters that Riley'd hired yesterday. She knew all the other men.

"You all right, ma'am?" came his yelled question.

Glory nodded. "I had no idea the wind was this strong. Thank you."

"Glad to help. Where you headed?"

She managed to get him to move one of his hands away from her by pointing toward the bunkhouse. "Out there."

Hatless, his dark hair whipped up onto its ends, adding to his sinister appearance. Suddenly, the man clutched her elbow. Glory caught her breath. And couldn't really say why her heart pounded as she looked up into his face. "You'd best allow me to escort you. A little thing like you is liable to get blown all the way to Texas."

Another gale-force gust rocked them, held them in place, robbed Glory of a chance to respond. Huddled in Papa's coat, her eyes squeezed shut against the pinprick sting of the blowing grit, she stiffened when the man hunched over her and put an arm around her. A protective gesture to anchor her against the wind. Nothing more. But Glory resisted. She didn't like him. It was that simple, that gut-deep. Opening her eyes to narrow, watering slits, she stiffened against him and pushed back. Raising her voice to be heard above the wind's howl, she called out, "I can make my own way."

"No, I can't let you do that." His iron-hard grip tightened around her as he braced them against a renewed gust.

Glory sucked in an alarmed breath. This danger was real, and her options were meager. She couldn't best him in a physical struggle. She wasn't about to make an excuse to go back inside, where only she and Biddy would be at this man's mercy. She therefore had to get to the bunkhouse, where other men, hopefully Riley among them, would be. As soon as the gust subsided, Glory pointed to the bunkhouse, signaling she was ready to make a dash for it.

"Then let's go," he called out, gripping her arm as he directed her steps to the ground. Frightened lest he carry her off, never to be seen again, Glory exhaled only when she realized the tall, squarely built stranger was indeed leading her to the bunkhouse office door. A man of his word, he opened the door, handed her in, and closed it behind them.

After the howling wind and the banging shutters and barn doors, the cramped and cluttered office was quiet. Too quiet. Filled with dust motes and leather tack and carelessly stacked papers atop a small desk, it was otherwise empty. Of men. Of help. Then so be it—she was on her own. Despite her fear-weakened knees wobbling with each step, Glory crossed the room to stand behind the desk. Not much of a barrier, but it made her feel better.

She turned to her escort, noting with relief that he'd stayed by the door. He ran a big, thick-fingered hand through his hair and smiled at her. "That's some wind, ma'am."

Struck by his rough, craggy appearance, and contrasting it with his straightforward actions, Glory barely managed a nod of acknowledgment for his words. She reached up and smoothed her completely undone and knotted hair from her line of vision. She had to get ahold of herself, had to quit jumping at every noise, at every—The man was watching her. Not simply looking at her, but watching her. Like a wolf did its prey before it roused itself for the kill.

Show no fear, Glory. Lifting her chin a notch, mustering all the authority she could, she said, "I'm Glory Lawless. This ranch is mine and my sisters'. You must be one of the hands Mr. Thorne hired last evening."

The man grinned at her, showing big, square teeth. "Yes, ma'am. Name's Carter Brown."

Glory nodded, didn't know what to say next. So she busied her hands with straightening piles of invoices on Smiley's desk. There was something else about this man. The way he talked. His voice. *That's it.* Glory raised her head, saw he hadn't moved, and called herself glad for that. "You're not from around here, are you, Mr. Brown?"

He shook his head. "No, ma'am. I'm from back east."

Back east. Where Mama's family is. Wariness shot through Glory, tightening her throat. "I see. Where back east?"

"A small town outside of Boston. You probably never heard of it."

Boston? Mama's family lives in Boston. And Hannah's there. "You're a long way from home, Mr. Brown." *Be calm, Glory. Think. If he's one of the murderers, he'd lie about where he was from. Wouldn't he?*

Mr. Brown smiled, narrowing his dark eyes. "Yes, ma'am. A long way from home. But we all have our reasons."

Glory swallowed and nodded. "That's true." And realized she had no idea what to do or say next. The silence stretched out.

Carter Brown abruptly ended it. "I didn't know I'd be working for a woman. I thought Mr. Thorne was in charge here."

"Mr. Thorne is *not* in charge here. I am." Then it suddenly occurred to her that if she didn't like this man, she could fire him. Her fear remolded itself into angry authority, rendering her capable of looking him in the eye and informing him, "I'll be giving the orders, and you'll be following them, like every other drover here. If it's a problem for you, you're free to ride out under the same gate you rode in under."

Mr. Brown held up a big hand. "Easy now, little filly. I didn't say it was a problem. I just said I didn't know. In fact"—he raked his gaze up and down her—"I'm beginning to think it might be a most pleasing experience."

Glory's hands fisted at her sides as her heartbeat picked up speed. "Perhaps, Mr. Brown, you'd be better off to—"

The door from the bunkhouse into the office opened. Glory jerked toward the sound. In stepped Riley—*Thank you, God*—and, right behind him, a short man of slight build who pulled up short when Riley stopped suddenly. "Glory! What're you doing out here?" He then caught sight of the new man. "Brown, where've you been? I was looking for you."

Carter Brown smoothed out his hungry expression. "Sorry, boss—no, that's not right, is it? Seems Miss Lawless is the boss. Leastwise, that's what she was just telling me. I'm supposed to be following her orders. Not yours."

Silence met Carter Brown's words. Riley settled his brown-eyed, questioning gaze on Glory. She raised her chin in defiance of the heat blooming on her suddenly warm cheeks.

She'd meant only to make a strong point with the new hand—and she had, but perhaps she'd gone over the top a bit.

Riley's unreadable gaze shamed Glory. She barely stopped herself from looking down at her shoes. Ever the same Riley, though, he kept his thoughts to himself and said, "As long as you're out here, Miss Lawless, this is your other new hand, Abel Justice." He then stepped aside, bringing into view the beak-nosed stranger behind him.

Riley'd called her Miss Lawless. She'd hear about this later. Ready to look at anyone but Riley right now, Glory focused on Mr. Justice. Grinning and deferential, the gap-toothed drifter tipped his battered old felt hat to her. Now, this man she liked. All but chirping, Glory acknowledged his greeting. "Pleased to have you on the place."

"Yes, ma'am, and it's right proud I am to make your acquaintance. I have a heap of respect for the Lawless name. And I count myself proud to be one of your drovers. I'll work hard and do a good job for you, ma'am."

Glory turned a genuine smile on him. "I can't ask for more than that from a man, Mr. Justice." Sobering, she turned to Carter Brown. "Nor will I."

She'd no more than chilled the air with that before the door behind Carter Brown flew open. He jumped out of the way as it banged against the wall. Glory raised her arms protectively against an intruding blast of cold air. As if possessed of a mischievous will of its own, a whirlwind lifted and scattered the random stacks of invoices, adding them to the spiraling dance of dry leaves and twigs captured in its energy.

Also blowing into the cramped office was a sputtering, cussing Sourdough. Using both hands, the camp cook wrenched the door away from the wall, slammed it closed, and held it there until he was apparently satisfied that the wind would obey him and stay outside. Only then did he turn and rub his hands together. "That wind is so fierce that Ah'll swear and be damned if Ah didn't just see a hen out yonder lay the same egg twice."

His felt hat secured to his head and mashed down over his ears by his bandanna, which he'd knotted under his chin—

giving himself the appearance of a bonneted and incredibly ugly old woman in need of a shave—Sourdough glared out his displeasure with the nature of Nature. His gaze then lit on Glory. "There you are. What you doin' out here, Miz Glory?"

Stooping to retrieve yet another invoice from the floor, and taking those handed to her by Riley and the two new men, Glory straightened up, hands and invoices held at her waist. "I have every right to be out here, Sourdough. And if you don't think so, just look to see who signs the drafts to pay these." She held up a fistful of bills and shook them.

Riley stepped in between her and the old cook's defiantly puckering mouth. "I need to speak with Miss Lawless, Sourdough."

"Well, so do I, boy. Ah just come from the main house, lookin' for her. Miss Biddy said she seen her bein' all but carried out here by some big varmint of a man." He sized up Carter Brown. "Ah reckon that'd be you." He then went on with his story. "Miz Biddy said, from what she could see, Miz Glory here didn't look none too pleased to be in his company. So what with all the recent troubles, Ah thought it best if Ah made sure she hadn't come to no harm."

The air thickened at the end of this remarkably long speech for Sourdough. Glory shifted her gaze from the cook to Riley. He studied her a moment, as if sorting out events, and then turned his head to glare at Carter Brown. "The main house? You want to explain what you were doing over there when I sent you out to the horse barn?"

Carter Brown shifted his weight and hitched at his belt. A gunbelt, Glory noticed. "I thought I saw something."

Riley narrowed his eyes, mirroring the skepticism he voiced. "You *saw* something? Maybe Miss Lawless here? I'll say this one time, Brown—stay away from the main house. And especially stay away from Miss Lawless."

Carter Brown turned his lip up in what some might call a grin, and others a sneer. His black eyes alight with challenge, he looked from Riley to Glory and then back to Riley. "I will, if *she* says so. She's the boss lady. And the way I hear it, she's the one should be giving orders."

Glory's heart plummeted to her feet. Riley might be the one standing in the middle, but she was the one in the hard place. Four sets of male eyes stared at her, waited for her comeback. She had no choice. Caught like this, there was only one answer she could give. And it would seal Riley's place here and extend his authority over Lawless concerns.

Exhaling her reluctance, and not liking this one bit more than she knew the Lawless hands would when they heard about it, Glory stated, ''Mr. Thorne acts on my behalf, Mr. Brown. You'll take your orders from him.''

Chapter 7

The heated flames behind her in the great room's fireplace were nothing compared to Glory's flare of temper. She stopped her pacing and turned to Riley. "The man is dangerous. I don't like him. I was this close to firing him when you came in. Why *did* you hire that Carter Brown? Better yet, why did you hire either one of them? Mr. Justice seems fine, but still, you're the one who told me I should be letting men go, not taking on more over the winter."

Riley shrugged. "Turns out you were right and I was wrong. You do need more men. This winter's going to be a hard one—just look at the thickness of the horses' coats. Smiley let go too many hands after the fall drive. All I did was make up for his mistake."

"His mistake?" Loyalty to the longtime Lawless foreman pricked Glory into defending him. "Smiley doesn't make such mistakes."

Riley firmed his lips into a straight line. "He did this time."

She narrowed her eyes, but decided to let it go for now. Mr. Rankin and Riley both had burrs under their saddle blankets where the other one was concerned. "All right, say he did and he was wrong. But until ten minutes ago, out in *Smiley's* office, you didn't have the authority to hire anyone."

Seated on the oversized brown-leather couch that faced the stone fireplace behind her, Riley crossed his legs, resting an ankle atop his opposite knee, stared at her, and didn't say a word. In the silence, Glory could hear Biddy puttering around in the kitchen.

Glory huffed out her breath. This being "in charge" was a rough business. No wonder Papa always seemed to rage around in a temper, with Mama right on his heels and calming him. "Out there, Riley,"—Glory pointed in the direction of the foreman's office—"I was forced to acknowledge that you have a say in Lawless matters. You saw Sourdough's face when you told him to settle in those two new men. The rest of my hands aren't going to be any happier to take orders from you, either. Why, I'll be lucky if any of them stays on now."

"They'll stay."

She met his patient, knowing stare. "How can you be so sure?"

"Because they're loyal to the Lawless brand. Have been for years. This place is their home. And you're their family."

His words pierced through to her heart, evaporating her anger. The terrible weight of her new responsibility further weighed her down. Not sure that she was, after all, equal to this task of preserving the Lawless ranch, Glory looked down at her feet. "So many people are counting on me, Riley. And I don't know what to do half the time. Sometimes I wish someone would come along and take this burden from me."

Riley's quiet words brought her head up. "There's no one but you, Glory."

She nodded. "I know, and that scares me." Another thought occurred to her. She put it to Riley. "But you don't have to be here. And yet you are. There's nothing keeping you here. And yet you stay. Why?"

Riley uncrossed his legs and scooted forward to the cushion's edge. "I've got my reasons." Pausing for a moment, he then went on in a mellower tone. "Don't doubt yourself, Glory. That's the worst thing you can do. That's when you start making your biggest mistakes. Just decide and act on it, right or wrong. If it's wrong, just learn from it and go on." He looked down at the woven carpet under his feet, ran a hand through his black hair and again focused on her. "You need to think like a man."

Glory blinked. "And how do I do that?"

Riley's expression softened, smoothing out the worry lines in his forehead and around his mouth. "In some ways, you already do. You're doing a good job here, better than you realize. I'm surprised, but I guess I shouldn't be. To me, you're still that shy little girl in pigtails with an apron over her dress who used to hide from me. I keep forgetting you're a . . . grown woman now."

Glory knotted her fingers together at her waist and concentrated on forcing out words she knew she shouldn't say but couldn't stop. "I wasn't sure that you'd noticed."

A light sparked in Riley's brown eyes. His black-fringed lids lowered a fraction. "I've noticed."

Feeling suddenly as shy as the girl he remembered, Glory all but whispered, "I've noticed you, too."

Riley chuckled. "I guess you have."

Heat burst upon Glory's cheeks. He meant last night, her seeing him without his clothes on. She glanced at him from under her lowered lids. "I liked what I saw."

Riley sobered and lay back against the cushions, his fingers laced over his abdomen, his knees spread apart. Looking like a lolling panther, he stared up at the ceiling. His Adam's apple bobbed under the taut skin of his muscled neck. "You're playing with fire, Glory."

She had no idea how to respond to that. So she didn't. Riley rolled his head until he sighted on her. "You know what that means?"

Glory shook her head, felt a length of her wind-tossed hair fall forward over her shoulder. "No," was all she could mumble out as she looked away from him to the brightly patterned Cherokee blanket hanging on the room's far wall.

"Yes, you do. Every grown woman knows."

With a jerk of her head, Glory was again staring into his assessing brown eyes. "I do *not* know what you're getting at, Riley Thorne."

A lazy, taunting grin, showing white and even teeth, emphasized his grand good looks. "Come here and I'll show you."

Shocked, and yet wildly curious, Glory raised her chin and didn't move one step closer. "I will not."

Still grinning, Riley shrugged his broad shoulders. "Suit yourself."

That did it. Glory stomped over to him and, leaning over, smacked his arm. "Do you know how hard it is to talk to you?"

Riley suddenly jerked forward and, with a swiftness that left her gasping, grabbed her and pulled her onto the sofa and under him in one smooth movement. His arms closed around her, cradled her, did anything but reassure and comfort her. "Then quit talking to me," he advised, looking down into her eyes. "Kiss me instead. Or am I hard to kiss, too?"

Her heart pounding, her eyes widening, his weight pressing into her from her chest to her toes, Glory could only stare up at him and shake her head. Riley's intensifying stare quickened a sharp thrill of desire in the vee of her legs. His hardness against her . . . down there—even through the thickness of their clothes—only excited her more. It was all so horribly, wonderfully forbidden.

"You're all I can think about, Glory. I've been wanting to get you like this since the day Jacey left and I saw you standing on the verandah with Biddy. It shocked the hell out of me, seeing you after all that time." Glaring at her as if she'd done something wrong, Riley lowered his head and captured her mouth.

Glory made no pretense of protesting. She wanted this, too. Wrapping her arms around his neck, she pressed him to her, instinctively arching into him. Which seemed to be what he wanted, judging by the low-pitched noises in his throat. His growl of need fed Glory's desire. She answered with a gasp of her own and opened her mouth to the hungry plundering of his.

Not even caring that her clothes were twisted, that her hair was tangled, that she was pinned under him, and more than willing to let him go farther, Glory clutched spasmodically at his thick, dark, and waving hair. She smoothed her hands over his cheeks, needing more, wanting to feel more of him but unable to because his weight trapped her. Only she didn't feel trapped. She felt secure, safe . . . wanton.

Riley broke their kiss only seconds before Glory was sure she'd faint dead away from rampant desire and a lack of air. Breathing in gasping pants that matched his, she clutched helplessly at him, even as he reared back to look down at her. In the reflected firelight, with an errant lock of almost-black hair falling over his wide brow, Riley's high cheekbones stood out in sharp relief, emphasizing the dark hollows under them. His expression remained wholly intent on her. Glory's heart fluttered, skipped a beat.

Then Riley's husky voice captivated her attention. "That first day I got here, you said you didn't have these feelings for me. But we both know you were lying. I want you . . . in the way a man wants a woman. And now I know you feel the same way. It's killing me, sleeping two doors down from you. I burn up at night with wanting you. I can't sleep, I can't think. Let me come to you, Glory. Tonight. To your room."

Her mouth open and wet with his kiss, her world defined by this moment, by this man, Glory suddenly and clearly saw herself—as if she stood across the room—lying here under him. She a Lawless, he a Thorne. Breathing in gasps of air, she gave in—belatedly—to pangs of regret and sanity. "Oh, Riley, what are we doing? I can't. We can't. It's not right."

Above her, Riley stilled, a muscle twitched in his jaw. He closed his eyes and took a deep breath . . . several deep breaths. He then opened his eyes and ran his gaze over her face. "It *is* right, Glory. You're the only damn thing in my life that is right."

Scared now, ashamed and wanting to get up, Glory shrank back into the pliant leather's softness, jerking her head sideways. Her words came out on a sob. "You're scaring me, Riley."

A very long stillness marked the steady ticking of the mantel clock. Then Riley lowered his head, gently resting his forehead against her temple. His voice was no more than a whisper that feathered softly, seductively over the shell of her ear. "It's all right, Glory, it's all right." He pulled back, smoothing his fingers down her cheek. "Will you look at me, honey?"

Glory turned her head but, reluctant to meet his gaze, looked instead at his neck, at the rapid pulse beating there. She wanted to kiss it, to taste him. But she didn't dare. Even in her innocence, she knew that the least gesture from her right now would unleash a torrent of passion that she couldn't stem, couldn't control. She finally sought his gaze. "I'm sorry, Riley."

Riley shook his head and grinned. He planted a tender kiss on her forehead. "You didn't do anything, sweetheart. I did. I'm the one who's sorry."

With that, he bunched his muscles, pulled his arms away from her and levered himself up. On his feet now, he immediately turned his back to her, hung his head forward, ran a hand through his mussed hair and exhaled a long breath.

Struggling against her skirt, Glory sat up, feeling awkward but also strangely weightless after having supported Riley's heavily muscled self. Swinging her legs around to the floor and sitting up, she rested her elbows on her primly clamped-together knees and smoothed her hair away from her face. *What in the world does one say now?* she wondered. *Mama didn't cover this situation in her etiquette sessions.*

Saving Glory from further wondering was the sound of hurrying feet and Biddy's crying out, "Riley! Glory! Are ye in here?"

Biddy'd no more than shouted their names before Glory was on her feet and rounding the end of the couch. Riley went the other way. They met the apron-strings-flapping nanny at the same moment, each taking an arm to support her as she bent forward in relief. "There ye are, the heavens be praised. Come quick, the two of ye. There's somethin' the matter with Skeeter. He's barkin' and bayin' to wake the dead."

Glory stared at Biddy, then her words sank in. She flicked her gaze to Riley. He let go of Biddy and took Glory's arm. "Stay here with her. I'll go."

"No," Glory cried. "I'm going, too." She herded Biddy

toward a leather chair adjacent to the couch. Over her shoulder she called, "You wait for me."

Biddy stopped where she was and pulled Glory's hand off her arm. "Go on, child. 'Tis only winded I am from hurrying. I'll be fine. Now go see what's got that hound in an uproar. I'm afraid yer the only one he'll allow near him. Ye be careful, ye hear me? An' stay with Riley."

Glory cupped Biddy's full, soft cheek. "If you're sure. Now, you sit right here and don't you move." With that, she turned to the doorway. Riley was gone. Not the least bit surprised, Glory held her skirt up with both hands and ran for the back door. She tore through the kitchen, her mind's eye noting the raw makings of supper spread on the counter.

Not even stopping for her sheepskin coat, she wrenched open the back door, flung it aside, and leaped from the landing to the ground. Not even the tormenting, stinging-cold wind slowed her down. Indeed this time, it seemed to blow in the direction she ran, seemed to urge her on, to ease her way.

Fighting her hair, which whipped across her face, Glory could see them now. Riley outside the wooden gate of the family cemetery. A short man—was that Abel Justice, the new hand?—inside the fence and cornered by a back-humped, hair-raised Skeeter. Stumbling and tripping her way up the hill's slope, grabbing at her skirt, trying to suck air into her lungs, Glory nevertheless heard Riley shouting, heard Skeeter's answering snarls and baying.

Jerking to a winded, stumbling stop beside Riley, she clutched at his arm and hung on. Riley righted her as if he wasn't aware of doing so, so intent on Abel Justice was he. Holding Glory upright, he called out to the terrified man. "Don't make a move, Justice. That dog'll take you apart."

Glory saw the whites of Abel Justice's muddy brown eyes as he nodded. The man's prominent Adam's apple bobbed up and down. He never once looked away from the threatening hound dog.

"What are you doing up here?" Glory called out.

At her side, Riley advised, "Call Skeeter off, Glory. We

can talk then. I just tried to coax him, but he's not having any part of me today.''

Glory bit at her bottom lip as she tried to think this through. Reflexively, out of ingrained habit, she swiped her hair out of her face. And then became aware that the wind had suddenly died down. For once today she didn't have auburn tangles blurring her vision. That was one blessing. Maybe she was due another. She pulled away from Riley and walked toward the gate. "I'll go get him. Skeeter hasn't been himself since Old Pete was killed.''

A hand clamped around her arm, eliciting a surprised cry from her. Riley spun her around. "You're crazy, if you think I'm going to let you go in there. Skeeter might turn on you.''

Glory jerked in his grip, but to no avail. "I'm going in, Riley. Take your hand off me.''

Riley's face burned with determination. "No." He pulled his Colt from his holster. "You call him from here. If he goes for you, I'm going to shoot him.''

Glory froze. "If you shoot him, I'll never forgive you.''

Riley's mouth firmed in a straight line. "That's your decision. But if it's you or him, Glory, I'll shoot him.''

Glory stood where she was, staring up at Riley. He was right and she was wrong, and she knew it. His way was the logical, sensible way. But this was Skeeter. Old Pete's dog. The hound she'd helped raise from a pup. Old Pete was gone forever. Mama and Papa were gone forever. And no one was going to shoot Skeeter.

"Let go of me, Riley," she warned in a low voice, looking him right in the eye. "He'll listen to me, I know he will. Just don't follow me in there. That'll excite him. Give him a chance, Riley. One chance.''

Riley's gaze roved her face as he apparently assessed her determination. Then, he exhaled and relaxed the barest fraction, loosening his grip on her. "One chance. But nothing's changed. If it's you or him, Glory, I've got to end it.''

Glory glared at him and stepped up to the gate's latch. Her chest rising and falling with exertion, anger, and no small amount of fear, she opened the gate and sidled into the square enclosure. Taking a deep breath, she bent over and clapped her hands together softly, calling out, "Skeeter, come here, boy. It's okay. It's me—Glory. Come on now, settle down. It's okay." Keeping her voice lowered to a croon, Glory slowly advanced on the riled-up hound.

Skeeter turned his big head in her direction. Glory stopped where she was. With no sign of recognition in his eyes, the dog lifted his black muzzle, showing her his razor-sharp teeth—a clear warning. Glory sucked in a breath. She cut her gaze to Abel Justice, noted he hadn't moved, and then she looked around, seeing the uneaten scraps and the water bowl. No sense trying to ply Skeeter with food.

Then, knowing Riley stood behind her, his gun in his hand, Glory glanced at him. His sober expression met hers. She took a deep breath, watched him shift his weight as if impatient. Scared that he would shoot at any moment, Glory took her life into her own hands and walked purposefully toward the dog. By her third step she was foolishly between Riley's gun and Skeeter. Behind her, she heard Riley's sharp intake of breath, heard him cock his gun.

Not taking time to think too deeply about her actions, Glory used a different tone of voice with the offended animal. Whereas before she'd been coddling, now she was firm but cajoling. "Skeeter, it's me—Glory. Look at me, boy. It's me. No one's going to hurt you—or Old Pete, okay? Now, come here, Skeeter. Come to me."

Skeeter stared up at her, his black eyes roving over her. He then suddenly made a mock-lunge for her, woofing but not growling. Glory tensed up but didn't move, didn't retreat. "Stop that," she shouted, the words coming from her gut reaction to his behavior. "Stop that right now, Skeeter. Old Pete would be ashamed of you, jumping at me like that. What's gotten into you?"

Skeeter cocked his head, lifting his ears slightly, perhaps curiously. Glory ran the tip of her tongue over her fear-dried lips. *All right, you've got his attention. Keep talking to him.* "Come here, Skeeter." She dropped to her knees, held her arms out, making herself completely vulnerable to attack. "Come here, boy."

Skeeter's long tail wagged halfheartedly. Glory let out her breath. "That's a good boy. Come here, honey. Come to Glory."

The dog drooped his head and tail and slowly padded over to her. When he nudged her shoulder with his nose and licked her, she grabbed his big, floppy-eared head to her chest and hugged him fiercely, tears of relief standing in her eyes. "Good boy," she told him, rubbing him vigorously.

Over the dog's head, she nodded to Abel Justice, indicating for him to climb over the fence behind him. The man nodded and then clambered over it, taking off as if a pack of wolves chased him.

Glory stood up, kept Skeeter at her side, and turned to Riley. He'd holstered his gun and was standing where she'd left him, a knee bent, his hands at his waist. He was shaking his head at her—and fighting a grin, she noticed. And suddenly it was funny to her, too. She grinned openly at him. "I told you I could do it."

Riley broke down and chuckled. "I never doubted it for a minute."

Riley stepped into the warm kitchen that evening. Hungry and tired, but freshly washed up and his damp hair combed back, he nodded to Biddy at the stove and then to Glory. She cast him a shy, green-eyed glance, took a steaming bowl of something that smelled wonderful from Biddy and hurried over to the old sawbuck table with it. She sat it at the place he now thought of as his and returned to the stove, waiting on Biddy to hand her another.

Riley liked it that they ate in here, instead of that big, dark dining room around the corner. The kitchen was more cozy, had more of a family feeling to it. His gaze sought Glory's back. Anytime he thought about a family in his future, she was in the picture's center. Suddenly feeling self-conscious just standing there staring, Riley greeted the women. "Evening, all. It sure smells tempting in here."

Stirring a big, steaming pot, Biddy beamed at him. Her smile lit up her kind and rounded Irish face. "I thank ye, Mr. Thorne. And may I say yer looking right and proper for yer evening meal? We're having a beef stew and cornbread that'll stick to yer ribs. Here, Glory, take this one. Careful now, 'tis hot."

"I know, Biddy. Just give it here. The cornbread will be cold by the time we all sit down. In fact, why don't you sit down and let me do this? You've only been out of bed this day."

Biddy puffed up. "And a good thing I am, too. We'd have been up to our ears in mess, had I not, miss. I pity the man who marries ye, I do. Like as not, he'll starve."

Riley grinned broadly, thoroughly enjoying this bit of play. What with Ma being the only woman at home, he'd not witnessed female teasing before coming here. But then, Glory winked at him. Surprise wiped the grin off his face. She felt comfortable enough with him to let him in on this family fun?

Her bright and playful, green-eyed gaze still on him—but speaking to Biddy—she cupped another bowl of stew and again made her way to the table. "The man I marry won't give a fig for how good a cook I am. He'll be too busy laying presents at my feet and buying me anything my heart desires."

"Ha," was Biddy's opinion of that. She wagged her ladle at Glory for pointed emphasis. Splotches of dark broth pocked the puncheon floor. "And 'tis something more besides a beef stew he'll be wantin' in return from ye for all them baubles. Am I right, eh, Riley?"

Riley nearly choked on his own spit. He flicked his gaze from Biddy to Glory's stiff back as she sat the bowl down, and then back to Biddy. "Umm, yes, ma'am. I suppose."

Biddy laughed knowingly at him. "Ye suppose? Well, suppose this, me fine young man—'twas this close Glory was to organizing a search party for ye just now. It was that worried, she was."

Glory spun around. "Biddy, you hush." She then turned to Riley. "I was no such thing—worried or thinking about hunting for you. Why, you're a grown man and can take care of yourself.'' She wiped her hands down the front of her apron. ''But a body'd think you'd have the decency at least to keep me informed of your whereabouts. We've had enough troubles without you wandering off.''

Her obvious concern for him, despite her words, hung in the air. Glory suddenly looked away from him and made her way back to the stove.

''I'm sorry I worried you. I was just one place and another this evening, it seems.'' Riley's words followed her. She didn't acknowledge them, but still he grinned, pleased that she'd missed him.

Watching her help Biddy, and with their attention off him, Riley used the moment to study Glory, noting her neatly combed-back hair. It wasn't in a bun. Instead, a bright-blue ribbon held her masses of rich reddish-brown hair loosely at her nape. Without warning, she turned around, a third bowl in her hands. Her gaze met his. And held it . . . for a tenuous second. Then ducking her head, as if against a wind, she walked back to the table.

Riley grinned, more to himself than to her. What would it take to get her to admit she wanted him as much as he did her? As if an answer lay in her individual features, Riley caressed her with his gaze. Short, curling tendrils that framed the delicate oval of her face captured his attention. Emphasizing her evergreen eyes and full, pink mouth, the curls spoke of a softness about her, a vulnerability that wrenched his heart.

Glory thumped the bowl down on the table and poked out her bottom lip. ''Why are you staring at me like that? Is something wrong?''

Riley snapped out of his reverie to announce, ''No.'' But the more he tried to concentrate on the moment, the more his mind kept going back to earlier that afternoon . . . to the couch. To them on the couch. Every time he recalled the feel of her under him, moving against him, kissing him, he almost busted out of his britches—

''Riley?! You're doing it again—you're staring at me. Did you get into some *loco* weed?''

Caught and roped and branded by his bedroom thoughts,

Riley shook his head and looked away from her, the source of his befuddlement. "No. Sorry. I guess I'm just tired."

Biddy whooped out her opinion. "Tired, is it? Is that what yer callin' it nowadays, Riley, me boy?"

That damned Biddy. Heat burst upon his cheeks like the Fourth of July fireworks he'd seen up in Kansas once. "Yes, ma'am. I mean, no ma'am."

Still, Biddy's knowing expression cooled his . . . thoughts. Which was probably her intent. He wrenched his chair out and abruptly sat down, scooting it loudly all the way up to the table. Only when his bulging lap was out of plain sight did he chance a look at Glory.

Her face as red from Biddy's teasing as he figured his was, Glory sat down with studied motions and kept her gaze on the steaming bowl of stew in front of her. In silence, he waited with Glory for Biddy to join them. When the beaming, bustling older woman seated herself, he reached out his hands and joined his with theirs, so that they formed an unbroken circle.

On his left, Biddy's hand felt warm, comforting. On his right, Glory's was tiny, fragile. Riley bowed his head, tried not to squeeze Glory's hand too hard, and listened to Biddy's short, Irish prayer for the Lord's bounty and this meal. Following the amens, a quiet clattering of dishes and silverware and murmurs of please-pass-me-this-or-that ruled the next moments. But once they were settled and eating, Glory broke the silence.

"Did you talk to Abel Justice about what it was he was doing up at the hill, Riley? He took off so fast after I grabbed Skeeter that I never got to ask him."

Riley watched her talk and then nodded as he buttered his cornbread. "Yeah, I spoke to him. He said he was paying his Christian respects."

Biddy tsk-tsked. "Ye cannot fault a man for that."

"I suppose not." Riley dipped up a mouthful of stew.

Glory made a disbelieving noise. "Paying his respects? I find that hard to believe. He was up to more than that for Skeeter to get so riled up. I've never seen him act like that before. Never." Then some other remembrance quirked her features. "Oh, drat. That's another thing I forgot to check. Did Smiley and the men make it back?"

Riley swallowed and nodded, remembering the men's pointed silence in his presence and Smiley's grumbling about the two new hands. "Yep. They rounded up about twenty head of cattle, near as I could count."

"Why, 'tis glad I am they're back, what with this devilish wind blowing winter right to our doorstep."

Riley looked at Biddy, saw Glory do the same and then noted her laughingly quirked mouth. Biddy pointed at her. "I know what yer going to say. Ye keep a civil tongue in yer head, young lady."

Glory grinned openly and turned to Riley. "She's sweet on Mr. Rankin."

Biddy's spoon smacked into her bowl, slopping some broth over the edge and gaining her both Riley's and Glory's amused expressions. "The devil ye say! I'm no such thing. Me—at me age? Why, I've no time for such nonsense."

"Yes, you do," Glory egged.

Biddy picked up her spoon and wagged it drippingly at her. "An' yer a fine one to be talking, miss. Don't ye be carrying tales, lest yer wantin' some of yer own naked stories to come back at ye."

Naked? Riley glanced at Glory. His gaze stuck. Naked? Him, perhaps? She'd told Biddy about that? Yep. Her wide-eyed, stricken expression spoke volumes. She stared at him and then became intent on her meal.

"Just as I thought," Biddy pronounced, settling down some and turning her attention and a change in subject on Riley. "Ye didn't sound too convinced a moment ago, either, about that new hand's Christian intentions."

His forearms resting against the table's edge, Riley met her gaze squarely. "I like to give a man the benefit of the doubt."

Glory snorted her opinion of that. "The truth is, Riley, he had no business out there. None. Where was he supposed to be?"

Riley focused on her. "I'd set him to work in the tack room."

"Then that's where he should've stayed."

Riley's eyes narrowed. He knew a rebuke when he heard one. "Was that a Lawless commandment? You're saying I should've kept my eye on him?"

"You hired him," Glory came right back. "And I've been thinking about him. The first words out of his mouth were condolences to me about my folks. How'd he know about our troubles here?"

Riley stilled, speaking carefully. "The Lawless name is a well-known one. He could've heard talk on the grub line, traveling from one ranch to the next."

She made a face, allowing him that point. "I suppose. But he couldn't see the crosses readily from the bunkhouse or the barn. He'd have to do some snooping to find them." She then leaned forward to make her next point. "Same as Carter Brown right before that. He was out back of the house, too, when he spooked me at the kitchen door."

Her words met with silence, which Biddy broke. "Merciful heavens. Are ye thinking the two are in some sort of cahoots, child?"

Glory shrugged. "They could be. Carter Brown did tell me he's from Boston."

Biddy gasped and turned to Riley. "That's where Hannah is at this moment. With her mother's family. And the Lord knows the Wilton-Humeses are a sorry lot. Except for my Catherine. And her grandmother Ardis."

Before he could digest that, Glory caught his attention. "I've been wondering . . . did Brown and Justice ride in together, Riley?"

Uncomfortable with where this was headed, he shook his head. "No. About an hour apart."

Glory nodded, as if deep in thought. Then she tilted her head at him. "No reason why they couldn't have split up and ridden in separately, right?"

"You've made your point, Glory." Riley's jaw tightened against his clenched teeth. "I hired them, and I'll be responsible for them. If they need firing, I'll take care of that, too."

Chapter 8

In the next two weeks, Glory had more than one disastrous reason to recall Riley's words about firing the two new hands. Or not firing them, more accurately, since both of them still rode for the Lawless brand. Standing in her father's office, her arms crossed under her bosom, she peered out at the blackened wall of the horse barn. A fire. The latest reason.

The gray day was no match for her mood or for the smoke rising from the hay the men pitchforked out into the barn's service court. When heavy, booted footsteps announced someone's approach, Glory turned from the window and toward the sound.

Bringing an acrid smell with him, Smiley turned into the room, his hat held in his hands, his face grim and soot-smeared. Without preamble, he launched into his report. "We were lucky. We caught it early and there wasn't much damage to the barn itself that some nailed-up boards won't repair."

Glory nodded. "And the horses?"

He shrugged. "Skittish but none burned or lost. Thorne's got some of the men turning them into the far corral while we clean up."

Glory exhaled her breath in relief. "Thank God the horses were spared." Then she stared down at her brown lace-up shoes, giving them undue consideration. Keeping her gaze lowered, she asked her foreman, "What's your thinking on this, Smiley?"

He was quiet for so long that Glory finally looked up at him, taking in his dingy denims tucked into his muck-smeared boots and his unbuttoned coat. He wasn't going to tell her a thing—not without being prodded. Glory eyed him levelly and encouraged, "I asked, so you may as well tell me."

Frowning, obviously uncomfortable, Smiley ran a hand over his balding pate and voiced his opinion. "The fire was set, plain and simple, Miz Glory. Fires in three different parts of one structure just don't start on their own. Somethin' or someone has to spark 'em. And there sure-as-shootin' wasn't no lightning about to do the job."

Glory pressed her lips together, which seemed to constrict her chest. "No, there wasn't. And that fire in the cook shack last week—I'm not so sure anymore that was an accident. Or an oversight on Sourdough's part, like we've been thinking."

Smiley nodded and quirked up a corner of his mouth. "I never have knowed him to set his own kitchen on fire."

"Me either." Glory took a deep breath and let it out. Above the knotted bandanna tied around his neck, Smiley's expression spoke volumes. Her spirits dragging, Glory prompted, "There's more, isn't there?"

"Afraid so. A fight broke out last night in the bunkhouse."

His words slumped her spirit. She needed to sit down. Circling the desk, she pulled out the leather chair and sank gratefully onto its padded seat. Rubbing her temples, she said, "Go on."

"Carter Brown and Heck Thompson got into it over some missing money. Heck said he caught Carter going through his things and then found some money gone, money he'd set aside to send his folks. Carter said Heck's saddlebags fell off his bunk, and he was just putting them back and didn't know nothin' about no money. I made both men turn out their belongings."

Glory nodded. "What'd you find?"

Looking disgusted, Smiley made a gesture of helplessness. "Nothing. It's one man's word against the other."

"Like every other incident in the past two weeks."

Smiley sniffed, giving her a sidelong glance. "Yes, ma'am."

Pretty sure she knew what he was thinking, and what he wouldn't say, Glory pressed on. "All starting about the time Mr. Thorne hired Brown and Justice."

Now Smiley stared at her straight-on. "Yes, ma'am."

Glory waited, but Smiley didn't offer more. So she urged, "Smiley, I know if Papa was here, you'd tell him everything you're thinking, and you wouldn't hold back. You're going to have to treat me the same way, if we're going to survive. I promise you, I won't break."

Smiley considered his hat a moment, scratched his stubbly jaw and then nodded. "I reckon yer right." He met her gaze. "There's no solid proof that either man had a guilty hand in these troubles. Not the sabotaged equipment or the downed fences and loose cattle we had to round up. Not even this here fire or the one in the cook shack. But I do know this—none of these things was happenin' before those two came."

Glory frowned as she sorted through everything Smiley told her. Then she admitted, "I've thought the same things. Still, I hate to fire just one of them. What if I don't get the right one?"

"Then you fire the other one, too, Miz Glory. It's that simple."

A prick of temper flushed her cheeks and sharpened her voice. "It's *not* that simple. Not for me. Yes, Brown and Justice always seem to be in the area when the troubles happen. But so are a lot of the other men. You want me to fire them all? Would that be fair to any of them with winter coming on?"

Smiley pinched his lips together. Whitened lines appeared at each corner of his mouth. "Miz Glory, you got to be hard-nosed about this—just like yer pa was. You got to think like a man. You cain't worry yerself about every drifter that rides through. Now, I know yer no more'n a girl, and yer trying to do yer best. And I know you ain't got no experience runnin' this place. But I've been hirin' and firin' men since before you was alive. Yer pa trusted my judgment. And my gut tells me these two hands hired on by Riley Thorne are trouble.''

The foreman paused, as if allowing Glory to absorb that, and then added, ''You can trust the men I've brought onto the place. We ain't never had no trouble outta any of them.'' Despite her best efforts, Glory felt the sting of hot tears at his rebuke. Perhaps Smiley saw them glitter in her eyes because he looked down at his hat, twisted it in his hands, and then jammed it back on his head.

From under its brim, he considered her in a sober fashion. ''Well, I've had my say. Except to add that it ain't helped none that you've placed Riley Thorne over me. The men don't like it, but they respect you. And that puts 'em smack-dab in the middle betwixt me and Thorne. As a result, there ain't much gettin' done without first a heap of cussin' and discussin'. Now, I don't know what can be done about that, but just think long and hard on it, if you would.''

Lowering her gaze to the desktop, Glory swallowed a fistful of emotion. Smiley's words sounded like they came straight from Papa's mouth. And everything he said was true. Sitting there in her father's too-big chair, feeling his absence like never before, Glory forced herself to meet her foreman's eyes. ''Are you telling me that you're thinking of quitting?''

Smiley ducked his head. ''No, ma'am.''

Glory exhaled, but the moment stretched out, became too long. She stood up. ''Thank you for that. I know you have a lot to do. I won't keep you.''

Smiley glanced up at her, surprising her with a whiskery smile. ''Look, Miz Glory, it'll take some time, and yer goin' ta make mistakes. But you'll find yer way. An' we . . . all us men . . . we're behind you. We ain't a one of us leavin' you.''

Tears sprang again to her eyes. He should've said he quit and was taking all the men with him. That's what she deserved. Sniffling, clearing her throat, Glory all but whispered, ''Thank you.''

''Yes, ma'am. I'll just go see to . . . the men now.'' With that, he turned and strode out of the room.

The second his retreating footfalls no longer echoed across the hardwood floor, Glory relented on her earlier promise to

Smiley. She broke. Falling limply back onto her father's chair, she covered her face with her hands. And cried.

Riley backed away from the kitchen porch, making room for Smiley, who shoved open the door from inside and came stomping down the well-worn steps. Riley nodded his tight-lipped greeting to the foreman, who returned it and wordlessly stepped past him. Riley spared the man a glance and a hard thought as he entered the same way Smiley had just exited.

Inside the orderly kitchen, Riley stopped. Empty. He frowned. Hadn't Smiley been in here speaking with Biddy about the fire? That's where he'd said he was going. But the clean, dry counters and cold stove told another story. No one had disturbed this room since breakfast. He knew, because no one could talk to Biddy without getting fed or at least having a cup of coffee.

Not liking the feel of this, Riley reasoned where Biddy might be. Most likely, that sweet old lady sat in the parlor doing her mending—and looking out the window, hoping for a glimpse of Smiley. What she saw in the man, he'd never know. Well, it was none of his business. But what was his business, the way he saw it, was what Smiley must have been in here telling Glory about the fire today and the altercation last night in the bunkhouse.

Every story has two sides, and she needed to hear both. Cursing this state of affairs, Riley went in search of Glory. He checked the other rooms as he passed them, but he figured she'd be in J. C.'s office—the last place he wanted to be. That room, to him, still smelled of the former outlaw's cigars and his greed. But if that's where Glory was, then so be it. As he approached the open door of the office, Riley became aware of a sound inside. He stopped out in the hall and frowned. Was that somebody crying?

His mind flashed him an image of Smiley, showing him the man as he'd looked just now—stiff, grim, unspeaking. *If he so much as*—Not even taking the time to finish his thought, Riley crossed the threshold and stepped into the room. Greeting him were the oversized desk, two facing armchairs, a wall of books . . . and one curled-up and crying Lawless girl in a chair meant to hold a much larger man.

Dammit. Guilt over his part in her tears had Riley scrubbing a hand over his face. Then he lifted his Stetson off his head, flung it to a chair, and shed his coat, sending it the same way. Finally, with great tenderness welling up inside him, he went to Glory and picked her up in his arms. She clutched at his shirt, and clung tightly to him, turning her face against his neck. Careful of his fragile, precious burden, Riley turned, sat them both in J. C. Lawless's chair, and held the man's daughter next to his heart.

More undone by her tears than he'd ever thought possible, Riley remained still and stared at nothing across the room. Every now and then he'd kiss the top of Glory's head and maybe rest his cheek there a moment. But for the most part, he let her cry it out. It'd do her good. She'd been holding in a lot lately.

Lately? Two whole weeks now. She'd avoided him except when it was impossible to do so, like at the evening meals. There'd been no more hungry kisses in the kitchen or lustful scenes on the leather couch. Only polite distance and sidelong glances. He could name about fifty reasons why they'd come to such an impasse, but probably the main one was that she blamed him for the troubles on Lawless land. And looking at things from her point of view—or even her foreman's—Riley figured she had every right to.

Glory shifted her weight on his lap. He looked down at her. And smiled. Her cheek snuggled against his chest, her arms loosely encircled his waist. She sniffed and blinked and stared—like he'd been doing—at nothing across the room. A sudden shuddering breath escaped her and nearly shattered him. Tightening his grip around her, he gritted his teeth against the sudden bolt of protectiveness that shot through him. If Smiley had hurt her, he'd kill him. That's all there was to it.

Edging a shoulder up to get her attention, Riley looked down into her splotchy face and grinned at her red and runny nose. "You want to tell me about it, sweetheart?"

She sniffed loudly, scrubbed a finger under her nose, and

then curled her hand into a fist, which she buried in her skirt's folds. "I'm nineteen and alone and it wasn't supposed to be like this."

Her hurt and watery voice, as much as her words, brought a frown to Riley's face. "What wasn't supposed to be like this?"

Without lifting her head from his chest, she waved her arm in a big arc that encompassed the entire room. "This. All of it. Mama and Papa. Jacey and Hannah. This ranch. The men. I can't do it. I let everybody down. I don't make good decisions. I don't have anybody to talk to about it—"

"You can talk to me."

She shook her head. "No, I can't. You're part of what's wrong."

Riley exhaled, knew the truth of her words, and said, "You think so?"

"Smiley does. Or says he does."

"Smiley." Riley snorted. "I could be a foot-deep solid vein of gold lying exposed on the ground and he'd find fault with me, Glory. You know that."

She nodded against his chambray shirt. "I do. He also found fault with me. He said I need to think like a man—the same thing you said two weeks ago. I don't know how to be a man, or think like one. I don't even know what you mean by that."

Riley quirked a grin. *Well, you asked for this, now didn't you, old son?* he thought wryly. Then, sobering, thinking about what he wanted to say, he launched into his explanation. "I mean you make decisions with your head and your gut. Not your heart. Know what you want, decide, and stick with it. This isn't a contest for likeability. It's about being the boss. It's hard. And you have to be, too."

Glory didn't say anything for a minute. Riley contented himself with the cozy feel of her on his lap, with her warmth snuggled against him. Then she raised her head and met his gaze. "Then I know what I'm going to do."

He smiled down at her. "That fast, huh?"

She nodded. "Yes. I'm going to replace Heck's money that

was stolen. And then, at first light, I'm going to fire Abel
Justice and Carter Brown."

Her words stunned Riley into a second's stillness. He then
slowly shook his head from side to side to emphasize his
words. "You can't do that, Glory."

Her head cocked to one side, her face mirroring stubbornness and maybe a trace of suspicion, she asked, "Why can't
I? I'm the Lawless here. Not you."

Standing out in the darkened hallway, right outside the closed
door of Riley's bedroom, and knowing he was in there, Glory
clutched at her chemise nightshirt. Her own words from that
afternoon came back to haunt her. *I'm the Lawless here. Not
you.* Poor Riley. All evening he'd slouched on the leather sofa
and stared at her so hard she hadn't been able to keep her
mind on the book she'd been reading. Even Biddy had noticed
the tense quiet between them and had excused herself early.

Glory blinked back to the present, to the closed door, and
put a finger to her mouth, thoughtfully biting the nail. She
couldn't just knock. She couldn't. This was wrong. No matter
what she told herself her real reason was for being here, her
pounding, fluttering heart told her otherwise. *You want to kiss
him. You want him to kiss you. You want him to hold you in
his arms and—*

The door opened. Framed in the doorway, his hands moving
to his lean waist, Riley didn't appear the least bit surprised.
But Glory—wide-eyed, barefooted, and trapped—couldn't
move. Or speak. Then Riley chuckled and shook his head, as
if at some joke. "Glory." That was all he said. Just Glory.

The man's quietness irritated her. She never knew what he
was thinking. *Well, you're caught now. Say something.*
"Umm, I thought you were asleep."

Undressed down to his combination suit and denims, his
feet bare, Riley raised an eyebrow. "Well, I'm not."

He was doing nothing to make this easy, darn him. He just
stood there looking all big and finely formed and . . . big and—
a sigh escaped her—and handsome and sleepy-eyed. Glory's
guilt and agitation—and Riley's suddenly hot-eyed stare—

wriggled her toes on the hallway's carpet runner. *Say something.* "I just came to . . . say good night."

Making a slow, lazy circuit of her entire body from her head to her toes and then back again, Riley finally met her gaze and shook his head. "No, you didn't. You're not dressed for good night. You're here to play with fire again."

Glory sucked in a breath at his forwardness, but still felt her nipples harden, her womb stir. She folded her arms over her telltale bosom as best she could. "I'm doing no such thing."

Riley grinned and leaned a shoulder against the doorjamb. He crossed his arms over the expanse of his hard chest, bent a knee—a picture of complete male ease—and stared down at her from under his lowered lids. "All right, you're not. Then . . . good night, Glory."

She swallowed and notched her chin up. "Good night, Riley. I hope you sleep well." With that, she turned in the direction of her bedroom two doors down.

But that was as far as she got before Riley clutched at the back of her gown and pulled her stumbling to him. "Come here, you."

Shocked, titillated, Glory gasped and found herself spun up against his unyielding body. And held there by arms strong enough to support the weight of her world. Momentarily robbed of speech, she stared up into his brown-eyed, handsome face. Her mouth open, her body shamelessly afire, she shook her head no.

"Don't tell me no, Glory. It's too late for that." His husky voice slipped over her skin like whispering fingers, undressing her. "You come stand outside this door almost every night. I hear you. I know you're there. This was one time too many. So tell me what you want. Tell me."

Scared of what she wanted, Glory could say nothing. She could only cling to his warm, solid length and . . . want.

"Tell me, Glory, say it," Riley urged, his darting gaze roving over her face. "Look at you barely covered up in your nightclothes. And your hair all undone like only a husband has a right to see it." He ran his hands through her curls, bringing a fistful up to his nose and inhaling the fragrance. His eyes closed. His expression changed to intense pleasure.

Then he exhaled, opened his eyes. "Do you know I can *feel* when you walk into a room? I don't even have to look to know you're there. But when I look across the table at meal-time and see you, it's you I smell . . . you I taste. You're a cool spring day and a hot summer night all rolled into one."

Glory's mouth dried, her eyes drooped closed. These words of his. All day long Riley didn't say two words. He kept a close guard on his thoughts and emotions. But when he was like this? She never could have dreamed he'd have such words. Like poems they were. So unexpected, so precious. This was what she wanted. She wanted his . . . words, his wanting her.

Weak-limbed, too warm for her chemise, when she should have been cold from the drafty hallway, Glory laid her head against his chest, felt a button under her cheek. Its round hardness didn't matter. All that mattered was the way Riley's body felt and the things he was saying . . . and doing.

He released her trailing hair and ran his long-fingered, questing hands over her nightshirt, down her ribs, her waist, her hips. It was too much, his touch. Glory shrank against him. Only his hands held her upright. If he let her go, she'd fall in a broken-doll heap to the floor. "You're everything I want. I dream about you, about making you mine. I see you in my bed. My wife. I see our children—"

Stark, raving reality struck Glory cold, stiffened her in Riley's arms. His words and his hands both stopped. Why, his dream was hers. Hers. But *his* wife? *Their* children? Her—a Thorne? No. That wasn't her dream. In her dream, she saw herself with a husband and children, yes. She saw their home. The house was always this one, but . . . who was the husband? Whose face did she put in her dream? Was it Riley's, dear God?

Afraid to look into her mind's eye for the answer, or into his face for the living truth of it, Glory held tightly to Riley's arms and turned her cheek to his chest. Underneath her ear, his heart beat slowly, steadily. But he said not a word. Not one. He didn't even move a muscle. He waited for her, she knew it. Just like all the other decisions around here, this one was up to her.

Decision? Nightmare was a better word. How could it be Riley she wanted? How? It wasn't fair. She tried to picture them wed . . . and greeting her sisters when they came home. Hannah would die of shock to find her married to the son of Papa's enemy. And Jacey? She'd most likely shoot her. Glory shook her head. She couldn't do this. She couldn't. Finally pulling away from Riley, she looked up into his square-jawed and serious face. "Riley, I—"

He held up a hand. "I know. You can't. You can tease me. You can want me. But you can't love me. Me—a Thorne." He closed his eyes, his jaw jutted, and he mouthed, "Dammit." Then, looking again at her, his brown eyes so dark and serious, his generous lips firmed to a thin line, he said, "Your father's feuds don't have to be yours. Think about it." With that, he released her and stepped back into his room, closing the door in her face.

Blinking in shock, her cheeks heating up, Glory covered her mouth with her hands. She just didn't understand any of this. What was she doing outside Riley's room in her nightclothes, for heaven's sake? It was as if her body had taken over her mind, was telling it what to do, was forcing her to seek him out. She wanted him to hold her and kiss her and say those pretty words to her. But Riley wanted something more. A lot more. He wanted all of her.

A heavy aching between her legs told her she wanted him to *have* all of her. Defeated, feeling like a traitor to her family, Glory closed her eyes and heaved out a sigh laden with unfulfilled edginess. Opening her eyes, she bit at her lip and stared at his door. She had to get away from here before he opened it again. Or before she did.

Feeling anything but sleepy, Glory knew she couldn't go to her room, to her bed. She'd just toss and turn and cry and be miserable. No, what she needed was a good stiff dose of cold air. Mind-clearing air. Body-chilling air. *Now.* She took off at a sprinting, skipping pace down the hall and then down the stairs, clinging to the bannister for support, as if a pack of wolves were chasing her and she wouldn't be safe until she was outside.

Actually fleeing by the time she crossed the moon-silvered great room and raced for the door, her arms outstretched, Glory firmly believed that real wolves, their eyes red, their fangs bared, did nip at her heels. She pulled the bolt back on the heavy lock and twisted the brass knob. Wrenching the door open, she sucked in a mouthful of cold, cold late October air. In only three steps she crossed the wooden verandah and stood gasping, clinging to its low railing. Her thin gown billowed like a laundered sheet hung out to dry.

Instantly sober, alert, and over her ache of desire, Glory hugged herself, hunkering down to a shivering posture. She concentrated on the nightscape revealed for her by the starlit, full-moon night sky. *Beautiful*, she called it, turning in a slow semicircle, her bare toes curling against the hard wood under her feet. Not a thing moved in the yard. Or up on the hills. All around was quiet. Still. Calming.

Still hugging herself, still shivery, Glory made herself a promise. She'd do this more often. She'd get out of the house more. She'd ride Daisy more. Surely the little chestnut mare was getting fat and lazy without the exercise she was used to. Paying the invoices could wait. The hard decisions that required her to think like a man, when she was barely used to thinking like a woman, could just go hang themselves.

Because no one—not Mama, not Papa, not Hannah, not Jacey—expected her to lose her mind trying to hold this place together. Glory smiled. She'd have a little fun, that's what she'd do. But right now, she was going to go inside before she froze to death. A smile for her own silliness in coming out here lifted her spirits as she started to turn toward the open front door.

But then . . . from behind her, and as if conjured from the night, a hand clamped over Glory's mouth, a viselike arm gripped her around the waist. Jerking in shocked and fearful reaction, falling back against her captor's thickly padded, fully clothed body, she could only suck in air through her pinched nostrils and scream inside her head.

Stunned by the unexpectedness of the attack and stiff with horror, every nerve-ending alive, Glory clawed at the hand over her mouth. She kicked barefooted at her abductor as he began dragging her back and over to the wraparound veranda's dark side. Out of the moon's light. Out of eyesight of the guards posted at the gate. *The guards! Where are they?*

In the next instant Glory realized that, for some reason, the guards weren't at the gate. Had they been, they would've seen this man long before he got to her. And no one in the house knew she was out here. So her life rested in her own hands. And if the man dragging her got her into the shadows, he'd kill her. Glory twisted and wrenched in his grasp.

Her attacker tightened his hold around her waist, nearly cutting off her air. She had to stop him. But how? *Think, Glory.* She needed a weapon. She had none. Then she realized that she did—and right under the hand clamped over her mouth and cutting off her air.

Instead of tearing ineffectually at the grunting man's claw-like fingers, Glory jerked her head from side to side, finally forcing him to shift his position the slightest bit. That was all she needed. She opened her mouth, pressed his palm against her teeth . . . and bit down hard. A yelp of shocked pain preceded her being let go and shoved forward.

Stumbling, she fell to her knees, but instantly was on her feet and running for safety. Crying out in sharp little gasps of terror, her heart pounding against her ribs, Glory expected at any second to be grabbed again.

But by some miracle, she made it inside and got the door closed and locked without the groping hands seizing her again. Outside noises captured her heightened attention. Bootsteps running across the verandah. Glory jumped away from the door, backing farther and farther into the great room.

The clumpy, distorted shadow of a man, like a great winged raven, passed suddenly in front of the casement window. Glory flicked her unblinking gaze to the matching window on the door's other side. No shadow passed. She focused on the door itself. Her breathing stilled. Just then, the door shook in its hinges, the lock rattled, and the knob turned.

Glory pulled her hands away from her mouth and screamed.

Chapter 9

Doors behind her opened. Glory jerked around and, still stiff with fright, made a stumbling dash toward help. "Riley, Biddy, come quick! Help me! There's a man outside. At the door. Hurry!"

Just as she stumbled against the leather couch's padded back and gripped it desperately, Glory saw Biddy emerge from her bedroom and come bustling and tying her wrapper over her ample waist. "Glory! What is it, child?" Then she called over her shoulder. "Riley, come quick. There's something the matter with Glory. Riley!"

Footsteps thudded down the stairs, accompanied by Riley's cry of "I'm coming. I heard her. Get Glory and get down, Biddy. Stay away from the door."

The door. Glory jerked to the door, listening. Nothing. Silence. He was gone. Or was he?

She turned back to Biddy and saw her in a waddling run, coming fast toward her. *She'll give herself another heart spell.* More afraid now for her nanny than herself, Glory shook her head. Her long and heavy hair swished about her face and shoulders. "No," she cried out, running to the plump woman and grabbing her by her arms. "Biddy, do as Riley says. Get down. He could have a gun."

Biddy lurched to a stop and clutched at Glory. Puffing in and out, she managed to gasp out, "A gun? Who? Riley?"

"No, Biddy, the bad man outside. Now come on with me."

With that, Glory began tugging a suddenly befuddled-looking Biddy with her around to the other side of the couch. At that moment, Riley sprinted past them, startling a whoop of surprise out of Biddy. Dressed the same as he'd been earlier, but with his Colt gripped in his fist now, he slowed only as he approached the door.

Slinking into a shadowed corner, he disappeared in a way that raised the hairs on Glory's arms. The man outside had done that—come at her from out of nowhere. In a split second, Riley emerged as a silhouette which became a solid man with his back to the wall. He slid along it to the first window. Only when he was in place there, his gun raised, did he look over at her. "How many?"

"One. He tried to hurt me, Riley." Her chin quivered. "Be careful."

"He's the one who better be careful." His tone of voice—as cold and hollow as the wind—chilled Glory to the bone. The sound of him cocking his pistol carried to Glory's ears.

She closed her eyes and exhaled. *Please, dear God, watch over him*, she prayed. Only when Biddy's hand closed over hers did Glory realize she'd clutched her nanny's arm at some point. Suddenly needing her solace as much as she had when she was a little girl, Glory fell into Biddy's grandmotherly arms. "I was so scared," she whispered and sobbed.

"There, there, child, I know ye were," Biddy soothed, just as quietly. "But yer fine now." Then she cupped Glory's chin, forcing her tear-dampened face up to her concerned, apple-cheeked one. "Ye are . . . *fine*, aren't ye, Glory Bea? That man didn't . . . take ye against yer will, did he?"

Glory shook her head, then jerked tautly, same as Biddy, when the lock bolt was jammed free and the door slammed against the inside wall. Jumping, clutching at Biddy's wrapper, Glory saw Riley crouched in the open space, his arms extended, his Colt waving this way and then that. Glory's breath caught in her throat. A tense moment passed, when even the mantel clock didn't seem to tick-tock.

Then Riley relaxed, released the Colt's hammer, straightened up, and turned to them. "Whoever it was, he's gone."

"Thank the sweet Lord," Biddy entoned. "I thought me heart would pop right outta me chest."

Over her initial fright, and with nagging questions swirling in her head, Glory kept one eye on Riley as she pulled away from Biddy, freed her own nightshirt's tangling folds from under her knees, and stood. She then helped Biddy do the same while watching Riley close and lock the door. Looking her in the eye now, he stuck his pistol in his waistband and said, "You two go to Biddy's room and lock the door. Stay in there until I come back."

Glory frowned at his words. "Where are you going? Surely, not out there, not knowing where—"

His hand raised, halting her flow of words, Riley started for the stairs. "Don't argue. Get to Biddy's room with her, Glory, and stay put. Do it. Now."

An angry protest poised on her lips, Glory jerked in his direction. But Biddy's hand on her arm stopped her. "Do as he says. 'Tis a man's place now."

A man's place? Glory's bottom lip poked out as she watched Riley take the stairs two at a time. *We'll see.* She freed herself from Biddy's grip and took the older woman's arm, walking her to her downstairs bedroom. Once she'd ensconced her nanny in her bed and settled her covers around her, Glory feigned a look of surprised remembrance. "I just recalled something very important about . . . that man outside. I must tell Riley before he goes outside."

"Then go, child. Run. Catch him."

Momentarily startled—no sermon, no questions, no nagging—Glory stared at Biddy. And then spun away from her, held her nightshirt's hem up, and dashed for the door. Just before she closed the door from the outside, she poked her head back in. "Keep this closed, Biddy. I'll be right back."

She then closed the door and took off for the stairs, like Riley had—taking them two at a time. Once upstairs, puffing from her exertion, she took determined strides toward the smoky lantern-light spilling into the hall from Riley's bedroom. Stopping just short of the open door, Glory steeled herself with a chest-expanding breath. Then, fisting her hands at her sides, she turned into the open doorway, spied Riley, and spoke in a level no-nonsense tone. Men seemed to respect that. "I'm going out there with you."

Seated on his bed, tugging his boots on by the mule-ear straps, Riley looked up at her. "No you're not."

Glory stifled her first inclination to stomp her foot and yell. Childish behavior. A man wouldn't do that. She took another deep breath and a step inside the room. "Yes I am. This ranch is *my* place, I'm responsible for everything that happens here, and I'm the one who was attacked."

Riley stood up, stomped his feet to settle his boots, and smoothed his hands down his denim-covered thighs to straighten his jeans. He eyed her and then reached for a heavy chambray shirt draped over the back of a caneback chair. "You're not going."

Glory bit down on her tongue until she believed she tasted blood. *Be calm, even-tempered.* Watching him slip his arms into his shirt and shrug it across his shoulders, watching him button it—all while ignoring her—Glory wondered why exactly it was she thought she had to be in here telling him she was going. Why didn't she just do what he was doing—get dressed and go? Quirking her mouth with her decision, one she didn't intend to share with him, she turned on her heel. She'd just get dressed and grab a gun from the case in Papa's office and—

Riley gripped her arm and spun her around. "That was too easy. What's going on inside that head of yours?"

Glory wrenched her arm free. "I could ask you the same thing. And another thing, how do you know who you're hunting? I'm the one he attacked."

Riley's eyes narrowed. "*Do* you know who it was? Did you see his face?"

Glory's defiant posture slipped as she admitted, "No."

"Then tell me how *you'd* find him."

Her mouth insisted on twitching with her lack of definite answers. Then she blurted, "Well, you tell me how you're going to do it."

Riley's clenched jaw worked as he cut his anger-glittered

gaze to a far wall. Glory could tell he waged an internal battle for control. Finally he looked back down at her. "I'm wasting time here, Glory. The man could be to the border by now."

He snatched up his gun from off the bed, stuffed it into its holster, and strapped on his gunbelt, settling it low over his right hip and tying the rawhide thong around his tensed thigh. Every movement was deliberate, no wasted motion. He then grabbed his heavy buckskin overcoat, threw it over his arm, reached for and donned his Stetson, and then grabbed her arm.

That surprised her. "Where are you taking me?"

Not deigning to answer, he marched her out of his room. His long-legged strides forced her to hop-skip along beside him in the lamp-lit hallway or be dragged. He handed her into her own bedroom, stepped back, grabbed the doorknob, snatched the key out of its hole, and said, "Here's where I'm taking you. You *stay put*, Glory Bea Lawless, or I'll turn you over my knee again."

Outrage with his high-handedness caused her to forget her "manly" ways. Glory sucked in a breath and ran for the door as he edged it closed. "Don't you dare, Riley Thorne. I have every right to"—he closed the door in her face—"go with you," she shrieked at the impassive barrier. Gritting her teeth, she dove for the knob and tried to turn it. It wouldn't turn. Glory beat on the door. "You let go of that knob right now, Riley Thorne, you hear me?"

No answer. Glory stepped back, her head tilted at a listening angle. Bootsteps receded down the hallway. She eyed the knob and attacked it again. It didn't turn. Sure enough, that darned Riley had locked the door from the outside. Fairly bursting with temper, Glory flung herself upright and stared at nothing in particular, trying to think this through. What would a man do?

She turned to stare at the gable window across the room. And grinned. It opened onto the verandah roof. She could carefully edge her way down the sloping shingles, grab onto a verandah support beam and climb down that.

She took a deep breath as her smile faded. *Well, Jacey could.* And had on several occasions when they were young girls—and then named her a 'fraidy-cat when she wouldn't follow. Glory frowned at the memory. *If I were a man, I'd already be climbing out that window*. She blinked at the locked door. *If I were a man, I wouldn't be locked in here to begin with*.

That settled it. Glory tugged on her clothes over her night-shirt. Mimicking Riley's swift yet controlled motions as best she could, she readied herself for the outdoors. Stockings and her lace-up boots completed her wool-skirt-and-blouse outfit. She then stomped over to her armoire and snatched out the first heavy coat she touched—a fancy, maroon satin-serge coat—and tugged into it.

As she tore for the window, she swooped up her fringed shawl from the end of her bed and flung it over her hair, twisting and turning it until it formed a hood. The cold night air and Riley Thorne be hanged. Opening the window, Glory ate those words as the intruding cold wind sent shivers through her, in spite of her clothes. Still, she pulled up the bottom sash as far as it would go and then bent over and climbed outside.

Immediately sitting down, remembering now why she hadn't attempted this before—it was so high off the ground—Glory took a deep breath. And then another. Steeling her resolve, telling herself to be a man, she scooted on her bottom—at great snagging expense to her satin and ruffled coat—to the very edge of the eave. Exercising extreme caution, and swallowing hard, she peered over the roof's lip.

Right into Riley Thorne's upturned face down below. *Blast and drat*. Hands to his waist, a knee bent, Riley called up, "Took you long enough."

Riley watched to make sure Glory made her way back inside her room. *Ornery, stubborn, little . . . woman*. He grinned. Just what the hell was he supposed to do with her? Several steamy options presented themselves instantly.

Jerking in his denims, tamping a lid on those images, Riley turned away and made his way to the bunkhouse . . . although, he didn't really see any need to, at this point. Like as not, whoever'd attacked Glory was either innocently back in bed or halfway to Kansas or the Indian Territory by now. That's how long she'd delayed him. Lucky for the guilty bastard that she had, too.

The son-of-a-gun better hope he took off for parts unknown. Because if I find out who it was, I'm going to kill him, plain and simple. That was twice, Riley reflected, that he'd said he would kill a man. Both times had to do with Glory. As the darkened windows of the bunkhouse loomed larger, Riley focused on their blank facade and wondered if he *could* kill a man. In his life he'd only seen one man killed—that cattle rustler Pa had shot. Riley again heard his father explaining how necessary the killing was. But the sight hadn't set well with twelve-year-old Riley. It'd also done something to his feelings toward Pa after that. There had to be another, better way, that's all.

Or so he'd thought until tonight when some bastard hurt Glory. No one had to tell him that if she hadn't freed herself, he and Biddy would've awakened to the sight of her body on the verandah. A gut-weakening throb of dread made Riley misstep, but strengthened his resolve. *I'm capable of taking a man's life if he so much as lays a hand on Glory. It's that simple.*

And that hard. He frowned for what it all meant. For both families. He loved Glory. Always had. Always would. In fact, if she said it was best he go away and never see her again, he was prepared to do that, too. The West was a big place. A man didn't ever have to see another person if he so chose.

Glad he'd reached the bunkhouse door, so he could abandon his thoughts of loving or leaving Glory, Riley opened the heavy door and stepped inside. He closed it quietly behind himself. And wrinkled his nose. After the fresh, bracing air outside, the warm, close air inside reeked of the noxious miasma of unwashed men and their other more-lingering scents.

His way lit by the fire in old wood stoves, one at each end of the narrow building, Riley walked quietly among the snoring men in their bunks. He peered at each one, checking to see if he really slept. He examined boots and clothes. If a man's boots were muddy and his clothes felt cold, he'd just been outside. Almost to the end of the bunks, Riley turned when a kerosene lamp was lit in the office and the door opened with a squeaking of hinges.

His eyes widened. Smiley Rankin stood there. Fully dressed, down to his hat and coat. Curious. Riley stepped out into the aisle between the two rows of bunks. The older man sucked in sharply, clearly startled, and then signaled for Riley to come to him. Riley's eyes narrowed . . . his thoughts exactly. He stalked down the aisle, toward the man, suddenly realizing that the foreman had more of a reason to suspect his presence out here than Riley did his.

Once at the open door to the office, Riley stepped through when Mr. Rankin backed out of his way. Closing the door behind Riley, he turned to him. "What're you doing sneaking around in the bunkhouse, Thorne? We already had one fight over stolen money."

Riley's temper flared enough to heat his cheeks, but he held it in check. "It's not the Thornes who're the thieves, if you'll remember back enough years, Mr. Rankin."

The man's long face set into hard lines and shadowed hollows. "It's late, and I ain't wantin' to git into that with you."

Riley met his gaze. "You brought it up."

Mr. Rankin clenched his jaw and stepped behind his desk. "Suppose you tell me what it is you're doing out here in the middle of the night. You're liable to git yerself shot, bein' as how everyone's so skittish."

Riley quirked his mouth as he considered the foreman. No matter what he thought of the man, Smiley Rankin was loyal to the Lawlesses. To a fault. To death even, he suspected. In some convoluted way, that put them both on the same side. "I'm out here looking for the man who attacked Miss Lawless less than fifteen minutes ago."

Rankin straightened up, his face sobering to the point of showing pain. "What the hell—attacked Miss Glory? She okay? Where'd this happen? What—?"

Riley held up a hand. "Hold on. She's fine. I locked her in her room."

The foreman's gray and bushy eyebrows rose. "Locked her in her room? What in tarnation for?"

"Safety. Hers and ours. She wanted to get a gun and help find the man responsible. But that's what I'm here to do. I was checking the bunkhouse to see if I found anything suspicious."

"And did ya? Like maybe one of them two hands you hired?"

A jet of impatient anger narrowed Riley's eyes. He notched his Stetson up and looked away long enough to calm down. Only then did he continue. "Maybe. It was either someone already here, or someone who came onto the place after the lights went out. Those are the only two explanations."

Smiley scratched his head and nodded. "Yep, guess so. But like as not, we'll never know which . . . since you pulled my guards off the front gate. They'd have been the only two to see anything."

Riley met the older, shorter man's accusing stare and said, "I didn't pull anybody off their posts. Who said I did?"

"Yer own two hires did. Brown and Justice. They both came in at dark and said you was speaking for Miss Glory and she didn't see any need to have men out in the cold."

Riley cocked his head at this bit of information. "I never said such a thing. And neither did Miss Lawless, that I know of."

Smiley's expression clouded. "That's interestin', I'd say. And maybe just about all the proof you'd need of their dishonest and lazy ways."

Riley liked this turn of events less and less. "You're right. I'd expect it of Carter Brown. But not Abel Justice."

"Well, it was Abel as did the talkin'."

Riley's mouth worked right along with his brain as he put all this together in a matter of seconds. "I aim to find out right now on whose orders they were acting."

The old foreman nodded as Riley spoke and even relaxed his dogged expression some. "So, while you was looking around in there, did you see anything to make you think we got a skunk in the flowerbed?"

Riley shook his head. "No. But I hadn't exactly finished looking around when you came in." He narrowed his eyes. "No offense, Mr. Rankin, but what are you doing up at this hour and dressed for the outdoors?"

Smiley's face colored. His mouth worked. He looked down at his desktop, moved a few papers around. And finally admitted, "I go out to see ole Skeeter of a night before I turn in. That dog's behavior is the dangedest thing I ever saw." Then as if realizing with whom he was sharing this observation, he sniffed and frowned. "But I didn't see or hear anything out of the ordinary. Or I would've come runnin' right then."

Riley nodded. "I know you would. Then that means whoever did it is long gone . . . or still here."

It was Rankin's turn to nod and meet Riley's gaze. "Yep. I reckon so. May as well stir the men. It's been a long day, what with the fire early this morning. They ain't goin' to be none too happy about gittin' up."

Riley stepped out of the foreman's way when he shouldered past him to the closed door. "I reckon they won't be," he finally said when Smiley's hand was turning the knob, "But then, Miss Lawless isn't any too happy about nearly being killed, either."

The older man's hand stilled on the knob. Keeping it there, he pivoted to look into Riley's eyes. "I've said it before, and I'll say it again. It weren't none of these things happening until you came to stay and then hired on Abel Justice and Carter Brown."

Riley suddenly had a crawful of this man's bellyaching about the two hands. "If you can show me one shred of proof that points to either man, beyond being lazy, then I'll fire them both. And I'll leave with them, come sunup."

Smiley notched up his stubbly chin and raised an eyebrow. "You're on, Thorne. You just start yer packin'."

Fighting a nightmarish shadow she couldn't elude, Glory wrenched awake with a sharp cry and sat straight up in her bed, blinking and staring at the opposite wall. Her heart pounded, but her mind soothed, *It's okay, Glory, you're awake. You're in your room. There's no one here but you.* Deep breath after deep breath began calming her. Until she looked down at herself and frowned. She was fully dressed, including her satin serge coat twisted all about her. She fingered the fringed shawl around her neck. What in the—?

Sudden remembrance and fear clutched fistlike at her heart, held her in its grip. Her hand went to her mouth as she saw it all again. The verandah. Dark. A man grabbing her, choking off her air. Her getting away. Riley locking her in here. It was all so horrible, and she'd been so angry at him. But then— her frown deepened—she'd simply fallen asleep while Riley searched the place for her attacker. How long ago was that?

She turned to the gable window. Bright daylight streamed in, dappling the hardwood floors with warm yellow. Morning. Late morning. Where was Riley? Was he unharmed? Glory began scooting off her bed, telling herself she had to—The doorknob turned, freezing her in place, centering her attention on the closed door. Riley, at long last, no doubt. Glory reached back for a pillow. Let him show his face in here. She'd give him a thing or two to think about.

But it was Biddy who popped in when the door opened. "Well, the good Lord be praised—'tis awake she is. I've checked on ye twice before now and found you snoring away, I did."

Vexation met with Glory's eyebrows, lowering them. "I don't snore."

Biddy cackled as she crossed the room. "Look who yer talkin' to, child. I raised ye from a babe. But let's have a look at ye." Trundling up to the bed, she gripped Glory's chin, firmly turning her head this way and that as she considered her in critical appraisal. Finally, the older woman announced, "Yer none the worse for wear, I s'pose, seein' as how ye slept right through the excitement."

Glory tugged her chin free and clutched her pillow to her stomach as she flopped back, groaning, onto the remaining pillows at the bed's head. "Please, no excitement. Not today, Biddy. I can't take anymore."

Creaking floorboards announced Biddy's shifting stance. Glory opened her eyes and saw the beloved older woman fluffing her wide flower-printed skirt out around her, like so many feathers, as she perched her weight on the side of the bed. "Well, then, can ye maybe do with 'less,' if 'more' is such a bother?"

Glory impatiently brushed tangle after tangle of her long hair out of her face as she cocked her head at a questioning angle. "What?"

Biddy self-importantly pursed her lips and clutched her hands together over her ever-present apron. " 'Tis 'three less' I'm talking about. If ye didn't lay about all day, ye'd know these things."

Glory bopped Biddy on the arm with her pillow, drawing a snort of displeasure from her nanny, which she ignored. "Just tell me straight out, Biddy. Have mercy. I was nearly killed last night."

Biddy slapped her hands over her heart. "Are ye tryin' to put me in me grave, child, with such talk? Now, ye just sit there and listen. Mr. Rankin himself told me only this morning when he came in for—well, never ye mind why. The truth is we're still not knowing who it was who attacked ye last night. But it appears there was enough reason—as well as yelling, I don't mind tellin' ye—to fire those two men Riley hired. They're already gone, they are."

Surprise jerked Glory to a sitting position. "Who fired them?"

"Why, Riley himself. And then he came up here and packed his things, saddled that gray horse of his, and without so much as a word, rode right outta here this morning, he did."

Glory sat openmouthed, her hands flattened over her tripping heartbeat. "Riley left? But why, Biddy?"

Biddy pulled back in a dramatic show of surprise. "After all the fussin' and evil-eyein' between ye two, now yer goin' ta be upset about his leavin'? Why, the only times ye were decent to each other was when I sent ye out to see to Skeeter and to pay yer respects to yer folks and Old Pete . . . may God rest their souls."

Glory lowered her head for Biddy's sort-of prayer, but from

under her lowered lids, she cut her gaze over to her nanny. And immediately looked away, afraid the sharp-eyed old dear would see the indecent truth written on her face. She and Riley had come very close to being just that—indecent—on more than one occasion. And the last time, they'd approached complete indecency. Glory picked at the fringe on the shawl wadded up in her lap, and wondered if Riley's feelings for her had anything to do with his leaving.

About halfway home, and flanked by Abel Justice and Carter Brown, Riley's temples pounded in time with the horses' hooves as they loped over the autumn-browned hills. As tired from a lack of sleep as he was from his troublesome thoughts, he concentrated on the flat, treeless horizon of the trail ahead and hoped that looking forward, instead of over his shoulder, wasn't a fatal mistake.

Because he couldn't trust either of the men behind him any farther than he could see them. But a deal was a deal. And mud was mud.

Both Brown and Justice had mud on their boots last night. Mud not yet dried to clumps. Each man had a different story, though. Brown said he'd gone out to relieve himself shortly before the bunkhouse was roused. And Justice said he thought he'd heard something and went to investigate. He said he hadn't seen anyone beforehand, but considering Brown's story, figured as he'd most likely heard him going outside.

Not for the first time, Riley noted, the men backed each other's stories. Were they the strangers to each other they pretended to be? Hadn't Glory raised that same question? Riley's thoughts pricked his conscience. Could everyone else see something he was determined not to see, because he'd hired the men? Was his stubbornness clouding his judgment? Riley knew he'd never forgive himself if his mistake or carelessness hurt Glory in any way.

But a search of the Lawless yard, incomplete at best with nothing but moonlight to aid them, yielded only the two men's boot prints around the bunkhouse, exactly where they'd said they were. No suspicious hoofprints leading on or off the place. Nothing missing or disturbed. Well, except for Smiley. He'd been pretty disturbed when he reminded Riley this morning of his pledge to fire the two men and also to leave himself.

A man of his word, Riley'd done just that. He'd fired Brown and Justice, only to immediately rehire them as Thorne hands. How better to keep an eye on them and know their whereabouts?

And now here they were, riding for the Lazy T and a sure-fire confrontation with his father. Because the last thing the Thornes needed were two more hands, two more mouths to feed, two more horses to pasture. *And speaking of pasture* . . . Frowning, Riley reined in his gray gelding and stared off at a knot of cattle grazing contentedly enough in a shallow, grassy depression between two hills.

Brown and Justice drew up beside him. Riley eyed each man in turn, saw their questioning looks, and figured he knew what was coming. Sure enough, Abel Justice spotted the problem and gave voice to it. "Ain't them cattle over there sportin' the Lawless brand?"

Riley kept his gaze on the livestock and nodded. "Yep."

Then Carter Brown chipped in, "We ain't off the Lawless holdings *yet*? We been ridin' a good three hours."

The incredulous tone in his voice narrowed Riley's eyes. "You could ride three more in any direction and not be clear of the Lawless range. Leastwise, this used to be Lawless range. And not more than a few weeks ago, at that." He nudged Pride forward in a canter, reining again at a crude wooden sign staked into the ground. It hadn't been here when he'd ridden for Glory's on the day Jacey left. He recognized his father's handwriting on the sign.

Abel Justice again spoke up. "It says this here is now Thorne property and we're trespassin'." He turned his questioning gaze to Riley. "Or we would be if'n we weren't in yer company, I suppose."

Riley notched his Stetson up. A muscle worked as he clenched and unclenched his jaw. It had started. The range war. The trouble was here. And not surprisingly, it had started at his home. "Let's ride," Riley told his two new hands. He then put his heels to Pride.

Chapter 10

"To *hell* with all the Lawlesses, I say. And especially to Glory."

Red rage flashed in Riley's eyes about a second before he turned from unsaddling Pride and rounded on Henry, punching him hard enough to send him sprawling in the dirt. Standing over his younger brother, his own features set in stone, Riley pointed down at him and gritted out in a husky voice, "Don't ever speak of the lady like that again, you got me, Henry? There're hard things happening at the Lawless spread, things that no one should have to go through. And you're just lucky that, tired as I am, I don't kick your ass all over this yard."

Henry achingly pulled up on an elbow. He put a hand to his jaw, tested it, glared up at Riley, and then sprang to his feet. At twenty-three, only two years Riley's junior, he was every bit as big and hard-muscled from farm labor as his brother. "You just go ahead and try, Riley. Because I mean every word of it. The only good Lawless is a dead Lawless."

"You son-of-a-bitch," came Riley's answering snarl as he bunched his muscles, reared back, and then stepped into his brother with a big fist to Henry's stomach, doubling him over, and then another blow to his jaw that wrenched him sideways and staggering, blood seeping from his mouth.

"Riley—stop it! Dear Lord. Ben, come quick. Riley's home and he and Henry are at it already. Hurry!"

Riley heard his mother's frantic yells, heard running feet

coming their way at the horse corral, was aware of the still figures of Brown and Justice behind him, but he didn't look away from Henry. He shook his aching hand, worked his fingers, and then pointed at his younger brother. "Say anything like that again—especially about Glory—and I'll take you apart, brother or no."

Down on one knee and bent over, heaving and groaning, a hand on the ground for support, his other to his belly, Henry turned his glittering gaze and his blood-smeared face up to Riley . . . and just kept on. Barely able to speak around his swollen lips, he nevertheless mouthed a particularly vile curse about what Riley could do with Glory.

Murderous rage flared in Riley's heart and launched him forward. But seemingly from out of nowhere—so focused was he on Henry—his other brothers and his father materialized to grab his arms and hold him back. His father stood in front of him, his big, work-roughened hands on his son's chest. "No, Riley. No more. You'll kill him."

Struggling against his captors, Riley stilled at the sound of his father's commanding voice. Then, as if a bystander to the scene, he watched his mother bend over Henry to assess his injuries. Forcing himself to calm down, Riley took several deep breaths, and then nodded to his father.

Ben Thorne notched his chin up as he flicked his gaze over Riley's face. "Yeah? It's over? You done now?"

Riley nodded again. "I'm done . . . if he is."

"He is," Ben said, turning around and ambling at a hitching gait to his wife's side. Speaking over his shoulder now, he called out, "Son, you're not likely to find anyone hereabouts as feels any different than your brother about them Lawlesses. You can't use your fists on 'em all."

Staring after his father, hating the limp the white-haired, overalled man had to live with—thanks to a crippled leg caused by a Lawless cowhand's bullet years ago—Riley clenched his back teeth and then shrugged against his other brothers' hold on him. "I'm okay. You can let go."

They didn't. Held in place as effectively as any roped dogie, Riley focused on the boys in turn, looking from Caleb to John and finally to the youngest, Zeke. "I said I'm okay. I'm not going to hit him—unless he opens his mouth again."

"I'll hit him for you, if he does," fifteen-year-old Zeke offered as he, with his brothers, stepped back from Riley. As always, the boy's shaggy brown hair hung in his grayish eyes. "He's been hogging all the blankets at night, anyways, and I owe him one. I won't miss him none when he gets hitched to Janie Sutfield come December."

Still feeling the pounding of his blood through his veins and his temper's hold on his thoughts, Riley forced his body to relax, to ease down from his rage. Finally he managed a deep, almost normal breath, a glance at Henry who was standing up now with his parents' help, and a question for Zeke. "Hitched? When did this happen?"

Zeke shrugged and deferred to nineteen-year-old Caleb, no less a big-boned, hard-hewn, dark-haired specimen than any of the other Thorne sons. "About a week ago. He rode on over to the Sutfield place and just asked her. She said yes."

At this point, John, the seventeen-year-old Thorne, cut in with "Well, hell yes, she said yes, you big coot. How else could there be a wedding?"

With that, two more fights nearly erupted before Louise Thorne bustled over, waving a broomstick at her sons. "I'll light into the next one that says a word. Just see if I won't. Now, you young'uns have said your howdys to your big brother, so get on about your chores. The body that says he doesn't have any can just see me for more."

That cleared the yard of Thorne younger siblings. While Ben helped Henry over to the water pump to clean himself up, Riley faced his mother and hugged her. "I'm sorry about my homecoming being like this, but I couldn't abide the way Henry was talking."

Returning his hug and then putting her hands to her sturdy hips and shaking her head, Louise opined, "That boy. You'd think Henry'd learn he can't best you. And I'll swear if John doesn't have a smart mouth just like him. If I had a lick of sense, I'd marry off the lot of you to the first wagonload of women that rolled by."

Riley grinned. "If you did that, you'd have to do all the chores yourself."

She hooted out her amusement. "There wouldn't be none without you boys." She then sobered and looked past Riley. "And who would these two stray dogs be? They follow you home?"

Riley turned, realizing he'd forgotten about Abel Justice and Carter Brown. Looking scruffy and unsure of themselves, Riley thought, *Two stray dogs. Fits them perfectly.* But maybe their seeing the physical way of things here might help keep them in line some—especially the big man, Carter Brown, whose way with words was like Henry's.

"These are two hands I brought with me from the Lawless place." He pointed to each man as he said his name. "Abel Justice and Carter Brown. This is my mother."

The men nodded their heads and touched the brims of their hats in greeting, each one mumbling, "Ma'am."

Louise nodded back at the men, looked them over with a critical eye, and said, "Lawless hands, huh? Well, you're here. You may as well stay. You can bed down out in the barn. That's the best we can do."

With Riley, she watched them collect their mounts and walk away before she again spoke. "I'll leave you and your pa to sort out what we're going to do with two more mouths to feed. I'm sure you have a good reason for bringing them along." Then she was silent a moment as she looked him up and down. "As well as for yourself being home."

"Yep, I do." Riley looked from his mother to his father's distant figure and gestured toward him. "I'm going to go talk with Pa a minute."

"You do that," Louise agreed. "It's been hard on him without you here. Mind you, he doesn't complain about working, but he relies on you, son. And you know your brothers—they work hard, but they've got to be told what to do. I guess you heard we're losing Henry to Janie Sutfield? It'll only make things harder." Suddenly she quieted and squinted up at him, shading her eyes against the cool afternoon sun. "I'm trying to say I'm glad you're home."

Riley looked from her to his father and back to her, and smiled. "I know, Ma. Things took such a turn at Glory's that it looks like I'll be here for good."

Louise Thorne shook her head, as if saddened by his words. "Well, I can't rightly say how I feel about that, Riley. About you and Glory, I mean."

Riley's snort came out a chuckle, but not of humor. "There is no me and Glory. She and I . . . well, there's just too much between us, her being a Lawless and all. And me a Thorne. Damn shame, though."

With that, he walked away, heading for the water trough and Henry and his father.

Hurting for him, Louise watched her son's retreating back. Riley walked as if the weight of the world was on his shoulders. Knowing how to lighten that load, she made up her mind and cast her gaze heavenward. *Catherine, forgive me, but I've got to break my promise to you about Glory. I'm going to tell Riley the truth. It's the kids' only chance for happiness. So, if you don't want me to do this, then you'd best have the Good Lord send me a sign right now.*

Louise stood where she was in front of her rough and low dwelling. She dutifully waited a respectable amount of time for something to happen. Nothing did. She figured that was her sign—that it was okay to tell. She brought her hand to her mouth, suddenly staggered by the enormity of the secret she was about to divulge to her oldest son.

She turned and saw him with his father. They were still standing by the wooden water trough. Riley had his booted foot on its edge and was leaning forward, his arms crossed over that knee. He nodded at something his father said and then both men looked off the way Ben pointed.

Louise watched Ben turn from Riley and head toward the barn. She glanced back at her eldest, saw him watching his father's departure before he strode off in the opposite direction, toward the corral. Louise shook her head. Her firstborn. So strong and true. And quiet and capable and willing. A tear came to her eye. *Thank you, Lord, for such a son. And please*

*give me the right words to tell him that Glory Bea Lawless
. . . is no Lawless at all.*

Riley heard his mother coming up behind him before he ever
saw her. She loudly directed everyone's chores as she approached him. But he didn't turn around. Instead, he remained
facing the low, brown hills of the prairie that dipped and
swelled for hundreds of miles. Beyond more than a few of
them, and warmed by the same sun, chilled by the same wind,
Glory was going through her day. And he wasn't there.

That knowledge ate at his gut. He shook his head, mouthing,
Damn you, Glory, for making me care. A foot up on the split-
rail corral fence, his arms crossed atop its highest rail, he
frowned out his unsettled feelings at the dozing horses en-
closed there.

Just then, to his left, his mother joined him. He looked down
at her, saw the troubled set of her features, and knew he was
somehow responsible for the lines to either side of her normally cheerful mouth. A surge of love swept over Riley. She
was everything he could ever hope to be as a person. Strong,
loving, firm, capable. Dressed in plain homespun, her patched
skirt and blouse covered by an old coat of her husband's, she
was a rock in time of trouble. He smiled down at her. "Is
Henry okay?"

Louise Thorne shook her head and pursed her lips. "That
boy, I swear. I'll dance at his wedding come December just
because I'll be so glad he'll be Janie's problem from now on.
Bless the girl for saying yes."

Despite the turmoil roiling his gut and the throbbing in his
knuckles, Riley grinned. "Then I guess he's okay?"

"He's beat up pretty good. But none the worse for wear.
Your pa sent him out to check on them yearlings. He took
them two hands of yours with him. They may as well start
earning their keep right off."

Riley nodded. "I reckon so. I'm sorry to bring all this home,
Ma."

Louise frowned up at him. "Just what did you bring home,
son?"

"Trouble. A whole heap of it. I just wish I didn't—" Riley bit back his words, turned his attention to the waving tallgrass, denied that his heart thumped leadenly in his chest. He just wished he didn't care so damned much for Glory Bea Lawless. Day and night, he saw her face, felt her body move under his hands, tasted her kiss, tasted . . . her.

From his side, his mother touched his sleeve. "Look at me, son." When he did, she went on. "I want you to listen to me. I've got something to tell you that will most likely change a heap of things around here. Or maybe not, I don't know. All I know is you need to hear it."

Riley frowned at her seriousness, felt his gut clench, but he nodded. "All right. Go on. I'm listening."

His mother's face crinkled into a gentle smile. "You always do, son." Then, and to Riley's surprise, given his mother's eternal forthrightness, she looked suddenly uncertain, glancing away from him, and knotting her fingers together at her waist.

Riley straightened up, turning away from the corral and the nodding horses there. He gripped his mother's sleeve. "What is it? What's happened?"

Louise covered his hand on her arm, squeezed it, and shook her head. "What happened, son, happened nearly twenty years ago."

Riley drew back, went back to leaning on the corral. "Twenty years? About the time of the range war? J. C. Lawless taking the land?"

Louise shook her head. "No. That was before what I have to tell you. I swore I wouldn't, but I don't see now how I can keep my word to Catherine Lawless any longer."

"Catherine Lawless?" Riley ducked his chin in confusion. "What about her? Say it right out, Ma."

To his further surprise, she shook her head and turned her back to him. All Riley could do was wait her out, his heart thumping in mixed fear and anticipation of her news. He studied her graying hair, knotted tightly in a thick bun. The set of her broad shoulders, the rigidity of her stance. "Mother?"

As if she waited to hear that one word, his mother spun to face him. "Glory is no blood Lawless at all."

"What?" The word was torn from him. As if he'd been gut-punched, Riley stiffened against the next blow. "Glory's not a Lawless? What do you mean?" Then, a seeping numbness settled over him, causing his brows to frown low over his eyes, firming his lips to a straight line. Her words sank in. Speaking barely above a whisper, he asked, "How can that be?"

"I'm tryin' to tell you. Her real name is Beatrice Parker. When J. C. brought her home with him from Tucson nearly twenty years ago . . . and him trailing that danged nanny goat and its kid—"

"Nanny goat?" Truly lost now, Riley could only frown.

"To feed the baby—Glory. Glory was the baby he brought home."

Riley held his hands out in defeat. "Brought home? Where the hell did he get her?"

Louise shrugged, frowning as if trying to remember exactly. "Somewhere down in the Arizona Territory. Some mountain pass named after the Apache."

Strength seemed to leach from Riley's muscles as he muttered, "Arizona? That's where Jacey went."

"I know. That's what scared Biddy—finding that Lawless gang spur in the house and then not being able to stop Jacey from leaving. It's why she sent for you to watch over Glory."

"I've got to sit down." And then he did, perching his butt on a low fence rail. Pitched forward, he rested his elbows on his denim-clad knees and stared at the hard-packed dirt between his scuffed boots. He felt his mother's touch on his shoulder and looked up at her. "I'm okay. Go on."

She nodded. "Maybe I'd best start at the beginning. One day whilst I was visiting Catherine, and you boys was here with your pa, J. C. rode in trailing that nanny goat and holding a sweet-faced baby girl. With no more'n a how-do-you-do, he just up and handed the child to Catherine."

"Just like that?" Riley asked, hardly believing any of this.

"Just like that," she assured him. "Well, at any rate, Catherine took one look at that beautiful, squalling child and said something like 'Glory be, a little girl.' And that's how she got her name. Catherine changed the 'be' to B-E-A—short for Beatrice, her real name, you see?''

Riley nodded that he understood. His mother continued. ''Well, let me tell you, Hannah was thrilled. She acted like her daddy'd brought her a new doll. But Jacey—only two years old—clung to her mama's skirt, her thumb in her mouth. She didn't want no part of that noisy little critter. She said she wanted a puppy instead. We all laughed about that.''

Riley stared up at her. ''Go on.''

''Well, the next time I paid a call, I took you and Henry with me—I was carrying Caleb at the time. You were six years old and curious enough about that baby to stick your nose right in her face. She grabbed it with her tiny baby fist and scratched the fool out of you. You jumped back and blurted out your first cuss word. And got your britches tanned for your efforts. Why, after that, you were much obliged to keep your distance from her.''

Despite himself, Riley had to chuckle. Glory'd been scratching him and getting under his skin ever since, the way he saw it. He looked up at his mother, who'd leaned her back against the corral fence. She wore a faraway look, one that told Riley the scene she saw in front of her was a different one, in a different time. ''What happened then, Ma?'' he gently urged.

Louise glanced at him as if surprised to see him there. ''Nothing. That's the whole of it. J. C. brought the baby home. And Catherine took right to it, claimed it as hers.''

Riley shook his head, lifted his Stetson, ran a hand through his hair, and resettled his hat on his head. ''I'll be damned. But who is Beatrice Parker really? Do you know?''

His mother nodded. ''Oh, yes, I know. Her folks was killed by Kid Chapelo, J. C. said.''

Surprise brought Riley to his feet. ''Kid Chapelo?'' The hair stood up on his arms. ''From J. C.'s own gang? Legend says that man was pure evil. Heartless.''

''And I reckon he was. J. C. said what The Kid did to the Parkers convinced him he didn't want no part of being an outlaw anymore. He never rode out again with his gang. After that, he settled down to being a cattleman and family man.''

Riley shook his head, put his hands to his waist. "Just what did he do, Ma? The Kid, I mean."

Louise shook her head. "J. C. never would talk about it. But the little I know is The Kid ambushed a young couple in that mountain pass and just cold-bloodedly killed 'em. Then he robbed 'em and left the baby there to die."

"*Damn* him," Riley spat out, sick to his stomach. "I guess, then, that J. C. went and got her? But how'd he know?"

Louise shrugged her uncertainty. "I'm trying to remember. It seems he—The Kid—came back to the hideout bragging on what he'd done. And one thing led to another, ending with J. C. killing the man. He then went to get the baby and came home."

Trying to absorb all this, Riley frowned and shook his head. Then something else occurred to him. He turned to his mother, saw her worried expression, and knew . . . just knew . . . that what he suspected was true. "Who else knows about this? Glory doesn't, does she?"

Louise raised her hand, as if being sworn to secrecy. "Lord no. Hannah and Jacey don't, they were too young to remember. And I know, but only because I happened to be there when J. C. rode in. He and Catherine talked about it, deciding not to tell her. J. C. worried about The Kid's family seeking revenge through Glory. But luckily, that never happened."

Suddenly feeling like bleached bone, Riley said. "Yes it did happen, Ma. It happened the day J. C. and Catherine were murdered. Jacey found the evidence—that broken silver spur. And it happened again last night. Someone tried to kill Glory." His mother gasped, but Riley went on. "She didn't see who, but a man grabbed her from behind when she was out on the verandah. He'd have killed her for sure if she hadn't bitten him."

Louise jerked her hands to her chest, covering her heart. "Dear Lord above. Is she okay?"

Riley nodded. "Yeah, she's fine. It was dark, but we searched the whole place over. Didn't find anything—not even a bite mark on any man. So, either she didn't bite him hard enough to break the skin or, whoever it was, he's not there now.''

His mind focusing with deadly singularity on the unknown man, the object of a growing hatred within his heart, Riley narrowed his eyes. His next words poured forth in a voice so husky he barely recognized it as his own. ''What you just told me about Glory? It changes things. The murders. J. C. and Catherine.'' He shook his head. ''Their kin back East aren't the only ones responsible. I've felt it in my gut all along.''

After a moment's silence, he added, ''Whoever tried to kill Glory didn't do it because she's a Lawless. But because she's *not*. It all makes sense now. And it's worse than I thought.''

''Oh, son, how could it be worse?''

Riley glanced at his mother and then looked across the yard. Saw his father and brothers coming out of the barn. And thought of the land feud. He closed his eyes against a kernel of truth wanting to plant itself in his mind. He swallowed back the bile rising in his throat. Taking a breath, he turned to look down at his mother. ''Does Pa know any of this . . . about Glory?''

Wide-eyed, suddenly stricken, her features crumpling, Riley's mother nodded. ''Yes. I told him and I made him swear on the family Bible he'd never tell or use it against her. But what are you thinking, son? I see something in your eyes I don't like.''

''There's something in my gut I don't like, Ma. Promise to you or not, Pa knows Glory's not a Lawless. That means there's no Lawless on her spread. The place isn't hers. She can't hold it.''

''Yes, she can, Riley. All them men loyal to her and her sisters on that spread? Why, there's not a rancher around here who doesn't know or remember what it's like to face Lawless hands. The whole lot of your Pa's friends ain't got the stomach for much more than talking about that old feud. I hope.''

Riley's expression hardened to match the tone in his mother's voice. ''That may be. But I'm saying the range war heated up the minute Jacey left—the last legitimate Lawless on the place. And Pa knows that. I'm saying the ranchers' meetings took place right after that. On our land.''

Louise waved her pointing finger at Riley's nose. ''Don't you say another word, Riley Eugene Thorne. Your Pa had nothing to do with attacking Glory Lawless. He might go after the land that was his once. But he'd never hurt that girl. Never. Besides, he'd have no cause to. If he wanted to hurt her, all he'd have to do would be to tell her the truth. And he ain't done that, nor told no one else, either. You ask yourself why, son.''

Riley firmed his mouth, thought about it and then almost grinned. ''Because you'd box his ears, if he did?''

Louise nodded. ''That, or worse. I loved Catherine Lawless and her girls. Especially Glory. Your Pa knows that. And *he* loves me.''

Riley chuckled at this insight into his parents' relationship. But then, it faded as he thought of his brother Henry's hot head and even hotter words, words that told plainly enough of his hatred of anything Lawless. Riley fisted his hand, felt the swollen pain in his knuckles. He rubbed his hand and looked pointedly at his mother. ''Maybe Pa wouldn't want to see her hurt. But there're others who would, others who'd want to please him.''

Riley hated that his mother's face paled to the color of cream. She put a shaking hand to her heart. ''You don't think Henry would do such a thing? Tell me you don't.''

''I can't do that, Mother. I pray to God he wouldn't. But God won't be able to help him if he did.''

Tears filled his mother's eyes. Staring at her, seeing that she couldn't deny it, a sudden sting of wetness filled Riley's eyes. A dampness clogged his throat, hampered his breathing. Hands to his waist, he turned his back on his mother, lest she see. ''And there's not a damned thing I can do to help Glory, either. Not without telling her. Not without destroying her myself.''

Chapter 11

Glory smiled as she stroked Skeeter's bony head. Perched on her knees next to Old Pete's grave, all but lost in her father's sheepskin coat, she crooned low to the hound. "I'd feel much better if you'd eat something, Skeeter. It's not nice of you to worry me like this. Old Pete would be the first one to want you out running the hills and hunting your own meals."

Skeeter thumped his tail, blinked his big brown eyes, and stared up at Glory. A sigh escaping her, she reached over to his tin plate of food and picked up a meat scrap. Offering it to him, she said, "I'd be the happiest woman in the territory if you'd eat this."

The dog sniffed the meat chunk and turned his head away, resettling himself atop his slain owner's grave. Glory tossed the scrap back into the plate. "You don't fool me." She stood up and pointed an accusing finger at the hound. "Look at you. You're not near as scrawny as you were a month ago. So you're eating sometimes, and I'd bet you even get up off this grave. Like it or not, you're getting better. So there. What do you think about that?"

Skeeter raised an eyebrow, sending her a baleful look before he stretched out on his side in the pale November sun, effectively dismissing Glory from his presence. "Fine then, Mr. Skeeter." She chuckled around her words. "I'll leave you be."

With that, she stuck her cold hands in the coat's deep pockets, felt the steely comfort of the small pistol she now carried, and stepped around Old Pete's grave, making her way to the next two. She then spent the next several minutes paying her respects to her parents, before exiting the fenced-off cemetery.

She was about half the distance from the back of the main house, and deep in thought about last night's attack on herself and Riley's abrupt departure earlier that morning, when she heard her name being called out. She looked to the narrow back-porch landing and saw Biddy framed in the doorway. The round little Irishwoman waved what looked like a letter in her hand and she all but bounced up and down.

Glory acknowledged her nanny's wave and headed for the porch, all the time thinking, *What now?* Wasn't it enough for one day that Riley'd left so abruptly, and so had those two men he'd hired? Good riddance to Carter and Brown, but she missed Riley. And admitting that did nothing for her mood.

"Glory, come quick, child. 'Tis a letter from Hannah."

Absorbing that news, Glory cried out, "Hannah!" as if her oldest sister herself stood there. Her spirits instantly lifting, Glory clutched at her skirt, ran all the way to Biddy, and pounded up the wooden steps. "Who brought it? When did it come? Let me see it."

"And here it is." Biddy handed over the letter. "That nice Mr. Jessup stopped by the post office in Kansas and brought this with him on his way home. Easy now, child, have a care to what yer doing—like as not, ye'll tear up Hannah's words before we can read them. And look at you—after last night, what are ye thinkin', being outside by yerself?" As she fussed, Biddy tugged Glory into the warm kitchen with her and closed the door behind them.

"No one would bother me out there in the open, Biddy. But if they did, I'm ready. I loaded one of Papa's old pistols and stuck it in my pocket." Glory worked at opening her sister's folded letter as she spoke.

"The saints preserve us. The child's carrying a gun now."

Glory looked up. Defiance narrowed her eyes and edged her words. "Yes, I am. And you should be, too."

Biddy waved a hand in dismissal of that idea. "Me with a gun? Why, child, I'd be a bigger danger to meself than I would be to anyone else. Like as not, I'd shoot meself in the foot, as sure as I'm standin' here."

Glory's expression softened as she chuckled at her nanny and lowered her gaze to Hannah's written words and said, "Maybe she's writing to say she's coming home."

"We'll never know—now will we?—if ye don't read what she has to say." With that, Biddy hovered around Glory's elbow, her faded-blue eyes showing she was as agog with anticipation as Glory was.

Glory lovingly smoothed a hand over her sister's neat lettering. Then, suddenly afraid of what she might read, she headed for the trestle table and pulled a chair out. "I've got to sit down . . . in case this is bad news." She did just that and then frowned up at Biddy. "She addressed it to me and Jacey and you. Hannah'd be in a tizzy if she knew Jacey wasn't here."

Biddy pursed her lips and raised an eyebrow. "An' we'll not be telling her, either. But never mind that. Read Hannah's words before I do it for ye." Biddy scraped out a chair and joined Glory at the table. She prayerfully folded her hands together atop the table's smooth, worn wooden surface and waited.

Glory impulsively squeezed Biddy's hands and grinned in excitement. "I just know she's coming home." She then turned her attention to the silent reading of her sister's words. Her smile faded. Her expression darkened. Her mouth slacked open. She looked up at Biddy. "Sweet merciful heavens, Biddy. Hannah's married."

Biddy jerked back in her chair, nearly sending herself over backward. She grabbed the table's edge to steady herself. "The devil, you say!"

"Near enough," Glory said. Her heart pounding with shock, she added, "She married Slade Garrett!"

Biddy's broad, apple-cheeked face drained of color. She stared right through Glory. "Hannah married a Garrett? 'Tis the worst thing possible."

"I agree. How could she do that? His name is the very one on that burned piece of stationery we found here with Mama and Papa. Why, he's in cahoots with Mama's family."

Biddy turned her gray-bunned, wispy-curled head to look into Glory's eyes. " 'Tis worse than that, child—worse than ye can know."

Glory's fist crumpled around the pages and Hannah's words. An unnamed fear clutched at her heart. "What do you mean? Hannah just wouldn't marry him if he had anything to do with the . . . murders. She just wouldn't. Why, she says in here how much she loves him."

Biddy shook her head. " 'Tis not the murders I mean. 'Twas a Garrett—near to twenty-five years ago—who attacked my Catherine one night in her room. 'Twas a Garrett who had her fleeing Boston—and me with her—after the scandal of such behavior. 'Twas a Garrett who put us in Arizona Territory and got Catherine kidnapped by the Lawless Gang."

Shocked into silence, all Glory could do was stare into Biddy's faded-blue eyes as she added, "And even though it turned out well, seeing how much yer mother loved yer father, 'twas a Garrett who did all that. A Garrett. And now . . . Hannah's married one."

Her hand over her aching heart, able only to take shallow breaths, Glory all but whispered, "I've never heard any of this before. Why didn't you tell us after the funerals—*before* Hannah left for Boston to hunt this man down?"

"Yer mother didn't want ye girls to know. And I never thought Hannah'd *marry* the man, for heaven's sake." Biddy covered her face with her hands and shook her head. "That poor child," she mumbled between her fingers. Then, lowering her hands, she flapped one at Glory. "Read what else she has to say. Maybe she'll explain."

Putting aside her questions about the Garretts, Glory nodded and looked back down at the letter, smoothing it as best she could. Reading Hannah's words, telling them to Biddy, she said, "Her marriage isn't the worst of it. She says be wary of strangers because someone is having us watched. She doesn't know who or why, but she calls them trackers. She says one followed her to Boston. Slade Garrett's men caught him and killed him. That's how she knows.''

Frowning her face into deep lines of worry, Biddy cocked her head questioningly at Glory. ''Trackers, ye say? Like hunters?''

Glory nodded. ''I guess. Only these men track people. Us.''

Biddy put a plump and trembling hand to her bosom. ''Merciful heavens. This explains the attack on ye last night, child. I'm sure of it.'' Then her eyes widened, she intoned, ''Jacey. The girl is out there all alone.''

Dry-mouthed with fear for her sister, but wanting to reassure Biddy, Glory quipped, ''I'd worry more about any shootist facing Jacey than I would her.'' Seeing her nanny's brave smile, and knowing it was for her benefit, Glory sobered. ''Those two men that Riley hired—Abel Justice and Carter Brown? Suddenly I wish they were still here, just so we could keep an eye on them. I got so angry when Riley hired them. But now I'm sorry he fired them.''

When Biddy offered no comment, Glory stared pointedly at her. Something in the older woman's expression pricked at Glory, made her sit up straighter, and lean toward her. ''What?''

Biddy lowered her gaze to her lap. A moment later, she raised her head, revealing a stricken expression. ''There's more I need to tell ye, child. And yer not going to like it.''

A sudden sickness swept over Glory. Whatever Biddy had to say—she just knew it—had something to do with Riley. She raised her chin. ''Go on.''

''Well, 'tis the land, child. Smiley says he's not so sure that yer folks and Old Pete . . .'' Biddy's voice trailed off. She took a deep breath and started over. ''He's not sure that only yer mother's family back east is responsible.''

Glory took a moment to absorb Biddy's words and then leaned over the table, gripping her nanny's hand in hers. ''What are you saying?''

Biddy's gaze slipped away from Glory's face. ''There's talk again of the range wars. And the talks are going on at the

Thorne place. The ranchers are wanting their land back . . . land they say yer father took from them.''

Glory sat back, fisted her hands on the tabletop. She stared at the wood stove across the kitchen and said, ''I've heard that all my life . . . that Papa stole hundreds of acres by force. Did he, Biddy? Did he become successful by forcing others off their land?''

From the corner of her eye, Glory could see Biddy nod. ''Aye. That he did. But that's not what concerns me today, child.''

Fearing she was turning to stone, so cold was she inside, Glory swallowed the hard lump of truth in her throat and all but whispered, ''Tell me.''

''Smiley says he and the men believe that . . . maybe some of our own neighbors, umm, helped the murdering scum that day with their foul deeds.''

Glory jerked to her feet, sending her chair toppling over backward and skittering across the barewood floor. She leaned stiff-armed over the table, pressing her palms flat onto the tabletop, and peered into Biddy's eyes. ''Are you saying that the Thornes helped murder Mama and Papa?''

Biddy shrank back into her chair, her eyes widening. ''No, child, I don't know that. Neither does Smiley. He only suspects—''

''When did Smiley tell you this?''

Biddy's eyes cut this way and that, then she snapped her fingers when it apparently came to her. She pointed at Glory. ''That day ye and Riley went riding out over the land.''

Glory frowned. ''Why didn't you tell me then?''

Biddy shrugged, shook her head. ''I didn't want to worry ye, child. Ye've so much on yer shoulders as it is. Besides, naught could come of this.''

''And that's the point. Everything *is* on my shoulders. I'm the only Lawless here, so you have to tell me these things. You can't protect me. In fact, Smiley should have come to me with his concerns.''

Then Glory remembered Smiley doing just that—that day in Papa's office after the fire in the barn. And what had she done? Cried to Riley—the very man Smiley was upset with. She put a hand to her mouth in defeat. Then something else jumped into her consciousness. She turned to Biddy. "It couldn't have been the ranchers. There was the Wilton-Humes stationery and the spur like Papa's gang wore. Our neighbors couldn't—"

Biddy held up a cautioning hand. "I made them same points to Smiley. He said he believes only that the other ranchers might know something, might have heard something afterward. And aren't saying."

Glory needed to sit down. Turning around, she retrieved her overturned chair and pulled it up to the table. Sitting heavily, feeling as old as Biddy, she rested her head in her hands. "Land wars. Trackers. Hannah marries a Garrett. Mama and Papa dead. Jacey riding off to Tucson. Someone tries to kill me. Riley Thorne takes off the very next morning. I just don't know how all this is connected."

Feeling as baleful as Skeeter had looked earlier, Glory stared at her grandmotherly nanny. "Is there anything else I need to know? Anything you're keeping from me—something that could sneak up on me and bite me when I least expect it?"

Biddy sat stockstill. Unmoving. Unblinking. "No."

Two days later at dusk, and hard on the heels of Hannah's letter, a package of another sort arrived at the Lawless gates. This one made it no farther than the sentries posted there. The first Glory knew of it was when a knock sounded on the front door, she opened it, and found Heck Thompson standing on the verandah, his hat in his hand.

"Why, hello, Heck." Glory smiled, remembering the man's gratitude when she'd replaced the money stolen from him in the bunkhouse. His craggy face no longer bore the signs of his fistfight with Carter Brown the night before the barn fire of a few weeks back. "What is it?"

"Sorry fer botherin' you, ma'am, but there's a rider here what says he has a parcel for you. He's come all the way from the Arizona Territory with it."

"Arizona?" The word shot fear through Glory. Despite the cold and swirling wind that chilled her skin in the dying day, she felt a dampness under her arms. She clutched at the door-knob, leaning into the door itself. "Send him up to the house."

Heck ducked his beard-stubbled chin. "Yes, ma'am. We done taken his firearms off him, so's you don't have to worry none. And we'll be right outside the door here if you need us."

Grim now with worry, Glory nodded. "Thank you. Just send him up." She stayed at the door, watched Heck sprint back down to the arched gateway. Then, stepping out onto the verandah, she hugged her arms around her waist, a meager defense against the November evening's blustering winds. But she didn't really mind the cold. Or this new rider and whatever news he brought.

Anything was better than aimlessly wandering the house day and night, missing Riley, wanting to see his face, to touch him. Why, more than once she'd found herself in the room he'd slept in and had curled up on his bed. She fancied she could still smell his masculine scent in the sheets, even though Biddy had stripped the bed and replaced the linens.

Worse than missing Riley was the nagging fear that maybe somehow he was guilty in Mama's and Papa's murders. Or of the attack on her. Or the fires and the missing cattle. Or the sabotaged equipment out in the tack room. With that thought came a vicious gust of wind that whipped Glory's hair across her cheeks. She tugged it out of her face, telling herself that the sudden tears in her eyes were from the wind and her hair. And not from missing Riley Thorne. Or worrying about his guilt or innocence.

Glory abandoned her dispirited thoughts when, flanked by Heck and Pops Medley, the lone rider approached the veran-dah. Putting on her best Lawless-in-charge face, she somberly nodded her greeting to the man—boy, actually—who tipped his hat to her. Locking her knees against the fear that he bore bad news about Jacey, that perhaps his parcel contained her belongings—all that was left of her sister—Glory silently waited for him to dismount. Her nails dug into her palms, but she gave away nothing of her inner turmoil.

"You Glory?" the red-haired rider bluntly asked from the bottom of the verandah steps.

"Yes."

Rumpled and dirty under his ankle-length saddle coat, the young man nodded. "You don't look a thing like Miss Jacey. But then I don't reckon that should surprise me none."

Thinking that was a strange thing to say, but more focused on his mention of Jacey, Glory allowed his comment to pass, asking instead, "You know my sister?" Dropping her pose, she hurried to the edge of the verandah, clutched the wood railing, ignoring a few splintery pokes into the soft flesh of her palms. "Is she okay? Is Jacey all right?"

The boy nodded. "She was when I left Tucson a while back." He gestured to his saddlebags. "I got a parcel for you from her." He then looked over his shoulder to the armed and scowling men not too far away, and back at Glory. "I'd like to get it for you, if you think it'd be all right."

Glory waved a dismissal to Heck and Pops. "It's okay." They nodded and turned away, walking back toward the gate. Glory turned her attention to watching this messenger from her sister as he opened his saddlebag and pulled out a slim leather case, no bigger than a good-sized book. Rampant curiosity clouded her features—and got the better of her. "I didn't get your name," she called out.

The young man turned to her. "Name's McGinty. James McGinty. My pa rode with the Lawless Gang for a summer. Rooster McGinty was his name."

Shock and fear warred for the upper hand in Glory's stomach. She knew the name, knew the story of the scared boy who thought he wanted to be an outlaw. And she knew Jacey was in Tucson tracking down the Lawless gang members looking for the one, or ones, guilty of . . . something. At least of stealing. But maybe worse.

And now, here stood the son of a former gang member, saying Jacey sent him. But wait . . . Jacey would never have given away the exact location of her home to anyone she suspected. Nor could that information have been tortured out of her, so stubborn was she. So this James McGinty had to be telling the truth.

"Ma'am, are you all right? You look a might peaked."

Glory exhaled, remembered her manners. "I'm sorry, Mr. McGinty. I'm just cold. Please, come in."

"Call me James, if you would. When you say Mr. McGinty, I expect my grandpa to be behind me with a switch." James's disarming grin even pulled one from Glory's lips. His long legs carried him effortlessly up the wide steps and saw him towering over her on the verandah.

Suddenly at a loss, given the way he was looking at her— the same openly admiring look all men gave her—Glory waved him inside and closed the door behind them. In the polished wood entryway of the great room, lit by the kerosene lamps, she took James's duster and hat, hanging them on the coat rack. She then directed him to the leather couch, motioning for him to sit, which he did. "Can I get you anything to drink?"

Blushing to his roots, he looked her up and down—in a shy, boyish way that amused Glory rather than offended her— and then shook his head no. "I'm fine, thank you. I'm just glad I'm here finally." He then considered his surroundings. "I can't rightly believe I'm actually in J. C. Lawless's house."

Smiling her response, Glory sat on a facing leather chair and folded her hands in her lap, her attention remaining focused on the soft-sided leather case James McGinty still clutched in his hands. Since he didn't seem about to hand it over, she opened with, "I hope I don't sound rude, James, but why did Jacey send you, instead of coming home herself?"

James focused on her once again. "She can't. Kid Chapelo's son took her to Mexico. Some say she's his prisoner."

Glory nearly fainted dead away. She clutched her wingback chair's upholstered armrests. "Did you say my sister's a . . . prisoner?"

James nodded, even grinned, his expression somehow emphasizing the riot of freckles covering his face. "Yes, ma'am. But I wouldn't worry none if I was you. Zant Chapelo may be an outlaw—and a more fearsome one even than his pa— but he's a gentleman when it comes to the ladies.''

Glory blinked. ''James, I'm sorry, but that does not make me feel better.'' All she could think about was how Papa had killed Kid Chapelo about the time she was born. No one ever said why, but she knew that whatever had happened, Papa had quit being an outlaw after that. And now, here Jacey was—in The Kid's son's clutches. And James McGinty didn't think she should worry.

Glory's gaze flickered to the packet in his gloved hands. She pointed to it. ''Is that for me? Did Jacey give you that?''

James jerked the parcel up, as if startled to realize he still held it. He scooted forward on the couch and stood up, leaning over to her with the package held out. ''Oh, yes, ma'am, I plumb forgot—even after riding all this way just to give it to you. I guess I'm still befoozled about being in the Lawless stronghold.''

Glory had no idea what befoozled meant, but figured she probably was feeling somewhat the same thing as she accepted the parcel and held it in her hands. First Hannah's letter two days ago. And now this from Jacey. It could be nothing but bad news. She rubbed her hand over the soft leather of the thong-clasped parcel. Whatever was inside this package was so important that Jacey had sent someone directly here, despite the encroaching winter.

She didn't realize that she'd been quiet so long until James cleared his throat and recaptured her attention. She looked up at him. ''I'm sorry, James. It's just the shock of your being here.'' She held up the package. ''And this. I'm almost afraid to open it.''

''I've ridden quite a ways with it, and it ain't bit me yet.''

Glory laughed at his words—and at herself. ''You're right. I'm being silly.'' But still she didn't want to open it with him here. ''Perhaps you'd like to see to your horse and settle in out at the bunkhouse? You're welcome to stay as long as you like. It's the least I can do.''

James ducked his head. ''I thank you kindly, miss, but I'd best light out for home on the morrow. No telling how long the mountain snows will hold off.'' He turned and indicated the front door. ''You wouldn't mind putting in a good word for me with those men outside, would you? I'd hate to get shot trying to accept your hospitality.''

Glory jumped up. ''Oh, of course not. I'm sorry. We've just had . . . some troubles here. Everyone's edgy.''

''Yes, ma'am. I seen that when I rode in. And I heard tell of the . . . killings here. My grandpa spoke with Señor Estrada about it. I'm right sorry for your losses.''

''Thank you. But who's . . . Señor Estrada?''

''He owns the cantina where Jacey was staying in Tucson.''

''Cantina?''

''Saloon, I guess you'd call it.''

Surprised shock brought Glory's hand to her heart. She glanced towards the kitchen, listening to Biddy's singing and pot-banging. Until this mention of a saloon, she'd been going to call her nanny into the room to meet their visitor. But maybe not just yet. *If Biddy hears of this, I know exactly how the old dear's grave will read: Jacey slept in a saloon. Here lies Biddy Jensen.*

Glory redirected her attention to James, forcing an attentive expression on her suddenly stiff features. ''Jacey stayed in a . . . a saloon?''

James nodded. ''Yes, ma'am. She worked there with Rosie—Señor Estrada's daughter.''

''I see.'' But she didn't. *That darned Jacey. Leave it to her.* ''She worked there? Umm, exactly what did she . . . do in this cantina?''

''Do?'' James frowned at her, but then his face blushed as red as his hair. ''Oh. No . . . uh . . . not *that*. Señor Estrada is a Christian man. He wouldn't allow that . . . not that Miss Jacey wanted to. She tended bar some. Once or twice she did serve the men out on the floor.'' He smiled, then apparently heard his own words because his eyes went hoot-owl round. ''*Drinks.* Served the men drinks. That's all. I swear it.''

Tearing up with embarrassment, Glory cleared her throat, didn't know where to look. But suddenly galvanized by embarrassment, she ushered James to the front door. He snatched up his duster and hat, donning them with all haste. Glory recovered enough to say, "Thank you for coming all this way. I don't know how to repay you."

"Don't worry none about that. Señor Estrada paid me to make the trip. I'm glad to do it."

"Oh. Well, this way then." Glory opened the door and stepped outside, braving yet another gust of freezing wind. Behind her, James stepped outside and pulled the door closed behind himself. Glory signaled to Heck, who sprinted up to her.

"Yes, Miss Glory?"

"Heck, this is James McGinty. He's a guest. You can give him back his guns. And will you see to settling him in at the bunkhouse?"

"Yes, ma'am." Heck turned to James, nodded his greetings. "Get your horse and follow me."

The sound of James's scuffing bootsteps across the verandah and down the low, wide steps made Glory turn to him. "Thank you again, James. We Lawlesses owe you for your kind deed."

James grinned, touched the brim of his floppy felt hat in a parting gesture. "Don't mention it, miss. The way I see it, J. C. Lawless done my pa a favor by making him hate the life of an outlaw. Otherwise, I doubt he'd have lived long enough to marry and have me and my brothers and sisters. I figure we're even now." He stood there a moment longer, looked undecided about something, and then apparently made up his mind to say it. "I'm just sorry about your folks. It must be painful to be orphaned twice over."

Before Glory could absorb that, much less ask him what he meant, James untied his horse from the hitching post and followed after Heck. For long moments, Glory watched his slim, departing back. Finally, hugging Jacey's packet to her chest, she thought to ask herself, *Orphaned twice over? What does that mean?*

Chapter 12

Laura and Seth Parker? Who are these people? And why would Jacey send me the woman's belongings? Laying down the age-yellowed pages, smoothing her hand over the journal's ragged spine, Glory frowned, wondering why the words on these pages brought a lump to her throat. Wondered why she felt a kinship with this long-dead Laura Parker. Wondered why she felt like crying for the woman and her little family. It was all such a mystery. And just like Jacey to present her with one.

Thinking of her sister, Glory picked up Jacey's accompanying letter and reread it. In it, she introduced the young courier, James McGinty, and wrote that Papa had Señor Estrada keep these papers for him all these years. She went on to say, with no further explanation, that she felt Glory should have them. Glory shook her head and huffed out a breath laden with curiosity and frustration—and no small amount of fear for her sister. Because Jacey confirmed James McGinty's words of last evening—she was riding for Mexico with Zant Chapelo, The Kid's son.

Glory looked up from the troublesome words and flopped into a slumping posture that matched her mood. Perched cross-legged atop her bed in her morning-sunshiny bedroom, she stretched, trying to work out the remaining soreness in her muscles from fighting her attacker three nights ago. But it seemed her mind could wander to no place that offered her comfort. Certainly Biddy wouldn't console her once she learned that her precious baby had kept their visitor and this packet a secret from her all last evening.

Glory pushed aside that coming scene and found herself again reading through Jacey's words—which she figured she must've read twenty times between last night and this morning. But still no light had shed itself from her first reading to this one. Because, she admitted, reading Jacey's letter was like talking to her. Abrupt, unemotional, and short on details. Except to echo Hannah with regard to watching out for strangers.

Jacey also wrote of trackers, saying they'd been hired from Tucson, and that she was riding with Zant Chapelo to find out the who and the why of it. *One less thing I have to worry about—Jacey knows about the trackers, so she'll have a care for herself.* Glory put a hand to her thudding heart and stared at the far wall. What a turn their lives had come to, when she couldn't be certain that either of her sisters was alive.

A sigh escaped Glory as she looked around herself at the jumble of letters atop her quilted bedspread. She fingered a sheet or two of age-yellowed writing paper, but didn't realize she'd left her mind open to errant thoughts until . . . *It's too bad that Riley fired Abel Justice and Carter Brown before James McGinty arrived. After all, they're the only two strangers to come around since Mama and Papa were . . . murdered. And James is from Tucson—where Jacey says the trackers were hired. It sure would have been interesting to see if he recognized one—or both—of them. Especially in light of me being nearly killed the other night.*

She allowed that notion free rein, wondering if it was merely a coincidence that Riley and those men left before James arrived. Glory put her hands to her suddenly warm cheeks. She was sitting here casting doubts onto *Riley*, half-believing that he was in cahoots with the two suspicious drifters he'd hired—without consulting her or Smiley.

Glory shook her head, refusing to believe she was even entertaining these thoughts. Because how, she argued with herself, could they have known James was coming? Well, the answer was . . . they couldn't have. Besides, had they known, and if they were guilty, they'd have killed him long before he ever showed up on her doorstep.

A gasp escaped Glory. Her mind seemed determined to point a finger of guilt at Riley. But she refused to believe it. Riley involved with those two men? Why, it was a ridiculous notion. What reason would he have to want her dead? None, of course. *Unless you think about the land feuds, Glory. Remember what Biddy said Smiley told her about the other ranchers?*

Glory clutched at her head, as if she could squeeze out her awful doubts. *Stop it. Riley is not guilty of anything. Think about something else.* Forcing herself to do just that, she spread out the packet's contents over her quilted bedcover and eyed them. She couldn't deny it—they struck a deep chord inside her. In some very personal way. Some way that made her feel sick at heart.

Why couldn't Jacey just tell me why she thought I should have them? Why just me? The more she thought about it, the more frustrated she felt with her sister, and she blurted, "Oooh, I'd give you such a smack if you were here."

"And who is it yer talkin' to, child?"

Her heartbeat leaping at the unexpected sound of Biddy's voice, Glory pivoted on her bed to face the open door. "You startled me. Come in. I was talking to Jacey."

Two steps into the room at Glory's invitation, Biddy stopped, stared at her, and then looked around as if she expected a spirit to be in the room. A hand to her blouse's collar, she ventured, "Jacey, is it? And why would ye be fussing at yer sister?" Not giving Glory a chance to answer that, she pinched up her lips and narrowed her eyes. "Could it have something to do with the young man from Tucson who's eating in me kitchen, even as we speak?"

Guilt brought a smile—a sickly one, she was sure—to Glory's face. "I was going to tell you."

Biddy folded her plump hands over her round, apron-covered middle. "When, pray tell? I'd not know yet if Sour-dough hadn't sent the boy inside for a late breakfast, seein' as how yer tired guest slept through the men's meal. He's askin' if ye have an answer for Jacey's letter. Imagine me surprise upon learnin' he's been here since yesterday evening.''

Glory didn't quite know how to answer all that, so she diverted her nanny's attention with the letters and the journal. ''Well, now you know. Come here. See what you make of these.''

Curiosity apparently getting the better of her insulted snit, Biddy waddled to the bed, her gaze riveted on the papers. ''And what are they?''

''I'm not sure, except for Jacey's letter. One good thing— she knows about the trackers. She writes that they were hired in Tucson.'' Glory hesitated long enough to take a deep breath before telling her nanny, ''And she's on their trail.''

Biddy squawked and clasped her hands together over her heart. ''That darned Jacey. She'll not rest until she gets herself killed. And just ye wait until I get me hands on her, if she does.''

Fighting an ill-timed fit of chuckles, Glory bit down on her bottom lip and reached for the aged letter closest to her. Thinking to distract Biddy from a day-long, pot-banging, house-cleaning tirade brought on by news of Jacey's antics, Glory held it out to her nanny. ''Here. Look at this. I have no idea what it is. Well, I know it's an old letter. But what I don't know is why Jacey would send it to me.''

Her face a mask of curiosity, Biddy took the offered letter and eyed it. ''Well now, let's see what Miss Jacey thinks is so important that she'd send that nice young man downstairs here at this time of year.'' As she ran her gaze over the page, she perched an ample hip on Glory's bed and then sank into a deep—somehow disquieting—quiet. After a moment, she flipped the page over to the signature, read it, and cried out, ''Sweet merciful heavens.''

And then she fainted dead away, slumping off the bed and landing with a bouncing *thunk* on the braided oval rug. Squawking in shocked surprise, Glory jumped up and then knelt beside her nanny. Lifting the older lady's gray-haired head onto her lap, Glory patted her nanny's pale cheek, and cried out, ''Biddy! What happened? What's wrong?''

Nothing. Biddy was out cold. Glory thought frantically—
she needed to get help. But who—? Then it came to her.
James McGinty was downstairs eating. Carefully scooting out
from under Biddy's limp form and grabbing a lacy pillow from
off her bed to place under her nanny's head, Glory scrambled
to her feet, lifted her skirt out of her way, and ran to the door.
Tearing down the hallway to the head of the stairs, she leaned
over the balustrade and called out, "James?! Come quickly.
Biddy's fainted. Hurry!"

Before she could've counted to ten, James's long-legged
bounds had him upstairs and helping her. Glory quickly gathered up the old letters and the journal, set them aside, and then
helped James heft Biddy onto the bed. Leaving him sitting
with the elderly woman, Glory hurried to the water closet at
the hallway's other end. There she wet a facecloth, and in only
moments was back in her bedroom and applying the soft rag
to Biddy's forehead as she roused and thrashed about.

"What brought this on, Miss Glory, if I may ask?" James's
blue eyes were round with apparent concern.

Glory shook her head and coo-cooed to Biddy. "There now,
Biddy dear. Just be still." She then met James's gaze. "I don't
know. I simply asked her to look at these letters Jacey had
you bring me. She took one look, called upon the heavens,
and then fainted dead away. I was hoping you could shed some
light on all this."

His eyes popped open even wider. "Me, ma'am? I don't
rightly know as I could. I cain't read a'tall."

Her hands pressing against Biddy's shoulders to keep her
from falling off the narrow bed, Glory shot James a look.
"Well, perhaps you can tell me what you know from Jacey
and that Mexican saloon owner—"

"You mean Señor Estrada?"

Glory nodded. "I suppose. What do you know about all
this, James?" Before he could answer, Biddy clutched at
Glory's hand, drawing her attention down to her. "Oh, thank
the stars, you're awake. What happened, Biddy?"

Red of face, hair all but undone, Biddy shook her head.
"There's naught he can tell ye, child." Biddy then surprised

Glory with a show of strength that sat her up. She focused a hard expression on young James. "Is there, young man? Ye know nothing."

Completely stumped by this behavior, Glory frowned from Biddy to James, and saw him fidgeting about. He swallowed hard enough to bob his Adam's apple. "Yes, ma'am. I don't know nothing about them papers. I swear it. All's I know is what I've heard all my life about J. C. Lawless and Kid Chapelo—"

A loud snort from Biddy cut off his words. She swung her short, skirt-tangled legs over the side of the bed. Her hands clutched at fistfuls of bedcovers. "And ye'll not go repeatin' idle gossip, now will ye, lad?"

James backed up, as if fearing an attack by the Lawless nanny. "No, ma'am. I shorely won't. My grandpa'd skin me alive, if'n I did."

Biddy relaxed . . . just a bit. "There's a good lad. Now, go on about yer meal. I'm fine. Just a tetch of weakness from climbing the stairs. I'll be along directly, and we'll talk more."

James was already on his way out the door. "Yes, ma'am. But you don't need to hurry none. I've finished my vittles, and my horse is all saddled. I'll just clear on out of yer house." He turned to Glory. "I thank you for yer hospitality, ma'am. You got a reply for Miss Jacey?"

Unable to think straight at the moment, Glory shook her head.

"It's probably just as well that you don't," James said. "Because I ain't about to venture onto Calderon land to deliver it. Well then, I'm headin' out."

"But James," Glory protested, extending a hand to him. "Wait. I want to talk with—"

But James had already rounded the door's casing and disappeared from sight. Out in the hallway, his rapid footfalls, muffled only slightly by the woven runner carpeting the hardwood floor, told their own story—James McGinty was all but running away from Biddy's wrath.

Glory swung her disbelieving gaze back to her nanny.

"Margaret Biddy Jensen, you scared the life out of that young man. What's gotten into you?"

Red-faced and perspiring, Biddy fluffed and pulled at her heavy skirt, and tucked her wispy hair back into its bun. "Nothing."

Downstairs, the front door slammed. Glory put her hands to her waist and gave Biddy an accusing look. "Nothing? That's all you have to say? Why, he *fled* from here. I wanted to ask him about those trackers. Jacey mentions them in her letter, as did Hannah."

A wide-eyed look of relief claimed Biddy's features. "Oh, the trackers. Is that all?"

"Is—?" Glory narrowed her eyes at her nanny. "Is that all? Biddy, those men are *tracking* me and my sisters. They could kill us. And all you can say is 'Oh, the trackers'? I wanted to describe Brown and Justice to James. He might have recognized them both. Or at least one of them."

Biddy blinked a few times. "And if he did, child? What then?"

Glory cast about for an answer. "Why, I suppose we could . . . kill them. Or something."

Biddy sat up straighter, looking more and more sure of herself. "Kill them, is it? And who're ye appointing to do that? Not yerself?"

It was Glory's turn to straighten up. "If I have to. Papa always said a good leader's willing to do the same as he's asking his men to do."

A whoop of disbelief shot out of Biddy. "And will ye look at her—she's a leader of men now. You listen to me, Glory Bea Lawless. Those two drifters are gone from here. And good riddance. I'm glad Riley took them with him when he left. 'Tis not our concern now—"

Glory grabbed Biddy's arm. "What did you say?"

Biddy pulled back, studying Glory's face. "About what?"

Glory tightened her grip. "Don't play coy with me. You said Riley took those men with him, didn't you?"

Her nanny's expression crumpled into eyelash-batting and looking everywhere but at her charge. "Why, I don't know that for sure. They were behind Riley as they rode off in the same direction. But they could've gone their separate ways at any point.''

Glory let go of Biddy and headed for the doorway. ''They didn't. And you know it.''

As Glory turned into the hallway, Biddy called out, ''Where are you going?''

''To the Thorne place. And don't you try to stop me.''

''The Thorne place?'' came Biddy's screech. Heavy, hurrying footsteps told of her pursuit. Indeed, no more than a few steps down the hall, Glory's arm was grabbed and she was spun around. ''Ye cannot go there, child. 'Tis one thing for Riley and his mother to come here, where they're welcomed. But another matter entirely for a Lawless to set foot on Thorne property. No tellin' what might happen.''

''Biddy, let go of me,'' Glory warned. ''I'm going, and I'll be fine. No Thorne's ever hurt any Lawless before.''

Biddy took a deep breath, closed her eyes, and opened them again. ''Aye, 'tis true enough, they haven't. But the Lawlesses have injured the Thornes. Think of the old man's crippled leg. And think on this—yer father's not here to protect ye and to make them think twice. Besides, there's talk of—''

''The land feud. I know. I'll be careful—I swear it. I just want to talk to Riley. I have no intention of losing my temper and shooting anyone.''

More than three hours later, and nearing the dividing line between Lawless and Thorne properties, Glory reined in her chestnut mare, stared at the unbelievable words scrawled on the crude wooden sign stuck into Lawless dirt, and thought back to her parting words to Biddy. *I have no intention of losing my temper and shooting anyone.*

The unusually warm and windless day seemed to pale as she sat there staring, absorbing. Someone—no doubt a Thorne—had proclaimed this land to be Thorne property. As the shock of discovery melted away, an aching sickness of the heart had Glory's hands shaking. Surely, the merest gust of wind could blow her off Daisy. As if the mare read her mistress's thoughts, she stomped a foot, signaling her impatience. Glory tightened her grip on the reins, glared at the contentious property marker, and dismounted.

Thorne land? We'll just see about that. She stalked over to the sign and two-handedly gripped the wooden stake, much as she would someone's throat. Then, with grunting effort and much pushing and pulling, she finally exerted enough temper and strength to yank the hated sign up out of the hard ground and heave it as far as she could.

She watched the marker hit the ground and slide—words down—into a dry gully. A smile of grim satisfaction narrowed her eyes. With that—and once her breathing returned to normal—she mounted Daisy and rode hard for the Thorne place.

Only when their homestead loomed into view did she slow her mare. Then, steeling her courage with a deep breath and a check of her sheepskin-coat pocket for her pistol, Glory guided Daisy into enemy territory. Past the weathered corral, the red barn, the wagon yard. Right to the front door, where she reined in. Immediately, the door opened. Glory's grip on the reins tightened as she waited to see who was coming out to greet her.

Mr. Thorne and his four younger sons stepped outside and, in watchful silence, ranged themselves across the front porch. Zeke, John, Caleb, and Henry. As Glory looked them over, she experienced the strangest feeling, as if she were seeing Riley at different stages of his growing-up years. When she settled her gaze on Henry, she noted that he bore the bruises and swellings of a recent fight. Then she nodded to Ben Thorne. "Morning, Mr. Thorne. I'm looking for Riley."

"He ain't here." With that, Ben stepped to the edge of the porch and spat in the dirt, right in front of Daisy.

Stiffening with shocked offense, Glory forced herself to look directly into the older man's eyes, so much like Riley's that it hurt. "I see. Well then, can I speak with Mrs. Thorne? I've come a long way—"

"I know exactly how far you've come from your place to mine, young'un. Now just turn that horse of yours around and get off my land. Ain't no one hereabouts that wants to speak with you."

Despite her roiling guts and sweating palms, Glory kept on. "Perhaps I could speak with Mrs. Thorne?"

"Mrs. Thorne ain't at home. She's over to the Sutfields. Will be all day."

After that, except for a shifting of weight or the occasional sniff from one of the sons or their father, no one said anything. Glory exhaled a breath laden with defeat and no small amount of fright. "All right. Well, I'll just be going then. Tell them I came by, please."

The men said nothing, gave no sign that they'd relay her message. Quirking her mouth, Glory edged Daisy into turning around. But her next thought had her reining the mare. Once again, she faced the tall, white-haired man that was Ben Thorne. "I'll thank you not to put up signs on my property. I took down the one I found on the way here. When I get home, I'll be sending my men out to ride the line and look for more. Let's hope they don't find any."

Her words had the Thornes standing tall, looking ready to reach for their guns. Wondering if what gripped her belly was sadness for this turn of events or smugness for having stirred a reaction from them, Glory kneed Daisy, turning the mare back the way they'd just come. Showing the Thorne men her back, she nudged her horse into a canter that quickly gained them the safety of the open prairie. Only then did she give in to a hateful thought. *Darned Thornes. Riley and his mother are the only ones worth a—*

Two men, not too far away and laboring over a fence post two hilltops away, caught Glory's attention. Their hobbled horses grazed nearby. Glory's breath hung in her throat. She wrenched back on the reins, bringing Daisy to a dust-raising halt. The men straightened up, stared right at her. Saw her. Exchanged a look with each other.

Glory knew in her heart she should put her heels to Daisy and send her flying over the ground for the safety of the Lawless holdings. But she couldn't move. All she could do was stare at Carter Brown and Abel Justice, working on Thorne land. Finally, she wrenched around in her saddle and stared back in the direction she'd just come. It was true, then, all the talk she'd heard from Biddy and Smiley. The Thornes were somehow behind the trouble at home.

That thought, when no other one could, galvanized Glory. She spared the two men another look, saw they hadn't moved any, but still felt a need for speed and distance. Digging her boot heels into Daisy's tired sides, she urged the little mare into a gallop. Glory kept the mare's hooves flying over the hard, uneven ground until she outran her panic. Only then, and knowing she had to spare the animal or end up on foot when the mare's heart gave out, did Glory slow her to a canter and then a walk. Belatedly, she realized she'd reined Daisy at the exact spot where earlier she'd uprooted that property marker.

In a heartsick cold sweat that sickened her stomach, Glory slid off Daisy and collapsed onto the hard ground. Sitting in the billowing heap of her skirt, she cried. Just sat there, holding Daisy's reins, hearing the mare blow, feeling the horse's hot breath in her hair, and cried. Great, wrenching sobs with fat, hot tears. Not caring about passing time. Or the sun's path in the clear sky. Not caring about anything but the agonizing hurt in her heart.

"Glory?"

With a startled gasp, she twisted around, saw who was standing there, and took another moment to absorb that it was really him. She swiped at her eyes and rubbed her sleeve under her runny nose. "Leave me alone, Riley Thorne."

But he didn't. "I just came from home. My father said you'd been there, that you asked for me."

"I did."

"What'd you want?"

Glory sniffled, shook her head, watched him threading his horse's reins through his gloved fingers. Looking at him was painful, so she looked down at her skirt. "It doesn't matter now."

She heard Riley huff his breath out, heard him mutter, "Dammit." Then to her he said, "It matters to me."

Glory looked up at him, challenging him. "Does it?" But

her heart thumped with his flesh-and-blood nearness, with his air of belonging to this land, to owning this very patch he stood upon . . . and in a way that she, as a woman, would never be able to claim. "I was just told to get off Thorne land."

He firmed his lips together and then said, "I know."

Glory raised her chin. "Then you'll also know I mean it when I tell you to get off Lawless land. You're standing on it now—no matter what your . . . *damned* sign said. So if you're out here looking for it, I threw it in that ditch."

Riley eyed her from under the brim of his Stetson. Then he pivoted, billowing his ankle-length saddle coat, to glance back at the depression she indicated. Finally, and trailing Pride behind him, he came to her and squatted in front of her . . . near enough for her to push him over, if she so chose. "I don't care about any sign. I'm out here because of you. I want to know what's wrong."

His question was so absurd that she could only chuckle. "What's wrong? Look around, Riley. Look what I'm doing. And where I'm doing it. A better question would be what's right."

Riley tilted his Stetson back on his head and narrowed his brown eyes at her. "All right. What's right?"

Glory tilted her head in consideration of this Thorne man and his question. Reflected sunlight dappled his dark eyes with golden flecks, emphasized his wide, firm mouth. She took a deep, chest-expanding breath and slumped further into her heaped posture. "There's nothing right, Riley. Not in this world. Not where I live."

Remaining quiet, offering no solutions, he merely nodded, suggesting by his frowning stare that he was giving due consideration to her words.

And that annoyed her to no end. How dare he be so . . . so understanding, so reasonable? Without warning, and releasing Daisy's reins, Glory shoved Riley back onto his butt. His long legs jerked out in front of him, raising dust and Cain as he yelled and cussed out his shock. Pride startled, whinnied out his shock, and jerked back against Riley's hold on his reins.

Beyond caring, Glory leaped onto Riley's chest and, with

doubled-up fists, began pounding on him. "I hate you, Riley Thorne! Do you hear me? I hate you. How dare you hire those two men? How could I have trusted you, how could I have let you in my house?"

Caught off guard by Glory's attack, Riley lost his Stetson and his grip on Pride's reins. The panicked horse bucked wildly, mere death-dealing inches away. Crabbing sideways on his back, trying to take them out of range of Pride's sharp hooves—and praying the animal shied in the opposite direction—Riley captured her wrists and bellowed, "Dammit, Glory, you're about to get us killed."

"Don't you dammit-Glory me, Riley Eugene Thorne. I will never forgive you. How *dare* you make me love you, you—" She froze in position atop him. Surprise flared in her green eyes, widening them as she stared down at him and finished, "You . . . bad man, you."

Aware that Pride chose that moment to bolt away, but more concerned with the feel of her weight atop him, with her breasts pressed against his chest, with the look on her sweaty little face, framed as it was by her rat's-nest hair, and with her words, Riley took a moment to catch his own breath. Then he encouraged, "I'm listening. Go on. You were saying—"

"You shut up." Glory wrenched herself free of his grip and inched down his length until she was between his spread legs. There she pulled herself up to her skirt-covered knees, rested her hands atop them, and glared. Her shoulders, under her heavy sheepskin coat, rose and fell with each rapid breath.

Riley hoisted himself up onto his elbows and returned her look for look. He'd waited his whole life to hear her say she loved him, and now she had—while kicking his ass. Suddenly, his heart soared—with joy, with love for her, and at these ridiculous circumstances. He grinned. And then chuckled. And then laughed out loud, throwing his head back.

"There's not one danged thing funny about this," Glory fussed as, a hand pressing down on each of his thighs, she levered herself to her feet.

Riley knew he'd better not let her get away. So, almost

before she was on her feet, he was on his. And standing in front of her, gripping her shoulders. "I love you, too, Glory Bea Lawless."

When she opened her mouth—no doubt to protest—he wrenched her resisting body against his and claimed her mouth. A muffled squawk accompanied her stiffening in his arms. But kissing her now, Riley was lost. She tasted so damned good, even gritty and salty like she was. Tasted like the earth itself. The inside of her mouth was warm and slick . . . and hungry. Riley deepened their kiss and she began to yield to him. But again she stiffened, warning him with a gradual clamping down of her teeth—

Riley jerked his head back and stared down into her anger-puckered face. "You don't have to do that, Glory. All you've got to do is tell me. Tell me you don't want me to kiss you, and I *will* stop. Just say the words."

Tears sprang to her green and glaring eyes, her kiss-moistened mouth twisted, and her chin dimpled. But Riley's words, delivered in a voice huskied with want, hung in the air, remained unchallenged as she kept her silence.

"Well? Tell me to stop. Tell me you don't want me." He tightened his grip on her arms. "If you don't say the words, I'm going to see this through to its end. I've never felt before like I could tell you, but I love you, Glory, and I want you. You're in my blood, like a river carving out a valley in my soul. So if you think you're going to tell me you love me and then just walk away, you're crazy."

She shook her head and slumped in his grip. "I have to walk away, Riley. Don't you see? I can't love you. I just can't. You're a Thorne. And I'm a Lawless. Our families would never allow it."

Her words were a knife piercing his skin, stabbing through muscle, embedding themselves in the bone underneath. "I'm a twenty-five-year-old man, Glory. I don't give a damn what my family thinks. All I think about, all I care about, is you. You're all I've *ever* wanted. You're the only reason I've hung around this godforsaken no-man's-land all these years. I've just been waiting on you to grow up. And now you have."

Riley's heart sank when Glory shook her head, swirling her reddish-brown and tangled curls about her face and shoulders. "Don't say these things to me, Riley, please. It's so hard. I *have* to think of my family. Don't you see that? I'm a Lawless. Maybe even the last one alive. It's up to me to keep the ranch going. It's my parents' dream. My sisters'. Mine. I care, and I'm not leaving it."

Her words cooled Riley's blood, settled it in his veins. But hardened his soul. He released her and stepped back. "All my life I've heard the land comes first. And maybe it does. I've watched my father trying to hang onto it. I've stood by while it twisted his soul, Glory. I don't want to be like that. And I wasn't asking you to leave. I just wanted you to put me first, like I have you. But you can't. And it's right sorry I am for that."

Through saying his piece, Riley turned away, going to retrieve his Stetson. The intense quiet of the oppressive prairie settled over him, etching his features with disappointment as he bent over and snatched his hat up off the ground. He hit it against his thigh to shake the dust loose, and then reformed it with cutting motions of his hands. Finally, he fit it to his head and turned back to Glory. She hadn't moved or said or done anything to stop him from leaving.

Adding that hurt to his belly full of emotions, Riley suddenly blurted, "That land you care so much about doesn't give a damn about you, girl. It won't keep you warm at night. It won't give you those babies you want. And it sure as hell won't hold you in its arms in that big old chair in your daddy's office and promise you that everything's going to be okay."

Glory flinched. He saw it, but refused to muster any sympathy for her. With one long, last stare, he turned his back on her and headed for his horse.

"Riley?"

He stopped, didn't turn to look at her. "What?"

"Kiss me."

A shuddering breath escaped him. He put his hands to his waist, bent a knee, and stared out over the tan-brown and rolling hills of the Lawless holdings. And thought about what she'd just said. Then he spoke over his shoulder. "No."

"Yes. Kiss me. I want you to."

"This isn't a game, Glory. It's forever."

"I know. Kiss me."

"There's no stopping. No going back."

Silence. And then, "Kiss me."

His heart pounded, urged him to turn around. His legs and feet were already doing just that. Feeling like so much stone on the outside, but fluttering like a wind-borne feather on the inside, afraid to believe, more afraid not to, Riley faced her, narrowed his eyes. "You understand what this means? I want more than your kisses. I want all of you—your heart and your soul. Nothing less."

Glory never looked away from him as she jerked her father's heavy coat off and flung it to the ground. "I told you to kiss me, Riley Thorne."

Still . . . Riley hesitated, glancing at J. C. Lawless's coat lying in a lifeless heap on the cold, hard ground. Just like the man himself. The thought unnerved him. He sought Glory's gaze, saw her Lawless chin come up a notch. No—she wasn't a Lawless. What would she do when she found out? Would her spirit be crushed? Probably.

But maybe not—not if she had someone at her side to help her through. And by God, that someone was going to be him. She was offering, and he was taking. Out of love. Not hatred or bitterness. But love.

It was that simple. Riley chuckled, ducked his head in sudden embarrassment. He'd never had a woman seduce him before. Hell, he'd never had a woman kick his ass before, either. But he'd survived that, hadn't he? Hands again to his waist, his knee bent, Riley grinned at her. "Say it one more time, sweetheart."

Glory shifted her weight, looked uncertain. But then that stubborn chin came up. "Kiss me."

Riley ripped his hat off and sent it flying in the cool but windless November air. With long-legged, determined strides, he advanced on her. "Baby, I'm going to kiss you and one hell of a whole lot more."

Chapter 13

Glory had no time to think before Riley was upon her and holding her, kissing her. His arms slipped around her back, pulled her closer against his muscled length. Faint with wanting him, and not quite understanding the hot, pricking sensations happening inside her, things Riley caused with his nearness, with his kiss, she surrendered to his touch. And realized she could do that because she trusted Riley. Trusted him not to hurt her, not to betray her. Not to take more than she could give.

Riley broke his kiss. He pulled back enough to stare down into her face. "I've waited years for you, Glory. For this moment. I just hate that it's out here, out in the open like this. I wanted it to be special, to be something more . . ." His voice trailed off. He smiled, his expression baring his heart.

Glory reached up and stroked her hand down his tanned and smooth cheek. "It is special, Riley. It's wonderful. Because it's you."

She watched the effect her words had on this strong, strong man. Clutching at her hand, holding it to his mouth, kissing her palm, he closed his eyes, his mouth quirked into a tender line. His expression suggested he savored her words, as if each one were a treasure he could never recapture after this moment. As if this were his only chance to enjoy them.

Warmed to her core, despite the day's coolness, despite not having on Papa's coat anymore, Glory tugged her hand from his and slipped her arms under his duster and around his back. She then lay her head against Riley's chest. Even through the thickness of his flannel shirt and underlying combination suit, she could hear, could feel his heart beating right under her cheek. "Oh, Riley, I do love you."

Riley stirred, tensed. "Oh, damn, Glory," was all he said, his words no more than a husky whisper sighing off his lips. His arms encircling her more fully, he said, "I've got to feel you in my arms."

"I want that, too," Glory heard herself saying. "I want you."

Riley smoothed his hands around to her arms and held her away from him, looked down into her eyes. "Nothing and no one will ever stand between us again. I swear it to you right here, right now." With those words, and with suddenly feverish motions, Riley kissed her again with all the fierce longing for her that Glory knew he'd harbored for years.

Almost overcome with his intense passion, with his hands roving hard and fast over her body, as if her clothes were no barrier to his touch, she felt a faintness settle in her knees. And a hot heaviness in the vee of her legs. A throbbing pulse burned in her secret woman's place. The hurting ache of it, she somehow knew, could only be quenched by Riley's touch, his kiss. And so she put everything she felt into returning his kiss, into dueling with his tongue, into opening herself fully to his onslaught.

Riley broke away, breathing rapidly, staring down at her with an intensity she found both frightening and exciting. That she'd have this effect on such a man as Riley, one so normally cool and distant, so quiet and remote, was astounding to her. And very heady. Feeling suddenly wanton, wanting to make him feel more, Glory stunned even herself by beginning to unbutton her blouse. All without a word. And without breaking eye contact with him.

Riley watched her a moment, sucked in a breath, let it out in a shuddering ripple, and stood helplessly before her. Glory smiled . . . an ancient smile of female knowledge, of female conquering. "Make our bed, Riley."

Blinking—and not from anything to do with the warm beating down of the sun in his eyes, Glory suspected—Riley became a galvanized blur of activity. He all but ripped off his duster and spread it at her feet. Papa's coat was added to the nest. Riley then feathered it with his heavy flannel shirt. With hurried, fumbling motions of her own, Glory shed her blouse and fluttered it atop his shirt. Riley muttered a heated something as he stared at her. Then he frowned. "Are you cold, sweetheart?"

Glory nodded, hugged herself. Riley stepped over their makeshift bed and took her in his arms. "Let me warm you." And then he proceeded to do just that with the kisses he trailed over her jaw, her neck, across her shoulder, and down her chemise-covered chest. A shuddering gasp from Glory brought his head up, his dark eyes staring into hers. "Come with me." He pulled her down with him onto the bed he'd prepared for her atop a hill on Lawless land.

Lying in his arms, feeling his weight pressing into her, Glory closed her eyes, surrendering her will. Whatever he wanted from her was his. But she had no words to say what abided in her heart. She could only show him the way there. Marveling that she was unafraid, she flattened her palm against his chest, against the fabric of his combination suit, and smoothed her fingers under the unbuttoned neck, feeling for herself the warm, hard muscle there. The pulsing between her legs ticked off an aching beat, tore words from the depths of her soul. "I want you, Riley."

And those words were all it took. Riley tipped his forehead to hers and took several breaths. "All right, baby. All right."

In only moments, there were no clothes between them. No stitched fabric to hide behind. In only moments, they were as God made them. With His world as their witness, with the wind through the waving tallgrass as their music, with the sun shining its warm approval, with their horses grazing afar, Glory and Riley learned each other's bodies. And deepened their love.

Naked, long of frame, hard of muscle, and warm of skin, Riley covered Glory with his protective length, sheltering her in his embrace. His hands—so square and fine and capable—slipped over her skin, gliding like a soft wind over the peaks and valleys of her woman's body. Under his touch, she ached and arched, tossed and rippled. Riley bent his head to capture a nipple, even as his hand cupped the fullness of her virgin breast.

A cry rang from Glory when Riley's lips closed over her peaked flesh. She clutched spasmodically at his arms. Riley raised his head, looked with hooded eyes into her face. Glory felt the blaze of pain that was desire, that was lusting at its most beautiful. She needed this man, like she needed air, like she needed food. Like she needed love. Riley smiled down at her, seemed to sense these new and strong emotions tearing at her.

All while looking into her eyes, he smoothed his hand down her belly and cupped her femininity. Glory sucked in a breath and clutched at his wrist. Riley bent to whisper into her ear, kiss her neck, her cheek, her eyes . . . and moved his fingers. Stroking the slick and velvet folds of her desire, Riley softened her resistance, kept whispering to her, telling her of her beauty, of his love. Until Glory opened to him.

But it was Riley who made the noise at the back of his throat. Who reared his head back, his face reflecting the rapt pleasure he felt at pleasing her. Glory wanted to please him in return. But she didn't know how. As if he'd read her mind, Riley looked down at her under him and said, "Touch me."

A frown of confusion mirrored her lack of experience, of know-how. Riley smoothed his hand—that same hand which only a moment ago had her centered in its palm—smoothed his hand up her belly, captured her hand and placed it against his hard length. Glory gasped, her eyes widened. Riley smiled a deep and tender smile down at her. "It won't bite."

Glory lowered her gaze to his throat, caught her bottom lip between her teeth. A different heat, different from the hot, aching one of desire, suffused her cheeks. She absorbed the feel of him in her hand, allowed herself a moment to get used to this new sensation. And found she could make him gasp . . . if she only moved her feather-soft touch over him, up and down him. She chanced a look up into his face. Oh, he liked this.

After only a moment of stroking, Riley pulled her hand away, kissed her fingers, and pulled her arms up over her head as he lay himself across her and settled his hips in the saddle of hers. "Bend your knees, sweetheart. Wrap your legs around me."

Without thought or hesitation, Glory did just that. She marveled at the feel of him against her. He was so finely formed, so hard and handsome, so tender with her. He pressed himself against her, released her hands, and smoothed her hair back from her face as he captured her mouth with his, sipping hungrily of her. Glory's belly contracted with need, with a burning ache that nearly had her mad with desire. Breaking their kiss, she tossed her head impatiently, dug her nails into Riley's shoulders. "Please," she cried out, not even knowing for what she asked.

Riley kissed the tip of her nose and chuckled. "It might hurt."

Glory opened her eyes and poked out her bottom lip. "It hurts now. Do something."

Riley laughed out loud. Glory felt his belly laugh against her own abdomen. His muscles contracted and rippled over her softness. "Yes, ma'am. I aim to please."

With that, he began sliding himself inside her. Glory gasped, tensing. Riley stopped, looked deep into her eyes. "This is what you want, honey. This is what you're asking me to do. It'll make the hurt go away."

Glory blinked, felt dangerously close to tears, even closer to telling him no. She shook her head. Riley again soothed and aroused her with his whispered words in her ear, with his hot and trailing kisses down her neck. The tingling sensations he produced in her . . . so much lower down caused her to buck against him and tighten her muscles. Riley groaned, tensed . . . and slid in a little more. "You're so tight, baby. So wet inside."

Glory sucked in a breath—and Riley buried himself inside her. Glory went rigid, her eyes wide open, staring at the clear blue sky above them. It hurt. It hurt a lot. But she refused to whimper, to cry out. Instead, she bit down on her lip, felt certain she tasted her own blood. Riley looked down at her, seemed to understand. "It will never hurt again, sweetheart. Only good things now. You'll feel only the good things. I swear it."

Bravely, tearfully, Glory nodded, willed her chin to stop quivering. Riley placed a tender kiss there, rubbed his thumb over the dimpling flesh. "Don't cry. Just love me."

Glory wrapped her arms around his neck, mimicking her legs around his hips. "I do, Riley. Show me how."

And then Riley showed her. He rocked his hips against hers, using long, slow strokes that seemed to have a clutching end, a spur of hot, hot intensity at the end of each one, before retreating . . . only to do it again. After only a moment of this, Glory could take no more. She answered him in kind, moving under him, arching into him, until he made a guttural sound and picked up the pace to an excruciatingly agonizing one that wound Glory tighter and tighter, until she felt certain she would burst with wanting him.

And then, she broke, flowering into a shudder of ripples that paralyzed her in position, that threw her head back, and brought forth a sound from her that she'd never made before, a sound driven from her soul to echo in the cool November air all about them. Riley drove relentlessly into her, only increasing her pleasure, only killing her more and more . . . until he too went rigid over her. Until he too cried out and froze, poised above her. For an eternity.

Slowly, the shuddering ripples between them subsided. Brought them back to earth. Finally, Riley released himself from his position and collapsed atop her. Glory welcomed his sheltering weight, reveled in the feel of his warm, slick body atop hers. Knew then that she was on this Earth to love this man. She loosened her grip on his neck and his hips, felt limp with pleasure, fulfilled with his loving. "I never . . . knew, Riley. Never."

He dragged himself up on an elbow and grinned down at her. Glory's heart tripped over itself at the picture of male satiation he made. His face a heightened color, his teeth so white in his grin, a lock of black hair trailing over his forehead, his dark eyes dancing. "I know," he said.

Suddenly overwhelmed with the enormity of what she—they—had just done, with what had passed between them, the terrible intimacy, Glory turned her face away from his.

But Riley would have none of that. He gently tugged on her chin until she was forced to look up into his face. "Hey, you, I love you. What we did is good and right. Don't you go being ashamed."

"I'm not. I just—We're not—Oh, Riley, I'm getting cold."

The look he gave her told her plainly enough that he knew there was more to her feelings than what she'd admit. But he didn't press her. "All right."

With that, he slipped out of her and then off her. The sudden rush of cold air between their bodies brought home to Glory, more than anything else, the finality of their act. She was no longer an innocent. She'd just been initiated into womanhood. There was no going back. Only forward.

Riley stood up, perfectly at ease with his nudity. Glory's breath caught in her throat, her cheeks burned. He was . . . such a man. A glorious man, from his broad shoulders and tapering waist, to his muscled hips and down his long legs. And he was hers. A sudden stab of ownership, of possessiveness, entered Glory's heart. Riley Thorne was hers.

Just then, he leaned over her, held a hand out to her. Glory took it without hesitation, allowing him to bring her to her feet. He pulled her into his arms, holding her as close to his warmth as he could. Glory held him full-length to her, felt fulfilled by how perfectly they fit together in each other's arms. She closed her eyes. If only they could stay like this forever. But in only moments, the coldness of the afternoon skies forced her away from the comfort of Riley's arms. He looked down at her. "We better get dressed. You're a long way from home yet."

Feeling strangely out of place, out of time, Glory nodded

and stepped away. Turning, flinching in surprise at the soreness in her muscles, she sought her underthings. Spying them tangled at the foot of their bed of clothing, Glory squatted down to retrieve them. And gave a startled gasp at what she saw smeared on her thigh. "Riley, there's blood. I think we did something wrong."

Just then skinning into his combination suit, Riley stopped and stared at her. A slow grin spread over his face. "No, darling, we did everything right. There's always a little blood the first time."

"There is?" Then, Glory tilted her head questioningly at him. "How come you know so much about . . . these things? Who—? I mean, where did you—?"

Riley cleared his throat, looked everywhere but at her, and hurriedly stretched into his underdrawers, buttoning the one-piece suit up as he went. "Let's just say I misspent my trips up into the Kansas cattle towns—and leave it at that, shall we?"

Glory jerked her head down, stared at her coarse brown skirt and white blouse atop Riley's saddle coat, blinking through the white-hot tears of absolute embarrassment that reminded her she was squatting there as naked as the day she was born. *Riley's done this with other women.* That knowledge hurt to the bone, made her angry. Quickly she gathered up her clothes, donning her chemise and blouse and skirt with more ferocity than was called for.

Riley didn't say anything else. And it was just as well, she decided. Only when she was fully dressed, down to her stockings, lace-up boots, and the sheepskin coat, did she look over at him. He was dressed too, and reaching for his duster. That same streak of possessiveness fisted Glory's hands. "I don't want you doing that ever again."

Riley froze, but then straightened up slowly, shooting her a look of wariness. His knuckles, clutched around his coat, were white. "Do what?"

"This." Glory pointed to the ground where they'd just lain together. "With any other woman but me. Ever. Promise me."

Riley's mouth worked—Glory suspected around a grin. And

she knew he'd better not. Lucky for him, he didn't. Getting appropriately sober, he nodded. "I promise. I'll only make love with you."

Make love. Glory liked the sound of that, but she wasn't through with him. "For the rest of your life."

Riley darned near lost his battle with that grin. "For the rest of my life. Or how about just yours, in case you die before me?"

Glory stiffened. Then with a shriek, she launched herself at him. But he caught her handily under her arms and spun her around and around. This time, Glory's shriek was one of dizzy laughter. Finally Riley lowered her to her feet and held her against him. With her cheek pressed against his shirt's button, with her arms around his broad back, and warmed by his love, Glory felt all things were possible. Even a Lawless loving a Thorne.

Riley watched Glory ride away from him. Well, he'd lost that argument. Here he stood while she rode for home. He still felt the need to accompany her as far as shouting distance of the Lawless main house, just so he could know she was safe. But no, she'd shown him her pocket pistol and said she'd be fine— after all, she was on Lawless land. The pointed look she'd given him with those words made her position clear. So here he stood, alone with his horse and his guilt.

Guilt was a terrible thing. Weighed a man down. Again, he saw her as she'd looked only moments ago. Her sobering expression as she sat mounted on Daisy and looking down at him. The consequences were beginning to set in, he could tell. Second thoughts. Maybe even regret. Doubt, probably.

Riley slumped, shaking his head. Why in the hell had he allowed their lovemaking to happen? Before this afternoon, before he'd ever tasted her sweetness, he might have been able to keep his distance, to live his life without her. In the long run, that's what she wanted. She hated that she loved him. She'd as much as said it—today and every other day.

But now? Well, for one thing, he wanted to kick his own butt for thinking with the wrong head. But beyond that, now that he'd known her, had claimed her as his own, his life was going to be pure hell. Because he'd never let her go. Riley quirked a grin. He couldn't let her go—he'd promised not to make love to any other woman except her ever again. And he wasn't about to give up lovemaking.

A sober voice in his head reminded him that there was nothing funny about this situation. Riley's grin faded with his next thought. As much as he loved Glory, as soul-satisfying as the experience had been, why had he made love to her? Afraid of the real answer, afraid he'd hear that voice saying it was for all the wrong reasons, that it only made things worse—which he already knew, even if Glory, in her innocence—didn't, Riley turned his back on his conscience and sought out Pride. *May as well get home myself. I can't set her world to rights, but I can deal with my own kin.*

Feeling the tug of two worlds, of two loyalties, and thinking if he was smart, he'd ride away from them both, Riley spied his horse grazing in the shallow ditch, the same one where Glory had tossed his father's sign. Shaking his head, Riley whistled, caught the gray gelding's attention. Pride raised his head, ears pricked forward, and stared. Riley put his hands to his waist and called out, "Just come here. I don't need any looks from you."

Pride bared his big teeth and neighed his opinion of that, even as he plodded toward Riley, who felt compelled to mutter, "Yeah, I know. What else can I do to you—I've already gelded you. And the more Glory thinks about what just happened here, the more likely I am to join you."

Later that afternoon, with her home in sight, Glory reined in Daisy atop the very hill from which she'd last seen Jacey. Sitting there, aching from the unaccustomed activity with Riley and then this bruising ride home, she stared down on the Lawless stronghold. *So, this is what Jacey saw right before she rode away.* Glory swept her gaze across the bustling expanse of her family's home. Men going in and out of the barn, some leading horses, some toting their saddles. A stray kitten and a strutting rooster roamed the dirt-packed yard.

Fearing her heart would burst with the rush of love and with the compelling sense of ownership for all that she saw, Glory took a deep breath in and exhaled, feeling gripped suddenly by the fear that she was losing it all. The big, two-storied main house, the wagon yard, the barns, the grazing lands, the cattle. The family cemetery out back.

It seemed to her, sitting there astride Daisy, that time rushed forward, leaving her facedown in its path. As if all this land, these people she loved, were beyond her grasp. How could she ever keep it all together? Surely, loving Riley Thorne was a betrayal of all that Mama and Papa had built here, all that they stood for. No one need tell her there would be consequences.

Raising a hand to cover her mouth, Glory closed her eyes, squeezing them shut against the images of herself moving against Riley, against the images of the land spread out now below her, against the images of her sisters' faces as they'd made their blood pact to avenge their parents' murders. Feeling suddenly ill, she opened her eyes and moved her hand to her stomach as she took another deep breath to calm herself.

She was feeling these things today, she tried to convince herself, because of making love with Riley. *Making love.* What gave her the right to be out making love—with Riley Thorne, no less? Well, it was too late for that. She was changed now. Forever. A woman like she'd never been before. And of course she shouldn't be surprised that such a life-changing event would make a mishmash of her thoughts and her tummy.

It was that, and nothing else. But she didn't believe it, even as she thought it. Even as she urged Daisy down the hill's slope, even as she saw the men posted at the gate come to attention when they spotted her. Even as she felt the tears spilling over her lashes and running down her cheeks. She'd betrayed her family. And her inheritance.

Glory just didn't see how anything worse, in the whole rest of her life, could ever happen to her. Nothing she could ever do or learn or experience could be worse than this sense of betrayal of her family. She loved a Thorne—Papa's worst enemy. Glory hung her head. She didn't deserve to bear the name of Lawless.

Chapter 14

It's been two days now since Glory's taken to her bed, Biddy reflected as she grabbed up her shawl, knotted it over her bosom, and headed for the door at the back of the kitchen, *Enough is enough.* Taking the porch's wooden steps one at a time, tempering her determination with her bulk, she looked this way and that about the dirt-brown, wind-gusted yard. No Smiley Rankin.

Why could a man never be about when you needed him? At any other time, he was underfoot. Holding a stray wisp of gray hair out of her eyes, she pursed her lips. Perhaps he'd be in his office. Heading in that direction, her fear for her baby's state of mind forcing a frown to her face, Biddy fumed anew over Glory's traipsing over to the Thorne place and them sending her packing. *Why, the girl's will to live threatened to drain right out with her tears.* The nanny's worried thoughts carried her to the foreman's office door, which she wrenched open.

Inside, Smiley sat bent over some bit of leather he worked with a nasty-looking tool. His head popped up when Biddy breezed in. She barely hid her moment of pleasure at the heightened color that stained the man's cheeks and at how he jumped up, dropping his work and swallowing hard, when he saw her. Dragging a hand over his balding head, as if to straighten hair no longer residing there, he stammered out, "Miz Biddy. I'm right pleased to see you . . . ma'am."

Biddy caught herself already in a girlish simper and put a

hand to her fluttering heart. "Mr. Rankin. Am I interruptin' ye? I've a matter of some importance to speak with ye about, if I may."

"My time is yours." With that, Smiley rushed around the desk, banging his thigh against an edge, grimacing and limping now, but managing to drag a chair out from under its pile of papers and bridles and over to the desk for her. He ripped his bandanna out of his pocket and dusted the seat, and then gestured for her to be seated. "If you've a mind to set a spell, I'd be most pleased."

As if a grand lady in a ballroom, Biddy ducked her chin in acceptance of his invitation and flounced herself over to the chair. She perched her weight delicately on its edge. After carefully arranging her everyday coarse skirt into attractive folds about herself, she folded her plump, age-spotted hands in her ample lap. And waited for Mr. Rankin to sit again in his chair and give her his attention. Only then did she broach her subject. Taking a deep breath, she delved in. "I've come to speak with ye regarding my Glory. Only she's not really Glory, as we both know. Nor is she a Lawless."

Smiley stilled, put a big-knuckled hand to his chin, and rubbed it while he eyed her. "That's a pretty bald statement of affairs, Miss Biddy."

"I know. 'Tis the way of things, though. We'll not be able to keep the truth at bay much longer, I'm afraid."

Smiley shook his head. "You're right. I was afraid it would come to this. I think I knew the minute Rooster McGinty's boy rode up with that packet from Jacey." He firmed his lips together and raised a bushy eyebrow. "You going to tell me what he brought?"

Biddy sighed. "Nothing less than Glory's real mother's own letters and her journal. Some Mexican gentleman—"

"Glory's *real* mother's journal?" Smiley's mouth dropped open to a perfect O. "Great jumping Jehoshaphat."

Biddy nodded. "Aye. Some Mexican gentleman in Arizona had them all these years. That McGinty boy said J. C. himself asked the man to keep them. But he gave them to Jacey, and either he knew the truth, or Jacey—that one's smart as a whip—figured it on her own. But not a word of explanation from her to Glory about the what or the why of the packet. I fainted clean away when I saw Laura Parker's name signed to a letter.''

"You didn't tell Glory right then?"

Biddy primmed her lips together. "I just said I fainted clean away. When I came to, she was of a mind to leave for the Thorne place. And since she's gotten back, she's been in her room and crying. And won't talk to a soul. So, when was I supposed to tell her?''

Smiley appeared to study this, centering his gaze just to Biddy's right. After a quiet moment, he focused on her. "Yer right. You never got a chance.'' Then he snapped his fingers and pointed at her. "Wait a minute. There's yer answer. Jacey meant for Glory to figure it out on her own. So let her.''

"Ye suppose? Just let her? Where's the good in that?''

"Well, think about it, Miz Biddy—if you tell her who that Laura Parker is, and then tell her we've known all along that she's not any blood kin to the Lawlesses, just how do you think she's liable to feel toward you? And me?''

Biddy bit at her bottom lip as she met Smiley's serious gaze. Then she sighed. "Yer right—she'd hate us for sure. But she will, anyways, once she figures it out on her own . . . if she ever does. So what's the difference if I tell her meself or let her reason it out?''

Looking unsettled, Smiley ran his big-knuckled hand over his beard-stubbled jaw. "I see yer point. Do you want me to help you tell her? I will.''

Biddy managed a smile for the man. His hangdog expression told her plainly enough that he hoped she would turn down his offer. "Yer most kind to offer, but no. I've been handling the girls since they was born. I'll take care of this, too.'' Her next thought sent her gaze to her lap, where she picked at a loose thread in her skirt and softly said, "Thank ye for listenin', though. I didn't know where else to turn. With Old Pete gone, yer the only one left on the place, besides meself, who knows the truth of the matter.''

Smiley cleared his throat. Biddy looked up to see him grinning. "I'm right pleased that you confided in me. You know I love that child like she's my own. Feel the same way about the other two and . . . everyone else in the main house. Always have."

Before Biddy could say anything to that, the door from the bunkhouse opened into the office and in stepped Heck Thompson. He stopped when he saw Biddy, but she and Smiley both waved him in. Biddy indicated for the man to proceed with his business with the foreman.

While they spoke of some ranching concern, Biddy quit listening and pulled a hanky from her skirt pocket. It was just as well that Heck had interrupted because she was blinking back sudden tears, tears brought on by the layers of meaning contained in Smiley's words. She lived in the main house. So Smiley cared for her, too. And here they'd never before spoken of such things together, and yet were the closest things to grandparents the Lawless girls had. They'd wasted a lot of years, Biddy reflected.

She watched Smiley speaking with Heck, allowed her warm feelings for the foreman to surface. They had so much in common. Their loyalty and years of service to the elder Lawlesses, not to mention their love for them. The land, this ranch. Their home. And the three girls. They certainly had them in common. But Glory, no more than a stray little kitten when they'd first seen her, was special to them both, Biddy knew.

A little lost waif when J. C. brought her home, she'd been near to death and so tiny. Months of nursing her back to health, of sitting up holding her all night to make sure she breathed, of rocking her and crooning to her, of soothing the child's mewling little cries had forged a special bond. Only now did Biddy recall Smiley pacing back and forth outside, peering up at the house, asking through J. C. how the little one was.

Again Biddy could see herself and Catherine taking turns with the child—she at night, Catherine during the day. It had taken two mothers to replace her real one and to save the tiny baby that she'd been. Then, when she was older, Smiley had sent to the house—again through J. C.—wooden toys he'd whittled. For the baby, he said. It weren't no big deal. Just been bored, found himself whittling. That was all.

Biddy smiled. But it faded. And now, here the child was—grown up, healthy, but threatened again. And in some vague way that Biddy couldn't put a finger on, couldn't name . . . couldn't fight. That terrified her, and she needed help.

She dabbed at her eyes and stuffed her hanky back in her pocket. She focused on Smiley's strong yet kindly face as he nodded at Heck in dismissal. She exchanged a look with him, but waited with him in silence until Heck closed the door after himself. As soon as they were alone again, Smiley all but leaned over the desk toward her. "You all right, Biddy? Are you crying?"

Biddy sat back heavily against the slatted chair's support. He'd called her Biddy. Not Miss Biddy. Not Miss Jensen. But plain Biddy. She stored that away for later reflection. Right now she needed to concern herself with Glory. "I'm not cryin'—me at me age. But I . . . well, I'm having second thoughts"—she tested his name on her lips—"Smiley."

The foreman's eyes lit up. Biddy felt herself color. She rushed on. "I'm not so sure I can just let Glory—on her own—realize that her whole life has been a lie. Why, the realization could come to her in the middle of the night. Or out at the graves. And then what, with no one about to steady her? When she finds out she has no Lawless blood—and her with that stubborn pride? Why, she'll hate us all."

The pleased light in Smiley's dark eyes faded. "Maybe for a while, but not after she has time to think it through. Believe me, that stubborn pride of hers will stand her in good stead. She'll realize she's been raised no different from Hannah and Jacey, that's she's as much a Lawless in fact as they are in blood."

Unconvinced, Biddy pursed her lips. "I wish I had the same certainty in me heart as ye have, Smiley." His name was coming more readily to her lips. "But ye haven't seen her the past two days since she went to the Thorne place. She just stays in her room, mourning and calling for her mother. And she's havin' them nightmares again about the murders. Why, 'tis enough to put me in me grave. And all this without her knowing she has *two* mothers to mourn. What will she be like then?''

Smiley slammed a fist down on the desktop, making Biddy jump. ''Those damned Thornes—pardon my language. But I've a mind to take a bullwhip to every last one of them.'' He then cast a cautious, testing look Biddy's way. ''Well, except for Mrs. Thorne, that is. She's a good woman.''

Biddy smiled. ''Well now, 'tis glad I am to hear ye say that. But ye should know, I'm of a mind to send for Riley. Again.''

Smiley narrowed his eyes at her. ''You sure about that? It's been right peaceful-like without him here.''

''Hmmph. Mayhaps out here. But not inside there, I can tell ye.'' She pointed in the direction of the main house.

Smiley's lips worked, showing his unsettled state as he concentrated on Biddy's face. She smiled at him. He threw his hands up. ''All right. You know what's best for the young'un. Send for Riley Thorne, if you've a mind to. But remember, since Ben and Louise also know the truth, Riley might know by now. While I don't believe he or his mother would use that knowledge against her, who's to say what Ben might do? He wants this land awful bad. And if he gets it, we all lose.''

Smiley's words struck close to Biddy's heart. '' 'Tis my worst fear. We'd lose the only home we've ever known.'' Biddy pursed her lips together and shook her head as she came to her feet. ''I had no idea how much I had to worry about before I came out here. But now I see—'tis bigger than all of us. And who'd have thought it would all come down to Glory's slender shoulders to keep it all together?''

On his side of the desk, Smiley stood, too. ''What are you going to do?''

Biddy exhaled heavily, knotted her fingers at her waist. ''I'm going to tell her. 'Tis the right thing to do. But first, tomorrow morning, I'm going to thc Thorne place. I want to hear from Louise what happened to Glory there. And maybe I can talk her into coming back with me. I'd like her here, as Catherine's friend, to help me explain things to Glory.''

"Do you think that's wise?" Smiley spoke barely above a whisper.

Despite her warm feelings for the man, Biddy pulled herself up stiffly. "It may not be. But it's no less wise than you men fightin' over a piece of dirt. The Good Lord knows that all these years 'twas only Catherine's and Louise's friendship that kept J. C. and Ben from killing each other."

Having said that, she quieted, waiting for Smiley to dispute her words or to argue with her. But he remained silent. Biddy ducked her chin, finally admitting her own doubts. "I just hope the children—and the love I know they have for each other—are strong enough to withstand what's coming. Because the truth can kill us all. And not only Glory."

Mounted on Pride, Riley surveyed the stretch of flat land laid out before him, broken only by the washboard hills and waving tallgrass. It'd been three cold, November days now since he and Glory had found each other out here and made love. He hadn't been able yet to sort out his feelings regarding that because here he was sorting out Lawless cattle from Thorne cattle. And having to fight his father and brothers every step of the way.

Stretching in the saddle, feeling Pride's stamp of impatience, Riley turned at the sound of approaching hooves. With narrowed eyes, he watched Henry rein his lathered horse next to him. In wary silence he waited for his brother to speak.

Henry notched his felt hat up and spat between the two horses. Then he swiped a hand over his dust-and-sweat-grimed face and said, "Caleb and Zeke found about ten more head over in that next dry gully. Lawless cattle. I'll swear and be damned, Riley, I ain't never worked so hard to return cattle to someone I hate. If she wants her steers, let her come get 'em."

Riley inhaled and exhaled as if breathing required conscious effort. He'd been listening to Henry gripe since they'd started rounding up the herd yesterday. Too tired to bellyache with him again over the same issue, he ignored all but his brother's statement of fact. "Ten more head? Damn. How does this keep happening?"

"Well, it ain't like there's any fences. Cattle don't know the difference from one piece of dirt to the next."

Riley nodded. "True enough. Only, before the past couple weeks, it seemed like they did. Does it appear to you that someone is driving them over our way, just to start trouble?"

Henry stopped in the act of reaching for his canteen, looped as it was around his saddle's pommel. "Like who?"

A shrug and a sharp-eyed stare preceded Riley's answer. "I don't rightly know."

Henry took his meaning, judging by the way he sat up straight and narrowed his eyes right back at Riley. "I might be a lot of things, and I might not cotton to the Lawlesses, but I ain't a cattle rustler, Riley."

"I never said you were. But I'm glad to hear you say that."

Henry eyed Riley a moment before uncapping his canteen and bringing it to his lips to take a long pull. Watching him, Riley experienced a sudden flash of memory, of Henry as a scrawny boy, always making things harder for himself than they had to be. A grin tugged at Riley's lips. Despite his constant desire to pound some sense into his brother, he admitted to the rush of love in his heart. *Danged kid.*

As Henry recapped his canteen, Riley continued watching him. Next month, his brother would marry the girl he loved. At least this one thing was easy for him. Fall in love, get married, and everyone was happy about it. Then Riley thought of Glory, of his love for her. And how, right now, it looked like it could never be. Frustration gusted Riley's breath out of him. No sense dwelling on it. He turned to Henry. "If you're through sitting a spell while the rest of us work, show me where those ten head are."

"Me sitting a spell? You're the one up here overlooking our hard work, like you're some kind of king or something. What the hell have you been doing all morning?" Despite his challenge, Henry turned his horse as he spoke and led Riley, grinning behind his back, in the direction he'd just come.

For the next few hours, Riley helped his father and brothers sort Thorne cattle from Lawless cattle. It had taken him two days of arguing with them to get them out here and working. They all felt pretty much like Henry did about this venture. But he'd finally made them see that their looking like cattle rustlers, which by all the evidence was exactly what someone wanted them to appear to be, didn't help their cause—that of regaining their pasture lands. A range war was one thing in the eyes of their neighboring cattlemen. Cattle rustling was another.

Still, even though the work they did was right and good, Riley expected at any moment for Smiley Rankin and a string of Lawless hands to come thundering over the hills, guns blazing. Because he knew from afar it'd be hard to tell ''sorting out'' from ''mixing in.'' But when lunchtime came and that hadn't happened, Riley felt heartened some. Perhaps they could herd the cattle back to Lawless land without anyone being the wiser.

Reining in Pride a distance away from the chuckwagon, and on the side away from his congregated family and their few hired hands, he dismounted and hobbled the gray gelding, leaving the big horse enough length to graze and get to the water-filled rill for a drink. Thinking only of his own lunch, and how he was the last one in for the meal, Riley approached the wagon and was only two steps from rounding into view of the men, when he heard Abel Justice's voice rise above the sound of spoons scraping against tin plates.

What the man was saying abruptly ended the other quiet or teasing conversations going on at the same time. His words had the same effect on Riley. He stopped where he was, listened, and felt sure his heart would thump right out of his chest.

''Well, Mr. Thorne,'' Justice was saying, ''I ain't one to carry tales, but I heard-tell that Miss Glory ain't no Lawless a-tall. I been told her real folks was killed by that Mexican desperado what ran with the Lawless Gang. And he left her— no more'n a tiny baby—for dead. But J. C. Lawless brought her home to raise as his own. A good, Christian thing to do, is all I'm saying.''

"What the hell—?" That was seventeen-year-old John. "Miss Glory ain't even a Lawless?"

In less than a second, Zeke followed up his older brother's bold cussing with, "The hell you say!"

"That's enough. You two boys watch your mouths." And that was Ben Thorne's deep, authoritative voice. For the next few seconds only an occasional neigh from a horse or the lowing of the cattle broke the silence. Then Ben spoke again. "Where'd you hear that, Justice?"

Abel answered, "Here and there. Is it true?"

Keeping his presence a secret, Riley waited what he felt was a lifetime for his father's answer. He could only imagine the rapt looks on his brothers' faces. And the thoughts running through their heads. "I couldn't say if it was or not."

Riley exhaled the breath he hadn't realized he'd been holding. His father knew Glory's real story . . . and yet, he was keeping it to himself. Or at least he wasn't verifying it. And probably for no other reason than because Abel Justice was a stranger, not yet to be trusted. Still, noble or not, Riley was glad for his father's holding back the truth. He listened in when Abel Justice went on.

"Well, don't git me wrong, sir, I ain't meaning the lady no harm. She's a right sweet little thing, she is, and God-fearing, just like myself. Got a lot on her shoulders, too. I just think it's a shame, is all—her being a little orphan twice over. And all alone now on that big old ranch. It don't seem right."

After a moment of quiet, punctuated by a couple of metallic scrapes that told of the men continuing their meal, came Ben Thorne's soft reply. "No. It doesn't."

Riley became aware of the sweat pooling under his arms, despite the day's sharp coldness. This was the last thing he needed—Abel Justice firing up his father's vengeful juices. His first thought was to interrupt, but then he stilled himself, thinking he'd be better off right now to listen. Because if the drifter was telling the truth, that he'd heard Glory's story "here and there," then Riley needed to know everything the man knew. And then he needed to get to Glory before she heard it from someone else—when they came to take her land.

Thus riveted in place, he stayed where he was and heard Justice say, "Well, I just find myself wonderin' how—what with too-few men, and no real or legal claim to the land—"

"There's no law in no-man's-land to say what's legal and what ain't. A man holds onto what he can by might alone. Ain't that right, Pa?" That was nineteen-year-old Caleb, the Thorne who said what the others only dared think.

Riley rolled his eyes. *Shut up, Caleb.*

"That's right," Ben answered his son.

Justice added, "I reckon yer right, boy. By might—and by what others will allow or tolerate . . . the way I see it."

Dammit. Judging by the quiet on the other side of the wagon, Riley knew that Justice had just fed their thoughts of a range war. Thoughts that he'd barely been able to squelch lately. Riley found himself again wondering how Abel Justice knew the truth about Glory. Had the drifter overheard the conversation between himself and his mother when she told him? He thought back to that day and then shook his head. No, Justice and Carter had ridden out with Henry before that talk.

Eliminating that, Riley reflected on who else knew, but immediately discounted Biddy telling him. Smiley Rankin? He'd worked for J. C. Lawless since there'd been a Lawless ranch. He had to know. But two folks more fiercely loyal to the Lawlesses, you couldn't find. And they'd kept the family secret for nearly twenty years. Neither one of them would just up and tell a stranger.

So, with J. C. and Catherine—a terrible nagging in his gut accompanied the horrible conclusion Riley's mind forced on his consciousness—and Old Pete dead, no one else outside the family knew. Except for himself and his parents. And now his brothers and the other hands, thanks to Justice. Were the people involved being systematically killed off? It appeared that way. Riley's eyes narrowed. Who was doing this? And why?

Just then, a new voice broke into the discussion on the other side of the wagon. It belonged to Carter Brown. "Look here, Mr. Thorne, it appears to me you got five big old sons, which gives you a lot of blood-family and loyal firepower. And Miss Glory, for all Justice here is sweet on her, ain't got nothing but a handful of drifters and old-timers to count on. Seems to me it wouldn't take much to turn things in your favor. If that was yer aim.''

Riley's gut clenched. Then he heard his father say, ''*If* that was my aim.''

And again exhaled a breath he hadn't realized he was holding. Not until this moment did Riley realize the truth of what his mother always said—he was just like his pa to keep his own counsel. I have to pull thoughts and words out of you both, she always said. Right now, Riley counted that a good trait. Figuring he'd heard enough, he started around the wagon, but was stopped again, this time by the sounds behind him of a steadily approaching wagon.

He'd no more than turned around before he was joined on his side of the chuckwagon by his father and brothers, who looked startled to see him there. They were followed by the assembled hands, among them Justice and Brown. Riley spared those two only a hard-eyed glance, which they didn't return, before he too focused on the harness-jingling, clattering buckboard nearing them.

Then he recognized the rig. And the driver. The Lawless buckboard and Biddy handling the team's reins. His gut tightened. This could only be trouble. Apparently spying the assembled men in front of the chuckwagon, and the milling cattle arrayed off to a side, Biddy brought the team to a dust-stirring halt, still a good distance from the watching men. And sat there, obviously waiting. With the combined weight of his family's stares burning in his back, Riley turned to his father. ''I'll go talk to her.''

Ben wrinkled his nose in his grimace. ''Maybe that'd be best.''

Riley exchanged a charged look with his father and then broke away from the crowd of quiet men clustered around the chuckwagon. Breaking into a sprint, he caught up with Pride, unhobbled and mounted him . . . all under the watchful eyes of the Thorne men and their hired hands. With a muscle jumping in his cheek, Riley wheeled Pride and urged him into a loping gallop across the hard-packed, uneven ground. In only moments, he reined in beside the Lawless buckboard, saw the worry lines framing Biddy's faded-blue eyes, further shadowed by her gingham sun bonnet.

Controlling his restive mount with a firm tug on the reins, and ignoring the stark, blue cold of the day, Riley took the gloved hand Biddy offered him. "What brings you over this way, Biddy?"

"Oh, Riley, yer a sight for sore eyes. I thought I saw yer horse over there." Then she frowned, pulled her hand away, and pointed toward the milling cattle. "Is that the Lawless brand I see on some of them cattle?"

Riley didn't need to look where she pointed. "Yep. Someone's trying to make the Thornes out to be cattle rustlers. We're getting ready to drive them back to Lawless land."

Biddy swung her bonnet-covered head back to him, considered him a sober moment, and then nodded. "I'll say a prayer yer done with it before Mr. Rankin comes huntin' them cows."

Riley tipped his Stetson's brim to her. "I would appreciate it. Now don't tell me you came all this way as your foreman's advance rider."

Biddy gave a vigorous shake of her head, which set her plump little chins into motion. "No, not at all." Then she seemed to crumple into herself. "Oh, Riley, 'tis Glory. She's in a bad way, and I don't know what to do."

Riley exhaled, fearing he knew exactly what was wrong with Glory. He didn't know which hurt the most right then— his empty stomach or his throbbing temples. He heaved out a sigh, shook his head, and then focused on Biddy. "Wait here. I'll go tell my father I'm leaving. And then . . . I'll go to her. Don't try to keep up in your wagon, because I—"

"Don't worry about me. It's to yer mother I'm going." Biddy paused, gave Riley a considering look, as if she wrestled with some decision, and then blurted, "There's more. I don't quite know how to say it, but Glory's not really a—"

"A Lawless. I know about her real folks. Ma told me just the other day."

Biddy exhaled, slumped, put a hand to her cloak-covered

chest. "Thank the Lord for that. Yer knowing makes everything easier. I was right to come seek ye out. Ye go, Riley. I'll collect yer mother and we'll follow directly."

"All right. But why do you need my mother? I can handle—"

"Ye don't understand. After ye left, Glory got a packet from Jacey. In it were Laura Parker's letters and journals."

A spasm of surprise tightened Riley's grip on his reins. "Laura Parker? Isn't that—?"

"Yes, 'tis. Glory's real mother. Only Glory's not knowing it yet. She doesn't know any of this. At least, she hadn't figured it out before I left this morning." Biddy tsk-tsked and shook her bonneted head. "And what's more, Jacey warned Glory—just as Hannah did in her letter—about men hired to track the girls, maybe to kill them. The very thought just stops me heart. I know I'm asking ye to ride into a hornet's nest, but don't let that girl out of yer sight."

Riley firmed his lips, looked out over the low, brown hills in the direction of the Lawless ranch yard, as if he could see it from where he sat atop Pride. "I won't." He then looked down at Biddy. "You go visit with Ma, but don't hurry home. Give me some time with Glory. Alone."

Biddy raised her eyebrows and stared right into his soul. Riley's heart thudded. His hands, encased in his riding gloves, sweat against the soft leather as he pressed his knees against his horse's belly. Biddy's expression changed. She looked up at him from under suspicion-lowered eyelids. "Time alone with her? Is *that* what's wrong with her?"

Riley found reason to study his pommel, to stretch in his saddle, to look everywhere but at the Lawless nanny. "Yes, ma'am."

"Riley Thorne. Shame on ye."

Feeling his cheeks heat up, but refusing to admit he was actually blushing, Riley shot her a look. "You all that surprised, Biddy?"

She shook her head, pursed her lips. "I should be. But I'm not. Well then, be off with ye. Go. 'Tis ye she's needin' to see, after all. And not the rest of us.'' She gave a heavy, dramatic sigh. "Not for a while, at least.''

Riley understood. He grinned at the fearless, wonderful Lawless nanny. "I think I love you, Biddy Jensen. But don't tell Mr. Rankin I said that. I don't want him calling me out.''

Wide-eyed and brushing him off with a wave of her hand, she whooped out her girlish enjoyment. "Go on with ye, lad. Mr. Rankin, indeed. Ye've all ye can do to worry about one Glory Bea Lawless.''

The long shadows of the quiet afternoon—quiet because Biddy was gone to visit Louise Thorne—cast themselves over Glory's bedroom. Seeping in through the window, the graying beams crept across the floor, creating ripples of dark which tiptoed on cat's paws for the security of the corners.

Noticing one such dust-mote-laden beam, and watching its progress for long moments, Glory sighed and stretched her aching back. Sitting ensconced on her bed, her legs folded Indian-style, she eyed the scattering of letters and the old journal spread about her. Another day all but gone by as she pored through them, rereading them. And still, she could make no sense out of it all.

Oh, she had inklings of ideas, and various notes she'd made in an effort to correlate people and events, but still . . . what was Jacey thinking with her little mystery? It wasn't in her sister's straightforward nature to play such games. Which only frustrated Glory more, and suddenly told her this was no game. Maybe she was trying too hard, looking too deeply. Maybe the answers were obvious.

Glory gritted her teeth, shook her head. She wiped her dry, scratchy eyes and then blinked until she could focus again on Laura Parker's life. Why would Jacey send the woman's letters to her? If these brittle and yellowed pages were related in any way to the murders and the present danger, Jacey wouldn't have been this coy with them. She would've sent James McGinty at a tearing pace with an out-and-out warning. But she hadn't.

Why? In a tired, bored snit, Glory told herself she couldn't care less why at the moment. She folded her arms under her blouse-covered bosom and stared at her bedroom's open door. And frowned. Shouldn't Biddy be home by now? Glory shook her head, wondering at her nanny's determined haste to be gone this morning. And at her admonition to "Stay at them letters until they make sense to ye."

Glory's frown suddenly deepened. She sat up straight. Her heartbeat picked up speed. She heard again Biddy's words that she'd just repeated for herself. *Ye stay at them letters until they make sense to ye, Glory Bea. To me?* Did that mean they made sense to Biddy? Glory cast her gaze down to her lap, fingered the worn cover on Laura Parker's journal. And had the sudden urge to fling it across the room. But she didn't. Because she didn't want to pick it up, like she wouldn't want to touch a coiled snake.

Instead, she picked up her own notes she'd made of dates and names and places mentioned by the young woman almost twenty years ago. *Almost twenty years ago?* Glory's head popped up. She stared vacantly at her reflection in her vanity's mirror across the room. *Almost twenty years ago would be 1854. The year I was born.*

With suddenly shaking fingers, she gingerly picked up the journal. Turning the brittle pages one after the other, she found the one on which Seth Parker had recorded the date of his . . . Glory swallowed the lump in her throat . . . daughter's birth. And forced herself to read it again, even knowing what she'd see. *There it is. May 9, 1854.*

Instantly denying what she now realized she'd suspected all along, ever since her first reading of the journal, she closed it with an angry flip of her hand. The Parkers had a baby girl born on May 9. That was her birthday, too. So the Parkers' daughter was the same age as her. So? Almost defiantly, Glory awaited an answer, a conclusion, from her otherwise empty room. And got one. As if her conscience were another physical presence in the room, it leaned over and whispered, *So they named her Beatrice, Glory.*

Glory's lips quivered. She closed her eyes against the fat, hot tears threatening to flow. Almost of its own will, her hand sought her mouth, covering her lips to keep back the scream that billowed like a storm cloud over her heart. And still, she sat there. It was all very simple, wasn't it? In fact, obvious. *This* was why Jacey'd sent Laura Parker's letters to her without any explanation. *This* was why Biddy'd fainted when she saw the woman's signature. Jacey knew who Laura Parker was. So did Biddy. And now, Glory suspected, so did she.

Downstairs, a door opened and then slammed. It sounded like the back door. The one into the kitchen. *Biddy's home.* Glory absorbed the sound, listening as it faded into a memory, only to be replaced bare moments later by the scuffing sounds of someone slowly climbing the stairs. With a growing sense of bleak destiny, of bleached-bone finality, Glory riveted her gaze on the empty, open doorway to her room and waited for Biddy to be framed there.

She knew already what she wanted to ask her nanny. *Who did Beatrice Parker grow up to be?*

Chapter 15

But it was Riley Thorne who turned into her room. Glory lifted her chin and stared at the silent man. Even from across the room she could smell the life he brought with him, the benediction of his presence: horses, leather, the open plains, and the cleansing wind. Looking tall and serious in his long saddle coat, he looked into her eyes and then down at the papers spread all around her. A muscle in his jaw jumped. From under the low brim of his Stetson, he narrowed his eyes at her. And didn't say a word.

Glory hauled in a breath deep enough to raise her bosom. Holding it a moment, she then exhaled the spent air slowly and said, "You know, don't you? You know I'm"—she held up the ragged-edged journal for him to see—"this baby in here, don't you? Say it. Tell me I'm Beatrice Parker. Not Glory Lawless. I want to hear you say it."

Framed by the doorway, looking as serious as a gunfighter, he intoned, "You're Beatrice Parker."

Glory's heart plummeted, her blood ceased to flow, seemed to pool in her legs. She closed her eyes against the truth and concentrated on taking stunted breath after stunted breath. It seemed the world faded, taking her with it as she shrank into her bed's depth like she would a churning sea.

"But you're also Glory Lawless."

Glory opened her eyes, stared at Riley. "There is no Glory Lawless. There never was. She was a prideful girl, a made-up person. Someone who stuck her nose in the air and thought she was better than everyone else for being a Lawless.''

Riley quirked his mouth, shook his head. ''Just because Lawless blood doesn't flow in your veins, Glory, that doesn't make you less of a person. The Lawlesses aren't royalty. Or even something more than the everyday person—for all their thinking otherwise.''

Glory cocked her head as she considered his words. And what lay underneath them. ''You don't like the Lawlesses one little bit, do you?''

Riley shrugged, looked right into her eyes. ''Some more than others.''

Harboring a growing sense of betrayal of all that she knew, of all that she believed—about herself, her family, and her entire world—Glory kept on, wanting to hurt, wanting to make him hurt her. ''But I'm not a . . . a Lawless. So I guess you *can* like me even more.''

Riley moved, as if he meant to turn away, to step out of her view. ''I'm not going to do this, Glory. And I'm not going to let you do it, either.''

''Wait. Please.'' Glory held a hand out as if to hold him in place. The air around her seemed so paper-thin, so spider's-web fragile. If he took something as solid as a booted step away from her, she and her surroundings would shatter like dropped china, she just knew it. Already, porcelain shards of who she'd thought she was all her life cut into her belly, making her ill.

She then clamped that hand over her mouth and again closed her eyes. Swallowing the bitter bile of truth—a horrible, sour lump in her throat—Glory's first shudders of reaction stuttered inside her chest, wrenched her shoulders spasmodically. But before the first wail tore from her, Riley's footsteps sounded on the wooden floor, his weight sank next to her on her feather-stuffed mattress, and his arms went around her. Glory clutched at him, turned her face against his shirt, against his thudding heart. And knew if he turned her loose, she'd die.

But then, just as suddenly, she couldn't stand the closeness, the warmth and vitality of Riley's body against hers. With a violent wrench, Glory freed herself from his embrace and all but flung herself off her bed. She stood facing him, but backing away, pointing an accusing finger. Her long, dark hair, wild and curling around her face, blocking her vision, forced her to see him as if through a dark veil. "No," she warned. "No. Don't touch me."

Riley stayed where he was, stared at her, stark concern mirrored in his features. Then slowly he raised a hand and removed his Stetson, tossed it aside. Standing, but never looking away from Glory's eyes, he peeled off his saddle coat, sending it the way of his hat. And followed it with his gunbelt.

Glory narrowed her eyes at him. "What are you doing?"

"I'm getting ready for the fight."

"What fight?"

"The one you're starting. Glory, I didn't have anything to do with the lies told to you about who you are. I was only six years old at the time."

"But you knew."

He shook his head. "Not until a few days ago. I didn't know. I swear it."

"Who told you?"

"My mother. She was here that day your father rode in with you."

"My fath—He *rode* in with me?"

Riley nodded. "Yeah. He brought you with him all the way from Arizona."

"Why?"

"I don't know. Except maybe you were a helpless baby and he felt sorry for you."

Glory absorbed that for a moment, tried to feel something for the man she'd always thought of as her father. But found she couldn't, not right then. She cocked her head with her next question. "What happened to those . . . people?" She looked past him to the journal on her bed, eyeing it as if it were a writhing snake. "The Parkers. My . . . parents. What happened to them?"

Riley made a helpless gesture, then ran a hand through his hair. "Glory, I'm not the one you should be having this talk with. I don't know all the answers. Biddy does.''

"You tell me what you do know.''

Huffing out a breath, he put his hands to his waist, met her gaze. "Kid Chapelo killed them at Apache Pass. And left you to die.''

Glory grimaced at the sudden stab of pain in her chest. "Kid Chapelo? Jacey's with his son right now. And that man's father . . . left me to die? But Papa—no, he's not my papa at all—but *he* . . . saved me? And brought me here?''

Riley nodded. "That's all I know. You were raised as one of the Lawless girls from that day forward.''

Glory's arms dropped to her sides. "Do Hannah and Jacey know this?''

Riley made a gesture of uncertainty, spreading his hands wide. "I couldn't say. I don't know what they were told, if anything. They were so young. But looking back over the years, I figure they didn't know, or didn't remember. Because kids being like they are, they'd have talked. I can't speak for Hannah, but since Jacey sent you these things, she must know now.''

Glory nodded at the reasonableness of Riley's words, at his calm voice. He spoke as if the unraveling of her life, of her identity, were of no more consequence in this world than ordering oats for the horses. It was almost funny. Then suddenly her mind shied away from the precipice that was this news and took another path, one which led away from the sheer drop into insanity. "Where's Biddy? I want to talk to her.'' Glory turned away from Riley with her question, thinking to go find her nanny.

"She's not here.''

Glory stopped, turned to him, and stared, waiting.

"She's at my place. With my mother.''

"Why?''

Again Riley shrugged. "I don't know. All I do know is she came and found me, all upset about Jacey sending you these papers. Maybe she wanted my mother here when you figured it out.''

"Why?''

Riley's mouth quirked with evident impatience. "How the hell should I know? Maybe she expected you to fall apart." A punctuated silence followed his words. Then, "Are you going to? Fall apart, that is?"

Glory considered that. Was she? She focused on her body, felt suddenly alien in it, as if she didn't fit this skin. Then she shook her head. "No. I thought I was going to"—she pointed at the bed—"back there a minute ago . . . when you held me. But not now. What good would that do?"

Riley frowned, held out a hand to her, but withdrew it. "I don't like the sound of your voice, Glory. You sound like . . . well, like you're not in there somehow."

Feeling cold and dead inside as she did, Glory knew just what he meant. But swiping a hand over her face, clearing her vision of straggling curls, she shrugged her shoulders and denied it. "That's silly. I can't be anywhere but here, Riley." She looked down at herself, spread her hands wide to indicate her body. "It's me. Who else would it be?"

Then she heard her own words. Who else, indeed. What a question. One which made her chin quiver, one which forced her chin up a notch. "It's all been a lie, hasn't it? My whole life. Here I was, so proud of who I was, so proud to be the daughter of J. C. Lawless, famous outlaw, and Catherine Wilton-Humes, Boston socialite. When in reality, I'm nothing more than the orphaned offspring of two people I'd never even heard of before today. Seth and Laura Parker. Stupid enough to get themselves killed in some godforsaken place called Apache Pass, the last place Laura—my mother—writes about."

"Don't do this, Glory."

She put her hands to her waist, fought the welling-up inside her of a raging anger, a terrible sense of betrayal. "Don't do what? Speak the truth for the first time in twenty years? It must've been funny for everyone around to watch me prancing about, so full of my Lawless pride and my—"

"Stop it right now. I won't listen to this. Your folks loved you."

"My folks? Which ones?" Glory gritted her teeth, felt a

white-hot rage that brought beads of sweat to her forehead, that had her launching herself at Riley. "I never knew my folks."

Riley caught her by her wrists and held her. Glory struggled and fought, bit and kicked, yelled and raged. Dodging her blows, Riley held fast, like the solid trunk of a mighty oak against a swirling whirlwind. The more he held her, the more Glory fought, the more she wanted to hurt, wanted to hurt him, wanted to hurt him for knowing, for caring, for the look of sympathy on his strong face, for the love he held for her in his heart.

With that realization, Glory froze, stared up into his grim face, into his black and snapping eyes, saw and heard his labored breathing, even over the torturous sounds of her own efforts. Nearly out of her mind with an emotion she couldn't name, she screwed her face up into a snarling mask of hate. "How dare you love me, Riley Thorne? How dare you?"

His face reddening with his effort to hold her, Riley glared down at her. His grip loosened a fraction. "I didn't ask to, believe me. And right now, I wish to hell I didn't."

Glory wrenched a hand free, drew it back and slapped his face as hard as she could. The resounding echo of her transgression clapped like thunder in the otherwise still house. She stared openmouthed up at Riley, saw her handprint form on his face. She curled her offending hand and held it to her heart. "I wish you didn't, either."

Riley firmed his mouth, grabbed her by her arms, pulled her close to him. Glory sucked in a breath laden with the scent of horse, sweat, and angry man. "You're going to pay for that, Glory Bea Lawless. I'll see to it."

With that, he cast her aside and shoved past her, making his long-striding way out of her room. Glory scrambled after him, grabbed at his flannel-covered back, stopping him. "Don't you turn your back on me."

Riley jerked around, breaking her hold on him. "Get the hell away from me, or I won't be responsible for what I do. I came here because I care, Glory—and for no other reason. Because I was afraid of what this news would do to you. But you don't want my help. Or me. I'm a Thorne—not good enough. When am I going to learn that? When am I going to learn that—Lawless by blood or not—you're one of *them* through and through?''

He nodded down at her, looking like he hated the very idea of her existence. ''Oh, yeah, you're one of them. So quit feeling sorry for yourself. You just got some tough news, and I feel for you. But you haven't lost anything, Glory. Not one thing. Twenty years of being raised by the Lawlesses to think you're something special will get you through this. You don't need me.'' He stabbed a thumb at his chest. ''But me? I've lost everything by loving you. Everything. Now get the hell out of my sight.''

With that, he turned on his heel and stalked with angry strides down the long hallway. Glory didn't move, didn't speak as she watched him go. Her hands, gripping her skirt, clenched and unclenched around the woolen fabric. She couldn't even be sure she breathed, until the dull sound of his taking the steps in a near-run jarred a ragged breath from her. A voice in her soul cried out to her, telling her not to let him go, telling her to stop him . . . and to love him. Or be forever doomed.

''Riley!'' The anguished sound tore out of her soul, set her feet in a skittering run down the hallway, to the stairs, in a stumbling tumble down each step, close on his heels. But ahead of her, he never even looked around or slowed down. ''Riley!'' she called out, only to realize she was crying, only to realize that hot tears swamped her cheeks, made her feel hot all over.

Still, Riley never faltered. He strode across the great room, skirting with sure steps the hulking shapes of the leather furniture, and headed for the front door.

In soul-deep desperation, Glory chased after him, her hands held out to him in supplication. Only he couldn't see that. Because he wouldn't turn around. Glory caught him before he made it to the door. She grabbed his arm and, using all her strength, forced him to turn to her. Her hands now on his chest, she pushed him back against the front door and held him there.

Riley spread his arms as if in surrender. "What, Glory? What? I heard you call my name. It doesn't mean anything to me. It's too late. I can't do this anymore. I thought I could. But I can't. I won't. I won't clean up J. C. Lawless's messes anymore."

Glory's will to live shriveled with each word of his. She had to make him see, to understand. "What are you saying? I love you, Riley. Don't you see? I love you. I always have. It doesn't matter anymore about me being a Lawless and you a Thorne. I'm not a Lawless. I see that now. We can be together. We can go away, away from where anybody knows—"

Riley pulled her hands off him, held her wrists tightly, painfully. "Do you hear yourself? You're saying I'm good enough for you now because you're not a high-and-mighty Lawless. Well, let me tell you something, Glory—or Beatrice or whatever the hell your name is—the Lawlesses aren't anything. Nothing. J. C. Lawless was scum. A thief and a murderer. Decent folks wouldn't have anything to do with him."

Glory fought his grip on her. "Stop it, Riley."

"No. You need to hear this. Why do you think he lived here in no-man's-land? He didn't *choose* this place, this hard land. He was *forced* to settle here. And why? Because he wasn't welcome anywhere else. He'd have been hanged for the land-grabbing, cattle-rustling, murdering son-of-a-bitch he was. The only good thing ever to come out of his life was Catherine and your sisters. Damned fine women, Glory. Strong and good. I used to think you were all those things, too. But not now. You're feeling sorry for yourself for not being one of them—and so you think you can lower yourself now to love me. Well, to hell with that. And to hell with you."

With that, he pushed her back, letting go of her wrists. Seeing him through a waterfall of tears, through a chasm of hurt, Glory stumbled backward against a leather chair. She clutched at it, held on. And still she couldn't look away from him. Not when he glared his hatred at her. Not when he jerked around and tore the door open. Not when he stepped through the opening and slammed the door behind him.

Even still, she couldn't look away from the barrier of wood between her and Riley. Not even when she heard, from outside, a cry of animal anguish that had to have been torn from the depths of Riley's soul. Not even when she heard his shouting and cursing . . . at her, at God, at the ugliness that was the truth of their lives.

She didn't know how long she stood there, frozen in place as she was, watching the door, waiting for it to open, hoping against hope that Riley—hatless, coatless, without a weapon—would be forced to come back inside. She prayed he would. Dreaded that he would. And waited.

The shadows in the room deepened, as did the cold. No fire burned in the grate to warm her, to light her world. The shelf clock on the mantel ticked steadily, persistently, marking passing time with relentless patience.

Glory swallowed and put a hand to her blouse's collar, fingering it absently. Stared at the door. What had she done? Was Riley right? Had she said she could love him now that she wasn't a Lawless—as if to say her life was over and she needed to wallow in garbage? She thought back to her exact words, heard herself saying what he'd thrown back at her. Glory slumped, closing her eyes against her own rash words, against the raw emotions that had cost her—

The door opened. Glory opened her eyes, jerked upright. The last pink and purple rays of the dying day showed her Riley framed there, his hand still on the brass knob. Her heart thudded, her skin chilled with the skirl of wind that swept past him and danced around her. He had to be freezing. And yet he just stood there, his features lost in the darkness of the room between them. With her heart sinking, her knees weak, Glory clutched at the chair. And waited.

Without moving, standing with his legs spread, nearly as tall as the door's casing, nearly as broad-shouldered as its wood-framed opening, he spoke. For all she could see his face, his words could have come from the very air itself. But she knew they came from him. Because he said, "God help me,

Glory, I should have kept on going, kept on walking. But I can't. I'll take your love any way I can get it. Any way I can have it."

A mewling cry of relief escaped her. She couldn't have said if she took a step toward him, or if he came to her, but suddenly, she was in his arms and he was holding her . . . saving her, if he only knew it. Glory clung to him, fisting her hands around the flannel that covered his back, pressing her ear to his chest, listening to his racing heartbeat. "Oh, Riley, I am so sorry. I don't know what I was saying, why I would—"

"No, Glory." He tugged her chin up, forced her to look into his eyes. His features blended a great tenderness with a frown of anguish. "*I'm* sorry. You already have enough on your plate to deal with and to sort out, without me adding to it. Without me making this about the things that eat at me. I pressed you, I pushed you . . . and I got what I deserve. I said I came here to help. But all I did was cause more hurt. And I am so damned sorry. Can you forgive me?"

To hear Riley—usually so quiet, so spare with his words—pouring his soul out, whether in anger like earlier or in regret like now, made Glory realize the depth of his feelings for her, made her realize how much he'd been holding in all these years. And it made her love him all the more. She shifted in his embrace, moving her arms up and around his neck, holding him securely to her. "Oh, Riley, there's nothing to forgive. You only spoke the truth. It's me who should be begging for forgiveness. Me. I'm the one—"

"No." He looked deep into her eyes. "No, Glory. You're not the one guilty of anything here. All the rest of us—all of us, everyone who knew—we're all guilty of this hurt you feel now. All of us. Not you."

Glory's chin quivered, her eyes misted. "It hurts so much, Riley. It hurts. I don't even know who I am. How can I know what I feel?"

Riley tightened his grip, forced her to look up at him. "I can't tell you how to feel. But I can tell you who you are—at least, to me: You're the woman I love. That's who you've always been, and always will be. No matter what your real name might be, or who your real folks are—none of that matters. Not to me.''

Glory shook her head. ''I don't deserve you. I don't know how you can—''

He put a finger to her lips. ''Shhh. You'll work this out because you're strong. But no matter how you come to think of yourself, it won't change anything for me. I will always love you—no matter what you call yourself. If the day comes when you don't think you can count on anything staying the same, Glory, you think about that. You think about me. Because I will never change. And I will always love you.''

Glory soaked up his words, his love, and fell against him, weak with emotion. ''Oh, Riley, help me. Help me. I can't do this by myself.'' She heard the wrenching sobs, realized they were her own.

She then felt herself being lifted, knew Riley now cradled her in his arms. Felt the protection of his embrace, heard his softly whispered words of comfort, realized he was carrying her across the great room. Weak as a newborn, Glory could only cling to him, could only press her face against his neck and breathe in his scent with every breath, trust him with every step.

Up the stairs he carried her, down the hallway, and into her own room. Glory saw her bed, the journal and the letters scattered there. Riley's hat, coat, and gun lay atop them. She tensed, turning her face once more against the warm, muscled column of his neck. ''No,'' came her muffled whimper, no more than the mewl of a forlorn kitten. ''I can't see them now. Not the letters.''

''All right, honey. You don't have to.'' He abruptly turned around and exited her room.

With her eyes tightly closed, she could only sense where he headed now. But she believed he'd gone two doors down, to the room where he'd slept when he stayed here, to the bed where she'd curled up to feel safe once he left. Sure enough, when he bent over to lower her onto a bed, when she felt its feathered softness under her, she opened her eyes to find herself being deposited on what she called his bed. His arms slid out from under her. He began to straighten up.

Glory clutched at his arm, turned her face up to him. "Stay with me."

Riley stilled, stared into her eyes. Shook his head. "No. Not like this."

"Please. Don't make me beg."

He hung his head a moment, but then raised it, settling his gaze on her once again. His black eyes glistened with an unnamed emotion. "It wouldn't be right. Not with all the things you're feeling right now. I'm not sure I can stop with just holding you. And that would be the last thing you—"

"That is the only thing I need, Riley. I don't want you just to hold me. I need *you*. All of you. Please don't make me fight you." Then she surprised herself—and felt heartened—by a sudden sense of teasing and ridiculousness that came from out of nowhere. "You made me beg you last time, the first time. And now again. Am I going to have to force you for the rest of our lives?"

Riley's eyes widened and then his face erupted into a grin that crinkled the skin at the corners of his eyes. "Well, I'll be darned. The girl I love *is* still in there."

Glory bit at her bottom lip. She couldn't believe she was going to say this, but she did anyway. "Want to be in here with her?"

Riley stared openmouthed and then chuckled. "I knew you were going to be okay. I swear to you, Glory Bea—I love you."

Suddenly shy, Glory looked away, but managed to get out, "Big words, mister. Prove it." She then sought his gaze, purposely exposing to him her hunger for him, her naked heart.

Riley's chuckles mellowed to a warm grin, then to a sincere smile, and finally to a heavy-lidded, desire-laden gaze. "I'll prove it."

Glory scooted over as Riley stretched out next to her on the narrow bed. With the curtains still open, the silvery gaze of the moon cast the room into grays and whites, giving Glory enough light to see the tender yet taut expression on Riley's face. He leaned over her. She reached up to cup his cheek,

felt the smoothness of his skin, as well as the beginning rough-
ness of his beard. "I love you, too. I always will."

Riley stilled where he was. Closing his eyes, with the barest
of smiles on his lips, he pulled his head back, as if savoring
her words like he would a fine wine on his tongue. After a
long, quiet moment, he once again was looking down at her.
"You, Glory . . . your words, your love . . . you save me. You
save me."

Glory had time only to frown in wonderment of how she
could save him before he pulled her to him and kissed her.
Frowns, wondering, all thoughts except those of pleasurable
sensations fled her mind, left her straining toward him, wanting to feel more, wanting to touch more of him. But sensing
by the way he held her, by the tenderness of his kiss that he
meant to be gentle with her, to respect her fragility, Glory
found herself impatient.

She broke their kiss, pulled away from the swirling sensation of his tongue in her mouth, even knowing as she did that
it mimicked the union of their bodies on a much deeper level.
Tossing her head, tumbling her hair all around her, she told
him, "No. Not like that. No holding back. All of you. I want
this."

Riley's hold on her tightened. His voice was breathless.
"Oh, damn, Glory. You don't know what you're asking."

With a hand around his neck, and her other clutching at his
shirtfront, she held him to her, spoke through her desire-gritted
teeth. "Then show me. I want to feel it all. I want to know
. . . you."

As if she'd uttered magic words, some timeless incantation,
Riley stilled, looked into her eyes, roved his gaze over her
face. And exhaled a shuddering breath. His voice husky, he
smoothed his knuckles down her cheek and all but whispered,
"I've waited all my life to hear you say that. And yet I want
you so much, it scares me. You're so little, I'm afraid I'll
break you."

Staring up at him, her entire world defined by his strong,
handsome features, Glory smiled . . . and pulled him down to
her. This time, she took his mouth, claimed his kiss, swirled

her tongue with his, felt the answering ache and tightness in the vee between her legs. Like a tiny white-hot poker, her bud ached for him, for his kiss. A moan shook through Glory when Riley pulled away, but only to cover her more fully with his body, to trail-nipping kisses across her cheek, her jaw, her neck.

Drugged by the sensations he lavished on her, Glory cried out in protest when he suddenly rolled off her and the bed to stand beside it, his hand held out to her. "Come here, baby."

Frowning, but not questioning, she scooted over to the bed's edge, took his hand, and stood up, turning her face up to his. He smiled down at her and then put his hands on her . . . undressing her. The skin-prickling sensation of his warm, strong fingers moving over the fabric of her blouse, then against the silk of her skin weakened Glory's knees. She clutched at his arms. He followed his hands with his kiss, claiming every inch of her that he exposed.

Almost without realizing she was doing it, Glory unbuttoned his shirt, smoothed her hands over the feel of his combination suit, unbuttoned it, reveling in the sculpted, masculine feel of his chest underneath it. Riley helped her, shrugged out of his shirt. Glory captured his gaze, saw his tight smile, read the desire there, the pleasure of her touch to him. Her senses inflamed, emboldened by his tensing over her as he bent to kiss her neck where it met her shoulder, Glory sighed out, "Oh, Riley, please. I can't take it anymore."

"Yes you can," came his husky response as he expertly and gently undressed her, opening her like a flower, revealing each petal of her femininity to his gaze, his touch, his kiss. Until finally he was kneeling before her, his hands spread on her bare back, his mouth capturing first one budded nipple and then the other. The sensations that rippled through Glory made her throw her head back, made the back of her throat dry and feel thick with need. She felt the cascade of her hair caress her bottom, felt the burst of desire in her belly when Riley all but raised her off her feet to kiss the soft, dark curls that covered her woman's mound.

A crying sound she'd never before made in her life rang

out into the silent air of the room. On its echo, Riley stood up, and with Glory's fevered help, divested himself of his boots and clothes. In only moments, he stood before her in his naked glory, proud, aloof, and yet totally wrapped around her finger, his heart in her hand.

Glory realized that . . . and accepted it. This man was hers, given to her by God. She could uplift him. Or destroy him. Looking deep into his eyes, seeing his soul mirrored there, Glory lifted her arms up to him, invited him into the center of her womanhood, gave him the gift of her heart.

"Oh, Glory." He sighed. And again he lifted her, gently laying her on the bed. He joined her there, lying half atop her, half beside her, his leg thrown over both of hers, as he smoothed his hands over her body. Near to writhing under his touch, so intense was the pleasure, so close to actual pain were the sensations he wrought, that Glory sought to pleasure herself with the feel of him. He was like warm marble, like a pulsing sculpture under her hands.

"You are so beautiful, Glory," he breathed, even as he shifted, moving over her, moving down her, his hands and lips playing her body like a harp.

"So are you," Glory answered him, running her hands over his shoulders, his neck, and clutching at handfuls of his thick, dark hair just as he—her breath caught, her muscles tensed— kissed her *there*. An aching cry of primal pleasure tore out of her, but she was helpless in his hands, forced to absolutely surrender against his mouth. Riley sipped and swirled, kissed and prodded. Glory's every nerve centered on the throbbing between her legs. "No," she murmured. "No."

But her mouth slacked open, her eyes squeezed shut. Time ceased to exist. Only Riley populated her world. Glory had to wonder why people the world over ever did anything but this, so good did it feel. It was her last thought before his ministrations brought her to the peak and tipped her over the edge. A throat-tightening, guttural cry escaped Glory as she rode the crest of her climax, as she undulated with a soft violence against Riley's mouth, as her body opened fully to his onslaught.

Clutching at handfuls of the quilted bedspread under her, as breached and vulnerable as any woman ever could be, Glory didn't even move when Riley kissed his way back up the length of her and settled himself in the saddle of her hips. He gathered her in his arms and took her mouth in the same way he just had her core. "This is what you taste like. This is who you are," he told her. "This is what I think of when I think about you. This and so much more."

Lost, undone, Glory arched her hips against Riley's powerful legs. She wrapped her own legs around his hips, pushed on his shoulders. He answered her by probing her opening, by unerringly finding her center, and slipping inside her. As if the mere contact with her innermost self was more than he could stand, he jerked, lowering his forehead to her shoulder. A ragged cry, some jumble of words that Glory didn't catch, accompanied his rapid breathing.

And then . . . they were one, in perfect union with their souls, with their love for each other. Riley rocked his hips against her, Glory met each thrust with one of her own. In this way, she struggled to express the depth, the force of her love for him. She wanted to show him that she was the woman for him, that she was his match. That her love could equal his. And the only way she could do it at this moment was to use her body as a vessel, to offer it up, to allow him into the secret places of her heart.

And to hope that, in the coming days, in the coming trials, this love she had for him would be strong enough to survive.

Chapter 16

The old buckboard wagon, pulled by the obedient roans hitched to it, clattered over the rutted grooves of the trail that connected the Thorne land with the Lawless boundary. Above it, the winter sun bathed the dun-colored hills and browning tallgrass in its weak morning light.

Glancing at the huge and steadily rising sun, Biddy huddled in her cloak and threaded the reins through her fingers. Then, dividing her attention between the horses' plodding pace and Louise Thorne at her side, Biddy said, " 'Tis sorry I am to be dragging ye out in this cold. But 'tis glad I am ye would come with me this morning. I'm near to being out of me mind with worry for Glory. I only hope she survived the night, what with the truth of that journal staring her in the face.''

Louise Thorne reached over to squeeze Biddy's cloak-covered arm. "Now, don't you fret none, Biddy. You did the right thing staying overnight with me. You couldn't see your way home in the dark, and Glory's smart enough to figure out that you'd stay. Besides, what with Ben and the boys being out with the cattle, and me all alone, I was glad for the company.''

"It was nice, wasn't it—just the two of us?'' Biddy was quiet a moment, but then added, "I'm hoping yer menfolk get them cattle back onto Lawless land before Mr. Rankin finds them gone. There'd be no end to the troubles.''

Louise shook her head, disturbing the trailing bonnet ribbons tied under her chin. "Don't I know it. You're right, too—about them trackers you spoke of last night. Because someone's taking pains to make us Thornes look like rustlers of Lawless cattle. I'd bet the same man who tried to hurt Glory is behind this—and wantin' us all at each other's throats. It makes sense. I swear, I told Ben no good would come of all them meetings about the danged Lawlesses—"

Biddy cut her gaze over to Louise, saw her wide-eyed, guilty stare, and encouraged, "Go on. 'Tis all right."

"I'm sorry, Biddy." Louise slumped with her words. "Sometimes I forget."

Biddy pursed her lips. " 'Tis easy to do. But still, yer menfolk are going to miss ye. And they'll not be happy with where ye are."

Louise waved that away with a brush of her hand. "They don't tell me what to do. Besides, it'll do 'em good to fend for themselves a day or two. If we don't pass 'em on the way to your place, they'll see my note when they ride in. I'm not worried about them."

Biddy nodded and smiled, spared her friend a glance. "Yer a good woman, Louise Thorne. A fine and loyal friend."

Louise brushed that away, too, with a hoot of laughter. "I just do what I have to, Biddy, what I feel in my heart. And don't forget, my firstborn is tied up in all this, too. I'm thinking of him."

Biddy adjusted the reins in her hands and forced a light note into her voice. "Ye know, he and Glory have been . . . alone now this past night."

She didn't have to say more. Louise shifted about on the buckboard seat, her weight rocking it. "I know. I reckon Riley, being the man he is . . . that he and Glory, umm, *know* each other by now. You suppose?"

"That I do." Biddy was silent for a moment, as she considered the implications of Glory and Riley's aloneness, but then she said, "I'm only hoping that me Glory hasn't figured out yet that she's Beatrice Parker. We should have known— all of us—that the truth would come out. But I never thought it would be like this. Or at this time, when we're still so raw from the murders and all. Mark me words, Louise—all these happenings are for one and the same reason.'' ⟍

A serious expression rode Louise Thorne's broad features. ''You think so? J. C. and Catherine being gunned down? The unrest over the land? That attack on Glory? The cattle showing up on our land? How could they all be related? That's a big stretch, Biddy.''

Biddy firmed her lips. ''I just know what I feel. But worryin' me most right now is this journal showing up after all these years. Poor Jacey. She had no choice but to pass it along. And now . . . poor Glory.''

Louise put a work-roughened hand to her lips. Her frown dipped her eyebrows low over her nose. She lowered her hand to say, ''I swear if this don't beat all. At least Glory's not alone. Riley wouldn't let the first thing happen to her. Why, that tracker, if he's still about, would have to kill him to get to her.''

''Aye, and well I know that,'' Biddy agreed. ''But the troubles I mean are of the soul. When that child learns she's not a Lawless at all . . . well, I . . .'' Biddy's voice trailed off with her mounting sense of impending doom.

''Biddy, you listen to me,'' came Louise's strong, kind voice. ''No matter what happens, no matter what Glory learns, Riley is right there with her. He loves her, and he'll see her through.''

Biddy nodded, blinking back sudden tears. ''Yer right, of course. But with everything against them, I only hope that their love is enough. For us all.''

Louise stared at her a moment and then pulled a hanky out of her coat pocket and dabbed at her own eyes. ''Look what you've done. Now I've gone to blubberin' like a baby—''

''Louise,'' Biddy cried, cutting off her friend's words. ''Look over there. Two riders comin' this way—and fast, as if the devil himself is on their tails. I'm not likin' the looks of this.''

While Biddy managed the horses, Louise straightened up and looked in the direction she'd indicated. Louise didn't say anything, but she wadded up her hanky and fumbled in both pockets. Biddy eyed her efforts and asked, "What are ye looking for?"

Louise turned her serious, brown-eyed gaze Biddy's way. "I forgot my pistol. You got a gun on you or in this wagon?"

Biddy's heart picked up its thumping pace. She gaped at the looming riders, heard their horses' hooves pounding the ground, and then shook her bonneted head at Louise. "No. I left in such a hurry yesterday that I never gave it a second thought. Oh, dear Lord, I'm only hopin' that whoever they are, they're friendly."

Louise shook her head. "I don't think so. They just pulled their guns."

Biddy frowned, joined her friend in staring at the menacing presence of the horses aiming straight for them, like arrows shot out of a bow. Like bullets speeding toward their targets. "Hold on. I'll try to outrun them."

With that, she snapped the long reins over the broad backs of the roans hitched to the Lawless buckboard. "Hiyah! Git up with ye."

Why, it's nearly lunchtime. Where did the morning go, Glory marveled as she stretched like a lazy cat and eyed the mantel clock. Dressed still in her chemise and morning gown, and seated cross-legged on the leather couch in the great room, she grinned as she turned her attention to watching the play of muscles across Riley's back. Clad only in his combination suit and denims, he crouched in front of the huge fireplace, working at rekindling the blaze—the one in the grate—that he'd started a few hours ago before breakfast.

As she watched every movement of his with the keen intensity only a lover can muster, Glory reflected over the changes in herself. When Riley'd arrived last evening, she'd been a lost and crying little girl, absolutely torn up about her true identity. A sudden clutching in the pit of her stomach told her she still hadn't dealt fully with that knowledge. *But look at me now,* she rushed on. *I'm sitting here all calm and collected, like the lady of the house with her man home for the day.*

, That thought made her cock her head wonderingly at Riley's back. She'd slept all night with this man. *Well, not all night. Not slept, anyway.* A guilty grin tugged at her lips as she bit at her bottom one. But still, did that explain the person she was today? *Maybe.* Glory shied away from that hesitation to say it was so, settling instead for acknowledging that she now knew every inch of Riley Eugene Thorne. Every finely honed and muscled, masculine inch.

She shook her head in appreciation of all that he was, from his thick and wavy black hair, down that broad back of his, to his narrow hips and long legs. A sigh escaped her. *Papa'd kill him, if he was here, for having slept with me.*

The errant thought jerked Glory upright, causing a sharp rustling sound of her skin across the soft leather of the couch. Riley pivoted to face her, his own face aglow with reflected firelight. "What is it?"

Glory shook her head, smiled. "Nothing. I was just . . . I was . . . Nothing."

Riley's neutral expression bled into a frown. He studied her face, nodded his head. "All right." But continued to stare at her. And to wait for her to explain, she just knew it.

"I just—" The words spurted out of her on a guilty thrust. She swallowed, shrugged her shoulders, looked down to consider her fingers knotted together and resting on her lap. She then glanced up at Riley, saw he hadn't moved . . . or let her off the hook. Every line in his body said he was waiting. Glory took a deep breath and decided to try again. "I was just thinking that if . . . Papa was here, he'd kill you for having . . . slept with me."

Wide-eyed with her own words, she looked away from his unblinking brown-eyed gaze, looked down again at her fingers. But even so, and as if she could read his mind and know his thoughts, Glory knew he waited to hear what she thought about that. And so, she sought Riley's eyes, and admitted, "I wouldn't let him. He'd have to go through me to get to you."

Riley stared a moment longer, as if unwilling to proceed through time until he'd absorbed her words, until he'd clarified for himself this underlying shift in allegiance, this new willingness of hers to fight for him, for what she felt for him. After a moment, he grinned broadly, showing white and even teeth as he chuckled and looked away from her.

Glory's mouth opened with happy surprise. She'd embarrassed him. What a revelation. That he—so big and capable and strong—could be undone by simple words from her. There it was again—that heady feeling of power that she'd sensed last night with their lovemaking. And again this morning.

Feeling suddenly warm all over, and knowing it had nothing to do with the fire in the grate, but more with the man in front of it, Glory soaked up Riley's presence. This perfect moment between them couldn't last, she knew, but lost in its exquisiteness, she gave herself over to enjoying it to the fullest. As if he felt something of the same, Riley ran a big, square hand through that black hair of his, and stared at his feet, telling them, "I'd never ask you to take a bullet for me. And I'm glad it won't have to come to that."

There it was. All that was and remained between them. It couldn't come to that, to her throwing herself between Riley and her father, because Papa was . . . gone. Both Papa and . . . her father. Two different men, but each one responsible for her life, for her being here to think and to feel these things. And both denied to her by murderers' foul deeds. Glory sucked in a deep breath through her pinched nostrils. And stared at Riley.

Bracing his palms across his knees for support, he stretched up to his full height and grinned. "But I appreciate the thought," he added.

Just seeing him smile banished her sad thoughts. Glory chuckled and held a hand out to him. Riley took a step toward her, but that was as far as he got. Because a fierce pounding on the front door shattered the cocoon of quiet surrounding them. And jerked her and Riley's attention in that direction.

Shocked into rigid reaction, Glory stared at the door and then twisted to see Riley. She caught his reflexive motion, the putting of a hand to his hip, only to realize that it was devoid of gun and holster. He jerked his attention back to her. "That doesn't sound like anything but trouble."

Despite the fear that chased across her nerve endings and goose-bumped her skin, Glory began scooting off the couch. "I'd better get it before they break the door down. It's probably Smiley or some of the hands." Standing now, she looked Riley up and down, seeing him as half-dressed and not belonging here. At least, according to the Lawless hands. "Maybe you'd better go upstairs."

Riley stared at her a moment, then shifted as he apparently took her meaning. "No. If it's your hands, they already know I'm in here. I rode right past two of them last night at the gate. And the others will have seen Pride in the barn by now."

In her mind's eye, Glory again saw Riley leaving her briefly last night to stable his gray gelding. Only now, though, did she appreciate what her men's reaction, in the morning light, to that horse would be. "That's exactly what I mean. They know you're in here."

Riley stilled, stared at her, looked somehow diminished by her wanting him to hide. Ashamed of herself, Glory looked away from his face. Only moments ago, she'd as much as told him she'd fight Papa for him, but now, when faced with the reality of that conviction, she was asking him to hide. No wonder he looked at her with all the disdain that Skeeter did his supper plate. Clutching handfuls of her morning gown, Glory said, "I'm sorry, Riley. I didn't mean—"

The front door was kicked. Gasping, Glory spun to face it, saw the lock splintering in its wood casing, saw the door give some, heard men yelling. Riley stalked past her—weaponless but jaw seriously clenched—and put a shoulder to the door, forcing it back in its jamb as he worked the tortured lock and then jerked the door open. As if the suction surrounding the opening of the door drew them inside, Ben Thorne and his four other sons poured into the room.

Right behind them were Heck Thompson and Pops Medley. Heck sought her gaze. "We tried to stop them, Miz Glory, but it was either shoot them or—"

"It's okay," Glory cut in, raising a hand to stop the man's tirade before he could bring them all to gunfire.

Heck clutched his long rifle with both hands, his knuckles

white around the weapon. "You want me to get Mr. Rankin?"

Her heart knocking against her ribs, Glory eyed the Thorne men. Armed to the teeth and looking grim yet haggard, as if they'd ridden all night, they eyed her right back. Determined to show no fear, she angled her chin up and shook her head. "No. I'm sure there's no need."

Her words had the desired effect. The Thornes relaxed their stances and turned from her to focus on Riley.

"Pa, what are you doing here?" Riley looked from his father, to his brothers ranged behind the old man, and then back at Ben. And watched his white-haired father search the room with his disapproving gaze.

Finally, he settled his black-eyed seriousness on his oldest son. "Where's your ma, boy?"

Riley's gut tightened. "Ma? I don't know. I haven't been home since I rode out with you to sort the cattle days ago. I came straight here yesterday after sending Biddy on to our place. You saw me do that." Then, even though he knew the answer, he had to ask. "She's not at home?"

Ben raised an eyebrow, ducked his chin. "Would I step foot on Lawless dirt if your mother was at home?"

Riley heard Glory's gasping intake of breath. And knew in his heart that trouble had found them. Had found them all. He forced air past his constricted lungs and said, "Give me a minute. I'll get dressed and—"

An abrupt gesture from Henry caught Riley's attention, cut off his words. "I told you, Pa, that he'd be here playin' house with a Lawless while his own mother was bein' kidnapped. And probably by someone in *her* employ." He stabbed a finger in Glory's direction.

His hands already curling into fists, Riley took a step toward his younger brother. "If Ma's missing, Glory had nothing to do with it, Henry. What the hell makes you think—?"

Ben caught Riley by the arm, stopping him. "Look at this." From out of his coat's deep pocket he pulled a black-velvet bonnet that Riley recognized as his mother's favorite, the one she wore when visiting. Only now it was crumpled and torn.

"We found it on the way here. Run over by wagon wheels. On Lawless land." Before Riley could do more than frown over that, his father reached into his coat pocket again and produced a slip of paper. "And this. Yer ma wrote it. I found it at the house. It says she and Miss Biddy was coming here."

Riley took the note, stared at his mother's familiar handwriting. In the time it took him to read her words—no more than a few seconds—a thousand details tore through his mind. Among them . . . when had the note been written? When did Ma and Biddy leave home? Where were they now? Had there been an accident with the wagon? Were they alive? Had they met up with strangers? Or with someone they already knew? Why hadn't Pa and his brothers seen any other evidence of them, like the wagon, the horses? That they hadn't meant someone was holding them, most likely against their will. But who? And why?

Realizing that these same fears drove his family, only they'd had more hours than he'd had seconds to burn with these questions and to worry, Riley forgave all, forgave their pounding and kicking on the door, their abrupt entry, Henry's accusing Glory. He put aside all else except finding the two women. Handing the note back to his father, he said, "I won't be but two minutes."

When his father nodded his consent to wait, Riley turned, sought Glory, and saw she hadn't moved from in front of the couch. Her white-knuckled hands were fisted around the delicate fabric of her morning gown. Her stare was the wide-eyed one of shock . . . too much shock in one lifetime. Sure he could read her mind, that she believed she'd now lost Biddy—the last of her loved ones, Riley ignored his family's disapproving presence and went to her.

Taking her by her arms, holding her close, he looked down into her scared and pinched little face, so heart-wrenchingly beautiful and, right now, so pale. "She's fine, Glory. Whoever did this didn't mean her or my mother any harm. Or Pa and my brothers would have . . . found them. And the wagon. I'll bet there's some simple explanation for all this. Like they ended up at the Sutfields' or the Nettlesons' place."

But Glory shook her head and spoke just above a whisper, as if she didn't want his family to hear her. "No, Riley. It's the tracker. I just know it is."

Confusion knit Riley's brow. "Tracker? What are you talking about?"

"In their letters—Hannah's and Jacey's. Someone in Arizona hired some men to track us down. I don't know why. But I think he's the one who attacked me on the verandah. Oh, dear God, Riley, if he has Biddy and your—"

Riley's grip on her tightened with his reaction to her words. "Why in the hell didn't you tell me about this sooner? Never mind—just listen to me. We'll find them, no matter who has them, and they'll be fine."

Glory's chin quivered. "You don't believe that at all, do you? Don't lie to me, Riley."

Riley looked down at her, heard the shifting of weight amongst the men ranged behind him, felt the outside cold air blowing on the grate's fire, and exhaled. "No, I don't believe that at all. But I do know we'll find them. And we'll find that tracker. Or whoever's responsible. And he'll pay."

Riley saw her sudden grimace, felt her flinch, and realized he'd tightened his grip until it must be painful on her slender arms. He instantly relaxed his hold and hugged her to him, over the surprised sniffs and intakes of breath coming from the other men in the room—Lawless hands and Thornes alike. "I want you to stay put and lock the doors until I get back. And keep a gun on you at all times."

Glory pulled back, flattened her palms on his chest. Her upturned face, especially her eyes, took on the sheen of guilty panic. "Could this have anything to do with"—she cut her gaze over to his family and then looked back up at him—"me not being . . . who I thought I was? Riley, what if it is the tracker? And he's using Biddy and your mother to draw *me* out? I couldn't stand it if anything happened to them because of me."

Her words seemed to grip his chest as surely as her hands did, so painful was the sudden lurch of his heartbeat. Behind him, he heard the further stirrings and mutterings of his family, but again he ignored them for Glory. "Listen to me. Even if that's his plan—or their plan—it won't work. Because *we* know about it. And we'll get Biddy and my mother back, I swear it to you. Glory, look in my eyes and tell me you believe me."

As Glory stared up at him, her mouth thinned into a straight line, her grass-green eyes lit with a fierce light from within. "Look at *me*, Riley, and tell me *you* believe that."

All around them was quiet, as if Glory's words had brought a pause in individual heartbeats, had forced the evil plottings of others out into the open. As well as between him and Glory—to forge their new bond, to forge their new trust. To test their love. And that being the case, what could he say? What promises could he make? Riley smoothed his hands down her arms, captured her small, cold hands, and squeezed them, saying, "I can't."

He then turned away, heading for the stairs.

For long moments after Riley's footsteps on the stairs no longer echoed dully in the great room, Glory stared quietly at the Thorne men over by the still-open front door. She wished Riley would hurry up, and for more than one reason. It was bad enough she was in her night clothes. It was bad enough they were men and she was a lone woman. It was bad enough they were enemies.

But it was worse that they all knew what she and Riley had been doing . . . together. But even beyond that, she wanted them all gone because she fully intended to search for Biddy and Louise herself. Because whoever had them wanted her. She knew that as surely as she knew her real name was Beatrice Parker. She hoped this tracker was ready for her. Because she was coming. Alone. She'd not endanger any other lives—Riley's chief among them—for what she knew in her gut was her trouble. And hers alone.

As the Thornes formed a cluster and spoke together in quiet tones, in essence ignoring her and excluding her in her own home, Glory realized that here it was—her chance to keep her part of the blood oath with her sisters. A frown captured her features, but firmed into a grimace. *Yes. My sisters—no matter the difference in our blood.* Having thought it, she paused to mentally poke and prod at that truth with the sharpened stick of please-let-it-be, and realized what she felt was just that— the truth. She was a Lawless.

A sudden warmth spread through Glory and freed her heart, but weakened her knees. She locked them, forcing herself to remain stiffly aloof, and explored this new feeling inside her. She'd been raised as a sister to Hannah and Jacey, and she would remain one. The three of them had vowed they wouldn't rest until the murderers were found and were made to pay with their lives. Like Hannah and Jacey, she hadn't been here to help Mama and Papa and Old Pete that awful September day. But she was here in November to help Biddy. And nothing and no one was going to stop her.

But she'd learned her lesson the other night when she'd pitched such a fit with Riley to join the search for her attacker. She knew better than to do that again. No one was locking her in her room. This time, she'd say nothing of her intentions, wait for Riley and his family to ride out, and then she'd get dressed—

"I'm . . . sorry for yer recent losses, Miss Glory."

Glory jerked back to the moment. Ben Thorne's voice had broken the weighty silence in the room. Not sure she'd heard him correctly, she sought the other men's reactions. Judging by the surprised expressions on all their faces as they too stared at the older man, she knew she was right—she'd just lived long enough to hear Ben Thorne express his condolences to her, a Lawless. She narrowed her eyes. Did he know she wasn't really a Lawless?

Ben made a half gesture, cleared his throat, and added, "I mean yer folks an' all. I didn't hold no warm feelin's for yer pa. You know that. And I can't say I didn't wish him harm a time or two myself. But I didn't—we didn't''—he nodded to indicate his sons—"there weren't no Thornes responsible. I'm just real sorry. And especially for Old Pete and yer ma."

Glory clamped her teeth together against the mixed message in Ben Thorne's words. Knowing how he felt about Papa,

knowing how he'd stirred up the other ranchers since the murders, the last thing she needed or wanted right now was this
man's pity. But he was Riley's father, after all, and she loved
Riley. So, fisting and unfisting her hands, she made ready to
thank him for his . . . kind words.

But apparently Ben wasn't done. He thinned his lips together and ducked his head, twisting the crushed bonnet he
held in his hands. Momentarily, he looked back up at her and
exhaled heavily. "I just felt I needed to say that."

Seeing the pinched expression on the man's face, his worried fondling of his wife's hat, and despite her own wariness
of him, Glory's chest tightened with locked-away fears. She
and this man could very soon have a shared loss to grieve . . .
if their search for Biddy and Mrs. Thorne ended badly. So,
keeping her steadily blurring vision centered on Riley's father,
Glory relented, softened. "Thank you, Mr. Thorne. I appreciate that. I'll pass along your condolences to Hannah and
Jacey when they come home."

He gave a nodding jerk of his head and made a vague but
benign gesture toward her, as if to say he recognized the peace
offering she extended. He rushed on with, "Have you heard
from yer . . . sisters?"

He knows. From just the way he hesitated before he said
"sisters," Glory knew he knew that she was sister to no one.
She also knew that what this man chose to do with that knowledge could determine the course of the rest of her life. But
binding him, just as it did her, was his love for Riley. How
ironic that the truth of her birth could align her with Papa's
enemy. And make them both somehow responsible for the
other one's happiness. With all that crowding her consciousness, Glory still managed to nod and to get her words out.
"Yes I've heard from them. I've gotten letters."

Ben Thorne nodded his big, white-haired head, scrubbed a
finger under his nose. "I hope they're doin' fine."

Do you? It was a mean thought, she knew, but this sharing
of . . . pleasantries with Ben Thorne was still new to her.
"They are."

Ben nodded, cut his gaze away from her, half turned to his

sons, exchanged a look with them that she couldn't see, and then fell quiet. Thus, they all waited. Until the cold air swirling about her feet and legs reminded her that the door was open and her armed men were standing behind the Thornes. "Heck, you and Pops can go on back to your posts. But first tell Mr. Rankin what's happened and send him to me."

She waited. But Heck and Pops stayed where they were—stayed staunchly, loyally where they were. Glory bit the inside of her cheek to keep from grinning at their blatant behavior. When she felt more in control of her facial muscles, she assured them, "I'll be fine here with the Thornes."

She looked to the Thorne men for confirmation of her trust, saw Ben nod, and then focused again on her hired hands. Seeing Heck's mouth opening, no doubt to protest, Glory spoke with command in her voice. "Close the door after you."

"Yes, ma'am," Heck grumbled as he jerked his thumb to indicate for Pops to precede him outside. "But I don't like it none," was the man's parting comment. He closed the door just shy of a slam.

In the resounding silence, Glory raised an eyebrow at the congregated Thornes, hoping she'd just conveyed to them, by sending her men away, that she wasn't afraid of them. Not when she was fully dressed and armed—like a few days ago at their place. And not now—alone, in her nightclothes, and weaponless. But, oh, she wished Riley would hurry up.

Just when the silence in the crowded room stretched out with her last nerve, Riley's hurrying footsteps upstairs in the hallway turned a grateful Glory in that direction. Within seconds, he clambered down the steps, crossed the room and, leaning over her, encircled her waist with one incredibly strong arm as he pulled her to his chest and kissed her. When he pulled back, Glory gasped, put her fingers to her mouth, and stared up at him.

Riley's expression revealed he knew exactly what he was doing. Holding her gaze, his black eyes lit with determination, he whispered, "They need to get used to that sight." Then he released her and turned to his family, leaving Glory openmouthed and watching him cross the room with long-legged strides, his saddle coat billowing in his wake.

Shouldering through his family's midst, angling his Stetson on his head, and every bit in charge as his father and brothers stepped aside for him, he said, ''I want go back over the ground where you found Ma's bonnet. From there, we'll search the surrounding hills and fan out from there. I'll just saddle my horse, and then we'll ride.''

In a slightly dazed silence, brought on by his claiming her publicly, Glory watched him go. And bided her time. And plotted out her own search for the two women.

Chapter 17

Of all the things that could take her breath this day, Glory never thought it could be the punch of frigid air that rocked her back against the front door, which she struggled to close behind her. Firming her stance on the verandah, and gripping the knob with both hands, she finally banged the door shut. Turning around, she stiffened in surprise when Heck Thompson stepped around from the far side of the verandah to confront her.

"You're to stay inside, Miss Glory—Mr. Rankin's orders."

Frowning as much from the blue cold that shocked her unsuspecting body, even under the heavy fabric of her split riding skirt and Papa's sheepskin coat, as she did from Heck's near-command, Glory raised her chin a determined notch. "Mr. Rankin takes his orders from me, Heck. Not the other way around."

Looking momentarily taken aback, Heck nodded his head but persisted, "Yes, ma'am, I know. But not in this instance."

This was the last thing she needed. A wall of resistance from her own men. Glory narrowed her eyes at her hired and loyal hand. "In this and every instance—make no mistake." She stalked across the wood-plank floor of the verandah, heading for the wide steps there. "Don't try to stop me."

Booted footsteps echoed hollowly behind her as Heck trailed her. "No, ma'am. But, umm, can I ask where you're going?"

"To the barn."

"You're not thinking to follow after them Thornes, are you?"

Realizing that at least she could answer this truthfully, and already down the steps, standing on the hard-packed earth, Glory looked back over her shoulder. "No, I'm not."

Heck puffed out a breath which, coupled with his widened eyes, signaled his relief on that score. "Then perhaps I can just follow you out to the barn?"

Sucking in a stunted breath, which all but froze her lungs, Glory hunkered inside her clothes and wrapped her arms around her middle as she stared up at the man and tried to come up with a good reason why he couldn't. And frustratingly couldn't think of one. So, she shrugged her shoulders and turned around, heading for the barn. "Suit yourself."

"Yes, ma'am. It suits me to go with you."

The man's pigheadedness made her want to stomp her foot. "Where is Mr. Rankin, anyway? He never did come to the main house. Did you tell him I wanted to speak with him?"

Suddenly Heck didn't seem to be able to look her in the eye. Instead, he focused—innocently enough—on her chest. "Well, I tried to tell him. But I didn't git no further'n saying Miss Biddy was missin' afore he yelled for some of the men, and they all lit out, close on the heels of them Thornes."

Glory's breath puffed out in a distressed, white-cloud vapor. This was awful news. And good news all at the same time. Good for her chances of getting away by herself. But awful for them all, if her men caught up with the Thornes. Feeling time slipping away, Glory suddenly broke into a sprint, heading for the barn, for her horse.

Right behind her came the labored breathing and heavy footsteps that told her Heck dogged her every step. Maybe when she got inside she could come up with a sidetracking task for the big man that would allow her to saddle Daisy and to get away without having to conk him on the head or threaten him with her gun. She wasn't sure she could do that. Not to Heck, at any rate. But to whoever awaited her out there? Well, that was another story.

A flash of sanity asked her just what made her think she'd be the one to live in the coming showdown. After all, she was only one small woman who wasn't used to handling a gun, much less her fists, if it came to that. And yet here she was setting herself up against a trained and experienced killer. Glory's steps slowed momentarily with that thought. Forced into it, she admitted to herself that if she had a lick of sense, she wouldn't be trying to get away alone, but would stay put, just like Riley had ordered her to do.

Glory's eyes narrowed as she tried to picture, in her mind, this lurking, hired killer she intended to catch. Suddenly, a leering, broad and pockmarked face lurched into her consciousness. Glory bit down on her tongue to keep from crying out. Carter Brown. That big, obnoxious drifter that Riley'd hired the same day he had Abel Justice. She hadn't liked the man from the first moment he'd laid a meaty, unwelcome hand on her that windy day. And she'd liked him even less out in the bunkhouse office for trying to provoke a fuss between her and Riley over who gave the orders here.

Glory fumed at herself for not having realized before now that Carter Brown had to be the man behind all the troubles here, including the attack on her. Why in the world Riley had hired him on after firing him here, she still couldn't say. But her only regret was that her indecision back then had cost that nice Abel Justice his job, too. Well, when this was over, she'd find a way to make it up to the God-fearing man that Skeeter'd all but eaten that day at the graves. All he'd been doing was paying his Christian respects. Glory felt even worse for having treated him no better than the old hound had.

Her thoughts finally carried her to the huge and closed barn doors. Heck hurried around her to open one of them. With only a wave of her hand, Glory indicated for him to leave it open, once they were inside. The mingled, familiar scents of hay and leather and horse assailed her nostrils as she strode purposefully down the central passage to Daisy's stall. Once outside the chestnut's stall, Glory stopped short and turned to her escort.

The man drew back to keep from running into her.

"I'll be right here with Daisy, Heck." She reached into her pocket and pulled out her pistol, pointing it as non-threateningly as possible at his chest. "As you can see, I'm armed, too. So, I'll be fine here by myself. Go tell Sourdough I said to keep supper warm until the men get back. And tell him I don't want any of his bellyaching about having to wait on them. He's not to close the kitchen down until *after* the men eat. Take however long you need to make sure he understands I mean it, too. You got all that?"

What could the hired hand say? Glory's lips twitched around a triumphant grin. But Heck's mouth tilted down into a frown. "Yes, ma'am. I'll go tell him. I only hope he doesn't knock me in the head with his frying pan." With that, he turned away, but then he stopped and turned right back around to face her. "Don't you go nowhere, you hear?"

"I hear," came Glory's reply to the man's actual question. Yes, she did hear. She heard just fine, thank you, and had all her life. "Now, go on and talk to Sourdough."

Thus urged, and with essentially no choice, Heck nodded—his grimace reflecting this was definitely against his better judgment—and turned away, heading back in the direction of the opened barn door. Watching him, as did the few curious horses whose heads poked out of their stalls, Glory repocketed her gun and waited where she was until he turned a corner and disappeared from view. As if the animals knew the next move was hers, they swung their big heads back to her and waited.

She didn't make them wait long. Lifting the gate latch on her mare's stall, she stepped through and closed it behind herself. After greeting Daisy with a pat and some soothing noises, Glory hurriedly set about the task of bridling and saddling the fine-boned horse. But guilt kept her looking over her shoulder, expecting as she did to see Heck's scowling face appear outside the stall at any moment. But luck was with her. She finished her task without interruption.

Sighing out her relief, Glory clutched Daisy's reins. She was as ready as she'd ever be. Tugging her reluctant mount, who seemed only to want her warm stall and oats, out into the central passage, Glory all but tripped over one of the biggest surprises of her life.

Skeeter sat on his haunches in the aisle, his big redboned head cocked in curiosity and no small amount of censure at her.

Glory nearly cried out in shock and happiness. At the last second, she clamped a hand over her mouth and stared wide-eyed down at Old Pete's hound. Not letting go of Daisy's reins, Glory quickly knelt and hugged the dog, who fondly nosed her and came to his feet, his tail wagging.

"What are you doing in here?" Glory whispered, looking up and down the still-empty aisle before focusing again on the heavy-jowled dog. His tongue lolling, his intelligent eyes staring, he seemed to be asking her the same thing.

"Don't you look at me like that," she fussed. "And what about you? You pick now for announcing you're over your mourning and have decided to live? Well, I'm happy for you, but I have to go. You stay here."

With that command, she stood up and pointed down at the hay-strewn, dirt-packed floor. "Stay." Skeeter obediently sat down but again cocked his head questioningly at her. Glory raised an eyebrow at him. "You don't worry about where I'm going. You just stay here."

Not sparing him another precious moment, Glory mounted Daisy and urged her into a walk. Looking back over her horse's rump, Glory saw Skeeter sitting where she'd left him, a knowing expression on his face. Again, she shook her head. And that was the last she thought of him as she gained the outside of the barn, turned Daisy sharply to the right and dug her booted heels into the mare's sides.

The chestnut responded with a burst of speed that saw them pounding over the hard-packed ground of the service court and then out under the arched gateway of the fenced yard. Horse and rider all but flew past the two startled and quick-stepping hired hands who jumped out of the way. Posted at the gate, they called out to her, but Glory pretended she couldn't hear them.

She knew they'd raise an alarm among the remaining men,

but it couldn't be helped. She had to do this herself. She had to find the tracker—and Biddy and Louise before Riley did. If anything happened to Riley because of her, she just couldn't live. She figured he probably felt the same way about her, but except for his mother being held captive with Biddy, this wasn't his fight. It was hers. And hers alone.

Glory fought the stinging wind in her eyes and scanned the surrounding hills and tallgrass as best she could. Glad she'd tied her hair back to keep it out of her way, she was nevertheless aware of the heavy braid as it whipped across first one shoulder and then the other as she sought her adversary out on the unforgiving landscape. She knew he could position himself on the downslope of a near hill, take aim, and shoot her—all without her ever seeing him.

But she didn't really think he would. After all, if he simply wanted her dead, and he really was Carter Brown, then he'd already passed up a hundred or more chances at a clean shot at her—today and in the past weeks. No, make no mistake, Glory figured, this tracker wanted a showdown with her.

Thinking that, she reined her mare and wheeled the horse in a circle atop a hill. In a gritting whisper, she challenged, "Here I am, Carter Brown. You want me? Then you come and get me. But this time, I'm armed and ready for you. This time you won't sneak up on me in the dark. Come on. Where are you?"

Suddenly hearing herself, Glory reined Daisy and clutched reflexively at the saddle horn. Where had all this courage come from? This challenging? This daring a shootist to face her? Why, if she didn't know better, she'd think she was Jacey. Wasn't she dressed just like her? And armed just like her? Wasn't her hair braided back like Jacey's? Then Glory realized it wasn't only Jacey's spirit gripping her. It was Hannah's, too—Hannah's oldest-sister protectiveness and deeply ingrained sense of honor and duty to protect those she felt responsible for.

Only then did Glory realize that tears streamed down her cheeks. She'd just been born into the family. This is what it meant to be a Lawless. Standing up for yourself, facing down the enemy on your own. Protecting your own people. Bearing the terrible weight of their lives. Putting your own life on the line for theirs.

As if the oath she'd shared with her sisters, as if the mingling of their blood with hers had truly made them one, Glory wanted to cry out in a war whoop, wanted to challenge the sky, defy the earth, wanted to shout to Mama and Papa in heaven, and to Laura and Seth Parker, to tell them to look at her. And see what she'd become. Like Skeeter, who'd decided to heal and to live, here she—Glory Beatrice Parker Lawless—was ready to own up to the truth about herself, ready to begin living her life as her true self.

But first, she had to live through the next few hours. Quickly swiping away her tears and blinking back others that threatened, Glory forced herself to calm down and see her surroundings. Not only to look around but to see. Realizing she probably had only moments before the guards at the gate and Heck were saddled and on her trail, Glory again wheeled Daisy in a tight circle.

And this time was rewarded with the startling, gut-wrenching sight of a lone man standing atop a distant hill, facing her, and silhouetted against the blue expanse of the sky. Her heart tripping over itself, Glory hauled back on Daisy's reins, bringing the obedient mare to a stiff-legged stand. With all her being centered on the man, Glory watched dry-eyed as he raised his arms heavenward, as if challenging: *Here I am, come and get me.*

So her life had come down to this moment. She swallowed the sudden fear that clogged her throat. Focusing on her enemy, fighting the bitter sting of the wind, Glory frowned with the realization that the man was still too far away for her to identify him. All she knew was he hadn't been there a moment ago. Had he then sprung up from the earth itself? As she watched, the man lowered his arms to his sides, stilled into a gunfighter's stance. And waited.

Able only to suck in a shallow breath through her pinched nostrils, so tight was her chest with anticipation, Glory pressed her lips together. Almost immediately, as if at some predetermined signal, she dug her heels into Daisy's sides, leaning over her mare's neck and urging her into an all-out gallop over the undulating hills, racing ever closer to the man. Ever closer to the fight of her life.

Glory didn't know what she expected the man to do as her mare's pounding hooves covered the ground between them. Would he run? Would he go for his gun? Would he disappear over the side of the hill and lie in wait for her? Whatever he did, she'd have to be ready. But the nearer she rode, the more her sense of surprise, of wariness, grew. The man didn't move at all. He stood his ground and waited, never even looking away from her. Strange.

When she was almost upon him, but still too far away to see his shaded face clearly under his wide-brimmed hat, Glory was finally gripped by caution. Keeping her gaze riveted on the strange-acting man, she began reining Daisy to a walk. But never looking away from him, she kept on coming.

Suddenly, the man pivoted to peer down the far slope of his hill, as if something out of Glory's sight held his interest. Her breath caught. *Please, God, don't let it be Biddy or Mrs. Thorne.* She'd no more than prayed it before the man twisted back to face her. Almost certain now that this was a trap, Glory felt in her pocket for her pistol. Facing an enemy was one thing. Being stupid about it was another.

In the shallow dip between the hill she'd only just ridden over and the upward sweep of the next one the man stood on, Glory reined Daisy and dismounted. The man watched her as closely as she watched him. Then, he nodded at her and turned to make his way down the other side of his hill. Glory had a decision to make—to follow him, or not to follow him.

Weighing each option and its consequences, and finally deciding—she'd come this far, hadn't she?—Glory pulled her pistol out of her pocket. Feeling instantly comforted by its cold weight in her palm, she wrapped her finger around the trigger, dropped Daisy's reins, and followed him on foot.

Topping the hill, barely aware of the cold wind that blew, of the clouds that gathered, of the hushed silence of the prairie, Glory saw the man. And frowned, her mouth going dry. Up close, he wasn't big at all, not like Carter Brown. Then who was this? Keeping his back to her, he squatted down on his haunches at the hill's base. From what she could see, he appeared to be running his fingers through the loose soil at his feet.

Cautious curiosity had Glory raking her gaze over this stranger. Slightly built for a man. Not too tall. Dressed soberly. And too quiet to be Carter Brown. Then who? She decided to put the question to the mysterious stranger. "Who are you?" she called out, shattering the day's silence and startling two quail out of a nearby scrubby bush and up into the air. Their flapping wings emphasized her next words. "What do you want?"

Putting his hands to his knees and levering himself up, the man stood and turned around. His greeting carried to her on the wind. "Afternoon, Miz Glory. Fancy meeting you out here. And all alone, too."

Glory gasped and stumbled back a step, nearly falling over loose gravel under her heels. "Abel Justice! You?"

"Yes, ma'am." His eyes narrowed to slits. The conniving grin on his thin lips gave him the appearance of a crow. He pointed a bony finger at her gun. "What you figuring on doing with that shooting iron? You afraid of me?"

Glory's grip tightened reflexively around the weapon, but she ignored his questions, preferring to ask one of her own. "What are you doing out here?"

Under his sweat-brimmed felt hat, Abel Justice's skinny cheeks lined with his leering grin. "Waitin' for you. I knew you'd come."

His words hit her with the force of a blow. Her mind screamed for her to run away from this enemy, this tracker from Mexico that Jacey'd warned her about in her letter. She'd been wrong about Carter Brown. All this time it'd been Abel Justice. Scared beyond measure, almost beyond control, Glory blurted, "Where are Biddy and Mrs. Thorne?"

The man's grin broke into a smile that looked like pure evil to Glory. "They're hid away for the time bein'. But whether or not they live . . . well, that's up to you, Miz Glory."

Glory shifted her stance, willed her throat not to close with the spasm of fear that shot through her. *Keep him talking,* her mind screamed at her. "Who sent you?"

"Señor Calderon, down in Mexico. I work for him."

Glory recognized the name from Jacey's letter. Wishing she could dry her sweating palms on her skirt, but not daring to show this hired killer any sign of a fearful reaction on her part, Glory tightened her grip on her pistol and asked, "Did he send you to kill me?"

Justice shook his head. "No, I'm just to deliver you to my boss. Now, what *his* intentions are . . . well, I cain't rightly say. But you'd already know, if I hadn't been shot that day we ambushed yer pa. And time's been a-wastin' while I holed up and healed. But now I'm more'n ready to get on the trail. See, I got me a pile of money riding on yer head. And I aim to collect it." With that, Abel Justice advanced a step on her.

"Not so fast," Glory blurted. She raised her gun, pointing it at the man's narrow chest. He stopped where he was. "Don't move." A bone-deep cancer of hatred narrowed Glory's eyes. She wanted with all her being to empty her gun into this man's skinny gut, to uphold her blood oath with her sisters. He'd just admitted his guilt in Mama's and Papa's deaths. With her heart thudding, her palms sweating, Glory all but snarled, "If it weren't for you holding Biddy and Mrs. Thorne, you'd already be vulture bait, you . . . you bastard."

The tracker eyed her and then her gun. He spread his hands wide, purposely leaving himself open, and said, "If you shoot me, you'll never find them two old ladies. Leastwise, not until after they're froze to death. Or starved. Now, put that gun down. You and me's got to get on the trail back to Mexico."

"I'm not going anywhere with you. Now take me to Biddy and Mrs. Thorne. Or prepare to die. Right now. Right here."

Abel Justice looked her up and down, as if assessing her seriousness. Then he shrugged. "All right, I'll take you to 'em. Let's go."

His cooperation was unexpected. And most likely a trap. Glory cut her gaze around their barren surroundings. "Where's your horse?"

He stabbed a thumb back over his shoulder. "Beyond that next rise there." He then eyed her weapon. "Why don't you put that away"—his eyes hardened—"before I'm forced to take it away from you?"

Glory swallowed hard and blinked. "I wouldn't try that, if I were you. You'd be dead before you took another step."

Unbelievably, Abel Justice took another step toward her. And chuckled. "See? I ain't dead. We both know you ain't goin' to shoot me. Now why don't you just lower that there gun and put it away? I said I'd take you to the womenfolk, and I will. But not with a gun at my back."

With her arm aching and her breath coming in shallow gulps, Glory challenged, "And then what—after you take me to them?"

His answering leer stood the hairs up on Glory's arms. "We'll just have to see, won't we?" he crooned in a threat-lowered voice.

Glory gulped back her fear and frustration. She had no choice but to cooperate—not with Biddy's and Mrs. Thorne's lives hanging in the balance. So, trapped but not defeated, she lowered her gun and sought her pocket. "All right. We'll do it your way."

When she glanced back up, it was to see Abel Justice, his hands clawed and reaching for her, almost upon her. A startled cry tore out of Glory. She had time only to open her mouth in shock as she stumbled backward and fumbled in her pocket for her gun. But too soon, too late, he clutched at her arms, his momentum taking them both to the unforgiving ground. As Glory fell to the hard-packed earth, she cried out again as she saw the man's raised fist—in a time-slowed, molasses-thick moment—come arcing down toward her jaw.

Abel Justice's animal snarl, the feel of his surprisingly solid weight atop her, pressing her into the rocky ground, and his white-knuckled fist arcing down in a path aimed at her jaw were the last things Glory saw and felt before her world exploded into a burst of painful darkness.

* * *

No more than thirty minutes after they'd left Glory, still in her nightclothes and standing in the great room of the Lawless house, Riley reined in when his father and brothers did. He sought their eyes, but knew the answer even before he asked, "Right here? This is where you found Ma's bonnet?"

"Yep," Caleb answered him. "Right here."

Zeke chimed in with, "There aren't any other clues here. We looked. And we told you—the ground's too hard for wagon ruts or hoofprints to be left behind. Even the tallgrass has already stood back up from the wagon wheels."

Riley ignored Zeke as he huffed out his breath and scrutinized the ground around them all. But like Zeke said, not even a single, trampled blade of grass could he find to act as a clue. Nothing to point the way. Fearing defeat before he even got the chance to try, Riley notched his Stetson up. "All right. John, you and Zeke go on back home, wait there in case Ma shows up. In case she and Miss Biddy did just go off on a visit."

When the younger two of the five Thorne sons started to protest, Ben cut into their griping. "Do as he says. This ain't no time for arguing. In fact, Henry, you take Caleb and the two of you go get any of the men we can spare from the herd. And then ride for the Lawless place and meet me and Riley there. Now, get going—all of you."

Surprised at and more than a little worried by his father's words, Riley frowned as his brothers obediently paired off and wheeled their horses in the two separate ways Ben Thorne had just sent them. When only he and his father remained, surrounded by the quiet indifference of no-man's-land, Riley spoke his mind. " 'Meet us at the Lawless place?' What are you thinking, Pa?"

Ben shook his head and firmed his lips before meeting Riley's gaze. "I'm thinking that if there's trouble, we're going to need all the help we can get."

Riley's stomach clenched, as did his hands around Pride's reins. "No Lawless did this, Pa. You can't ride in there, guns blazing. Think about it—Miss Biddy wouldn't allow anyone to hurt Ma. And the Lawless hands sure as hell wouldn't hurt Miss Biddy.''

Ben's lined and craggy features hardened. "Who rode over to our place and got your mother? Biddy Jensen. She's in with them. They've got your ma. If your judgment wasn't clouded by your feelings for Glory, you'd see that.''

"That's crazy talk, Pa, and you know it. Miss Biddy plotting against Ma? She'd never do that. If *your* judgment wasn't clouded by your wanting the Lawless land above all else, you'd see that." For long, hard moments, Riley stared without blinking at his father, who said not a word in reply.

For a split second, Riley's thoughts turned inward. *Glory.* He saw her as he'd left her. Alone. Scared. The same look on her face she'd had the night someone tried to kill her out on the verandah. *Son-of-a-bitch. That's it.* Riley blinked, focusing on his father's grim face. "It's not Ma and Miss Biddy at all. Their being kidnapped was a trick to draw us all away. Pa, it's Glory he's after. Not Ma. Not Miss Biddy. But Glory. She's the target.''

Ben's thick, white eyebrows all but met over his nose. "Like hell she is. It's not Glory's who missing. It's your ma, boy. Your ma. Don't you have any concern for your own blood?''

Riley wheeled Pride until the gray gelding faced the direction of the Lawless spread. His muscles bunched with his effort to control the stamping, grunting animal. He pulled back sharply on the reins and all but spat out his next words to his father. "I'm telling you that it's Glory who's the target. And as sure as I'm sitting here and talking with you, she's been taken, too. I've never been more sure of anything in my life. When we find her—if she's not dead already—we'll find Ma and Miss Biddy. Are you with me, Pa, or against me?''

Ben's mouth worked. His dark eyes snapped. He looked over his shoulder, back the way they'd just come, and then turned in his saddle to stare toward home. Finally he looked again at his son. "I've got to go look for your mother, Riley. There's no Lawless I'd ever care to—''

"Glory's not a Lawless and well you know it." The words

exploded out of Riley. "She's never done a thing to hurt you or anyone else. Put aside your differences. J. C. Lawless is *dead*. There *is* no feud. No one to fight with anymore. But someone wants Glory dead. Now, I'm riding back for her, and I'm asking *you* to come with me. I'm asking you to choose between a piece of land and the woman I love. Choose between your hard feelings for anything Lawless and the life of an innocent girl."

Knowing full well the import of his words, Riley watched the play of emotions across his father's face. Ben looked once more toward home, took a deep breath, and turned to Riley. "You better hope to hell you're right, son. Because if you're wrong, and something happens to your mother as a result, I'll never forgive you. Now, let's ride for the Lawless place."

Chapter 18

Deserted. The Lawless spread appeared deserted. No one manned the arched gateway to challenge Riley and his father as they walked their horses under it. Not one soul inhabited the dirt expanse of the wagon yard. Only one narrow door stood open on the big horse barn. No smoke arose from any of the two-story main house's chimneys. No kerosene-lamp light shone from within, against the afternoon's growing darkness.

The quiet was downright nightmarish. Even Pride spooked, forcing Riley's attention momentarily back to his gelding. He then exchanged a glance with his father, whose grim expression mirrored how Riley felt inside. Then, fisting Pride's reins in one hand, Riley reached under his saddle coat with his other and withdrew his Colt from its holster. Ben Thorne did the same. The sounds of the two guns being cocked broke the silence.

"It's too quiet, son. Something's real wrong here."

Eyeing the main house just ahead, and forcing himself into a relaxed-appearing posture, Riley nodded "Yeah. I agree."

At Riley's right, his father shifted his weight in his saddle. "You think it could be an ambush we're riding into? I don't know about you, but I feel like I've got a bull's-eye painted on my back."

"I'm feeling some of the same," Riley admitted. But targets for whom—the Lawless hands? Or Lawless enemies? Had something unspeakable again happened here since they'd ridden out? With his heart thumping in time with each of Pride's dull, thudding steps, Riley tried to see everything at once, with as little outward evidence as possible of doing just that.

Then . . . he saw him. Just sitting on the verandah and staring evenly back at him. The sight forced Riley's blood through his veins at a heightened pace. He pulled back on the reins, bringing Pride to a halt. At his side, Ben reined in, too. "What is it?"

Nodding his chin toward the shadowed verandah, Riley said, just above a whisper, "Over there, Pa. On the porch."

Ben shot Riley a questioning glance and then turned to look where he directed. "What am I looking for, son? I don't see nothing but an old redboned hound dog."

"That's exactly what I mean. That's Skeeter. Old Pete Anglin's hound that was wounded the day of the murders last September. This is the first time I've seen him off Old Pete's grave since he just showed up one day with a healed wound. No one knows where he went to lick his wounds. But wild boars couldn't get him out of that cemetery since then."

"That's mighty interesting," Ben said, cutting his narrowed gaze in a slow circuit around the hard-packed dirt of the wagon yard. "And yet, here he is. On the front porch. If that don't beat all. It would seem, then, that something awful important drew him away."

Riley nearly slumped in relief. Pa understood—and was giving the Lawless folks the benefit of the doubt. "That's the way I see it," Riley commented as he searched the area for the metallic glint of an aimed gun, for the glimpse of a furtively scurrying man as he moved from one hiding place to another. But . . . nothing. Only a stray chicken or two, a couple of kittens, and a long-haired dog, his nose to the wind, went about their business.

Then, as if the quiet weren't eerie enough, Skeeter suddenly jumped up and began an awful baying as he paced the length of the verandah. Startled almost out of his skin, Riley jerked his gun up, aiming at anything that moved. His father mimicked his actions. Then Riley wheeled Pride, urging the gelding alongside his father's mount. With the gray's nose even with Ben's mount's rump, the men could turn their horses in a slow, defensive circle without anyone sneaking up on them. No one did.

"There's nobody out here—that's for danged sure. That baying would bring 'em running if there was. Go see what's eating at that hound, son, before I shoot him myself. He's setting my teeth on edge."

"All right." With that, Riley turned Pride and set him at a trot for the main house. Once there, he called Skeeter. The hound came to the edge of the verandah, to the top of the wide steps, and stayed there. Wagging his tail, the dog bayed his greeting to Riley, and then stared at him, as if waiting for him to understand the problem. Riley gave the dog an assessing gaze, then trained the same look on the main house's closed front door. Finally, he turned to look back at his father and the barn behind him.

Nothing had changed. Or moved. Focusing again on the hound, knowing this animal's keen tracking skills, Riley spoke softly and levelly. "She's not in there, is she? Find her, Skeeter. Where's Glory?"

Skeeter cocked his head at Riley. Then he wagged his tail hard enough to wriggle his long and lean body. Nervously, he moved in place with mincing steps, raised his big head, whuffed at Riley, and then jumped off the porch, tearing for the barn. Like a red arrow shot out of a taut bow, he covered the ground at blinding speed, never once wavering in his direction.

"Damn," Riley muttered, looking after the hunting dog. Then, digging his heels into Pride, urging the big, tired horse after the hound, he signaled for his father to follow them. Ben turned his mount and came at a fast clip behind Riley.

Once at the barn's open door, the two men dismounted and cautiously, leading with their drawn weapons, made ready to enter the dim interior. But before they did, Ben asked, "What the hell'd you say to that hound?"

Riley shrugged his shoulders as he cautiously moved to enter the barn. "I told him to find Glory."

"Hmm," Ben offered. "Well, let's see what's in here."

With that, the two men slinked inside, sticking close to the rough walls, their guns held at the ready. A few curious horses watched them flattening themselves against the walls and peering around corners. But it quickly became apparent that their stealth was unnecessary. The barn was as empty of folks as was the yard. Riley straightened up and holstered his gun.

Doing likewise, Ben asked, "Where'd that dog go?"

Before Riley could say he had no idea, Skeeter answered for himself with a throaty bark. Riley exchanged a look with his father and then turned toward the sound. There, about halfway down the central aisle of stalls, stood Skeeter, his tail wagging slowly. His big, dark eyes never looked away from whatever . . . whoever . . . was in that stall. And then, suddenly, Riley didn't want to see who it was.

If it was Glory . . . If she was . . . A hand squeezed his upper arm. Riley jumped, and felt suddenly sheepish when he met his father's knowing gaze. "It's okay, son. We'll go together."

Riley nodded, then moved to the open gate of the stall he knew was Daisy's, Glory's little chestnut mare. Only there was no horse inside. And no Glory. But Smiley was. The old foreman lay moaning and spread-eagled atop the hay. A blood-crusted lump just above the man's temple told its own story. Riley rushed over to him and knelt, helping the older man to sit up. "Smiley, what the hell happened here?"

Smiley blinked and clutched at Riley's sleeve for support. Frowning in confusion, breathing shallowly, he mumbled out, "Brown. Carter Brown. He knocked me on my head."

Riley jerked in surprise and sought his father's gaze. "That bastard must be the one who attacked Glory the night before I fired him and Abel Justice." His expression hardened at the same rate his heart did. He eased the Lawless foreman back down and jumped to his feet. "I'll kill him."

He didn't get any farther than one long-legged step before his father grabbed him by his arm. "Calm down, son. Going off half-cocked could get you and all three women killed."

Just then Smiley Rankin shoved to his feet and clutched at the stall side to steady himself. "Three women? Who—?"

"My wife, for one," Ben threw out before Riley could answer. "And Miss Biddy and Miss Glory. They're all missing. Do you know where they are?"

Smiley's eyes widened as he stared at Ben and then Riley. "Miss Glory's missing, too?" Almost absently, the old foreman rubbed at his head just above his temple and then frowned at the clumpy, dried blood on his fingers. "If this don't beat all." He then looked from Riley to his father again. "We got to find them right now."

Still gripping Riley, Ben held his other hand up to Smiley. "Not so fast. No one wants to find them any more than we do. But it was riding out with nothing more than piss and vinegar to guide us that created this mess. So, think for a minute, Smiley, around that headache of yours. What do you know about what happened here? How come there's not a man to be found on the place?"

The old foreman stared at Ben a moment, as if he didn't recognize him, but then shook his head, telling him, "After you and yours left, I gathered up my men and rode out to look for Miss Biddy. We didn't see nothing—the men are still out searching. But I had second thoughts about Miss Glory staying put, and so rode back myself to check on her. When I got here, Heck told me he'd left her here in the barn with her horse.

"I knew right then she meant to light out on her own search for her nanny. But when I came in here, hoping I'd catch her, she was gone. I'd no more than turned around before that damned Carter Brown came at me with the butt-end of his pistol. We struggled, but he got the better of me. And knocked me on my head. Then you two showed up."

"Damn," Riley spat out between his clenched teeth. He pulled away from his father's grip and stepped out of the stall. His back to the two older men, hearing them talking in low voices but not listening in, Riley put his hands to his waist and stared absently at Skeeter, who sat quietly on his haunches. *Carter Brown. And I hired the bastard.* But then he thought about Smiley's exact words and jerked back around.

"Did you say Glory was already gone when you came in here?"

"Yep," he confirmed. Then his eyes widened. "That means he doesn't have her, right?"

Riley nodded, rubbed a hand over his jaw. "At least not then, he didn't."

"Then, son, there still may be time."

Riley met his father's gaze. "I hope so. I didn't tell you before, but Jacey wrote Glory to warn her about some shootists hired to track down the Lawless sisters. Jacey didn't know the why of it when she wrote, but Glory's convinced it has something to do with her real folks. Carter Brown must be that tracker. And I hired the son-of-a-bitch, just brought him right into the fold, didn't I?"

"You didn't know, son."

"That won't make me feel any better if he kills—" Riley bit off his angry, fearful blurt when he saw the stricken look form on his father's face . . . a collapsing, vulnerable, old-man expression he'd never before seen there. Affected in ways he couldn't put into words, Riley made a helpless, apologetic gesture towards Ben. But the white-haired, older man abruptly turned his back on his son. For a moment, Riley didn't know what to do, where to look.

In the next moment, though, Smiley made a throat-clearing noise. Riley gratefully turned to him, saw that the foreman's face was regaining some color. It then occurred to Riley that someone else was missing. "Mr. Rankin, I didn't see Heck anywhere. Didn't you say he was here when you rode in?"

Smiley stopped in the act of brushing hay off his clothes to shoot Riley a look of dawning understanding. "Yeah, he was. He's the one who told me to come in here—where Carter Brown was. And Heck's the one who let Glory out of his sight—against my orders. I'll be danged. You think he's in with Brown?"

Riley shrugged, frowned. "He could be. I'd hate to think it, though, as long as he's been with you."

Holding onto the wide slats of the stall side, unsteadily groping his way out hand over hand, Smiley gritted out, "Help me find that boy. If he's anythin' but dead or just plain stupid, I'll shoot him myself.''

Riley quickly lent a helping hand to the determined foreman as his wobbly steps brought him to the stall's gate and then out into the aisle. Without a word, Ben Thorne positioned himself on Smiley's other side, also gripping his arm. Thus, the three men headed for the open barn door. From the corner of his eye, Riley saw Skeeter padding along obediently beside him.

As they headed for daylight, Riley's thoughts broke out into words. "This is just what we need, isn't it? By now Henry and Caleb will have our men all riled up and searching the prairie. And your men"—he stabbed a finger at Smiley—"are already doing the same. And each posse'll think the other one's got the women.''

Smiley gave a fatalistic nod of his head. "And if the two meet up . . . given all the years of bad blood between us . . . shootin' first and askin' questions later is bound to happen.''

"Yep. And I'm responsible for a lot of that,'' Ben Thorne threw in, surprising Riley. "But even with two of my boys amongst those men, I say we've got to take our chances on that outcome and concentrate on finding the women.''

Riley shot him a look, grateful that his father would meet his gaze. "I agree with you." He then turned to Smiley. "You think you can ride, what with that lump on your head?"

The foreman jutted his stubble-shadowed jaw out. "I can ride. My horse is out by my office. Just walk me there." Smiley muttered his next words, but loud enough to be heard. "Can I ride, he says." Then, pinching his features up into an insulted grimace, he raised his voice and eyed Riley. "Boy, when I can't ride my horse, you bury me—'cause I'll be dead.''

Despite himself and their dire predicament, Riley felt heartened by the crusty old man's gumption. "Then we'd best ride—and I mean now.''

Ben nodded. "Let's do it. But in which direction? The prairie's a mighty big place. More'n one man's hidden out here, never to be found if he so chose.''

Riley knew the truth of that. No-man's-land, while home to

a handful of law-abiding cattlemen such as themselves, was also an outlaw haven for the very reason his father'd just named. "And Carter Brown would so choose," he finally commented.

Ben Thorne's bushy eyebrows lowered over his deep-set black eyes. "But he ain't as familiar with this country as we are."

Riley nodded at that, adding, "Another thing in our favor right now is"—he cut his gaze to his father's face and just as quickly looked away—"he has three women with him. Who don't want to be. So he won't get far—at least not with the afternoon getting long on shadows. I figure he'll have to hole up somewhere pretty quick—somewhere he can easily corral Glory, Miss Biddy, and Ma."

Riley's chest tightened at the somber gazes his father and Smiley Rankin leveled on him. No one wanted to say it. No one dared say it. But they were all thinking it. *If Carter Brown still has the women with him. If he hasn't already killed them.* Riley took a deep breath and then spoke with a quiet confidence he didn't feel. "They're alive, Pa. They're with him. They have to be."

"I know, son," Ben answered, his eyes holding a suspicious moisture that had him again turning his head away from his son's gaze.

In the ensuing silence that ticked away at the minutes and added miles to the distance separating them from the tracker and his prisoners, Riley squinted in fevered concentration as he prayed for inspiration and catalogued what he knew, starting with Carter Brown. Where might he be holed up right now, what with three women to herd and with night approaching? That was the question that needed answering.

But Riley had also to consider that Brown was smart enough to know he'd be found out and would be hunted. Might he then *not* stick to the most direct route back to Arizona, his eventual destination? At the least, he'd cover his tracks. Maybe even leave an obvious but false trail behind.

After all, the man was a trained tracker. "What we need," Riley mused aloud, "is a tracker of our own, someone who can smell out the man's trail.'' The words were no more than out of his mouth before he stopped short, causing the other two men to do the same and to stare at him. Riley met their gazes and grinned, turning to stare down at the dog behind them. ''And there he is. The best nose in the territory. Can you do it, Skeeter?''

The big, redboned hound, a keen intelligence shining from his black eyes, stared back up at them. With no more than a disdainful blink for such an absurd question, he then padded around them, heading for the open barn door. Once there, he raised his nose to sniff the air and then turned to look back at them.

''Hot damn!'' Smiley Rankin blurted around a chuckle. ''Cain't man nor beast hide from that hound. I bet he's already got the scent.''

''Yep. And he's been waiting on us to figure that out.'' Riley grinned broadly as hope began thawing the cold that clutched his heart. Glory's sweet and smiling face suddenly popped into his head. She was quickly joined by his mother and Miss Biddy. *We're coming. Just hold on. Be strong. Do whatever it takes to keep yourselves alive*, Riley told them from his heart. He then settled his gaze on his father and Smiley Rankin. Pointing at the hound, he told them, ''If anyone can find them, he can. Let's mount up.''

Despite her dire circumstances, despite her shock at seeing Carter Brown again, Glory exhaled in relief. Biddy and Mrs. Thorne were indeed alive. She could now face anything that happened to her. And had to admit, anything could happen to her. Because here she was, relieved of her gun, tied up and gagged, and only moments ago thrust onto the hard-packed earth floor of a long-forgotten squatter's shack.

But this old place was on Lawless land, and only about a twenty-minute ride from the main house. Hope renewed itself in Glory's soul. They'd be found before nightfall. It was that simple. All they had to do was stay alive until then. She pictured it in her mind. The men would discover that she and Biddy and Mrs. Thorne were missing. They'd spread out and search for them. And sooner or later, they'd stumble onto this cabin.

Already feeling it in her bones, Glory tried to communicate some assuredness to the two older women. Bound and gagged just as she was, they lay on their sides, facing her. Their creased foreheads and fear-edged expressions, as they stared back at her, broke her heart. Glory could only blink and shake her head at them. *Don't be afraid. I'll do whatever it takes to get you freed. I swear it.*

It wasn't working. Glory slumped. They were as scared as she was. Still refusing to give in to hopelessness, she resolutely told herself to ignore her throbbing jaw, the chafing of the ropes that bound her wrists and ankles, and the foul stench of the dirty bandanna that all but cut off her breath. She couldn't do anything about them, anyway. Instead, she needed to be brave and to—Oh, who was she kidding? She was as defenseless as a newborn. All their lives were in danger.

Abel Justice had tricked her, had talked her into lowering her defenses. And now look at her. Tied up tighter than a hog bound for butchering. Stupid, stupid, stupid. When would she learn? And who was she to think of bravery and big plans of saving Biddy and Mrs. Thorne? Saving them—how? Why, these hired killers could decide to shoot all three of them at any minute. And if they did, what could she do about it?

Having thus chastised herself to the point of terror, Glory wriggled about until she could see—and keep an eye on—the two hateful men whose backs were to her. They hadn't moved. She exhaled a hot breath through her nose. Positioned one on either side of two narrow windows set in the east wall, Abel Justice and Carter Brown scanned the hills for riders. Glory didn't doubt for a moment that riders would indeed show up sooner or later. And when they did, more men would die . . . because of her.

Blinking back sudden tears, she struggled to rid her mind's eye of the vision of Riley falling wounded or dead from Pride's back. No! She couldn't bear it, she couldn't live if that happened. Why then hadn't she acted on her suspicions about these two men weeks ago? Why hadn't she asked more questions, taken more control? Acted more like the boss lady she'd fancied herself to be?

The guilt was hers. She admitted it. Everything. All of it. Her fault. Then why couldn't she be the only one to pay for her inexperience and bad judgment? Glory's brutally honest thoughts directed her unwilling gaze back to her two bound-and-gagged companions. Riley's mother and Biddy. The older women's mournful gazes met hers. And made her feel worse. And more determined to get them out of this drafty, falling-down old hovel alive—even if it meant her own life. She owed them that much.

Glory had no more than settled that for herself before the guttural sounds of the trackers' low voices captured her attention. She saw Carter Brown nod at Abel Justice. Then both men turned their heads to stare at her. Their expressions reflected a calculating slyness. Glory's throat all but closed. Her stomach muscles clenched. They'd been talking about her.

As if to confirm this, Justice spoke up again, this time taking no care to keep his voice down. "We got *her* now," he was remarking. "So we don't need them old ladies. Let's just kill 'em and ride for Mexico. If we hand her over to Señor Calderon, maybe it won't matter none that we messed up and killed J. C. Lawless. 'Cause it's *her* he wants—even more'n them two Lawless girls."

Carter Brown's expression could only be called dubious. "I don't know. We were forced to kill J. C., all right. He didn't give us much choice. Still, the boss ain't going to be none too pleased. You sure she's important enough that he'd overlook the mess we made of things here?"

Stunned beyond a reaction, beyond blinking, or even taking a breath, Glory stared at the two killers. She heard the gag-muffled, mournful sounds coming from Biddy's direction, but there was nothing she could do to help her nanny. It was all she could do to breathe and to look into the eyes of the men who had killed J. C. and Catherine Lawless.

"Hell, yes," Justice finally answered, nodding at Glory. "She's the one he wants. The old man's been planning this for years."

"That's exactly what I mean," Brown reasoned. "With J. C. dead, so's his plan. He ain't going to be none too happy."

Justice's face suddenly reddened and his voice rose. "I'm telling you, it'll work. Now, I'm for riding for Cielo Azul. You going with me?"

Carter Brown's jaw jutted. "No. I'm telling you—we got J. C. Lawless's blood on our hands. If we show up in Sonora—with or without her''—he stabbed a beefy finger at Glory—''we'll find ourselves buried alive up to our necks in the desert and feeding every ant and scorpion that happens by."

Justice exhaled gustily and thumped a bony fist on his thigh. "Then why in hell did we stick around until my shoulder healed and then stir up all the trouble we could before kidnapping these women? We can't ransom them. There ain't no one left at the Lawless place to ransom 'em *to*. So we're stuck. We *got* to take her to Señor Calderon and talk our way into gettin' him to pay us for her."

"Pay us?" Brown all but snorted. "He'll kill us—right along with her—is more like it. And I for one ain't about to die for something I didn't do, for something that wasn't our orders. *You* shot J. C. Lawless—not me. And I seen you do it. You back-shot him while he stood over his dead wife. And I'll be glad to tell Señor Calderon that."

Abel Justice's snarl robbed Glory of a response to Carter Brown's horrible accusation. "You-son-of-a-bitch," the smaller man gritted out. "We're both in this up to our ears, and don't you forget it. But if I'd knowed you was going to chicken out on me, I would've carried on by myself—and kept *all* the money we're due. It's rightfully mine, anyhow, and you just admitted it."

Brown jumped up so suddenly that Glory jerked back against the rough wooden wall behind her. She heard the sharp inhalations coming from Biddy's and Louise Thorne's corner, but didn't dare spare the two women a glance. Not with this scene unfolding in front of her.

"Who you calling a chicken, you skinny little turd?"

Brown was yelling as he hauled Justice up by his coat's grimy lapels.

"You," Justice answered calmly, for someone whose boots no longer came into contact with the ground. Before another second passed, he raised his arm, stuck his pistol's bore flat against a very surprised Brown's forehead, and said, "I shoulda done this a long time ago," and pulled the trigger.

Everything happened at once. The gun's muffled report jerked Brown upright, his blood spattered the wall behind him, he released Justice and wilted to the floor. Justice fell atop him but instantly scrambled to his feet. Glory sucked in a shocked breath through her pinched nostrils, felt ill, feared she'd vomit into her gag and choke to death. From their corner of the one-room shack, Biddy and Louise made similar noises.

And then . . . just as suddenly as the chaos had begun, all was quiet again. Until Justice, holstering his gun as nonchalantly as if he'd just shot his supper and not his partner, riveted his narrow-eyed gaze on Glory. And started for her.

Shaming herself by whimpering in fear and drawing her knees up to her chest, Glory tucked her chin against her shoulder and breathed in and out too fast. Her head all but swam with her worsening light-headedness.

But still the cold-blooded little man came closer and closer with each step.

As resigned and unresisting as any trapped animal that knows it's going to die, Glory prayed—screamed in her head—for courage and presence of mind. But felt neither of those things. Standing over her now, Justice looked into her face, and then flicked his gaze up and down her before drawling out, "What's the matter? You look scared."

Glory's jaw jutted convulsively against the smelly bandanna covering her mouth and knotted at her nape. She swallowed time after time, realized she was slowly shaking her head from side to side. And couldn't remember the last time she'd blinked, so dry and scratchy were her eyes.

Justice knelt beside her on one knee, his hands resting on his thighs, as he remarked, in a tone of voice all the more chilling for being pleasant, "It would appear there weren't no need to tie you up, after all. 'Cause we cain't stay here now. Not even for the one night.''

The implication of his words hit her like a slap. He meant to leave right now and to take her with him to Mexico, to Señor Calderon. Biddy and Mrs. Thorne instantly set up a muffled fuss. Glory cut her gaze toward the hoarse sounds, but made one of her own when Abel Justice grabbed her roughly, wrenched her away from the wall, and flipped her roughly onto her stomach.

Breathing in the musty scent of the dirt floor under her nose, Glory suspended thought as she concentrated on the feel of his callused fingers clawing at the rope securing her wrists and booted ankles. In another moment, she felt the ropes fall free and realized she could move her arms and legs. Some deeply imbedded survival instinct told her to lash out. But she'd no more than braced herself to do just that before Abel Justice grabbed her arm and flipped her over to face him.

His six-shooter—again drawn and this time aimed about two inches from *her* forehead—rid her of any notion of trying to overpower him. Coupled with that cold-steel deterrent was the certain knowledge that if she didn't win the upper hand in a struggle with him, she knew she wouldn't be the one he killed.

No, she was valuable to him—a bargaining chip and a pile of money—according to his own words earlier to the now-dead Carter Brown. If she resisted him, he'd probably shoot Biddy and Mrs. Thorne. And make her watch. So, helpless with fear of the man and fear for the other women's lives, Glory did nothing but tear her gaze from the pistol's black and round bore to stare into the man's dark-brown snake-eyes.

He arched a thin eyebrow at her. ''Get up, Miss Glory.'' As she struggled to comply, he grabbed the bandanna tied around her mouth and yanked it down, untying the knot. Stuffing it in his coat pocket, he then hauled her up with him, pulled her close against his sweaty self, and gritted out, ''One thing you need to think on, Miz Glory, is I ain't got no more use for them old ladies over there.''

Glory's stomach clenched. ''Then turn them loose.'' She

heard her own voice, no more than a dry husk of its usual timbre. "They're no threat to you."

Justice dragged a hand over his chin. "Well, I think they are. They know too much. An' it's all their own fault, too. They shouldn'a been out by theirselves this morning. Taking them wasn't me and Brown's plan, but they sure made a nice distraction. 'Cause here you are. And I'll bet them Thorne men and the Lawless men are out there right now a-killin' each other over them."

Before she could stop herself, even knowing as she did that it was foolhardy to rile this killer, Glory blurted, "Or maybe they're right outside, right now. Waiting on you to show yourself."

Far from riled, looking instead more considering—like a rattler thinking about striking—Justice cocked his balding head at her. "You think so? Well, won't they be surprised when they start shooting—and I throw you outside, right in the line of fire? That'd be plain tragic."

Wondering where this Jacey-like bravado was coming from, but not questioning it, Glory countered with, "More tragic for you than me, Mr. Justice. If I die, you don't get paid—or worse."

The man's features hardened. He gripped her arm, hauled her up to his face. "You ain't as smart as you think. See, Brown was supposed to ride to yer place and nab you while I guarded these old women. But when he didn't show, I set out to see why. That was when I spied you riding hell-bent-for-leather over them hills. And Brown was smart enough to head here when he seen you wasn't at home. So you rode right into a trap. No, not too smart."

Hot-eyed and tight-lipped with helpless anger, Glory silently met her captor's level stare. Let him brag on. Maybe, just maybe, Riley or some of the other men would happen along before she was forced to ride off with this hired gun. Now she hoped they would show up, would kill him. Because what he didn't know was she no longer needed him. Before, he'd held the upper hand. He knew who was behind her folks' murders. But now, he'd given her the only thing she needed—a name. And it was Calderon.

Justice blinked, breaking the spell between them. He then yanked Glory around until she faced Biddy and Mrs. Thorne. "Now we're back to these two. I don't need 'em no more, so if you give me any trouble, they're going to end up like Brown. But if you behave yerself and ride out with me all nice and peaceful-like, I just might leave 'em here alive. It's up to you. What's it going to be?"

Glory didn't even hesitate. "I'll behave. You just keep your word."

Justice snickered . . . an evil sound competing with Biddy's and Mrs. Thorne's renewed but muffled protests, which he ignored. "I cain't. I never gave it. But you'll just have to take yer chances and behave, won't you?" He then shoved her ahead of him and toward the door. "Let's go. Me and you's going for that little ride to Mexico I told you about earlier."

Chapter 19

I'll kill him. I'll kill him. I'll kill him. That one recurring thought, with Carter Brown's face on it, tightened Riley's white-knuckled hands around Pride's reins. And kept him sane as he and his father and Smiley Rankin, about thirty minutes out from the Lawless barn, sat immobile atop their horses, atop a tallgrass-capped hill. And watched Skeeter nose and nervously circle a patch of ground.

Repeating his pattern of the past half hour, the redboned dog lifted his nose high in the late-autumn air and sniffed. His black and wet nose fairly wriggled as he tested the air for a scent revealed only to him. Suddenly, the big hound stilled, his muscles shivered under his loosely hung coat of fur. Knowing what this signaled, Riley tensed, gripping his prancing gray gelding's belly with his thighs and knees.

In the next moment, and with a keen, bird-flushing, rat-scurrying bay, the hound announced his victory. A triumphant grin stretched his bewhiskered black muzzle as he turned sharply to his right and settled into a loose-jointed lope over the prairie's rocky terrain. On a course forever pointed away from the Lawless homestead, Skeeter ran, his long ears flapping in the wind like drying laundry.

Riley marveled at the dog's stamina. For weeks on end, the faithful hound had mourned atop Old Pete's grave, risking the cold and the wind, and refusing to leave it or even to eat. They'd all feared he would waste away and die before the month was up. Obviously, they were wrong. But still, today was the first time Riley could recall seeing the hound show any sign that he cared about living—except for when he tried to rip poor old Abel Justice apart for daring to pay his respects inside the Lawless family cemetery.

Skeeter bayed again, pulling Riley back to the moment. Under the low brim of his Stetson, he squinted at the big hound up ahead. The dog's healed shoulder wound, gleaming bone-white and arrow-thin against his reddish fur, bore witness to his rightful stake in this manhunt. A grim smile split Riley's face. Could it be that all this time Skeeter, probably under cover of night, had been stretching his legs and hunting his own supper, making himself strong and whole again so he could be a part of this final retribution?

No, Riley chided himself, that was just plain fanciful thinking. Dogs had no notion of hate and revenge . . . did they? Was Skeeter that intelligent, that conniving even, to stay out all night and then return before daybreak to take up his self-appointed post atop his master's grave? Had he fooled everyone—including Carter Brown?

Riley found himself hoping so. Found himself again in the grip of some newly forged hardness in his soul, born of the cold acceptance that, to love someone like he loved Glory, rendered him capable of taking the life of anyone who dared threaten hers. And take it without mercy. Without regret.

For Riley, shooting or not shooting the tracker no longer hinged on whether or not Glory and Ma and Miss Biddy were alive. Either way, that worthless scum was dying. Today. In fact, to him, Carter Brown had been a walking dead man from the first instant he'd put a hand on any of the three women Riley loved.

Just then, Skeeter bayed again and wrenched Riley back to the sting of the waning November afternoon's frigid air on his chafed cheekbones, back to his awareness of the aching soreness in the stiffened muscles across his shoulders. Slowing Pride, Riley sat up tall in his saddle, focusing on the dog. Skeeter took another sharp turn to the right and bounded to-

ward a far hill, a rocky one particularly higher than the surrounding dun-colored swells.

Its very difference captured Riley's attention, had him
throwing up a cautionary hand to his father and Smiley when
they bunched in their saddles, preparing to send their mounts
after the dog. "Hold on," he called out.

The two older men hauled back on their reins, setting off
an agitated prancing in their horses, already poised for a burst
of speed. Ben Thorne didn't like it any better than his mount
did. "Why'd you stop us? Skeeter's found something over that
hill."

"He sure enough has," Smiley Rankin seconded. "That
caterwaulin' of his means he's treed his varmint."

"I hear him, too," Riley assured them. Indeed, the dog's
throaty barking carried to them on the wind, and held an un-
mistakably triumphant note. "No one wants to find the women
worse than me—or put a bullet into Carter Brown. But what
are we riding into? It could be a trap."

"Well, hell, son," Ben entoned, yanking his felt hat off his
head and hitting his thigh with it—a signal, Riley knew, of
his father's anger or impatience. "If trouble was waiting over
that hill for us, that dog would already be shot dead."

Riley stuck to his guns. "Maybe not—not if it *is* Brown
and he wants Skeeter to lead us right into an ambush."

Ben had no comeback for that. He blinked and stared at
Riley, as if he hadn't thought of that, and then resettled his
hat on his head. Riley then turned to Smiley. "You know the
lay of this land better than anyone. Anything in particular over
that hill?"

The foreman frowned as he directed his attention to the far
hill. After a reflective moment he said, "Seems to me there's
a falling-down, old, deserted squatter's shack setting under
them oaks. Ran them dirt farmers off years ago."

Riley tensed. "Then this is it. That shack is exactly what
Brown would need to keep the women corraled—and to keep
a lookout."

Along with Ben, Smiley sat straight up in his saddle and
stared at Riley. "Danged if that ain't so."

"Wait here," Riley said, already dismounting. He handed his reins to his father. "I'm going to sneak a peak over the top there and see what's going on. Just watch for my signal."

Not waiting for an answer or an argument, Riley took off at a sprint. The crisp afternoon's cold air frosted his lungs and had him breathing hard by the time he reached the slope. Scrabbling up its near side, he dropped to all fours and then finally down onto his belly to slither to the top. Once there, he yanked his tall Stetson off and held it at his side while he risked a peek over the hill's crest. He swept the scene below with a quick, assessing glance. The only thing moving was Skeeter, who wagged his tail and bayed at the rough-cut door of a pile of sticks some would call a cabin.

But no horses out front. And no men. Or bodies. Calling that good, Riley next considered the sparse stand of blackjack oaks that crowded against the shack's walls. Leafless, spiny branches reached for the sky. But under them . . . was the Lawless buckboard wagon. Then something moved. Riley tensed, looked closer. A horse. A roan horse. And another one next to him. Looked like they were hitched together. Biddy'd had two roans pulling the wagon yesterday. His heartbeat picked up. The women were here.

Riley scooted a few feet back down the hill, scraping his hands on sharp rocks in his haste and sending loose gravel sluicing down ahead of his boots. Ignoring the stings of pain in his palms, he turned on his side and signaled for his father and Smiley. Waiting until they reined in at the hill's bottom, Riley told them, "They're here. That old buckboard and the team are out back in the trees. But no other horses. And Skeeter's barking at the front door."

Smiley Rankin nodded, frowned, and rubbed at his stubbly jaw. "That bloodhound wagging his tail?"

"Yeah."

"Good." Then turning to Ben Thorne, Smiley drawled, "Toss your son his reins. We can ride right in. Skeeter's tail would be stuck plumb up in the air stiffer'n an arrow, if he smelled trouble."

Heartened by the foreman's words, and willing at this point

to take any good news at face value, Riley came to his feet and accepted the reins from his father. He quickly mounted Pride and took his unopposed position at the head of the threesome as they wheeled their mounts to circumvent the hill. When they approached the cabin, Riley pulled his gun from its holster. Similar noises from the two men flanking him told him they had taken the same precautions.

Remaining vigilant, even in the face of Skeeter's relaxed stance and swinging tail as he turned his big head to stare back at them, the men rode in slowly, warily. When no shots rang out, when no one challenged them, they dismounted and looped their reins over a left-leaning hitching rail. And then just stood there, unwilling to meet each other's gazes. Riley thought he knew why. He was no more anxious than they were to face what might await them inside.

"Well," his father said matter-of-factly, drawing his and Smiley's attention to himself, "we ain't accomplishin' nothing standing out here. What's in there won't be changed none in a few minutes."

"True enough," the Lawless foreman chimed in.

When neither man still moved, Riley turned on his heel and, his pistol in front of him to lead the way, stalked to the shack's closed door. The crunching of the gravelly dirt behind him told him that his father and Smiley followed him. When he reached Skeeter, Riley leaned over, patted the waiting dog's shoulder, and mouthed, "Good boy." But only by suspending further thought and denying his roiling emotions could he make himself grip the door's crude handle and begin slowly to tug it down.

Not hampered by any such reticence, Skeeter excitedly pressed his furry body between Riley and the door. Taking a deep breath, telling himself he was ready for anything, Riley pushed it open, burst inside, and directed his pistol in a sweep of the dim, dank one-room interior. Skeeter bounded off to the left, toward what sounded like muffled cries coming from a corner obscured from view by the open door. Before Riley could even turn in that direction, though, his father and Smiley charged in behind him, taking up their positions to either side of him.

Then, it registered—what they were seeing directly in front of them. For a moment, to Riley, the muffled cries and Skeeter's whining yelps held no more meaning than a distant babbling brook might have. Because it was the blood spattering the back wall and running in a thick smear down the rough-cut wood, ending at the body slumped in a dead sprawl on the earthen floor, that held his senses prisoner in those first few seconds.

Finally, he sucked in a breath—laden with shock and no small amount of relief. "Son-of-a-bitch," he muttered. "Carter Brown. He's dead."

"That'd be my guess," Smiley Rankin offered over Riley's shoulder. "A bullet to the forehead's been known to do that."

As if the sound of the older man's voice broke a spell that gripped him, Riley blinked and exhaled. Turning, suddenly aware of the significance of the muffled cries filling the room, he holstered his gun and rushed with Smiley and his father to the room's far corner, where Skeeter backed off when the two older men quickly knelt in front of the struggling women to untie and ungag them.

Fury at seeing his mother and Biddy lying there, tearful and helpless, pumped through Riley's veins. Only relief that they were alive could supplant the knee-weakening emotion. But the trouble wasn't over. Not by a long shot. His first thought when he saw Carter Brown dead was that, by some miracle, Glory had shot him. But that couldn't be. Because she never would have left Biddy and Ma here like this. That meant . . . someone else was involved. Carter Brown had a partner. Who was it? That was all he wanted to know. Who was it, and did he have Glory?

In only an instant, but what seemed an eternity of waiting to Riley, the women were freed of the ropes and the gags. While Smiley helped Biddy to sit, Ben did the same for his wife. Riley's mouth worked around his emotion as he watched his father gather his mother in his arms and hug her tightly to his chest as she assured him she was none the worse for wear.

To Smiley's question of what happened, Biddy sought Riley's gaze. Her apple-cheeked face crumpled with emotion as she sobbed, " 'Twas Abel Justice. He's got Glory, Riley. He was in cahoots with Carter Brown. They had a fuss over money, and he killed him and took Glory."

Even as his father and the Lawless foreman jerked in shock and turned to look over their shoulders at him, Riley's senses quickened, honing in on Biddy's fright-glazed blue eyes. Her words sounded all the more ominous for her voice being hoarse and whispery. Riley's mind raced through a jumble of questions as he tried to sort all this out. But uppermost was the only question that really mattered at this moment. "How much of a head start does he have?"

Biddy shook her gray-haired head. "I'm not sure. Not long. Ye have to find her, Riley. That man . . . he—" Her voice broke, tears spilled out over her lashes and tracked down her grime-streaked cheeks. Smiley pulled her to him, gently tugging her head onto his shoulder.

Even though sympathy for the sweet old woman tugged at Riley's heart, he instantly turned to his mother. "Where's he headed with her?"

Her broad face strong and composed, she pulled back from Ben and said, "Mexico. He's taking her to Mexico."

"Mexico?" Ben Thorne repeated. "Then he's heading for the Cimarron Cut-Off. That'll take him to the Santa Fe Trail."

Nodding, already picturing the trail in his mind, Riley met his father's black-eyed gaze. And then frowned as he looked deeper. Surprise at what he saw reflected in their dark depths stilled him. Everything that was in Ben's heart, things Riley'd never suspected, things he knew the proud, stubborn man would never say to him, shone for a brief instant.

Then, Ben's mouth worked, his square chin dimpled. "I been wrong for a lot of years, son . . . like you said . . . about what's important. I see that now. And almost losing your mother like this? Well, I—You go after Miss Glory. We'll take the women to the Lawless place and then go call off the men." He paused for a deep breath and then added, "We'll wait for you there. Son, I . . . just know I . . ."

His voice trailed off. He sought his wife's gaze. Her soft smile seemed to encourage him. Firming his lips, he turned again to Riley, saying, "Well, you just be careful, you hear? Your mother'll be worried."

Moved in more ways than he could name, Riley squeezed his father's shoulder, and nodded at his mother. "I'll be careful." He then straightened up to his full height, adjusted his Stetson low on his forehead, and looked from one face to the other as the quiet foursome stared up at him. "The Cimarron Cut-Off, huh? He'll never make it."

Grim and tight-lipped, he turned on his heel. Calls of "Take care," "God speed, son," and "Watch yer back" followed him across the room. But accompanied only by Skeeter, Riley stalked out of the shack and headed for Pride. Before this day was done, Riley vowed to himself, justice would not only be served . . . but Abel Justice would be dead.

Glory wanted to cry. She wanted to give up, to admit defeat. Her bottom was numb. Her thighs ached. Her complaining spine refused to hold her erect in the saddle. Worse, her nose was running, her heart pounded with fear, and her cheeks burned from the cold wind. Add to that the rubbed-raw skin over her wrists, again roped together and secured around her saddle horn, and she was one sad girl.

She stared at Abel Justice's narrow back. Hateful man. He'd looped Daisy's reins to his saddle horn and was leading the little mare at a bone-jarring, teeth-rattling trot over the uneven and rocky terrain. As like as not, Glory feared, Daisy would soon tire and stumble and fall, crushing her in the saddle. Then what? Why, as determined as Abel Justice was to get her to Mexico, he'd probably stuff her broken body into a flour sack and deliver her like that.

Heading west as they were, Glory took note of the pale light cast by the afternoon sun. Judging by its position, she figured they'd left Biddy and Mrs. Thorne behind less than an hour ago. At least the tracker had kept his word about letting them live if she cooperated. Still, he'd not allowed her to untie them. Glory pursed her lips. Hopefully, they'd be found quickly and wouldn't have to spend the night in that cold, drafty shack with no food and water.

Even though their well-being was uppermost in her heart, her mind also clung to the knowledge that the sooner Biddy and Mrs. Thorne were found and could tell the men what had happened, the quicker they'd come after her.

Thinking of her own rescue, praying yet fearing to see Riley, Glory pivoted her shoulders first one way and then the other, trying to see behind her. Nothing but flat prairie and waving tallgrass greeted her straining efforts. A wave of dejection swamped her spirits, had her slumping in her saddle as she faced forward again. She couldn't do this, this bumping along for weeks on end. Nor could she face this Señor Calderon in Mexico, much less think about killing him. She was only kidding herself when she thought otherwise.

Shying from that image—herself in a death struggle with her enemy—Glory quirked her mouth around her next admission. She didn't really want to see Riley riding up to rescue her. His smiling black eyes, set in his handsome face, stared back at her in her mind's eye. Glory realized she felt warm inside, and tender, just thinking about him. He was so good and noble. And he loved her. So how could it be any worse? Because she didn't doubt for a moment that as soon as he found out what had happened, he'd be riding after Abel Justice.

No one would be able to stop him, either. He'd rescue her, or die trying. Glory grimaced, feeling the ache of physical pain from just the thought. She couldn't live if he was killed trying to save her. But as flat and open as this prairie was, offering no hiding places, no defensive shelter, the advantage and the odds went to Justice. All he had to do was wait for Riley to get close enough . . . and then shoot. As if she could already hear the sharp report of a pistol firing, and see Riley jerking backward off his gray gelding, Glory hunched her shoulders against the stab of tightness in her chest.

No. She couldn't allow that to happen. She'd rather die. This was her battle. And too many innocent people already had died trying to fight it for her. Well, no more. She'd not have another death on her head. She'd ridden out on her own, on purpose, this morning to prevent that very thing. And tied up and trapped though she might be, nothing in her heart had changed. She'd gotten herself into this predicament, and she'd get herself out. Somehow. Somehow soon—before Riley showed up and got himself shot.

Looking down at the rope around her wrists, Glory reminded herself of her mother's favorite saying. *The Good Lord always helps those who help themselves.* Lifting that prayer heavenward, Glory began picking at the rope's knots. Biting down on her bottom lip in concentration, frowning so deeply her head hurt, she divided her attention between her nail-breaking, frustratingly tedious efforts and Justice's back. If she got her hands free, she could use the rope, her only weapon, on the man. Maybe surprise him, get it around his neck. And then squeeze real hard.

A sudden memory from her childhood of the only time she'd seen a man being choked—two drovers got into a fight out in the wagon yard and Papa'd broken it up—had her gulping back her distaste. Again she saw that man's eyes bulging and his tongue poked out, his face turning purple. And remembered her screaming nightmares for weeks after. Could she overpower Justice and hold on until she'd actually choked the life out of him? Glory stole a glance at the back of Justice's scrawny neck, just visible above his coat's collar.

No. She shook her head. No matter how hard she tried, she just couldn't picture herself killing someone. Not in cold blood. But then she thought about what she knew of this man who was knowingly leading her, like a lamb to slaughter, to certain death in Mexico. For money. And he'd killed Mama and Papa. They were still Mama and Papa to her, even if they weren't her real folks. And he'd killed them. And caused Hannah and Jacey to be in danger.

He deserved to die. That awful truth had her tearing at the ropes, trying desperately, mightily to get a finger under one coil, just one. Her fruitless efforts only fueled her temper, her determination. Maybe if she was mad enough, then just maybe—She gasped. The rope gave. She stared at it, frowning. Did it give, or was it her imagination? She shot a glance at Justice. He rode on, unaware. Keeping her fingertip locked in its lifesaving place, Glory breathed shallowly, terrified the least movement from her would undo this tiny bit of hope.

Then bravely, she looked down and flexed her finger. And almost burst into tears when it slipped easily under the rope. Blinking, grimacing, totally rapt with what she was doing, she crooked her finger and tugged. What she saw slumped her shoulders in relief. The coil she'd managed to loosen was the one that sported the knot, the top one looped over the saddle horn. If she could work it loose and slip it over the horn, then she could get loose. All she needed now was time.

Just then she realized that Daisy was circling and slowing. No! She jerked her head up to see Justice reining in his buckskin and pulling in the slack on her reins. *No, not yet.* Glory frantically yanked on the rope . . . and watched the knot draw tighter. She couldn't believe her eyes. Look what she'd done— her rash actions had only made things worse. *Like everything else I've done since Jacey left.* That thought did it.

Glory stilled and closed her eyes, thinking that maybe she wasn't supposed to escape. Maybe she wasn't supposed to live. It was just too darned hard and nothing she did was right. This was hopeless, the whole thing. Opening her eyes, she saw Justice handling his canteen of water. Glory ran her tongue over her dry lips, watching the tracker take a deep swallow and then stare at her.

Refusing to let him see the need in her eyes, Glory cast a secretive look down at her finger looped through the rope. And then, with a complete swing in emotions, nearly burst out laughing. Could she be more pathetic? She looked up at Justice, saw him grimly squinting at her. Suddenly he didn't look as threatening as he did funny, what with his receding chin, skinny neck, and oversized hat. Glory swallowed convulsively, again to keep from laughing. She couldn't give in to it. For one thing, she feared she wouldn't be able to stop. For another, if she laughed at him, he'd most likely shoot her.

So she wisely looked away, seeking the low and distant horizon as a distraction. It then occurred to her that she'd just reaffirmed for her flagging spirit that she did, after all, want to live. Because she'd looked away to keep from laughing, to keep from getting shot. That had to mean something. Yes, it did. It meant for her to live, Justice had to die. She exhaled, bit at her lower lip in concentration. There it was again. She was going to have to kill him.

Could she? Glory considered her . . . victim. A cold-blooded, merciless killer by trade. Her eyes narrowed, her lips firmed into a grim line. If it came down to him or her, then she could do it. Because she had plenty of reasons to live. She had Biddy and her sisters. She also had the ranch—Mama and Papa Lawless's dream of a good life for their daughters . . . including her. She dreamed of making the ranch even bigger and better, and of filling the house again with the sounds of love and laughing children.

Which brought her steadily warming heart around to the love she bore for Riley Eugene Thorne. Right now he was out there somewhere, she just knew it, trying to find her. Because he loved her. It was that simple. Glory raised her chin as she blinked back tears she didn't want to shed. Who wouldn't want to live to be with a good man like Riley? Who wouldn't want to be worthy of him?

"You want a drink?"

A taut jerk of her head and Glory looked into Justice's brown eyes. No more than ten feet away, having drawn her mare close to his buckskin, his expression was open and asking, a simple question. Glory cut her wary gaze to his canteen, which he held out to her. And decided there was no sense in being stubborn and stupid. So she nodded. "Please."

Edging his buckskin in even closer, the tracker fitted the canteen's mouth to hers and tilted it up. Glory drank down gulp after gulp. She hadn't realized she was so thirsty. Justice pulled the canteen away before she was done. Water sloshed down Glory's chin and dripped onto her coat. She turned her head and raised a shoulder, clumsily trying to dry the water from her chin, but to no avail. Justice ignored her efforts while he stoppered his canteen and then looped its long strap over his saddle horn.

Done with that, he then didn't do as Glory expected, which was to set out again, heading ever westward toward the Cimarron Cut-Off to the Santa Fe Trail. Instead, he just sat his horse and stared at her. Her heart picked up speed. *What now?* Tied up and helpless as she was, all she could do was wait him out. And be ready. A moment later, Justice frowned, lining his leathery brow as if in reaction to some thought or realization that clearly nagged him.

Had he noticed that her finger was crooked around the rope, that she'd been loosening it? Only an effort of sheer will kept Glory's expression neutral, kept her from glancing down at her saddle horn and thus drawing his gaze there.

"I ain't got nothin' against you personally, Miz Glory," the tracker blurted, breaking the silence.

Glory's eyebrows winged upward, her mouth dropped open. She stared stupidly for long moments before repeating, "Nothing personal?"

Justice had enough of a soul to look uncomfortable, to lower his gaze to the reins fisted in his hand. He made a pretense of straightening them out.

An overwhelming urge to spit in his face seized Glory. *Don't make it worse*, her conscience screamed. *Later—when you're not tied up—then you can fight him. But not now. If he wants to talk, then talk to him. Find out what you can to help yourself.* Glory narrowed her eyes. All right, she'd talk to him. But that didn't mean she had to be polite. Even Biddy wouldn't require that, under the circumstances.

So, into the taut silence between them, Glory repeated—this time in a voice tight with anger, "Nothing personal? Look at me." She waited for him to comply before making her point. "I'm tied to a horse and being led to a slaughter. By you. And this is only the latest in a string of sins that you've committed against me and my family. If there's nothing personal in this, then it's only because you didn't know anything about me before you came here."

Abel Justice nudged up his felt hat's stiff brim. No trace of his former contrition or shame now marred his expression.

"That was a mighty fine speech, Miz Glory. But I expect I know more about you than you do."

Glory tensed. "What do you think you know?"

A smug leer split his lips open, exposing the crooked teeth in his mouth. "I know you ain't no Lawless at all."

Glory's pulse quickened. This was exactly what she wanted him to talk about. "I know that, too. I also know that my real name is Beatrice Parker. That my real parents were killed by Kid Chapelo. And that J. C. Lawless brought me home to be raised as his daughter." Glory paused, gloating over robbing Justice of his thunder. Seeing on his pinched-up face just how much he didn't like it either, she added, "But I expect *you* know that, too."

Justice eyed her a moment. But then some sly thought sharpened his expression, pulling the skin taut over his cheekbones. "I do—that and more. But here's something I'll bet you don't know. Saving *your* life near to twenty years ago is what finally cost J. C. Lawless his."

His words stabbed at Glory's very soul. Her stomach pitched sickeningly. "You're lying," she cried, the words ripping out of her on an anguished sob.

Clearly pleased by her reaction, Justice arched an eyebrow. "Now what reason would I have to lie?"

"You're just trying to hurt me . . . to unnerve me. It can't be true. It—"

"It is true. Every word."

Just the way he said it made it sound true. She searched his face . . . and saw the truth in his brown eyes, in his sober expression. Then . . . it was as if the life drained right out of her, slumping her over her horse's neck. Glory closed her eyes, tried to will away consciousness. How could she go on living? Mama and Papa dead. Because they'd taken her into their family. Hannah and Jacey would never forgive her.

How could she ever hope to make this up to them? For long moments, Glory thought of nothing. Instead, she concentrated only on feeling alive, on feeling the cold on her face, the heaviness of her braid as it hung down her back, Daisy's shifting under her as she stamped the ground impatiently. But slowly, Glory became aware that she was indeed thinking, despite not wanting to. She realized too that, somewhere in the space of the last few moments, she'd reached a decision, one that changed everything. She opened her eyes, stared at Daisy's coarse chestnut-colored mane, and formulated a plan.

She needed to know what Justice knew. Every detail. Then, armed with that knowledge, she'd rid herself of him—and thereby save Riley from having to do it. That part hadn't changed. Then on her own terms, not like this—tied up and helpless—she'd find and face the man who'd ordered all this tragedy. And then she'd kill him. Or die trying. For Hannah and Jacey. She couldn't bring back Mama and Papa, but she could avenge their murders. And if she lost her own life in the process? Who would care?

Riley's handsome face popped into her head. Then she saw him raise his hands to her, as if begging her not to do this. Glory shook her head. *No, Riley, don't try to stop me. I have to do this. Don't you see? It's the only way. Just know that I have always loved you.*

Done then with her good-byes, Glory raised her head, narrowed her dry and burning eyes, and met Justice's gloating gaze. She'd gone through so many emotions in the past few moments that she'd almost forgotten his presence. Amazingly, he'd waited her out, hadn't moved or said a word. Amazingly? Or because he enjoyed watching people suffer? Glory felt she knew which one. "Tell me how you know all this."

A smirk of superiority lit his muddy eyes. "I've worked for Señor Calderon for more'n ten years. That's how I know. I know everything about you."

"Then tell me what you know. All of it."

He pulled back, ducking his chin, looking askance at her now. Perhaps he belatedly weighed the wisdom of sharing his boss's secrets with her, of giving her this proof of the señor's guilt. Or perhaps he'd noted the change in her. The dead calm. The quietness. The unblinking stare. Or perhaps she gave him too much credit. Maybe he was just gathering his thoughts. Because he eagerly blurted, "Back then, after J. C. killed Kid Chapelo and pulled you out of that wagon and headed for home, it took a while for word to get back to the old don down in Sonora—''

''The old don? Who's that?''

''Señor Calderon. He's a don—some Spanish noble title. Rich as all get-out. Powerful mean, too. As like to shoot you as look at you.''

Some of the dead emptiness lifted from Glory, sharpening her intuition. Here it was. She could feel it—what she'd not been able to figure out before. This Calderon's connection to her. Before, she'd been trying to figure out his connection to Mama and Papa. But now, thanks to Justice, she knew better. ''What does he have to do with me?''

Justice frowned, managing only to look prissy. ''I'm getting to it. Now, like I was saying, word got back to Señor Calderon and his daughter. Well, she took to crying and moaning something awful. Carried on like that day and night. Said she didn't want to live no more.''

Glory thought she could understand the feeling. But not the reason—not for this Calderon daughter, anyway. ''Why? I don't understand.''

''Ain't it obvious? Because she loved Kid Chapelo. Well, her pa put up with her antics for a spell. But then he arranged a marriage for her to some rich Spaniard. When the man came for her, she'd have none of him. And he sure didn't want her like she was—all crying and crazylike, so he left. That's when the beatings began. After one particular beating, she took her own life.''

Justice paused there, as if he expected Glory to be upset or saddened. She was both, but she showed him nothing. He shrugged and went on, this time almost thoughtfully. ''Well, that put an end to it for years. Kid Chapelo was scum, and the old don hated him, but his daughter purely loved him, I suppose. But she was the only one. Still, I would've thought that his boy'd turn out better.''

Another prick of intuition quickened in Glory. Tidbits of Jacey's letter began coming back to her. ''His boy? What boy?''

''Kid Chapelo's bastard by Señor Calderon's daughter.

Named him Zant. The old don loves that boy. Raised him himself. But Zant's a wild one, like his pa—always in trouble. Fought at every turn with his grandfather. Until the last time. About five years ago, I suppose, Zant just up and told the old man he didn't want nothing to do with him and then rode away. Señor Calderon hunted all over for him. And finally found him in a jail in Mexico a few months back. Paid his way out. But the boy wasn't grateful. He told the old man he still didn't want his money and his title. And left again. Shoulda let him rot in jail, if you ask me.''

With that, Justice surprised and frustrated Glory by wheeling his horse, playing out Daisy's reins, and setting them off at a westward walk. Glory glared at her captor's back. He hadn't told her the one thing she needed to know the most. Namely, how any of this was connected to *her*—directly and with enough force to nurse a twenty-year grudge that evidently just exploded one day. What could have happened?

Obviously there was more to it than what Justice had just told her, some one thing that made this Señor Calderon hate her and all things Lawless. Which brought her thoughts to Jacey. Thinking of that brave little spitfire in Señor Calderon's clutches, and wondering if she was still alive, if she suffered horribly, evoked a whimpering cry from Glory. In the prairie's otherwise quiet, marked only by the horses' plodding hooves, her gasp pierced the air, echoed loudly.

Justice pivoted in his saddle and stared at her. Glory stiffened her spine and met his gaze with a level stare. After apparently satisfying himself that she wasn't up to anything, he faced forward, toward the west and the lowering sun.

Sighting on it herself, Glory spared a thought for their eventual destination. Sonora, Mexico. It hit her then with considerable emotional force, like it hadn't before hearing Justice's tale, that if she didn't free herself soon, she'd be facing this Señor Calderon in the same circumstances as Jacey already had. A prisoner. And at the mercy of a man with no mercy in his soul.

Chapter 20

Glory's heart thumped heavily around that eventuality. She peered around her at the lengthening shadows that slipped slowly over the surrounding hills. Long, fingery shadows that seemed to be closing in on her with malicious intent. Fingery shadows. Fingers. That reminded her—she glanced down at her tied hands, smiled at her finger still looped under the rope.

And began in earnest to work on freeing herself. Several minutes of surreptitious tugging and pulling, made all the more difficult by the steady numbing of her fingers and the raw chafing around her wrists, finally produced results. The rope gave. Glory sucked in a breath. She jerked her head up, waited a moment, and then exhaled in relief. If Justice had heard her, he gave no sign. Not daring to look away from him now, Glory eyed him as she slowly, steadily raised her wrists.

And nearly fainted dead away when the rope uncoiled itself from her pommel. She was halfway free. In her excitement, she nearly unseated herself. Glory tensed her legs around Daisy's belly and clutched at the saddle horn. She took the few seconds she needed to settle herself into the swing of her mare's gait, to steady her balance with her knees. Then she brought her wrists up to her mouth and worked the knots with her teeth.

If Justice turned around now, she was dead. That certitude kept her sighted firmly on his bobbing head as she gnawed like a little mouse on the rough coils of the thin rope. More than once she scraped her gums. More than once she bumped her bottom lip between the rope and her teeth. More than once she tasted her own blood. But not once did she stop, not once did she allow any second-guessing to undermine her determination.

So intense was her concentration that she didn't immediately realize what it meant when she pulled her wrists away from her mouth . . . and the rope remained captured between her teeth.

For a split second, Glory stared at her hands. Shock caused her to bite down on the rope that dangled limply, like a dead snake, from her mouth. She was free. To prove it to her disbelieving mind, she flexed her fingers, straightened out her cramping arms. Then the enormity of what she'd done struck her like a blow. She really was free. Her belly quivered with victory. But the giddiness was short-lived. She was also now committed to her plan to kill Abel Justice. Just thinking his name settled her gaze on the man's neck.

Hardening her heart to what she had to do, Glory plucked the rope out of her mouth and coiled it in loops, like she would a lasso, around her hand. She'd have to be careful to make Justice think she was still tied up. Because her only weapons, against his superior strength and his gun, were this length of rope and the element of surprise. With Daisy tied to the buckskin, Justice controlled her every movement. So, Glory reasoned, her one and only chance would be when he stopped them again—probably for camp tonight—and came unsuspectingly back to untie her so she could dismount.

In her mind's eye, Glory saw herself kicking at his jaw and knocking him out. Or leaping out of her saddle onto his chest, stunning him and knocking him to the ground. She'd try for his gun, of course, but couldn't depend on coming up with it. What if it went flying? Or if he came up with it? She shook her head. No, she couldn't risk that. If she got it, great. If not, she'd better be ready with her rope.

A stab of doubt caught Glory off guard. All of a sudden it seemed to her there were too many details, too many events she couldn't control, things that could go wrong. And not the least of her worries was that once she successfully got away from Justice, she'd have to find her way back to that squatter's shack, in case no one had found Biddy and Mrs. Thorne yet. But she'd have to do it on a tired horse. In the dark. Alone.

Girlish fear cramped Glory's stomach muscles. She'd never been out on the prairie at night by herself before. But well she knew the nasty sorts of hungry creatures that hunted—sometimes in packs—an easy meal in the moon's light. That decided it for her. She couldn't wait until tonight, couldn't wait for Justice to decide to stop. Couldn't think about her grand plan to ride for Mexico with vengeance in her heart, like Jacey had done, if she was afraid to be out alone after dark.

Glory pushed that future worry out of her mind, concentrating instead on her more immediate problem. Abel Justice. Checking the sun's position again, she calculated she had another hour or two of daylight left. Which would put them a good three to four hours away from home by the time Justice stopped to make camp later. She couldn't risk that, so she had to create her own opportunity—she had to act now.

First, she looked heavenward, sending up a silent prayer. Then she blinked, realizing what she was doing. Was it okay to pray to God to help you kill someone? Probably not. She looked heavenward again, this time praying for courage, strength, and His will. There. She'd done all she could do. Another deep breath, and she'd be ready. Glory clutched the rope in her fear-slickened palms, ignored her pounding heart, and opened her mouth, preparing to call out to Abel Justice—

He jerked around to face her, hauling back on his buckskin's reins. Daisy, as well-mannered as always, stopped, too. But Glory's eyes popped open wide. She very nearly screamed. Had he read her mind?

"Did you hear that?" the tracker called back to her, his voice sharp with attentiveness, his gaze roving the landscape they'd only just traveled.

Glory let out her breath. He'd heard something. *He heard something?!* Someone was coming. Glory allowed hope to fill her heart, to light up the dark and despairing places in its corners. But only for a moment. Riley was coming. And Abel

Justice would kill him. No! She'd waited too long to act. And now Riley would die, too, because of her.

She couldn't let that happen. So, thinking to mask a rider's approach, she quickly shook her head. "No. I didn't hear anything. And I still don't."

Justice waved her to silence, cocked his head at a listening angle. Glory mimicked his pose. And strained her hearing. At first, nothing came to her. Then she heard it. Far away. No, it was nothing. There! Was that—? Glory almost forgot herself and raised her hands to her throat to massage it, since it insisted on trying to close. She gripped her pommel tighter, pivoted more in her saddle. And heard it again. This time, there was no doubt. She concentrated on the hoarse pinprick of sound, tried to identify it.

Then she had it. Shock straightened her atop Daisy. There was no doubt in her mind. That was the baying of a hound. And not just any hound. That was . . . *dear God, could it be true? . . .* Old Pete's Skeeter.

Goose bumps swept over Glory's skin. She swallowed convulsively, blinked back tears. Skeeter was coming. Glory shot Justice a look. Miracle of miracles, he gave no indication of having heard anything beyond that first time. Glory almost cried out in triumph. Her mind began to race. She had to do something to keep Justice from hearing the dog for as long as possible. But what?

How about what she did best? Talking. Before she lost her courage, Glory blurted, "At the shack back there, with Carter Brown"—at her mention of his late partner's name, Justice riveted her with a look that rivaled a bald eagle's for intensity—"before you killed him, you said something to him that's had me thinking."

He didn't even blink. Didn't move. "What?"

But Glory blinked. She shifted her weight in the saddle, too, remembering to keep the coiled rope atop her saddle-horn-clutching hands. And said the first thing that came to her mind. "You said you 'messed up' when you . . . killed my father— umm, J. C. Lawless. What'd you mean by that?"

Justice's expression changed to that of a tattling child, his voice whined. "It wasn't just me. I ain't takin' all the blame. There was four of us sent here. But it was to nab you and the Lawless girls and take you back to Señor Calderon. We wasn't supposed to kill nobody."

A cold fury swept Glory. She leaned forward in her saddle, yelling, "You liar! First you say Papa was killed because of me. And now you say you weren't supposed to kill him. Which is it? And why'd you kill my mother? And Old Pete and all his animals? How could you be so cruel?"

Justice pulled back, looked surprised, and began shaking his head. "We didn't kill no one but J. C. Them others did all that other killing. And that's the truth. They killed that old man and them animals. We seen 'em do it. They killed yer ma, too. Not us. Don't you go tellin' Señor Calderon we did, neither."

Glory met his words with a stunned silence. She looked at him. She saw him. Certainly, he hadn't moved. But she couldn't shake the terrifying impression that he was rapidly moving away from her, and all the while was speaking in a language she'd never heard before. "What others?"

Justice shrugged and sat up straighter. "Some dandies from back East. The four of us ambushed 'em up in the hills and killed 'em. Went through their stuff. Found a little painting of some pretty lady on one of 'em. Rafferty kept it, took it back to Mexico with him. We found some fancy papers on 'em, too, but tossed 'em away. All's we kept was their money and their horses. This here buckskin's one of 'em."

Glory could only stare at Abel Justice. She and her sisters had never considered that Mama and Papa had been killed separately by different murderers with entirely different motives. But it appeared Hannah and Jacey were both right. Mama's family must have had her killed. And Papa's outlaw past in Arizona had caught up with him. And both on the same day. Glory finally roused herself enough to order, "Tell me about the spur."

Justice sat up and took a deep breath. "All right, but you listen good, so's you can tell Señor Calderon how it happened. Because I don't cotton to bein' separated from my life for something that weren't my fault. It ain't fair.''

Glory's head snapped forward. She stared wide-eyed at the killer. "Fair? You dare talk about fair? Why, I've never known such a low-down person as yourself—to hide behind God and call yourself a Christian, like you did when you first came around. You weren't up at Papa's grave paying your respects that day Skeeter cornered you. *You're* the one who killed him. You're the one who pulled the trigger—or you wouldn't be so worried about facing Calderon, just like Carter Brown said. I'm right, aren't I?''

"Why, you little whore bitch. I'll cut them ropes off you and pull you off that horse and beat you to death. I swear I will." Abel Justice dismounted with a jump to the ground. Reaching under his coat, he quickly produced a wicked-looking knife and advanced on Glory.

Who reacted on pure instinct. From her superior position atop her horse, she threw the harmless rope at him, saw his start of surprise—no doubt at learning she'd untied herself—and used that moment to clutch Daisy's coarse chestnut mane, and dig her heels into the mare's sides. Yelling and kicking, Glory startled her horse into a sidestepping dance that had her bumping Justice's buckskin. Instantly panicked, he showed the whites of his eyes and erupted into a dust-stirring, hoof-flashing, bucking melee that took Glory and Daisy with him.

With no reins to control her mount, all Glory could do was grip the mare's belly with her legs and hold onto her handfuls of mane. And pray that the grunting, squealing buckskin would bolt and run off, leaving Justice here. But maddeningly, the terrified horse didn't. Instead, he made one outraged and bucking circle after another.

Dizzy from this dangerous dance, jerked and snapped about until she felt like a pudding sack of loose bones, Glory glimpsed only flashes of Abel Justice. Fleeting images of him, crouched and circling, dodging kicking hooves, and taking slashing swipes at the horses with his long-bladed knife settled themselves in her mind's eye. That same detached and functioning part of Glory's brain warned her that if he connected, if he cut one of the horses, no doubt it would rear, perhaps topple them all, and throw her.

She'd no more than thought it before Justice proved to be the least of her worries. Because the buckskin, with yet another panicked toss of his head, sent his trailing reins cutting through the air. Glory saw them . . . time slowed . . . she opened her mouth to scream. The buckskin lowered his head . . . and stepped on his reins. He went down hard. Glory stiffened as Daisy jerked back in reaction, but tied as she was to the fallen horse's saddle horn, the little mare never had a chance. Her screaming squeal as she went to her knees matched Glory's as she went sailing over her horse's head.

I've been thrown. I'm going to die. The thought was so clear, so calm. And brought Glory down to the earth, to a thickly grassed, soft and sandy patch of ground. She didn't die. She didn't even pass out. But she did slide and scrape and roll and thump to a mind-numbing stop, ending up on her back, spread-eagled—stunned, hurting all over, and staring up at the sky. She blinked. The blue overhead was replaced with Abel Justice's ugly face as he invaded her line of vision. He stood over her, straddling her, his big knife in his hand.

And there wasn't a thing she could do about it. Especially with the earth spinning like it was. Glory grimaced. What was that loud ringing in her ears? And why were those horses screaming? She thought she heard a dog's baying, too. But she couldn't be sure, not over the sound of Abel Justice's raised voice.

Gesturing angrily with his wicked blade, his face red and contorted, he leaned over her, a triumphant gloat riding his ugly features. "You ain't so high and mighty *now*, are you? You want the truth? Here's the truth—I killed J. C. Lawless. Me. An' I'll be famous for it, too. I surprised him in his own house and shot him—whilst he was bending over his dead wife. I'd have killed her too if she'd still been alive.

"That's your truth, little girl. An' I weren't lying before— they're dead because of *you*, all right. Because J. C. Lawless killed The Kid over *you*—nothing but a whining, sniveling orphan. The Kid shoulda dealt with you right then—the same way he did yer folks. But now it's up to me to do it. And Señor Calderon will thank me for it.''

With that, he drew his arm back in a vicious arc, sparking a star-bright glint of reflected sunlight off his sharp blade. Glory's eyes widened. Her mind cleared, understanding dawned. If she didn't do something—and right now—he was going to kill her. But the thought had no time to translate to action before Justice began the downward arc—a knife-wielding arc that would end at her chest.

''No!'' Glory cried out, crooking an arm up in a defensive posture. It was all she could do, what with him dropping down atop her, a knee gouging into her belly. Helpless, seeing lightning-flash images of home, of Mama and Papa—happy and alive, of Hannah and Jacey, and Biddy . . . and Riley . . . *Riley, I love you* . . . cross her vision, Glory waited for the pain, waited for death.

But it didn't come. Instead, a snarling growl . . . a solid thud . . . a man's hoarse yell . . . and Justice's weight lifted off her. Stunned, not quite convinced she was still alive, Glory lay there a moment. Then scared reaction sat her up. Breathing shallowly through her mouth, turning her focus inward, she took mental stock of herself, and realized she was okay. Unhurt. But her split skirt was twisted annoyingly around her legs.

She tugged at its folds, but caught a movement out of the corner of her eye. Her hands stilled as she looked more to her right. There, a little ways off, stood Daisy and the buckskin. Their coats were lathered and dirt-streaked. Their heads drooped tiredly as they blew and snorted, but miraculously they appeared to be fine. Glory slumped. A smile of thankful relief tugged at her mouth—

But died when a man's hoarse scream behind her forced a yelp of surprise out of her. Glory twisted around, flattened a palm on the grassy hilltop to brace herself, and found a pitched battle of flailing arms and legs and flapping ears and stiff tail. Her breath caught, her jaw sagged. She put a hand over her thumping heart. *Skeeter!*

Instantly, her mind latched onto the obvious—the hound

had knocked Justice off her before the evil little man could kill her. Old Pete's hound had saved her life. And now, the big dog had Justice down on the ground, on his back—and twisting and digging his bootheels into the dirt as he crabbed spasmodically and helplessly in the hound's grip. Again, his piercing screams and pleas for help split the air.

Glory looked closer. Skeeter's powerful jaws were clamped around the man's arm. With vicious shakes of his head, he effectively tore at the coat sleeve covering flesh and bone. No doubt some of the dog's long, sharp teeth had broken through. But it wasn't the killer's knife arm he'd bitten down on.

Glory's breath caught. Skeeter needed her help. Tripping once, clawing at the ground, she finally scrambled to her feet. She saw Justice raise the knife and stab desperately at, but miss, the tugging hound. *Not while I'm alive!* Sucking in a vengeful breath, Glory—skirt flying, hands fisted—quickly closed the distance between herself and the two combatants. And leaped into the fray.

Son-of-a-bitch! Riley's heart pitched over with what he was seeing. Up ahead, on the crest of a low and grassy rise, was the woman he loved—and Skeeter—rolling around in the dirt with Abel Justice, who flashed a pretty big knife. Riley didn't wait to see more. He dug his heels into Pride's belly, urging the gelding into a gallop. The horse responded instantly with a burst of speed that chewed up the ground at a dizzying pace.

Almost before he knew it, Riley was atop the same hill as the grunting, snarling battle. He hauled back on Pride's reins. Before the horse could shudder to a stiff-legged, dust-raising halt, Riley shook loose of his stirrups and vaulted out of the saddle. He hit the ground running, never taking his eyes off Glory as he yanked his Stetson off and his heavy saddle coat, tossing them both aside. He wanted nothing to hamper his movements.

Then his heart nearly stopped, his feet stumbled. "No!" he cried, stretching a hand out as if he could prevent—Too late. He jerked to a standing halt, not believing this. Justice and Glory and Skeeter rolled as one over the hill's crest and disappeared down its far and sloping side. Out of Riley's sight.

With fear and exertion clamping his teeth together, Riley bolted into flight again. He thought of his gun. Dismissed the notion. Might hit Glory. He could fire it in the air, get their attention. No. Not with that knife flashing between them. Had to get the knife, had to get Justice. Riley pictured grabbing Glory first to haul her to safety.

Every protective urge in his body screamed at him to do it. But if he did, then for long and vulnerable seconds, he and she'd both be wide-open targets for the killer's knife. No, had to get Justice. Had to avoid Skeeter, too. Lost in his blood lust, the dog might attack anyone who came within range of his sharp teeth.

With those thought-bursts carrying him to the hill's crest, Riley topped it and started over, his arms out to his sides for balance. Half slipping, half sliding, with the crunch of gravelly ground under his boots announcing his progress, he prepared to join the battle. And to end it.

But before he'd descended more than half the distance, he saw Glory shove to her feet—her back to him—and haul a knifeless, bloodied, and limp-limbed Justice up with her. Skeeter circled, snapping and lunging at the hired killer's legs, as Glory fisted her hand, drew her arm back and, with a mighty grunt of effort, windmilled a punch right to the man's jaw and sent him sprawling.

Startled into stopping where he was, Riley stared open-mouthed, splitting his gaze between the downed man, the bristling dog hunched threateningly over him, and the triumphant Glory. Seeing that Justice wouldn't be getting up anytime soon, Riley settled his disbelieving gaze and his tender smile on Glory.

The little hothead was shaking her right hand and rubbing her knuckles. No doubt she'd just learned that brawling hurt either way—if you got hit or did the hitting. She then leaned over, bent her knees slightly, and rested her hands atop them, allowing her head to droop tiredly between her shoulders. Her long auburn braid, all but undone, hung over her shoulder and swung gently as her back arched and sagged with each deep breath.

Undone by the sight of her, by the depth of his love for her, Riley quietly folded his arms over his chest and shook his head. His little champion. She'd kicked Justice's ass. Riley suddenly recalled an afternoon several weeks ago when she'd done the same thing to him. That thought evoked a smirking grin out of him. He'd best be careful how he let her know he was here. She might jump him too.

A lump settled in his throat, and seemed to make his eyes want to water. Riley's mouth worked, finally settling on a manly grimace. He dragged a finger under his nose in a rough gesture and, feeling more in control, broke his silence. "Glory?"

She gasped as she straightened up and turned to him. For long moments, she stared up at him, didn't move. Behind her and to her left, Riley caught a glimpse of Skeeter. He too had raised his head and was staring. Riley shifted his gaze back to Glory, only to see her crumple in on herself. A tender emotion tugged at his heart, pulled at the corners of his mouth. Here it came—reaction to everything she'd been through.

He started down the hill toward her, saw her hold her arms out to him and begin to run. "Riley!" she called as she stumbled and staggered up the hill. Riley broke into a loping sprint, meeting her with his own arms open, ready to embrace her. Glory never slowed. Her arms outstretched, the raw, abraded skin over her wrists exposed, she ran right into his arms.

His heart breaking for her injuries, for the swelling bruise on her jaw, for the multitude of scrapes and scratches that dared mar her china-doll face, Riley lifted her off the ground, pressing her beloved body to him and swinging her around and around. She clung tightly to him, wrapping her arms around his neck, nestling her soft but cold cheek against his.

Nothing had ever felt so right to Riley in his entire life. He emptied his heart of words. "I love you, Glory. I was so damned scared for you. I swear I'll never let you out of my sight again—never. I'll never let anyone hurt you again. Ever. I swear it."

"Oh, Riley," Glory cried, pulling back until she could look into his face. Riley lowered her to the ground and roved his gaze over her precious features, loving each and every one, as she stared up at him, cupped his cheek, and cried, "I was so scared. I thought I'd never see you again. When I didn't think I could go on, when I didn't believe I was going to live, I'd picture your face, Riley. And I'd hold on. Because I love you, too."

His world completed by her words, by her nearness, Riley lowered his head to kiss her, but before he could capture her lips, a big, reddish, bloodhound head nosed its whining way between them, wriggling until it separated them. Still holding Glory by her arms, Riley stepped back and teased, "Dammit, Skeeter, can't I even kiss my woman?"

Tail wagging—alternately slapping against Riley's leg and then Glory's skirt, Skeeter *arr-ooh*ed his baying opinion of that. And got himself laughed at for his efforts. Glory pulled out of Riley's embrace to kneel down beside the dog and hug his great head to her chest. She laid her cheek atop his furry brow and turned her green eyes up to Riley. "I'd be dead if it weren't for him. Skeeter saved my life."

Riley firmed his lips and stroked the big dog's back. "So would my mother and Miss Biddy be, if not for Skeeter's nose. He led us right to them."

A gasp of relief brought Glory to her feet. "Then you found them? They're okay?"

"Yeah. They're fine. Maybe a little sore from being bumped around. But fine. My father and Mr. Rankin took them back to your place. We're to meet them there."

Glory nodded her agreement to this plan, but something else bothered her, narrowed her eyes, tugged at her mouth. She quickly looked down and absently fondled one of Skeeter's long, soft ears. "And ... Carter Brown? You saw him ... there?"

Riley pressed his lips into a grim line. "I did. I take it Justice did that, that these two are in cahoots?"

Glory nodded, still with her gaze lowered to the dog's head. Riley feared the reason she wouldn't look up at him. Did she blame him for all this, for hiring those bastards in the first place? He needed to know. "I brought on a lot of this, Glory. I know that. I can only say I'm sorry."

A taut jerk of her head had Glory staring up at him, her emotions exposed in her clear, green eyes. She shook her head. "No. It's not your fault. Not any of it. You didn't know." She paused, her eyes teared up. "It was me, Riley. Papa got killed because . . . because of me. They were looking for me. Justice said so." She lowered her head to stare at her boots. "I don't see how Hannah and Jacey can ever forgive me."

Riley was suddenly very afraid for Glory's heart and mind. His own heart hung heavy in his chest as he stared at her. He reached out to squeeze her coat-covered arm. She still wouldn't look up at him. Riley died a little inside but persisted. "This is not your fault, Glory. You can't believe anything Justice says, and you know it, honey. He's just trying to hurt you. Don't let him."

She raised her head, showing him a face so scraped-up, and yet so beautiful, so heart-wrenchingly vulnerable, framed as it was by baby curls at her hairline, by long wisps of reddish hair that had escaped her braid. Her mouth quirked, her chin trembled. Riley prayed she didn't cry. Her tears right now would drive him to his knees. But she didn't give in to tears. She started to say something, but Skeeter's sudden movement stalled her.

The bloodhound jerked, his ears pricked. He turned his head to look up the hill behind Riley. Riley felt his heart pick up speed, his gut tighten. He sent Glory a warning look as he slowly reached for his gun. Settling it in his grip, he jerked around, aiming his deadly Colt at . . . Pride. The winded gelding, alone at the top of the hill, arched his gray neck in surprised reaction.

Relief coursed through Riley. He relaxed, holstered his pistol, and called out to the top of the hill, "Dammit, Pride." That was all the provocation Skeeter needed. With a last nosing of Glory's hand, the bloodhound loped up the hill, as if to visit with an old friend. Riley shook his head and started to turn to Glory, only to realize she'd stepped up beside him.

Seeing the worry lines that etched her brow, he turned to her and used a thumb to smooth them out. "You feel up to a ride? It's going to be dark soon. We need to find shelter."

Glory nodded. "I'm fine. But what about him?"

Riley pivoted, saw Abel Justice hadn't moved. He turned back to Glory. "I'd like to put a bullet in him. Or leave him here for the wolves. But I reckon we'd best take him with us. There's plenty of time later for dealing with him—when we're rested and you're safe at home."

Glory blinked up at him and then turned away to face the hill. She looked down at her hands, picked at a fingernail. "I'm not sure I'm going home, Riley. Well, maybe I need to for some rest and some supplies. But I'm not staying. There's something I have to do . . . in Mexico."

"Mexico?" Riley blurted in surprise. "What do you have to do there?"

At his side, Glory said, "I have to even a score. I have to . . . kill Señor Calderon. For killing Papa. I swore it with Hannah and Jacey."

He'd heard all he needed to. "Dammit, Glory." He gripped her arms and turned her to face him. She raised grass-green and troubled eyes up to him. Seeing them, Riley's deep anger, tempered with the very real fear that he could still lose her, warred with his need to handle her gently and yet to speak firmly. "Listen to me—you're not going to Mexico. It's over, Glory. Enough. This revenge oath between you and your sisters. Look what it's done—it's torn your family apart. It's taken you away from each other when you need each other the most. You can't even say if Hannah and Jacey are still alive. Now, do you really think this is what your folks would want, Glory?"

She looked down, shook her head the least little bit.

Heartened, Riley pressed on: "Too many people have died, Glory. Or have come close to being killed—my own mother among them. How many more will be enough? Are you not going to be happy until you're dead and my heart is broken, too?"

She slowly raised her head to look up at him again. Impossibly huge tears rolled to the edges of her black lashes, spiking them together like glistening stars. Riley's knees weakened. In her hands, faced with her tears, he admitted he had as much spine as one of her big soggy balls of pie dough. But any sign of weakening on his part and he'd lose her, perhaps forever. So, he shook his head no and narrowed his eyes at her. "Cry all you want. You're not going to Mexico. I won't let you."

Glory opened her mouth, as if to say something. But a metallic click cut her off. Riley frowned at her, and then stiffened with the dread of dawning realization. He knew that sound. That was a gun being cocked. Behind them. Abel Justice had the drop on them. Riley stared hard into Glory's eyes, squeezed her arms in a parting gesture . . . and shoved her backward.

Chapter 21

Yelping with shock at the sheer unexpectedness and force of Riley's shove, Glory stumbled backward, her arms windmilling. A part of her brain recorded that Riley was falling in the opposite direction. Glory screamed, wanted to reach for him, but couldn't. Her heel caught, her ankle turned. She lost her balance and fell, meeting the unyielding ground with a grunt of pain and a flurry of flying skirt. Landing on her back, she lay there for a stunned second, unblinking and staring up at the sky.

And then she heard it. The *pop-pop-pop* of a gun being fired. Fright fisted her hands, digging her fingernails into the prairie's soil. She turned her head, bit at her lip, and huddled against the ground, trying instinctively to make herself a smaller target. As if to prove she'd failed, the gun barked again and a bullet scudded into the ground not ten feet from Glory's hip. Gasping, her heart pounding, she rolled in the opposite direction.

When she did, something hard in her coat pocket gouged painfully against her pelvic bone. Glory grimaced as she levered herself up enough to turn her head so she could see and assess what was happening. Frantically, she searched the boulder-strewn and uneven ground of the small valley between the two hills. Off to her right, she found Abel Justice.

Protected by an exposed and jutting ledge of rock, he peered out from behind its safety and was firing away—to her left.

She didn't need to look to know he was gunning for Riley. Glory's face twisted with hatred. She would kill Abel Justice herself if she only had a gun. Finally looking to her left, she saw who she knew she would. Riley. Lying on his stomach on open ground—totally exposed and firing back. But blessedly, he was alive.

Relief swamped Glory, had her head sagging between her shoulders, her forehead resting against the ground. Tiny sharp rocks poked against her skin. She knew if she could find a rock big enough, she'd throw it at the hateful Abel Justice. And then she'd throw one at Riley for what he'd done. He'd shoved her out of the way, hoping to draw Justice's fire to himself. And for the most part, it had worked.

Glory cursed Riley's noble act as stupid, stupid, stupid. If he sacrificed himself like this, if he got himself killed, did he really think she'd want to go on living without him? She'd no more than thought it before a deafening quiet descended on the prairie. Glory divided her darting gaze between Justice and Riley. Had one of them been hit? Was one of them—? No! Riley was trying to reload. He was still alive. Glory sucked in a huge breath—which whooshed out of her when she saw Justice jump up and begin running. For Riley.

She cried out to warn him. He spared her a glance as he fumbled frantically at his gunbelt. Sheer terror seized Glory. He didn't have enough time to reload before Justice would be upon him—so close there'd be no chance of him missing. Glory shot a look Justice's way. There he was. Running, leering, aiming. "No!" Glory screamed, scrambling to her feet. "No! It's me you want. Me! Leave him be!"

She didn't realize she was running toward the hired killer until he turned to stare at her and called out, "Stop right there. Stay where you are."

But she couldn't stop. Panic and fear for Riley pushed her, carried her stumbling and crying toward the killer. "No! Don't kill him." But she suddenly lost her footing and fell face-first to the ground.

Again, whatever was in her pocket threatened to embed itself in her belly, so hard was it. Glory flattened her palms against the ground and tried to push herself up. But found she couldn't. Something, someone was holding her down. Slowly she realized what . . . who it was. Abel Justice had his foot in the middle of her back. And his gun cocked at her temple.

"Like I said, stay where you are, Miz Glory." Then he called out to Riley. "Throw yer gun down and get up, Mr. Thorne. Nice and slowlike. One wrong move and I'll kill her. You know I'll do it, too."

"No, Riley—don't! He'll kill me anyway. Don't listen to him." A sob wrenched out of Glory. She managed to raise her head and swipe her hair out of her face. Only to see Riley throwing his useless gun down and hauling himself up. "No," she cried again. "I love you, Riley. Please don't."

But he did. Unarmed, he stood tall and still, his hands raised. Glory couldn't look away from his face, even though what she saw reflected there was too awful to bear. His expression was grim, calm . . . fully prepared to die for her. Helpless to stop him, Glory gave up. Crying, she sagged back to the ground, her cheek against the hard, unsympathetic earth. With each shuddering sob, she choked on grit and grass.

But the sound of Riley's voice broke through her sorrow. Quieting instantly, she raised her head, tried to strain upward. But couldn't. Justice pressed her down more with his boot against her spine. Stabs of nerve pain shot down the backs of Glory's legs, rendering her all but paralyzed, reducing her to nothing more than an unwilling witness to whatever happened next. And so, against her will, she listened.

"Let her go, Justice," Riley was saying. "Pick on someone your own size for once, you yellow-bellied coward. Or can you only fight defenseless women?"

"Shut up," came Abel Justice's snarl. He cruelly ground his bootheel harder against Glory's spine. She jerked and cried out, but more from the sudden jab against her pelvic bone than from Justice's actions. What was that in her pocket and tormenting her so?

The thought was fleeting as she again strained to hear Riley's words, his unrelenting taunting of Justice. "Go on. Shoot me. What's stopping you? The fact that if you do, I've got four brothers and a father who'll hunt you down and kill you? They're out there right now, hunting for us. They could be just over that hill. Why else do you think Skeeter isn't down here chewing on your leg? You think it might be because someone's holding him up there?''

"Shut up, Thorne. And stay where you are. You think I'm stupid? There ain't nobody up there. I said stay there. One more step, and you'll get to watch Miz Glory die.''

Riley's voice lowered with deadly intent. "You don't want to do that, you sniveling little bastard. Because if you do, I'll be on you before you can raise that gun again. Only I won't kill you. Not for a long time. I'll keep you alive and carve pieces off you—one chunk at a time. I'll see that you suffer. After a while, you'll beg to die. And only then will I kill you.'' He paused to glare at Justice and then added, "Let Glory up. And just maybe I'll let you go.''

"You'll let me go? Are you *loco*? I'm the one with the gun. And that bein' the case, I'm through talking.''

Fright surged through Glory. She felt the gun move away from her temple. In only a second, that same gun would take Riley's life. She arrowed a quick prayer for strength heavenward and then wrenched hard to one side, crying out, "Now, Riley!'' as she did. It worked—she'd caught Justice off guard. His yelp of shock accompanied his bootheel lifting off her back. Glory completed her roll and scrambled to her feet, expecting to see Justice on his back and Riley atop him. But no. Not today. Not on this day of alternating hope and despair, minor miracles and major setbacks.

Justice had obviously regained his balance before Riley could move. Because there he stood, snarling and cursing, swinging his pistol's bore from her to Riley and back to her. "You shouldn't have done that, Miz Glory. And now yer goin' to pay. You can watch him die.''

Again the threatening pistol was swung toward Riley. Panicked, Glory clutched at Papa's coat she wore—and felt that hard something in her pocket. She instantly fumbled for it. She'd throw it at him, maybe hit him, knock his aim off. Plunging her hand in the deep pocket, she yelled out, "Justice!'' Amazingly, he turned to her, pistol and all. She froze. Riley's flying body entered her field of vision. He collided with Justice.

The gun discharged. Glory screamed, bringing her hands to her mouth. Had Riley been hit? Her wide, unblinking eyes forced her to watch, to see the men hit the ground together and instantly fall apart. They both lay on their backs, still and unmoving. Glory couldn't be sure that her heart beat in that tense second of suspended time. But then . . . both men wrenched, grabbed for the other one. Glory stiffened. Riley was alive. So was Justice—but did he still have the gun in his hand?

That fearful question galvanized Glory into action. She took off at a run, intent on reaching the fighting men, determined to do something to put an end to this most awful of afternoons. As she ran, ignoring the agonized protesting of her abused muscles, she felt that hard something bumping against her leg, that same object that had gouged her belly when she fell. Not slowing down, she plunged her hand into her coat's right pocket—Papa's sheepskin coat. Her fingers closed around the cold steel she found there.

Glory stopped as suddenly as if she'd hit a barn wall. She stared vacantly toward the horizon, not seeing the deep shadows of afternoon or the browning tallgrass all around her. Because every fiber of her being focused on what she felt in her hand. Could it be? Snapping out of her shock, she jerked her hand out of her pocket. Her mouth dropped open. Sure enough . . . Papa's pistol. The very same one she herself had loaded and put in there weeks ago. And had forgotten. She'd had it all this time.

Cursing herself for such forgetfulness, she clutched at her weapon and turned her attention again to the men. *It's time to die, Abel Justice.* Two steps closer, Glory again stopped. She stood there, her arms hanging loose at her sides at she stared at Riley lying on the ground. On his stomach and unmoving. She was too late to help him. Just then, Justice moved, began staggering to his feet. He was bloodied. His thin coat lay open.

A smear of red covered his chest. But whose blood was it—his own or Riley's?

Glory's heart sank. She refused to allow any thought to form that might try to tell her Riley was dead. She'd know soon enough. But right now, she had some unfinished business to attend to. Stepping closer to the two men, she called out, "Justice?!"

The man righted himself and turned to her, his fists raised as if he expected another fight. Glory clutched her weapon in both hands and raised her arms stiffly, sighting on this killer of innocent people. With no thoughts of mercy in her heart, she watched his eyes and smiled in a purely grim way when she saw what she wanted. When she saw the realization dawn—that exact moment when he knew that she held a gun. His muddy-brown, flat, and soulless eyes widened until white showed all around their dark irises.

A tic of triumph jerked a muscle in Glory's cheek. She took another step closer to Abel Justice. She didn't want to miss. And told him, "My only regret is I don't have enough bullets to shoot you once for every time I owe you. I will tell you this—the name of J. C. Lawless will be on the first one."

Her Papa's killer dared raise a hand in supplication to her and cry out, "I ain't armed. You cain't shoot an unarmed man."

That was the wrong argument. Glory raised an eyebrow. "Why not? You did. Carter Brown—your own partner—didn't have a gun in his hand when you put a bullet through his head. But more important to me—and worse for you—the other was my papa." Through talking, Glory shifted her weight, distributing it evenly on both feet. Her finger tensed around the trigger.

"Glory, don't."

The soft voice calling out to her startled her. Gasping, she jerked a quick look to her right. Miracle of miracles, Riley was on his feet. A surge of love and intense relief—and fear gripped her. Riley was alive, but his shirtfront was also covered with blood. "Riley! Oh, thank God you're alive! Are you shot?"

She glanced back at Justice, saw he hadn't dared to move, and then jerked her attention back to Riley. He was shaking his head. "No, it's Justice's blood. He shot himself when I hit him."

Glory again sought the tracker. Now she noticed the blood oozing wetly down his shirt. "Good. I'm glad. Then all I've got to do is finish him off."

Justice's mouth opened to a dark O. His eyes held that fearful look a trapped animal gets when it sees the trapper and knows its death is imminent. Good. Glory narrowed her eyes, ready to complete the deed.

"No, Glory. Don't," Riley called out, again stopping her. "He's already dead. He just hasn't fallen down yet. Listen to me. I don't want you to kill him."

"How can you say that? He killed Papa, Riley. He was unarmed. And this coward killed him when he was lost in his grief and was bending over Mama. How can I just forgive him?"

"No one's asking you to forgive him," was Riley's reply. "I know what he did, honey. But he's not armed now. Look at him."

She did. She flicked her gaze up and down Abel Justice. Terrified and sniveling, he held his empty hands up for her to see. She called out to him. "Where's your gun?"

"I don't know," he cried, his voice thin and reedy. "Don't shoot me, Miz Glory. Please. I'm already done for. Just let me be to die on my own."

Before Glory could even react to that speech, Riley recaptured her attention by calling out, "I don't think he's lying, Glory. He's got a bad wound and will probably die pretty quick. But it's not him I'm concerned with. It's you. You don't have to have his blood on your soul. You don't want to live with that."

"No. I have to shoot him," Glory screamed, suddenly tired of everyone telling her what she could and couldn't do. "But first he's going to give me some answers. There're a lot of things I still don't understand. I have questions about that day—that day when he killed Papa."

"I understand. But are you sure you want to know more, Glory? Look where you are now, this minute, for all your knowing. Look at the hurt it's caused you. Maybe there're just some things that are better not known. Honey, you may never know the whole truth. And that may be a good thing. So let him be. Let him go die."

Everything Riley said made good sense, she admitted. But good sense had nothing to do with vengeance. "You may be right, Riley, but he tore my family apart. He killed my Papa and hurt me and my sisters. And what about Biddy and your mother? Look what he did to them. He was going to kill me, too. And you. He deserves to die."

"Yes, he does. And he will . . . by his own hand . . . as it should be. Not by yours. He's not worth what killing him would do to you, Glory. I'm asking you—please, put the gun down. Because I love you, and I don't want to see you suffer later for this. Do it, Glory. For me. I'm asking."

Glory gulped back a sob and a whimper. Suddenly overwhelmed with it all, she looked over at Riley, wanting only for him to hold her, to make the hurt in her heart go away, make it quit aching.

As if he sensed this, he held his hands out to her, inviting her to take the steps that would have her in his embrace. "I love you, Glory. And your sisters do, too. You can be proud—you kept your promise to them. Abel Justice is dying right now because of the brave things you did to keep my mother and Biddy and even me alive. You never gave up, you risked your own life, doing what you had to do to fight for us. We owe you our lives. But it's over now. Put the gun down . . . so we can start our lives over. But this time, together. Forever."

Staring at him, hearing his words of love, knowing she wanted the same things, Glory weakened, suffered second thoughts. Her arms felt heavy, slipped down a notch.

And that notch was apparently big enough for Riley to see, because he jumped in with, "You'd be doing the right thing, Glory. There's a Higher Justice waiting to deal with him. Let Him. It's not your place. One man's quest for revenge—it's what put Abel Justice on the trail here from Mexico. That same wrong desire took your sisters away from you, too. I asked you before, when will it be enough? When, for God's sake, are you going to be through hating?''

Glory blinked at the note of impatience in Riley's voice, and bit at her bottom lip. Finally, she called out, "Riley, I don't want to hate anymore, can't you see? I don't want to be afraid. I want my sisters home. I want my life back and some happiness again. I want you, Riley. I want our babies."

"I want that, too, sweetheart. More than anything in the world."

Riley's warm words and tone pierced the tiniest hole in her heart's armor, her defense against the shattering grief of finding Mama and Papa dead that September day. Her awakening heart spoke to her, telling her that only by talking this out with Riley would she be able to finally let go—of the hurt, the hate . . . and the gun. "Riley, I don't want to do this anymore, but I can't put the gun down. I can't. Help me. Talk to me."

"Will you give the gun to me, Glory?"

"No!" Her grip tightened. She leveled her Papa's pistol again at Justice, saw that he was pale and sweating. He licked at his lips and stared unblinking at her. She frowned, thinking, *He certainly is hanging on pretty good, for someone who's supposed to be dying.* "Talk to me, Riley," she cried out.

"Okay. Just listen to me. Think of our babies. They'd be beautiful, Glory, just like you. And think about how happy Biddy'd be. And Smiley. They'd be like grandparents to our kids. Just like my folks. Honey, there's no more land feud— not between my family and yours. My father apologizes. We could live on your land or mine. We could build our own house."

"No, I want to live in Mama and Papa's house, Riley."

"We can do that, too. All of us. Me, you, our ten babies, Biddy, Hannah, and Jacey, and their families when they have them. And Skeeter, too. Don't you think he'd like lots of babies pulling on his ears and playing with him?"

Glory grinned at that. Somewhat against her will, but a grin nevertheless. This picture Riley was weaving . . . she'd thought this before. Her dream. The realization struck her with the force of a slap. And Riley Eugene Thorne knew it, understood it . . . had said it. He was also the center of it. With his love in her life, she could face whatever she had to.

Even bad news. Even if it was about her sisters. No! They'd come home. She couldn't bear anything else. They'd come home and find her married to a Thorne. Well, Riley came first in her heart now, not her sisters. And they'd have to understand and accept him. Glory blinked at that thought. It was true—Riley was first in her heart.

A sudden notion assailed her. She was a grown woman now, no longer clinging to the loyalties and affections of her childhood. She wanted Riley. She belonged with Riley. It wasn't the ranch at all. Not the land, not the house. They weren't home. Because wherever Riley was, that was her home. Her love for him and his love for her—and only that—could save her, could finally take away this hate that threatened to crush her soul.

Thinking of hate brought Abel Justice into focus. Cowardly, merciless, wounded . . . pitiable. No, she couldn't do it. Not in cold blood. Not like this. It was wrong, plain and simple. She'd be just like him if she ended him like this. That was what Riley meant. It was over. Glory gave up the fight. She relaxed her shoulders, bent her elbows, and raised the gun until its barrel pointed harmlessly at the sky.

Only then did she look over at Riley. He smiled and nodded at her. And then he put his hands to his waist, let his breath out, and closed his eyes, obviously relieved. A smile for him began to form on Glory's face, but died at the sound of Abel Justice's voice.

"You stupid little bitch—you might just as well be a Lawless for all yer gutlessness. You stand there with a gun in yer hand and talkin' about love and babies. I knowed you didn't have the gumption to shoot me."

Glory stared at the gun in his hands. He must have had it behind him, stuck in his waistband. Wherever it had been didn't matter, because at the moment it was now pointed at her. That gloating look was back on his face. "I ain't shot up half as bad as he thinks. Hell, I'm going to live. But not him''—he indicated Riley—''and not you. Because you'd rather talk than do somethin' about it. All that sappiness about love. Here's how much I care about love.''

He then made the mistake of pointing the gun at Riley. Who was a picture at that moment of helplessness. He was also unarmed. Glory didn't even think. She raised her Papa's gun and fired, hitting a very stunned-looking Abel Justice in his left shoulder. Glory saw Riley jump back out of the way and knew he wouldn't say one word this time to distract or to discourage her as she faced her enemy.

''This is J. C. Lawless's gun I just shot you with,'' she explained to the tracker in a murderously calm voice. ''And that bullet in you is for J. C. Lawless. You had your chance to walk away. You should have taken it.''

She fired again. ''This is for Catherine Lawless.'' She didn't stop. Not when Justice jerked and finally dropped his gun. ''This is for Peter Anglin, a crippled old cowboy who never hurt anybody.'' Justice spun around as the next bullet hit him. ''And this is for all the animals he loved. And for Skeeter, who lived to hate you and to hunt you down.''

Finally, Abel Justice fell to the ground, spread-eagled . . . and dead. But still, Glory advanced on him, pulling the trigger again and again. ''For Hannah. For Jacey.'' When all she got was the metallic *click-click-click* that told her the chambers were empty, she kept squeezing the trigger. And might have continued to do so forever had someone not gripped her shoulders and turned her away.

She looked up, blinking in confusion. Riley's handsome face filled her vision and her world. ''He left you no choice. You did what you had to do, what I should have done a long time ago. It's over now.''

Glory's mouth worked. She heard him, she nodded. Riley then pried the gun out of her fingers and stuck it in his waistband. Watching him as intently as she was and loving his every move—knowing it meant he was blessedly alive, Glory startled when something wet and cold nuzzled her palm. Looking down, she saw Skeeter. When had he come back over here? She smiled down at the big hound, who turned soulful eyes up to her. "He's dead, Skeeter. He can't ever hurt you again. He can't ever hurt any of us again. It's over."

Skeeter blinked, appeared to think about what she'd said. Then, he swung his large, squarish head to stare at Abel Justice's unmoving, bloodied body. A low woof escaped him, and he humped his back. Padding away from Glory, he adopted a stiff-legged walk that seemed to raise the hair on his back, and finally stood over the man who had shot him. He sniffed the body and then raised his head to bay loudly, to announce this victory, this triumph. His rich and throaty cry filled the air, carrying on the wind for all the prairie to hear and to know.

Watching him, Glory was suddenly moved to tears. Her fog lifted. Her eyes filling with the hot and salty drops of long-held emotion, she turned and stepped into Riley's warm and loving embrace. The smear of blood on his shirt didn't matter. Not now, when she needed so badly to rest her cheek against his broad chest and hear for herself his beating heart. Only this way would she believe that he was really and truly alive. And that she was, too.

Riley held her as tightly as she did him. He kissed the top of her head, smoothed her hair out of her face, and told her, "There's still a lot to be done, to be faced—and forgiven. I know that. But I'll be there with you every step of the way. I swear it. Every day and every night. I'll keep you safe and warm. I swear I will. But for right now, put everything else out of your mind, sweetheart. Right now, think only about how much I love you today. And about tomorrow—and how much more I'm going to love you then. And the day after that. Forever."

His words of love. Riley's for her. Could any woman anywhere, in any time, ever be loved so much? Glory blinked, her chin quivered, and again fat, hot tears spilled over and ran down her cheeks. She cried for all that had happened. For all that was yet to be. For her real parents' fates. For those of Mama and Papa Lawless. And for the as-yet-unknown fates of her sisters. But above all else, she cried for her happiness . . . for the love she'd found to help her through it all.

Pulling back in his arms, she turned her face up to Riley's, capturing for herself the depth of his love in his deep, dark eyes. "I love you," she whispered.

Riley smoothed away her tears and smiled down at her. In that instant, Glory knew that with him, her heart could finally rest. For, in him, she saw the cherished reality of all her dreams. "I love you, too. I always have," he answered her in that deep, quiet voice of his that chased gooseflesh over her skin, that voice that would be waking her every day for the rest of her life. He then raised his head and, looking around, considered the falling darkness. "The night's coming on. Everyone will be worried. I need to get you home."

Glory reached up to cup his cheek, to run her fingers over his lips, to draw his gaze back down to her face. "Riley," she said when he again looked into her eyes, "we need to go, yes. But in my heart, I'm already home. Because *you're* here."

Epilogue

"Well, Sutfield," Ben Thorne was saying, "we're all kin now. You, me, and the Lawlesses. What? Why, it is too true! See, your Janie married my Henry today. And Riley married Glory. The grooms are brothers. Yep, Lawless kin. Ha! You ever think we'd live long enough to say that?"

At his side, Louise Thorne tugged on his sleeve. "You hush up that loud talk. I don't want Reverend Bickerson hearing you and thinking you've had too much to drink."

"How's he going to hear me? He's in the kitchen with Sourdough and feeding the leftover food to Skeeter." He turned back to Sutfield. "That's what I was telling you. Riley says when the gunfire started, that danged Skeeter made himself scarce. Didn't show up again until Justice was dead. Turns out, betwixt those two times, he'd been sittin' on Riley's coat and chewin' on his hat."

The burst of laughter from the enthralled knot of friends and neighbors clustered around Ben and Louise Thorne, all of them dressed in their wedding finery, caught Biddy's attention. She and Smiley joined their group. "That Skeeter, he's a fine one. Has taken to sleepin' in me kitchen, he has."

Smiley teased, "She's spoiled that dog until he's worthless. Done the same with Heck Thompson, too, babying him over that lump on his noggin. Oh, you didn't know? We found him that night a week ago out in the bunkhouse, dazed and his scalp opened up. Yep—Carter Brown's doings. Wonder he didn't kill the boy when they fought over that missing money a while back. You didn't know about that, either? Where you been, Sutfield?''

Pressed into a group of well-wishers at Smiley's back, Glory smiled and nodded at her wedding guests' congratulations, saying how pleased she was they could make it on such short notice. As soon as was politely possible, though, she excused herself to seek her groom. Careful of her wedding gown, an ivory-satin creation Biddy and Louise Thorne had sewn feverishly to complete, Glory threaded herself through and around clusters of chatting folks in the gaily decorated great room.

Now where had Riley gotten to? Just then, as if she'd asked it aloud, the happy throng shifted. And Glory saw him. As always, her breath caught, her heart thumped. Across the room from her, he stood in front of the huge fireplace with his brother Henry. Next to him was his bride, Janie—a slender, blond-haired girl. If not for her quiet influence on Henry, Glory knew, she and Riley would have had to wait months for Reverend Bickerson's next visit before they could marry.

Her tall and handsome groom. Glory sighed, raising a hand to her chest. A possessive smile claimed her features. He cut quite a figure in his black Sunday suit and holding a crystal glass of whiskey. As she watched, he laughed at something Henry said, and Janie's face turned red. Glory shook her head. She needed to rescue her sister-in-law. Then it hit her, rooting her to the spot. She had a sister-in-law.

It was true. She and the Thornes, as of today, December 5, 1873, were now family. She prayed that the ties that now bound them together would hold strong *when*—she clung to "when"—Hannah and Jacey came home.

Glory blinked back her emotion and realized Riley'd spotted her, had apparently been watching her for a while. Because his dark-eyed stare questioned her, asked what was wrong. Glory meant to reassure him with a shrug and a smile, but they wouldn't come. Riley tensed, handed his drink to Henry, excused himself, and then started toward her.

Honing in on her, like an arrow to its target, he held her gaze. The sheer weight of his burning stare weakened Glory's knees, made her breathing irregular, made her wish they were alone as they'd been every night since . . . that awful day. As good as his word, he'd stayed here with her, slept with her, held her, but nothing more as they awaited their wedding day. And now, here it was.

Thoughts of the night to come had Glory clutching at her gown. And then, he was there and smiling down at her, holding his arms out to her. Eagerly, Glory stepped into his embrace. To her surprise, he swirled her around and around. Scurrying away and laughing, their guests quickly made way. Riley didn't bring them to a dizzying stop until he had her alone, over by the staircase. Then he turned her with him, and they bowed for the applause coming their way.

As the guests turned away, allowing the newlyweds their moment alone, Riley leaned back against a wall and circled her waist with a hard-muscled arm. Pulling her tight against him, between his spread legs, he gave her a private grin. "What was wrong with my bride back there?"

Glory shook her head, felt her trailing long curls caress her shoulders, which were bared by the gown's low-cut bodice. "Nothing. I just missed you."

Riley bent over her to place a nipping kiss on her nose. "Then you shouldn't have wandered away, Mrs. Thorne."

Batting him away, Glory teased, "I didn't. You did, silly goose." Then, caught up in Riley's infectious teasing, she circled his neck with a hand and pulled him to her, wanting his ear close to her mouth. Going up on tiptoes to reach him, she whispered, "I'll be glad when we're alone."

Riley pulled back, stared down into her eyes, and then leaned over her again to whisper, "Will you now? Does it have anything to do with . . ." He named an act so decadent that Glory squealed and pinched his arm, struggling playfully against him. But he held her rigidly in place.

She hit at his chest and whispered, "You're awful. People don't—do they? They do? I never—What if I can't? What if you don't like me . . . like that?"

Riley coughed, ran a hand over his mouth and chin. Then he assured her, "I think I'll like you just fine . . . like that."

Feeling suddenly very warm, just trying to picture what Riley'd suggested, Glory bravely plowed onward. "Well, I can only hope so. I promise to like you like that, too."

Riley gaped at her, burst out laughing, and hugged her to his chest, clinging to her as he all but collapsed against her struggling efforts to pull away. Which forced Glory to do her fussing into his stiff and starchy-smelling shirt. "Riley Eugene Thorne, you let me go this instant. What will our guests think?"

It was useless. He was too tickled to respond. But she didn't really want him to let her go, not with the heady scents of his clean and masculine musk reaching her with every breath. She wriggled against him, making a show of protest. But a grin tugged at her lips, a grin for Riley's rare happy abandon. He was always so serious. He needed to laugh more, Glory decided. And she would see that he did.

A week into Glory and Riley's honeymoon, the morning began like all the others, and yet was different. The winter sun rose to reveal a sprinkling of snow, like so much delicate lace, adorning the land. Feeble light bathed the main bedroom in ever-lightening shades of gray. And in the wide marriage bed, where before J. C. and Catherine Lawless had loved, now their Glory Bea learned how to be of one soul with her husband.

On fire with need, Glory moaned and writhed under Riley. With her legs wrapped around his hips, with her fingernails raking his back, she raised her head seeking his mouth, wanting even more. Riley obliged, claiming her lips, using his tongue to mimic the action of their hips. Glory clutched at his shoulders when she neared her moment. Riley's rhythm became fevered. Finally, the hungry needing burst.

She took Riley with her, pulling him deeper into her with each rippling, intense wave. He cried out, held himself rigid over her, gave himself up to her. And then, when he had no more to give, collapsed atop her. After a moment he slid out of her and rolled to lie next to her. Glory faced him, as spent and weak as he was. She grinned as she gasped for air. "I like this."

Riley nodded. "I know you do. You're killing me."

Glory's grin broadened. "Then maybe we'd better quit doing it."

Riley frowned. "Now you're really killing me."

Glory slapped at his shoulder and giggled. "Come on, get up and help me. I want to surprise Biddy and make her breakfast."

Riley blinked, didn't move. "Now you're trying to kill Biddy."

Glory sat up and bopped him with her pillow. He grabbed for her, but she squealed and rolled off the bed, dancing away from him. Across the room now and tugging into her nightgown, she begged from somewhere under its voluminous folds, "Riley, I have a good feeling about today."

She blinked in surprise when Riley tugged her gown over her head and helped her settle it over herself. Standing in front of her, muscled and gloriously naked, his big hands smoothing across her shoulders, he smiled but appeared hesitant. "You've said that every day since our wedding. Yet each day passes, and they don't come home. And then you cry. I hate to see you hurt, Glory."

Glory slipped her arms around his waist, resting her cheek against the black and crisp hairs sprinkling his broad chest. "I know, but I really feel it. You'll see. One of my sisters will come home. Because today is different."

The day wore on, cloudy and no different from any of the preceding days. The lacy snow melted away before a frigid cold gripped the land that afternoon, forcing man and beast to seek warmth and companionship. Out in the bunkhouse, the Lawless hands slept or played poker or cleaned gear. Inside the main house, Biddy and Smiley fussed over a game of checkers in the kitchen. Skeeter dozed at their feet. And Riley sat in J. C. Lawless's office, in the leather chair, poring over the accounts.

And Glory sat alone in Catherine's parlor, her hands folded in her lap as she quietly, lovingly looked around . . . and waited. Hour after hour.

Until . . . Skeeter's low warning woofs and the clicking of his nails against the hallway's wooden floors as he padded by the parlor wrenched Glory from her expectant pose. Could it be—? Her breath caught at the very notion. Then suddenly, Biddy and Smiley crowded the doorway, their expressions agog with hope. Behind them appeared Riley. Glory sought his dark eyes, begged.

Riley smiled. "You were right. Today is different. Someone's here."

"Someone's here," she whispered, tears springing to her eyes. Then she jumped up and began running. The threesome in the archway laughingly parted for her and then followed close on her heels. When she rounded into the entryway, she saw Skeeter nosing the front door, whining and wagging his tail. He turned his big head to her and barked. Glory reached the heavy door on the fly, yanked it open. Then, she froze, staring . . . not believing. "Hannah," she breathed.

The afternoon blurred into joyful tears and happy hugs. Everyone talked at once as the grand party—followed by four huge, quiet men Hannah introduced only as her damned Yankees— swept into the great room. Making them all laugh right off was Skeeter's instant fascination with Hannah's impossibly huge and playful puppy, Esmerelda. The dogs eyed each other, nosed each other, and then bounded off on a galloping, baying romp through the house—and promptly got themselves corraled and tossed outside for a spell.

Following that bit of chaos, Hannah pulled her tall husband, Slade Garrett, forward and introduced him to her family. And then spent a long time explaining him to Biddy—lady's maid all those years ago in Boston to Catherine Wilton-Humes, a young socialite who'd been wronged back then by his father. But she relented quickly enough, even hugging this handsome Garrett, when Hannah announced her expectant condition. Then they all exclaimed over Glory and Riley being married.

And finally . . . Hannah missed Jacey, and asked where she was.

The room quietened. Slade caught Riley's eye and the two men excused themselves to go oversee the unloading of the huge traveling carriages. Smiley followed them. Trailing him were the damned Yankees. Glory and Biddy eyed those quiet men curiously, drawing Hannah's laughter. They turned and saw she'd shed her bundling, revealing her loose clothing. Gone for the moment were unspoken fears for Jacey. Hugging and laughter accompanied patting "the baby" before the three women sat down to visit, as if Hannah'd only been away on a holiday.

Before the painfully avoided subject of Jacey could come up, Slade and Riley returned, each one drawing near to his own wife. Slade insisted Hannah rest, but she assured him she was fine, that she wanted Glory to catch her up on the past months here at home. She laughed, saying after the horrors in Boston, nothing could be better for her than to hear the everyday, unchanging news of home. She wanted to hear Glory tell her how boring the past months had been—except for her marriage, of course.

The room again got quiet. The moment stretched out until the day's shadows seemed to have lengthened before anyone spoke. Hannah looked in turn at Glory, Riley, and Biddy. What had happened here? And *where* was Jacey? Why wouldn't anyone tell her? At the mention of Jacey, Glory burst into tears again. She just knew it was because of her that something awful had happened to Jacey. Shocked at such a notion, Hannah asked how that could be.

Tearfully, Glory told of the journal Jacey'd sent her, how it revealed her true identity—Hannah's mouth dropped open— and how that related to Kid Chapelo, and ultimately Señor Calderon's elaborate plot against them. He'd sent the trackers who killed Papa. At this point, Hannah gasped and turned to Slade—this explained what the events in Boston hadn't. She urged Glory to continue. Glory then had to tell Hannah that Señor Calderon's grandson, Zant Chapelo—The Kid's son— had Jacey prisoner, the last she'd heard.

Stunned, not able to take it all in, Hannah sat numbly, sadly, for long moments. Then she quietly told Glory the truth behind Mama's death. She spoke of Cyrus and Patience, of their diabolical greed, of all the murders they'd committed and why—for Mama's vast inheritance. Not only had their great-aunt and uncle had Mama killed, they'd also murdered her estranged parents—and even her grandmother, the beloved Ardis, the one in the missing portrait. Her mention of Ardis sparked a memory in Glory. One of the trackers had taken the painting with him back to Mexico.

Why would he do that? Why would he want it? No one could come up with a logical reason. Which forced them to accept that between them, they didn't have all the answers. They lay in Mexico. Glory's troubles here pointed to the wickedness there . . . where Jacey was. So, until she came home, they could not lay to rest all their heartache, all their sorrow. When Hannah teared up, Slade knew why—he instantly assured her that they would not return to Boston until this feisty sister he'd heard so much about came home.

Later that evening, after a big supper, Riley and Slade took their whiskeys and settled in the great room, warming up to the blazing fire in the grate and to their topic of conversation—their wives. Meanwhile, Skeeter made a lovesick nuisance of himself by pining after Esmerelda, who ignored him in favor of investigating the house and, with happy swipes of her long tail, knocking over everything not nailed down. Biddy gave up herding the dogs and finally made a nuisance of herself by spoiling Hannah's "damned Yankees."

Upstairs, Hannah and Glory sat atop the quilted cover adorning the big bed in their parents' bedroom. Propped up with pillows at their backs, their legs stretched out in front of them, the sisters visited. Just the two of them, for the first time in a long time. "Riley and I've been . . . sleeping in here. But you and Slade can, if it's more comfortable for you. Do you want another pillow?"

Hannah chuckled. "I'm fine, honey. And we're fine in my

old bedroom. You're worse than Slade. He's worn me out fussing over me all the way here.''

Glory sat back and grinned. ''I like him. Have you noticed how much he and Riley look alike?''

Hannah nodded, ''Scary, huh? And they both look like Papa.'' Then she sent Glory a tender smile as she reached up to smooth a curl back from her baby sister's cheek. ''I've always thought Riley was the one for you. He's the only man around who didn't fall down at your feet in worship every time you batted·an eye. I just wish I'd been here for your wedding last week.''

''I wish I could have been in Boston for your wedding, too.''

Hannah startled Glory by bursting into laughter. ''There was no wedding. There was barely a ceremony—and a horrid one at that. Or so I thought at the time. I'll tell you all about it one day—after you've had time to form an unshakably high opinion of Slade.'' Having said that, she subsided into quiet chuckles and then pointed over at the journal in Glory's lap. ''Is that it?''

Glory nodded, met Hannah's hazel eyes as she handed over the worn journal. Riddled with guilt and fearful of Hannah's reaction, Glory lifted her chin defensively. Her voice, even to her own ears, sounded as harsh as her words. ''Here. Meet my mother and father, Laura and Seth Parker. Hello, I'm Beatrice Parker—the baby in there that got your father killed and quite possibly Jacey, too. I'll understand if you want me off Lawless land after you read this.''

Hannah's knuckles turned white around the slim book. Her expression clouded, reflecting a shocked grimness. Then, carefully, as if it were a living thing she didn't wish to awaken, she placed the journal next to her. Finally, she shifted her weight until she faced Glory and could take her hands. When she spoke, her voice quaked with emotion. ''First of all, Glory—this is your home. It always has been and it always will be. You and Riley will continue to live here. There. That's settled.

''Now—*how* can you think you got anyone killed? You

were a helpless baby. Papa acted out of compassion and good-ness. But some evil man twisted it into a bad thing. How are you responsible for that? Was Papa wrong to bring you home and let us all love you and spoil you? No, he wasn't.''

She pointed to the journal and said, ''What's written on those pages only tells you who brought you into this world. And we love them for doing that. But, Glory, it was Papa who gave you life. Papa. And Mama. And in my heart, you are my sister, my flesh and blood. Every bit as much as this baby I carry. Honey, I've already lived through all the pain that I ever care to. I've had to say good-bye and bury and give up too many people I love. So don't ask me to give you up. Because I won't do it.''

The tearing note in Hannah's voice as she broke off on a deep sob wrenched Glory into her arms, crying. She clung to Hannah, cried into her sister's hair. ''I'm sorry, Hannah. I've just been so scared for so long.''

''I know, honey. We all have.'' After a moment, she pulled back and held Glory by her arms. ''From this day forward, we're going to laugh together and love each other, Glory Bea. And we'll watch me get fat with this baby. And together, we'll wait for Jacey to come home.''

Hannah's sincere sentiment proved easier to say than it did to live with. Or to believe. Especially when the days of waiting turned into weeks. During that time, the damned Yankees took up residence in the bunkhouse, much to the narrow-eyed war-iness of the Lawless cowhands, who didn't cotton much to Easterners. In the main house, Biddy insisted that Hannah and Slade take her downstairs bedroom with its wide bed. ''Our little mother doesn't need to be climbing up and down them stairs, now does she, Mr. Garrett?''

With the blame put on him in that way, Slade made damned sure their belongings were moved to Biddy's room. She then insisted he and Riley wrestle Hannah's old bed downstairs and into the parlor for her. With Christmas almost upon them, she needed to be close to the kitchen. She had a lot of baking to do. Couldn't have Jacey coming home and no pies and cookies to greet her.

So, busy and hopeful, if not cheerful, they all pitched in to prepare for Christmas. Presents were made and hidden. The house was decorated, the tree was trimmed. The Yankees and the cowhands came in for singing and punch. And they determined to be happy. But it turned to an aching emptiness when Christmas came and went. Without Jacey.

Each snowfall, each howling blizzard, drooped their spirits further. The snows would only be heavier in the mountains Jacey would have to travel through to get home. That's what was keeping her, they told themselves, on New Year's Day, 1874. The snows in the mountains. Made them all but impassable until spring. So, they might as well relax and wait it out. But when January began to wear on, Slade and Riley declared themselves in a state of siege.

By late January, they were at their wit's end with trying to entertain their wives. One deeply cold and blustery day, they threatened to leave them and go find Jacey themselves, if Hannah and Glory didn't wear something besides long faces and moping spirits. The sisters stared at their angry husbands, looked at each other, and burst into tears.

Cursing, Slade and Riley threw their hands up. Biddy came running from the kitchen. On her heels, and stuck behind her bulk in the narrow hall, were the impatient Esmerelda and the love-besotted Skeeter. But when the dogs gained the entry, they didn't follow Biddy to the source of the noise in the great room. Instead they made for the front door, jumping at it, adding their baying and yapping to the general cacophony.

Riley split his gaze between his crying wife and the howling dogs. Then, with violence in his heart, he stomped over to the door to let them out before he could . . . well, he didn't know, but it'd be painful. "Get outside. Go." He yanked the door open and stood back, eyeing the hounds and waiting. But they just stood there, panting and staring up at him. Riley's eyebrows dropped dangerously low over his nose. "What's wrong with you?"

"Well, for one thing, I'm about to freeze my ass off, Thorne. For another, what are you doing in my house? And what the hell kind of a dog is that?"

Riley froze. Only one woman in the whole territory had a mouth like that. He wrenched around to face the doorway. Sure enough, there she stood—bundled up to her eyeballs and glaring at him. Laughing, Riley called over his shoulder, "It's Jacey! She's home!"

One second of follow-up silence shattered with the sound of running feet and joyous cries of "Jacey's home!" As happy as anyone, Riley nudged the dogs aside and grabbed her up in a big bear-hug—despite her loud protests—and swung her around. Within a second of being mobbed by her squealing family, he set her down and got out of the way. Glory, Biddy, and Hannah pounced on her, all but knocking over this orneriest of the Lawless sisters. Grinning broadly, Riley caught Slade's eye, but the man's grim nod to indicate the open doorway behind Riley sobered him into pivoting around.

He hadn't been there before, but just now entering the house, amidst a jingling of spurs and removing his Stetson, was a young, muscular, black-haired man who had gunslinger written all over him. Flanking him were two big, sombreroed Mexicans. All three were big and armed to the teeth. The biggest of the three closed the door behind himself. Riley settled his attention on the gunslinger, saying, "Howdy."

The sober, staring gunslinger nodded as he ran his hand through his hair. "Howdy."

In the space of the next few seconds, Riley made some snap judgments. Gunslinger type or not, this stranger had brought Jacey home safely. At this time of year. And she'd let him— this girl who didn't let anybody do anything for her. So, it had to mean something. Riley stepped up to the man, extended his hand in greeting, and said, "Welcome. My name's Riley Thorne. I'm Glory's husband."

A flicker of reaction raised the man's eyebrows, flashed through his black eyes. It was there and gone so quickly that Riley wasn't sure he'd seen it as the stranger clasped his hand, shook it, and said, "Pleased to meet you. This is Paco Torres. And Victor DosSantos. And I'm Zant Chapelo. Jacey's husband."

Riley froze. He heard the gasps and then the deathly quiet in the room behind him. Even the dogs, for once, didn't raise Cain.

This was a tough one. They loved Jacey and were overwhelmed with joy that she was home. They wanted nothing to detract from that—not harsh words or a thoughtless accusation of betrayal. No one wanted to hurt her, or make her feel unwelcome in her own home. But she was *married* to the son of Kid Chapelo, the grandson of the man who'd set events into motion that had nearly gotten them all killed. There had to be one hell of a story behind her marrying *this* man. That notion, coupled with their faith in Jacey, got them through the awkward afternoon while she and Zant settled in.

Even out in the bunkhouse, though, things didn't go smoothly. Smiley got an earful from his cowhands when he brought in the two huge Mexican men and their gear. Some of the Lawless men trailed their foreman into his office, closed the door, and complained they had a hard enough time trying to understand them durned Yankees' lingo, without him tossing in two Mexicans who couldn't parlay, in *any* brand of English. Smiley's advice was to see if they played poker—and then make the best of it.

Good advice for those in the main house, too. Following supper, they all settled onto the soft leather furniture in the great room, the girls sitting next to their husbands. Hannah and Glory briefly filled Jacey in on events in Boston and then here at home. The girls all marveled that they could be so wealthy now, thanks to Mama's inheritance. Then no one knew what else to say. All the pleasant surprises—marriages and babies—had been exclaimed over. All that remained were the hard parts. And so, the silence.

Until Biddy spoke up. "Ye poor things. Not a one of ye was spared. Onto yer young heads was heaped yer fathers' sins. Aye—yer fathers'. Yer troubles started over twenty years ago, not last September. But I'm hopin' 'tis over now. I'm hopin' yer done with hate, now that ye've seen what it can do. Just remember that it's love what's brought ye home—an' all one family now."

Another moment of silence followed. Then Jacey got up, drawing everyone's attention her way. So like Papa, even to her black eyes and hair. She fished in a pocket and finally pulled out the tiny portrait of their great-grandmother Ardis and held it up. "Here's what I went for—and I got it back," she said with a grin.

As they all exclaimed happily, Jacey proudly placed her keepsake atop the mantel above the fireplace. Then she turned around and spoke to Glory. "I take it you got my package?"

Glory nodded and slipped her hand into Riley's. "Yes. James McGinty brought it."

Jacey nodded. "Alberto said he was reliable. Good. Well, I didn't have this, at that time, to put in with your . . . things, but"—she glanced at Zant, who winked at her—"I have it now." With that, she pulled out of her skirt's other pocket a ruby necklace in an old-fashioned gold setting. The red gemstones sparkled in the firelight. She unceremoniously plopped it into Glory's hand, saying, "This is the necklace mentioned in that journal."

"But where—? How—?" Stricken with emotion, Glory stared at Laura Parker's necklace, and then curled her fingers around it. Tears blurred her vision as she raised her head and sought her sister. "I don't know what to say . . . except thank you. Jacey, I know this didn't come to you easy. You probably risked your life to get it."

Jacey nodded, shrugged like it was nothing. "What are sisters for?"

And Glory knew that was all Jacey would ever say about that whole Parker business. They were sisters. The hair stood up on Glory's arms, even as a warmth rushed through her. This was just like Jacey. Didn't say a word. Just went out and did it. Reckless and brave to the end, a fierce defender of all she loved.

And that brought them to the black-eyed gunslinger she'd married. Jacey pointed to him, saying, "Zant saved my life. And I saved his more than once. He's a good man. I find it hard to believe he could love me at all, that he could forgive us for Papa killing his father, that he could forgive me and love me—after I killed his grandfather."

Shocked gasps and turning heads all centered on Zant Chapelo. He kept his somber gaze firmly on Jacey. They hadn't considered things from his side. But Jacey was absolutely right. And then, Biddy's words seemed to hang in the air, words of hate and love and family. She was right—they'd all suffered. How could they judge him?

Jacey took up her story again. "Zant was never a part of Don Calderon's scheming—except to put an end to it. The old man was purely insane and evil. He killed Zant's mother and used to beat Zant until he got big enough to run off. But when he got wind of the old man's scheming, he went back to Mexico to stop him. And he took me with him to keep me safe. But the old man's dead now. And Zant's got the responsibility for rebuilding down in Mexico what his grandfather tried to tear apart. And I'll be there to help him."

That next morning, as the girls cleared away breakfast, Hannah said, "Now, Glory, you know Slade and I have to get back to Boston. I want to have my baby there. And Jacey and Zant are going back to Mexico. So it looks like the Lawless spread is all yours. But you shouldn't have to worry about a thing—or you either, Jacey—what with Mama's money. Slade's brought drafts for each of you. I suggest you sit down before you look at them."

Stricken, Glory put a hand to her chest. "Oh, Hannah, don't talk about land and money when you're leaving. I don't want you to go." She turned to Jacey. "And you just got here."

Jacey frowned and fussed, "Quit carrying on like we're riding out today. And neither is Hannah. We'll be here a spell yet."

"That's true," Hannah said, gripping the back of a chair as they stood around the dining room table. "But there's one thing I want us to do, now that we're all three together again.'' She paused, looking at each of her sisters in turn. "We need to go talk to Mama and Papa. And Old Pete.''

Jacey and Glory stood mute and sober and nodding. Then the three of them went to their separate rooms, got their coats and met again at the back door in the kitchen. Standing at the stove, Biddy silently watched them, seemed to know what they were doing. Her faded-blue eyes filled with tears, but she managed a watery smile for them.

Then, into the room filed Slade, Riley, and Zant. The men helped their wives bundle up. And then stepped back, holding Skeeter and Esmerelda by their collars. The sisters looked at each other and then went outside, closing the door behind them.

The day was cold and sunny, not as windy as it had been recently. The only snow was what clumped in dirty patches here and there. The three crosses at the top of the hill stood out against the winter-blue sky. Keeping their own private thoughts, Hannah, Jacey, and Glory trudged up the hill's slope. If they felt the cold, they didn't remark on it. Then, they were there and swinging open the squeaky gate, stepping inside.

Without word or design—but one on either side and helping the pregnant Hannah—they kneeled at the foot of J. C. and Catherine Lawless's final resting places. The girls' hands seemed to seek each other's of their own accord. Then, Glory and Jacey turned to Hannah, as they always had, and waited for her to say the words in their hearts. Hannah smiled and turned to the crosses.

"Mama, Papa, Old Pete, we're done with vengeance. We've fulfilled our blood oath to you. We know you're proud of us. We know you love us. We've felt your loving and protective presences with us, each and every step of the way. Know this: As long as we're alive, as long as your grandchildren and great-grandchildren and their children live, you'll be remembered. You'll live always in the love we bear you.

"In our hearts, we'll forever remain Lawless women. And this we promise you: To live well and to love well, as you've taught us. That is our new promise to you. And a new beginning for us all. So be it, and amen.''

Jacey and Glory, as one, repeated softly, "To live well and to love well. So be it, and amen.''

Bestselling, award-winning author

SHIRL HENKE

takes readers on magnificent journeys with her spectacular stories that weave history with timeless emotion, breathtaking passion, and unforgettable characters . . .

BRIDE OF FORTUNE

When mercenary Nicholas Fortune, amidst the flames of war, assumes another man's identity, he also takes that man's wife . . .

_____ 95857-9 $5.99 U.S./$6.99 Can.

DEEP AS THE RIVERS

Colonel Samuel Shelby is eager to embark on his mission to make peace with the Osage Indians. The dangerous wilderness is a welcome refuge from his troubled past — until he meets beautiful, headstrong Olivia St. Etienne . . .

_____ 96011-5 $6.50 U.S./$8.50 Can.

Start a love affair with one of today's most extraordinary romance authors...

HER SECRET AFFAIR

BARBARA DAWSON SMITH

Bestselling author of *Once Upon a Scandal*

It is Regency England. Isabel Darling, the only child of an infamous madam, is determined to exact revenge on the scoundrels who used her late mother—and uncover which one of these men is her father. As she sets her sights on blackmailing the Lord of Kern, his indignant son Justin steps in to stop the headstrong Isabel—and start a passion from which neither can escape...

"Barbara Dawson Smith is an author everyone should read. You'll be hooked from page one." —*Romantic Times*

HER SECRET AFFAIR
Barbara Dawson Smith
0-312-96507-9___$5.99 U.S.__$7.99 Can.

Haywood Smith

"Haywood Smith delivers intelligent, sensitive historical romance for readers who expect more from the genre."

—*Publishers Weekly*

SHADOWS IN VELVET

Orphan Anne Marie must enter the gilded decadence of the French court as the bride of a mysterious nobleman, only to be shattered by a secret from his past that could embroil them both in a treacherous uprising...

_____ 95873-0 $5.99 U.S./$6.99 CAN.

SECRETS IN SATIN

Amid the turmoil of a dying monarch, newly widowed Elizabeth, Countess of Ravenwold, is forced by royal command to marry a man she has hardened her heart to—and is drawn into a dangerous game of intrigue and a passionate contest of wills.

_____ 96159-6 $5.99 U.S./$7.99 CAN.

Read Cheryl Anne Porter's
BOLD NEW SERIES
About Three Passionate Sisters
And The Men Who Capture Their Hearts!

HANNAH'S PROMISE
Nominee for the Bookstores That Care "Best Love & Laughter Romance" Category
After she finds her parents brutally murdered, Hannah Lawless travels to Boston, vowing revenge on their killers. When sexy Slade Garrett joins her crusade, Hannah may have found her soul-mate—or the heartless villain she seeks...
0-312-96170-7___$5.99 U.S.___$7.99 Can.

JACEY'S RECKLESS HEART
As Hannah heads East, Jacey Lawless makes her way to Tucson, in search of the scoundrel who left a spur behind at her parents' murder scene. When she meets up with dashing Zant Chapelo, a gunslinger whose father rode with hers, Jacey doesn't know whether to shoot...or surrender.
0-312-96332-7___$5.99 U.S.___$7.99 Can.

SEASONS OF GLORY
With Hannah and Jacey off to find their parents' killers, young Glory is left to tend the ranch. And with the help of handsome neighbor—and arch enemy—Riley Thorne, Glory might learn a thing or two about life...and love.
0-312-96625-3___$5.99 U.S.___$7.99 Can.